I0675111

SPEED

GRAPHIC

Robert Brace

This is a work of fiction. All of the characters, organizations, and events portrayed in this novel are either the products of the author's imagination or are used fictitiously.

SPEED GRAPHIC. Copyright © 2022 by Robert Brace. All rights reserved.

Cover photograph, SIG Sauer P232 automatic pistol © 2022 Robert Brace
Cover photograph, background by Deleece Cook on Unsplash
Cover design by the author

First Edition: September 2022

Library of Congress Control Number: 2022904959

ISBN 978-1-7373192-4-5

Privately published, September 2022, New York.

www.RobertBraceAuthor.com

No part of this book may be reproduced or retransmitted in any form or by any means, electronic or mechanical, including photocopying, recording, or by any information storage and retrieval system, without written permission from the author, except for the use of brief quotations in a book review.

SPEED

GRAPHIC

I

WE WERE STANDING ATOP the pyramid, high above the jungle canopy, when I first heard the helicopters. I had not yet seen them but I knew from the sound they were not civilian—the rotors made that distinctive hard thump characteristic of heavy military helicopters. The Guatemalans sometimes use old Hueys to patrol their border, just a few miles west of us, but this noise was coming from the other direction, from inside Belize.

The Belizeans have no military helicopters.

I used the binoculars to scan the east—an endless sea of endless jungle rolling away to the horizon, uninterrupted except for the occasional patch of morning mist rising from a river valley. A red-tailed hawk soared nearby, searching for breakfast, and in the distance there was smoke from an early morning slash-and-burn clearing operation, but it was just past sunrise, and due east I could make out nothing against the glare. The sound was still low, a background bass you might miss if not attuned to such things, but from the slowly increasing volume I could tell that whatever they were, they were headed our way.

I considered gathering my group and retreating into the jungle.

Most of them were with me, roving among the intricate maze of royal apartments that top the Caana, the broad-shouldered 140-foot-tall pyramid that towers over Plaza B. Some of them had found a large scorpion sunning on the stones—guardian of the imperial tombs perhaps. I had warned them to take care since it was poisonous, and they were studying the creature with morbid fascination. Others were winding through the labyrinth of the palace or climbing the pinnacles or trying a hand at deciphering the pictographs on the stelae. The Caana is over a thousand years old but is nevertheless the tallest building in Belize. To gather the party together and get them back down the hundreds of steps to the bottom would take time, too much time.

I always end the tours in Caracol, and always at sunrise. By this stage the party is usually exhausted, invigorated by the adventure but worn down with the hard trekking of the previous five days. Caracol is a special treat, a way to end on a high note. On the last morning we break camp at first light, and after the best part of a week spent in the shade beneath the canopy the party emerges at sunrise into the wide-open plazas and sky-reaching ruins of the ancient Mayan city.

Down here in this part of the world it is usually Tikal, in neighboring Guatemala, that attracts the archeological tourists. Despite four centuries of Spanish conquest, Caracol had remained hidden deep in the jungle until 1938, when it was happened upon by mahogany loggers who must have been amazed at what they found. Serious excavation did not begin until 1985 and is not yet complete. The site is difficult to get to and is much less well known than Tikal.

All this is a blessing: there are no shops or souvenir stalls here, no guides touting their services, no mobs of charter bus tourists—it is the world's greatest attraction at which it is not possible to buy a Coke. There are few enough people at any time, but at first light the only other occupants of the ruined city are the howler monkeys. These last add nicely to the atmosphere, their ominous gates-of-hell screeching resonating throughout the jungle, incredibly loud, as if in urgent warning against entering a forbidden city best left undisturbed.

Not loud enough to cover the approach of those helicopters, however. Quietly, so as not to alarm anyone, I chambered a round in the .308 and then sat on a step to wait and see what transpired.

I DID NOT HAVE TO WAIT LONG. They came directly out of the sun, swooping in close by the pyramid, low and fast and suddenly loud, their roar deepening with the Doppler shift as they zoomed past us just above the treetops. There were two of them, the second flying behind and a little to the side, clear of the lead ship's rotor wash. If they had meant to arrive unseen, they could not have planned it better.

Now everyone was aware of their presence, and the people around me stopped whatever they had been doing to stare. The helicopters banked steeply to the left and turned back for a second pass. They were big and humpbacked, an airframe I knew well: Black Hawks. But this pair was painted in plain gray instead of camouflage pattern—Seahawks, then: the navy's version of the basic H-60 platform.

The second pass was slower, and I was able to get more detail for identification. There was a round pod protruding from the nose:

forward-looking infrared. Squadron markings on the fuselage, but I could not make them out. Two wing-like projections on either side of the airframe: hard points for the mounting of Hellfire missiles, currently unoccupied. But that is not to say that the helicopters were unarmed: the port-side doors of both aircraft were open, revealing crewmen in helmets with darkened visors crouched behind six-barreled Gatling guns—miniguns, as we used to call them, although there is nothing mini about the carnage they can wreak.

So the helicopters were HH-60Hs, a combat SAR and special forces variant with which I was well familiar. Armored, to withstand enemy groundfire. Night vision capable, to allow the aircrew to fly them into opposition territory low in the dark without radar. Heat signature suppression, to make it harder for shoulder-mounted IR-guided missiles to take them down. And finally those miniguns.

Miniguns are zone suppression weapons, designed to put down a mass of lead in a very short space of time. The idea is that with so much metal flying about the opposition will take cover rather than risk returning fire when the ship comes in to extract people of the type that I once was. They are 7.62 caliber weapons, exactly the same as my .308, except that miniguns sprout 4,000 rounds a minute, whereas my weapon's rate of fire was limited to how fast I could work the bolt.

A rifle was a waste of time in this situation—it could only make the gunners trigger-happy, and that would endanger my party. I ejected the chambered round and put the weapon down, bolt open, where it could be clearly seen from the air. I noticed the gunner on the lead ship nod, whether to himself or me I was not sure, but I could tell that he was thinking *wise move*.

They made several orbits of the site, like a dog circling a patch of ground before lying down.

The howler monkeys were dead quiet now.

Eventually, the lead gunship landed on the broad grassy expanse of Plaza B. The other continued to circle, minigun at the ready. Two men pushed past the lead ship's door gunner and out of the helicopter. Camouflage uniforms, tactical vests, M-16s at the ready—they were not sailors; they were marines. Their cammies were desert MARPAT instead of the woodland coloring they should have been wearing for jungle work. I wondered why; marines do not normally make mistakes like that. They trotted clear of the rotor wash and came to a halt halfway between the gunship and the base of the Caana. They stared straight up at me.

One of them stepped forward, cupped his left hand around his mouth, and yelled above the turbine whine.

"Captain?"

Not since the court-martial, but I guessed he meant me.

I turned to Eduardo. He was standing nearby, staring down at the scene in the plaza, his face bearing the universal look of wary distrust with which the downtrodden view all authority.

When I first decided to work down here I had begun at the marketplace of San Ignacio, the last outpost on the Western Highway before the Guatemalan border and the only town of any size in the Cayo district. San Ignacio conforms to the common pattern of provincial towns in the Third World—whether in Belize or Somalia or the Philippines they are all, apart from details of language and race and climate, much the same: concrete boxy buildings rarely more than two stories tall; in the center of town a jam of people and sidewalk vendors and small vehicles with rattling exhausts; then as you head out heaps of masonry, dogs running wild, folks standing or sitting, content to let time pass. Soon the streets turn into dirt tracks or simply end. And they all smell alike, a pungent mixture of diesel fumes and cooking grease, sweat and spice and sewerage—the results of poor plumbing and open-air cooking, but not as bad as it sounds.

If you want to recruit labor in such a place you begin at the marketplace, in this case a dusty expanse of ground with several rows of stalls under long thatched rooves. I had spoken with a few of the proprietors to put the word out, telling them what I wanted and where I could be found. Among the men who had subsequently shown up was Eduardo, somewhere between thirty and fifty years of age, short and stocky, skin the color of old leather, and with a past on which he did not elaborate but that I gathered had included several stints of delivering goods across the border without the inconvenience and expense of a customs inspection. That meant he knew the jungle, so I hired him. By the end of the first season—I only run treks during the dry—he had my confidence. Now, at the end of the second season, he had my trust.

"If I have to go with these people you're in charge," I said. "Don't alarm the guests, just give them my apologies and tell them I was called away in an emergency. Let them have their fill of the ruins, then drop them off at the lodge as usual." After Caracol we take them to a luxurious jungle lodge on the Privassion River to end the tour, an opportunity for a proper shower, a celebratory dinner, and a good night's sleep in a real bed before flying back home the next day.

Eduardo just nodded, a man who wasted no words. I shouldered the backpack and began the long descent down the broad steep staircase scaling the southern face of the Caana, much as prisoners destined for human sacrifice must have a millennium before.

The marines were waiting at the bottom. I stopped ten feet in front of them. The one who had called up to me was the older of the two, a black man wearing three chevrons with two rockers below and crossed rifles in between. A little gray among the stubble of his buzz cut. Long past his twenty; he was in for life. His name tape said Gandry. He held his M-16 in his right hand only, barrel-down. The other marine was an E-2, probably still in his teens, fresh from Parris Island and Infantry School, gripping his carbine like a security blanket, a kid who did not have the look yet. Gandry had brought him along to help toughen him up, I guessed—get him into a situation where he could not just blend in with the rest of the platoon.

My eyes reverted to the older man.

"What can I do for you, Gunnery Sergeant?"

"Captain Dalton? Captain Lysander Dalton?"

"Just 'Mister' now."

"Would you come with us, sir?"

He gestured toward the waiting helicopter with a jerk of his head and took a step in its direction, expecting me to follow. The PFC went the same way.

I remained where I was.

Gunnery Sergeant Gandry stopped. The private first class took a little longer to figure out that I was not following them.

Gandry nodded to himself and turned back around. Left hand on the guard now, right thumb at the fire selector. I doubted that he was even consciously aware of the changed grip—by this stage in his career that M-16 was as familiar to him as a limb, its use automatic, something accomplished without conscious thought.

He took a step forward before speaking again.

"Sir, I was imprecise. What I meant to say was that we have orders to bring you back with us. Sir."

He was right, he had been imprecise. *Would you come with us?* suggests choice, but in the Marine Corps anything that begins with the words *We have orders* means that there is absolutely no choice at all.

I stepped forward and ducked under the rotor blades.

EXCEPTING THOSE FOR THE AIRCREW, there were no proper seats in the Seahawk. Instead, there was aluminum-framed webbing which included lap belts that I had learned from long experience it was wise to wear. I strapped myself in and across from me Gandry did the same. The PFC was too busy slapping at mosquitoes.

I reached into my backpack and pulled out a plastic bottle of Skin-so-Soft. Pretty much all marines who do jungle work use Skin-so-Soft, a commercial moisturizer that has the unintended quality of also being an excellent insect repellant. It is favored over service-issue repellant not because marines like to care for their complexions but because it does not smell as much and so the odor will not give your presence away. Every PX stocks it. I wordlessly passed the stuff to the kid, but when he read the label he looked up at me in disbelief.

"So you just deployed down here," I said.

The PFC nodded dumbly. The gunnery sergeant looked annoyed—like any good NCO, he was not happy at having his people shown up.

The engine note changed, and the rotor began increasing RPM. The door gunner stayed by the minigun for the extraction. I shook my head in disbelief: all this firepower for a simple transport job—our tax dollars at work.

I caught Gandry's eye.

"Where are we headed, Gunny?"

"The Big Stick, sir"

At that moment the pilot came onto the throttle and pulled up on the collective, lifting us from the ground. The increased roar was too loud for me to ask Gandry what the "Big Stick" was.

II

I TRIED TO FIGURE OUT WHAT they wanted with me. The Big Stick was presumably the name of a base camp, probably just a landing field hacked out of the jungle somewhere. Back when I was a marine we used to do a lot of work in Central America, some of it public but much of it secretive and funded by creative means. I knew the DEA still operated down here, and all of a sudden I hoped that, whatever this was about, Eduardo was not involved. I had assumed that his off-season smuggling activities were of the benign variety, intended to bypass Guatemalan authorities who were notoriously corrupt, little more than criminals in uniform. But if the DEA was involved, that changed everything.

Maybe it would be something simple, perhaps just a friendly request to keep an eye out for signs of illicit activity during my own long treks through the jungle, although if that was all there was to it then why send armed gunships?

The helicopters did not continue into the jungle. Instead, we headed directly east, toward the coastal plain. The canopy below gradually gave way to wide flat fields and broad brown rivers. Soon we came to the coast and Belize City, a twenty-minute interval to accomplish a journey that would have taken two hours by four-wheel drive.

We did not land in Belize City; the Seahawks continued straight past it and out over the Caribbean. Viewed from the air, the sea below revealed itself as a vast variegated sampling from the far end of the visible spectrum: lush turquoise in the sandy-bottomed shallows, vibrant jade-green around the coral reefs, and then the depthless dark indigo of the ocean beyond.

I suddenly realized what the Big Stick must be and looked at the patches on the door gunner's flight suit for verification. One of them had a trident symbol with "HSC-35" over the top: his squadron affiliation. A second patch bore the confirmation that I was searching for: "CVN-71."

In my day they had different nicknames, like "Big John" (*Kennedy*), "Battle Cat" (*Kitty Hawk*), and "Connie" (*Constellation*), this last always expressed with the particular affection that sailors retain for the name of the navy's first ship.

The aircraft carriers had changed and presumably so too had the nicknames, but what could the "Big Stick" be other than the *Theodore Roosevelt*, an embodiment in steel and fissionable material of the twenty-sixth president's famously expressed foreign policy: *Speak softly and carry a big stick*. Sure enough, a series of long white wakes came into view, dead straight lines cutting across the calm blue below, soon followed by the battle group itself: a sprinkling of cruisers and destroyers and frigates, a big supply ship lumbering along in the back, and at the center of the formation the vast flat deck of the great capital ship whose humble attendants they all were: the aircraft carrier USS *Theodore Roosevelt*.

The helicopter banked for the approach.

Helicopters do not land on an aircraft carrier in the way that might be expected: hovering above the deck and then gradually lowering themselves. Instead, they go into a hover by the ship's side, matching her for course and speed, but over the water rather than over the ship itself—that way if something goes wrong they will drop into the drink and thus not foul the deck for continuing air operations. Launch and recover—carriers exist for no other purpose, and they would rather lose a helicopter than allow anything to interfere. With the helicopter just above the level of the flight deck, the pilot edged it over and quickly landed, having spent the minimum amount of time over the carrier itself, and at a height where a sudden drop would have unlikely caused the ship any serious damage.

The deck crew rushed to chock and chain the aircraft. The pilots shut down the engines, but before the rotor had stopped spinning I was being escorted out and across the broad expanse of the flight deck, several football fields in size. The carrier had four catapults, but only the two at the bow were currently in operation. An EA-6B sat on one, about to launch, and an F-18 was being towed toward the other. The air smelled of brine and burning jet fuel. Between the wind and the turbine whine conversation would have been impossible, yet there was a mass of activity, much of it coordinated with hand signals, immensely complex and seemingly chaotic but actually it was just the opposite, something conducted with the precise choreography of a ballet. The carrier was steaming into the wind, as they always do for launch, and so great wafts of warm exhaust came washing across the flight deck from the two aircraft up front.

There was a sudden roar, the high-pitched howl of turbines throttling up to full thrust. The two marines and I stopped instinctively, turning to watch as the Prowler was launched, the deafening sound of its engines momentarily overshadowed by the almighty wallop from the catapult. The aircraft was briefly obscured as it dipped below deck level and then reappeared again as it gained airspeed and climbed. A carrier like the *Roosevelt* would weigh in at something like 100,000 tons, yet the blow from that mighty catapult reaching the end of its short run was sufficient to have sent a physical jolt throughout the entire ship, as if Zeus himself, perhaps feeling his own immensity challenged by that of the carrier, had suddenly chosen to slap it with a thunderbolt.

It was hard not to be impressed. What an awesome and terrible human achievement is a Nimitz-class nuclear-powered aircraft carrier.

We continued across the flight deck, around an elevator the size of a house coming up from below, and over the braided steel lines that span the plating: arresting wires that slow the aircraft when the tail hook catches them on recovery. Eventually we reached the starboard side and the carrier's one slender piece of superstructure: the island. We went through a clipped steel door and entered a new world: calm and quiet, comfortably air-conditioned, a startling contrast to the noisy hubbub outside. I was expecting to head down below into the bowels of the great ship, but instead we took a ladderway up.

Aircraft carriers have two bridges. The first is like that on any other ship: the place from which the vessel is maneuvered and the preserve of the captain. But there is another bridge—the flag bridge—immediately below the first. This second bridge belongs to the admiral, the man who commands the entire battle group.

I was led to the flag bridge. We came to a halt outside. Gunnery Sergeant Gandry opened the door and with a nod indicated that I was to go on in alone. My marine escort would leave me here—I guessed that they wanted nothing further to do with whoever lurked on the other side.

I stepped inside. The door closed, and I could hear the rasping scrape of metal on metal as the clips were closed tight behind me.

The bridge was L-shaped, the long side running parallel to the flight deck, and the short side in front running athwartships. Wide windows lined both, giving a broad view over flight operations and the seascape beyond. The space was fitted with the equipment usual on a ship's bridge: heading and gyrocompass repeaters, radar displays, a chart table and drawers, an array of microphones and squawk boxes. But there was no admiral's staff, indeed nobody at all apart from the lone figure occupying the large armchair that was raised high in the prime spot at the corner of the L—the admiral's chair.

Normally no one except the admiral himself would ever dare to sit in that chair, but the man whose corpulent bulk currently occupied it was no naval officer. He had not yet turned around but I recognized him, a creature only slightly less immense than the carrier itself, a man whom I knew well, but someone I had hoped never to see again.

III

I WALKED TO THE FRONT OF THE BRIDGE. Dortmund glanced at me dismissively—much as an entomologist might glance at a bug that properly came under his purview but which was too common to be worthy of extended scrutiny—and then returned his attention to the flight deck. His expression was not of interest in the air operations but rather one of concern, even dismay.

"I have been observing the activities below," he said after a while.

No greeting, no salutation. Perhaps he sensed that such an approach would have been rebuffed; more likely he thought me insufficiently important to warrant the expenditure of courtesy to begin with. He watched as the F-18 was hooked up.

"Do you realize that the planes do not take off in the normal manner, but are instead flung?"

"Catapult launch," I explained.

His face assumed a look of ever-increasing consternation as the preparations advanced. The jet blast deflector came up, the engines were brought to full throttle, and through the bubble of the cockpit we saw the pilot salute, giving the final go-ahead. A momentary pause and then the fighter was launched. The entire superstructure reverberated with the shock.

"Dreadful," Dortmund muttered.

"Dreadful?"

He huffed a little before responding.

"After our little *tête-à-tête* today, my presence will be required back in Washington—there has been an incident in Kamchatka that requires my attention. I had thought that nothing could be as bad as the mode of my arrival on this wretched boat, but now that I have watched for a while I realize that the departure will be even worse. I do not look forward to being flung."

I wondered what they would take him back in. Probably an old S-3 stripped down for cargo duty—he would be too fat to fit into a regular aircraft's cockpit.

As he continued to watch the flight operations I inspected him, a man who although not technically my enemy was nevertheless someone for whom I bore an unusual degree of ill-will. Massive bulk encased as always in the finest of hand-tailored suits, made from black priest-cloth and cut by a tailor skilled in lending dignity to avoirdupois. White button-down shirt and plain black silk tie. Black oxfords, highly polished but surprisingly small—like many fat people, Dortmund had little hands and feet. His hair was shot through with gray. The Richelieu-like mustache and pointed goatee were unchanged, as was the cold hard stare of those steel-gray eyes—in both face and temperament he remained a living avatar of the Iron Cardinal, a Machiavellian man who pursued the interests of state with a relentless and unapologetic ruthlessness.

He seemed not to have aged since the day I had last seen him, more than two years ago, at the Mayflower Club in Washington D.C.—despite being a government man Dortmund preferred to conduct business from his private club, where there were no visitors' entry logs or requirements to present a photo ID, just a discreet place in which his guests could remain unknown and unremarked. It also happened to be conveniently located a few blocks west of the White House, the maximum distance that Dortmund was capable of covering on foot.

At least there was one positive quality, previously unsuspected, that I could now attribute to him: physical courage. If I was in his shoes I would not have risked meeting me again without having those marines, armed and ready, in close attendance. But then perhaps he had no choice: Dortmund was the sort of man for whom human transactions were best conducted without witnesses.

He turned away from the flight deck, having seen enough.

"Captain Dalton, you have greatly discommoded me," he said. "What is it that you actually do down here in this malarial bog?"

Vintage Dortmund: he sends two gunships with armed marines in what was little more than a polite abduction and then demands an explanation from the abductee.

"Jungle tours." I did not expand on the answer.

"And your vineyard?"

This time I did not bother answering at all. Ever since my involuntary separation from the Marine Corps, many years ago now, I have lived quietly in my vineyard in northern Virginia, tending the grapes, reaping the harvest, turning it into wine. I have survived a number of challenges over the years, from ravenous gophers to armed assault. To resolve the former I built owl boxes in the nearby trees, whose grateful occupants soon disposed of the varmint problem; the armed assault I had to deal with myself. But then a new threat had come in the form of a tiny aphid-like parasite—phylloxera—barely visible to the naked eye, but a creature whose infestations rapidly destroy grape vines. American vines are resistant to the bug and for this reason the majority of the world's commercial grapevines are grafted onto American rootstock, as too were all the new plantings that I had made. But most of the vines on my property had been there when I bought the place, and they were not grafts but French-American hybrids. Each year I gradually replaced some, but not fast enough. Phylloxera came and infested the remainder, more than half the total production.

That put a temporary halt to my winemaking. I ripped out all the old vines and replanted by grafting cabernet sauvignon and cabernet franc scions onto 1103P or 110R rootstock, both of which suit the varietals and the soil, and are resistant to not just phylloxera but also nematodes, the other parasitic threat to grape vines.

But it takes three years for new vines to produce grapes suitable for table wine, five to reach full maturity. My bank manager was not going to put a three-year moratorium on the mortgage payments. So while waiting for the new vines to come in I sold the remaining harvest to other producers, and meanwhile looked around for a suitable way to supplement my income.

In the marines I had been a captain in force reconnaissance, the Marine Corps' version of special forces. In force recon you learn a lot of interesting skills but unfortunately there is little demand for them outside of the military. However, as I sat back among the ruins of the vines and made a mental inventory of my minimal marketable talents, I realized that one thing I did know was the jungle, particularly the jungles of Central America, where I had been involved in several operations. So during the dry season I began running specialist jungle treks into Belize—least corrupt of the Central American states—and which I restricted to the fit and adventurous: part eco-tour, part archeological expedition, part jungle warfare training. The groups are platoon-sized, mainly couples. The women are usually tougher than the men, confirming my long-held view that all military specializations, including combat roles, should be open to females. We begin in the appropriately named Hidden Valley, deep in the Mountain Pine Ridge area, and hike upriver to the base of a spectacular fifteen-hundred-foot waterfall, a magnificent sight inaccessible except by a combination of machete and climbing gear. We camp there for the first night, swimming in the deep pool at the bottom and showering under cool water cascading down from a quarter-mile above. The next day is spent working from the base to the summit, then further into the jungle, until after five days we arrive at the crown jewel: Caracol.

Meanwhile, the fecund immensity of the jungle was ours to savor: fabulous flora and fauna, from the smallest—like *Pyrophorus noctilucus*, a bioluminescent beetle whose twin thorax spots glow like little green LED lights, bright enough to read by—to the biggest: giant ceiba trees, two hundred feet tall, five hundred years old, with trunks like grain silos and massive root buttresses bigger than a man. In between, we experience everything that the jungle has to offer, eating fresh fruit and fish and occasionally fried snake, sharing sunset cocktails in the company of sociable toucans and chatty macaws, and sometimes confronting the fearful, like freediving through black water into a cave containing the burial jars of the ancient Mayans, a place whose flooded entrance has protected it from looters, and once having an unexpected encounter with a jaguar, an animal that after a long contemplation of my party had quietly turned and disappeared back into the undergrowth, leaving me thankful that I had not been required to shoot it.

All of this would have been lost on Dortmund. He thought of nature as he thought of everything else, without sentiment, something to be either used or destroyed at will, whatever happened to be most convenient to his purposes at the time.

After I failed to answer Dortmund nodded to himself, having gotten the message that the time for small talk was past.

"Perhaps we might be of service to each other, Captain Dalton."

"Perhaps you can start by paying me what you owe me."

Fifteen months ago I had run an operation for Dortmund. It was not until its conclusion that he had seen fit to reveal that the operation had been off the books, completely unauthorized, and intended to have been funded with gold bullion aboard a tramp steamer that by then lay at the bottom of the Atlantic Ocean. My fee, which would have paid off the mortgage and left me in full possession of my vineyard, was utterly unreachable, a mile beneath the surface of the sea. He cleared his throat before responding.

"I believe that an arrangement accommodating your requirements might be made."

Dortmund: accomplished master of the noncommittal double-talk that is the *lingua franca* of Washington D.C. I leaned on the window frame and looked out over the carrier's flight deck. The helicopter that had brought me was still there. They had not yet folded the rotor blades, a good sign.

"I'm ready for my ride back now."

"I ask that you first hear me out, Captain Dalton. After that, I will be happy to return you to the place whence you came."

If I could have walked out I would have done so, but on a ship at sea there is nowhere to walk to. I had no choice but to hear the old devil out.

"Okay, what do you want?"

"For you to recover a piece of missing property."

"What sort of missing property?"

"A notebook."

He reached over to a briefcase stowed in a rack on the bulkhead. It was of the old-fashioned type, thick leather, soft sided, and with a flap folding over the top that was held down with two brass-buckled straps. The leather was dark brown, scratched here and there, shiny like an old saddle with age and use. Dortmund unbuckled the straps and withdrew a notebook—octavo-sized, about six by nine—bound in blue and bearing a gold emblem embossed on the cover. He passed it to me.

"A notebook like this one," he said.

I inspected it. Three-quarters of an inch thick. The pages were lined but otherwise blank. Good quality paper, fine Morocco binding. I looked at the front cover.

It was not an emblem but a seal, circular, with an eagle in the center, wings spread and holding a banner in its beak that bore the familiar motto *E Pluribus Unum*. Around the circumference were the words *United States Senate*.

"Been stealing from the Capitol supply room, Mr. Dortmund? You ought to be ashamed."

"The missing notebook does not belong to me."

"Whose is it?"

But instead of immediately answering Dortmund sat back and sighed. I understood why. Until now he had told me nothing definite, nothing whose revelation in the wrong quarter could come back and bite him one day. But as soon as he uttered a name, he knew all that would change. I would possess knowledge then, a commodity that to Dortmund equates with power, and when it came to power Dortmund was a paragon of parsimoniousness. Like a starving miser reluctantly opening a cobwebbed wallet, Dortmund could only be separated from his secrets by the most pressing of needs.

"William Stolper," he said at last. "You recognize the name, I take it?"

"The senator, I assume."

Dortmund nodded.

Stolper was an up-and-coming politician from one of the deep Dixie states, Alabama or Arkansas or the like. Tough, ambitious, photogenic, someone who had raised himself to the front ranks of his party leadership in a short space of time. Staunchly conservative, but with a gloss of New South sophistication to make him more palatable above the Mason-Dixon line. Intelligent, articulate, and a phenomenal fundraiser, particularly from the K Street outposts of the defense industry. He was sometimes called 'Battleship Bill' because of his strong support for the armed forces, especially the navy. I wondered if that was how Dortmund had managed to have an entire carrier battle group placed at his disposal.

"Since the mid-term election, Stolper is the senior senator from Mississippi," Dortmund explained. "He has been given the chairmanship of both the select committee on intelligence and the appropriations subcommittee on defense—two very powerful positions."

Mississippi, of course: there is a huge naval shipyard in Pascagoula, easily Mississippi's largest private employer and a certain source of support every six years for any senatorial candidate demanding a bigger navy.

"I take it that the missing notebook was not blank."

"It was not."

"What was in it?"

"Notes for his memoirs." Dortmund gave a snort of contempt. "It seems that the honorable senator has convinced himself that posterity will be enlightened by a detailed account of his career, something that he believes may yet reach higher than the senate chamber. Accordingly, he keeps notes. Like a diary, apparently— something that he updates every day. I think he imagines the wretched things ending up in his own presidential library someday."

"And the missing notebook contains classified material?"

"Unfortunately, *classified material* is an understatement. As the intelligence committee chairman, Stolper is the recipient of the most sensitive information."

"Which he wrote down?"

Dortmund merely nodded.

"What was it?"

He took a deep breath before responding.

"Our country has entered into certain contingent security arrangements with respect to the containment of a particular rogue state. These arrangements were mostly negotiated with countries ruled by families. It is customary in such negotiations to offer the parties involved a *douceur*, appropriately cloaked in the guise of aid or some such. Since Congress holds the purse strings the funding for these must necessarily go through an appropriations bill, but of course the money cannot be held accountable since it is ultimately destined for the private Swiss bank accounts of those involved. Therefore the funding goes into an intelligence appropriations bill. The details of intelligence appropriations bills are kept secret from the public, and indeed from most members of congress, but unfortunately the chairmen of the house and senate intelligence committees must be fully briefed."

He shook his head in discontent at this last requirement. Dortmund had nothing but contempt for politicians, whom he regarded as irrelevant impediments to his own grand schemes. If in the unpredictable roulette wheel of representative elections a candidate's number came up, he believed that the winner should confine his activities while in office to shaking hands, smiling for the cameras, and raising funds for the next campaign, meanwhile leaving the serious business of statecraft to those fit for the task, meaning himself. Strange that a man who had devoted his life to the buttressing of American power should be such a fervent despiser of democracy.

There were only two rogue states with which the U.S. was so concerned, and only one of them was surrounded by family-ruled kingdoms, so I assumed that they were bribing the rulers of the Gulf states to help contain Iran. There was a certain irony to the fact that we were paying bribes to people already made immensely rich by our unquenchable thirst for oil.

"Stolper wrote it all down?"

"Everything."

"And lost it?"

"Yes."

"How?"

In response, Dortmund pulled out a manila envelope from the briefcase and passed it to me. I undid the clasp and withdrew the contents: a single glossy eight-by-ten photograph.

A woman. A portrait shot, professionally done. She had a sort of startling, in-your-face attractiveness: buxom and blond, smooth even features, wide smile revealing either naturally fortunate dentition or expensive orthodonture. Dimples, whose cuteness was offset by long gray eyes that saw much but gave away little. Fine skin: she was a woman who looked after her complexion. The slip dress she wore displayed the taut well-toned arms of someone who spends a lot of time at the gym.

Hard to tell much from a single photograph. Early thirties, I thought, but I am not good at guessing such things. I had the impression of someone with more cunning than intellect, but I often get women wrong, and she could have been a rocket scientist for all I knew.

Not a woman easily dismissed, that much was certain.

"Who is she?"

"Her name is Hanna Moran," Dortmund replied. "Stolper met her at a fundraiser six months ago. To cut a long and predictably tedious story short, he ended up installing her in an apartment in Washington. His wife and family remain at home when congress is in session. Apparently, he gets lonely in D.C."

Now I knew why they wanted an outsider like me. An official investigation would inevitably leak, in the way that they do. Stolper's core constituency was Southern conservative: godfearing souls who took the Ten Commandments seriously—they would not forgive such a blatant breach of item number seven. A passing lapse might be survivable, but installing a woman in an apartment was something else altogether. If the affair were revealed, Battleship Bill's political career would run aground. No shot at that presidential library.

"What's she got to do with the missing notebook?"

"She has it."

"Then Stolper should ask for it back."

"It is not just the notebook that is missing—so also is Miss Moran." Dortmund shifted his great bulk awkwardly, uncomfortable in the seat or perhaps just uncomfortable in revealing so much to me. "Stolper last saw her Wednesday two weeks ago. It was his habit to make notes of the day's activities each evening, and he did so that night when he was at her apartment. Either he inadvertently left the notebook there, or else she removed it from his attaché case before he left—he cannot be sure. The senator flew home straight after Thursday's senate session and remained there for the following week, the usual recess after Memorial Day. He returned to Washington this past week. When he went to Hanna Moran's apartment he found it empty. I assume that in the intervening fourteen days she went through the senator's notebook, probably only to see if there was anything about herself inside. Instead, she discovered that it contained a full disclosure of our containment strategy, including a detailed list of which countries had committed to what actions and how much they had been paid to do so. Undoubtedly Moran realized that what she possessed was something of enormous value. Now she will try to sell it, perhaps back to the senator, but as yet she has not contacted him. I think it is more likely that she will enter into negotiations elsewhere. Perhaps with the parties named, more likely with the rogue state in question."

"Are you watching the embassy?"

"There is no embassy to watch."

Confirming that it was Iran, a country with which we have no diplomatic relations.

"For obvious reasons, the senator could not go to the authorities," Dortmund continued. "The one wise thing he did in all this was to come to me."

Actually, it was probably the least wise thing of all. I could imagine it: a hastily arranged lunch in the dining room of the Mayflower Club, or maybe just a quiet drink in the library. Stolper doing the talking, explaining the situation with an occasional rueful shrug of his shoulders. Dortmund listening, nodding from time to time, saying little while rapidly calculating how best to take advantage of this delicious little morsel being unexpectedly delivered into his lap. What Stolper had done was to address one problem by creating a bigger one, because from that moment forward he would forever be in the clutches of Dortmund, a man who would be sure to wring from him every political favor he could grant.

"You must find Hanna Moran," Dortmund said. "Find her, and you will find the notebook, too."

I passed back the photograph.

"Sorry, I'm busy."

"Busy doing what?"

"I told you: jungle tours."

"I am assured that you only conduct these jungle tours during the dry season, Captain Dalton. I am further assured that the dry season down here is January through May. Since it is now the beginning of June, I therefore conclude that the tour you have just completed will be the last for this year."

I should have known better than to have imagined that Dortmund would inconvenience himself without having first ordered a thorough background investigation. Right now he probably knew my schedule better than I did.

"It doesn't make any difference. I'm an ex-marine; I don't know anything about tracking people down."

"You forget that I have access to your service records," Dortmund said. "All of them."

"That was different."

"Not really. You tracked people down, Captain Dalton, just as I am asking you to do. The only difference is what happened when you found them."

I did not respond. It was not a subject open for discussion.

Dortmund reached into his briefcase and removed another large envelope, this one thicker than the first.

"Everything you will need is in here: money and credit card, notes from the interview with Stolper, his copy of the keys to her apartment. Find her and recover the notebook, Captain Dalton, then you will be forever relieved of your mortgage."

"I've heard that song before."

"This time the funding is assured. The senator himself will insert the appropriate earmark into an appropriations bill. He gets what he wants, you get what you want, and you both have a strong motivation to see that the other is fully satisfied. A perfect arrangement, I think."

"And what do you get out of it, Mr. Dortmund?"

He almost smiled, a rare event.

"The senator has kindly undertaken to earmark further funds for some as yet unspecified future operations," he said.

So it was a three-way deal. Stolper saves his career, I save my vineyard, and Dortmund gets a slush fund. A cozy arrangement of mutual dependence conducted in classic D.C. fashion.

I would have liked to just turn and leave, ask the first person I saw for directions to Flight Control, then go and arrange a ride back to Belize. But in the special forces you learn to be a clear-eyed realist, and the hard reality was that these days I was at a greater risk of losing my vineyard than I had ever been and would remain so until those new vines started producing. The vineyard was all I had. Dortmund knew this of course—he had made a career out of the careful manipulation of other people, locating their vulnerabilities like little veins of precious ore, then relentlessly digging away until the lode was exhausted. He knew my weakness well, and he was mining it right now.

I took the proffered envelope.

IV

I SAT BACK IN THE BIG leather seat and ordered a drink.
I do not normally fly first class. I do not normally fly unrestricted
coach either, instead opting for the cheapest advance purchase ticket
available, but since Dortmund was picking up the tab I had upgraded
the return leg from Belize City, putting it on the credit card that had
been among the items in the envelope he had given me.

The card was a Visa. On the previous operation it had been an
American Express Platinum card, a credit card without restrictions.
Visa cards have limits. I wondered what it was on the one he had
given me.

The drink arrived. In first class they are free but in coach you have
to pay; it is expensive to be poor. The flight attendant looked
uncomfortable; I was the only passenger in first class wearing
combat boots and probably the only one with a weapon in checked
baggage.

We reached cruising altitude. The seat belt sign was extinguished.
I opened the overhead compartment and removed the envelope from

my backpack. There were three hours before arrival in Dulles to study its contents.

The documents inside were still curled—something that happens to all paper in the humidity of the jungle to which I had been returned after the interview with Dortmund—but at least in the bone dry air at 30,000 feet they had dried out. There was an interview record, several pages of bullet points summarizing what Stolper had told Dortmund, although neither of their names was mentioned, just Hanna Moran's.

According to the senator, she was a fashion model by profession. Originally from San Francisco, like me. Only child, parents dead, no close relatives—again like me. Thirty-five years old. Self-contained, according to Stolper. She was fond of music and the arts, a regular at the Kennedy Center. When she was not on assignment she spent her days in the museums or shopping or working out at the gym, keeping in shape as her profession required. Liked the finer things in life: designer clothes and expensive restaurants, although these last were usually off-limits to them together in case he was recognized. Apparently she had a deep affection for French fashions, something Stolper had discovered to the detriment of his bank balance. But he had not flinched at the expense of maintaining his mistress: her Virginia Avenue apartment alone had cost him three thousand dollars a month. I wondered how much U.S. senators were paid.

Whatever her real name was, it was probably not Hanna Moran. Dortmund had ordered a basic background check, intended to obtain a Social Security number while remaining shallow enough to ensure that no connection with Stolper was inadvertently revealed. It turned out that there were no Hanna Morans born anywhere in the Bay area thirty-five years ago, and the two that had been born during the proceeding five years (allowing for possible discounting of her age) were both otherwise accounted for. She was not a registered voter. She had no credit cards, nor even a credit record. And if she really was a model, then she had failed to file an income tax return for the last five years.

So Dortmund had been unable to get a Social Security number, the key that would have unlocked everything else about her. Stolper knew little of her background beyond the basics, and I guessed that most of their conversation together had centered on himself rather than her.

The fashion model part was questionable to begin with—fashion models live and work in New York or Los Angeles or Miami, not Washington, D.C. I wondered if Stolper, who was supposedly smart, had believed her. Perhaps; a woman can turn even the most intelligent of men into fools.

Apart from the photograph I had already seen there were no other documents. There was a set of keys to her apartment—the spare set that she had given to the senator—five of them on a split ring, three large, two small.

I sat back and thought about what I had learned. Possibly Hanna Moran had set up the senator from the beginning—going to the fundraiser with the specific intention of meeting him and then relying on a combination of good looks and subtly expressed willingness to achieve the rest. How many attractive young women have a genuine interest in politics, sufficient to attend a fundraiser? And the fact that she had lied about her name supported the idea.

But there could be other reasons to use a false name: perhaps she had a past that she wanted to put behind her or a persistent former lover who could only be disposed of by disappearing, at least temporarily. Maybe she was a model, and Hanna Moran was her professional name. Or it could be just that she did not like her real name and had simply chosen to use another. There are a lot of benign reasons for a person to use a false name, especially a woman.

Was she operating alone? Although Moran could not have known of Stolper's habit of diarizing state secrets, maybe someone else did. Perhaps that someone had sent her to the fundraiser specifically to meet the senator, hoping to spark a relationship that if all went well would eventually access the type of information to which Stolper was privileged.

It could not be ruled out, but it seemed unlikely. In the past when Dortmund and his Soviet counterparts had been busy playing spy-versus-spy it might have been a realistic possibility, but who today would have the imagination to come up with such a scheme, let alone the necessary combination of patience, resources, and finesse to pull it off? And if Hanna Moran had been a professional then it would not have ended this way. She would have stayed on, hoping to get more. Or if all she had come for was the notebook then she would have photocopied it and allowed Stolper to reclaim the original when he next came over. She would have betrayed no sign of having read it; would probably have expressed surprise when it was found. Later, she would have engineered a reason for disengagement—a quarrel, a long overseas assignment, or maybe just a desire to move on—something which would not have revealed the true purpose. That was half the game in Dortmund's world: not letting the other side know what you had on them.

Disappearing with the original was an amateur's move.

The more I thought about it, the more likely it seemed to me that Hanna Moran had been operating alone. In Stolper she had found someone who would keep her comfortable, at least for a while, and Hanna had probably been content to leave it like that until the day she had discovered the notebook and realized that she had stumbled upon a retirement plan.

Now I had to find her before she cashed it in.

V

HANNA MORAN'S VIRGINIA AVENUE address turned out to be the Watergate.

The Watergate is not a single building but a complex of them: shops, a hotel, two office towers, three residential blocks. It is a strange place, an architectural jumble of ellipses and rhomboids decorated with shark-toothed cornices and course strings. It took five years to build. The anything-goes design reflected the era in which construction had commenced: the 'Sixties, that period of great optimism beginning with JFK and which reached its zenith in the summer of 1967. By the time the Watergate was finished so was the optimism, crushed by assassinations and race riots and the Vietnam War, and with any remaining embers soon to be extinguished by an event that would occur right here. The Watergate is unique: a place whose name serves as the epitaph to its own age.

I walked around the site for a while, getting a feel for the layout. Ten acres in all. I soon realized why Stolper had chosen to install Hanna Moran here. The Watergate is a city within a city; it even has its own zip code. With so many people there is constant foot traffic; a lone man leaving late at night would not be worth a second glance. The buildings have multiple entrances and exits and so there is no requirement to pass by the front desk, as long as you have a key. Tourists, too: a place where strangers were to be expected. The Watergate was the perfect place in D.C. in which to stash a mistress—I wondered how a guy smart enough to have chosen it could have misplaced major state secrets, and misplaced the mistress, too.

Hanna Moran's building—2500 Virginia Ave., a.k.a. Watergate East—had a large lobby complete with a doorman and reception desk. A sign read *All visitors must be announced.* I circumnavigated the building until finding a rear entrance and, suspecting that Stolper would probably have used the same door, tried the keys. Sure enough, one of them fit. Breaking into the Watergate is an activity with a venerable past, although since I had the keys perhaps my uninvited intrusion did not qualify. But like my unlucky predecessors two generations earlier, I entered without permission and went in via the back door.

Moran's apartment was on the ninth floor. One bedroom. Hardwood floors. Views over the Potomac.

I had expected to find the apartment still furnished but it turned out to be completely empty—just a bare shell of walls and floor and windows. I went through the place anyway, checking kitchen drawers and bathroom cabinets and bedroom closets. There was nothing, not even dust. I could smell the lingering trace of ammonia and guessed that the realtors must have already had a cleaning service in, preparing the place for showing to potential new tenants. The cleaning service had done a thorough job.

After finishing the search I went out onto the balcony for some fresh air. The garden below was in full spring bloom and even nine floors up I could smell the flowers. The sun was high overhead. The ever-restless Potomac ran by, its surface broad and gray and uneven, as if it were shallow enough for rapids although in fact the river is very deep here. How unlike the lazy Rappahannock, which flows by my own vineyard, quiet and brown-green, as unchanging as a country lane. It was as if the Potomac's proximity to the political vagaries of Washington was sufficient to physically disturb the water.

There was nothing for me to find here.

I went back downstairs and entered the shopping mall. Among the stores was a dry-cleaning service. The man behind the counter was about fifty, Oriental, sorting through a pile of laundry left by the last customer. He bore the perpetually harassed look of a guy who runs his own business. I knew how he felt.

"I have to pick up my girlfriend's cleaning," I said. "But she didn't give me the ticket."

He looked at me with more annoyance than suspicion.

"No ticket?"

"She's away on a business trip."

I shrugged my shoulders in the universal you-know-women gesture that men use to succinctly express their frustrations with the fairer sex. He nodded his head in quiet understanding.

"Name?"

"Hanna Moran. She's in Watergate East."

I gave him the apartment number. He went to his computer and tapped the keys. Eventually, he looked back up at me.

"I don't have anything for her," he said.

"You sure?"

"Sure."

"Do you have the date she made the last pickup?"

His eyes reverted to the screen.

"Last Wednesday."

So Hanna Moran had been living here until last Wednesday at least. Today was Monday. That meant two business days for her to have moved out, returned the keys, and for the realtor to have brought in a cleaning team. The timing was possible but tight. The cleaning service might work Saturdays. Or maybe they had been in this morning, before my flight landed. Still, it was tight.

"She must have picked it up herself after all," I said. "Guess she forgot to tell me."

He said nothing in reply. I turned toward the front door, then stopped.

"Say, can I get a hanger while I'm here? I need some wire for my exhaust."

Now he looked suspicious. He reached under the counter and emerged with a hanger, which he passed to me.

"What do I owe you?"

"Nothing," he said. "It's on the house."

I RETURNED TO HANNA MORAN'S APARTMENT. I used a quarter to unscrew the retaining bolt on the shower stall drain and removed the cover. I untwisted the wire at the neck of the hanger and straightened it out as best I could, leaving only the hook at the end intact. Then I shoved it down into the drainpipe, hooked end first, until it came to the trap at the bottom of the U-bend. I made several explorations, twisting the wire, using different angles, but every time the hook came back empty. No hair, no soap chips, no sludge, nothing.

Every drain has something in the trap, unless it has been cleaned out recently. I wondered what sort of cleaning service it could be that they were so thorough as to have even routed and flushed the shower stall plumbing.

I replaced the drain cover and left the apartment. The door had a regular lock and a deadbolt, which accounted for two of the large keys. The building's rear door accounted for the third. That left the two smaller keys. On the way out I stopped by the mail boxes. One of the small keys opened Hanna Moran's mail box, but there was nothing inside. People usually get mail every day, most of it unsolicited. Hanna Moran must have placed a hold on her mail, something that confirmed what the empty apartment had already suggested: her disappearance was not impulsive; it had been carefully planned.

That left only the second small key unaccounted for. I assumed that it would be for a garage, but when I went down into the underground lot there were only open parking spaces, no enclosed garages.

There was nothing else for me to see. I left the Watergate, wondering what that second small key was for.

VI

I HEADED BACK TOWARD VIRGINIA, taking the Rock Creek and Potomac Parkway—a long name for a short road that winds along the river from Foggy Bottom down to the Mall. It was a high-skied hazeless day, too early yet for the oppressive humidity that envelops Washington during the summer, reminding you that it had all once been a swamp. I had the windows down and the air smelled of freshly mown pepper grass. The Lincoln Memorial lay ahead, cool marble in quiet repose. In the distance to the left rose the Washington Monument, and beyond it was the Capitol dome. To the right ran the river. I drove lazily, lost in thought about Hanna Moran, and so it was not until I missed the ramp for the Arlington Bridge that I realized I was being followed.

It was the same car that had pulled out after me when I left the Watergate, a Chrysler 300C that I recalled because the lights had been left on. Not just running lights, which some people illuminate for safety—all four headlamps were ablaze on high beam. And they were not the usual yellow-tinged color of regular headlamps but that piercing lightning-white of high-intensity discharge beams, an expensive option. I remembered thinking that the driver had probably chosen them just so he could leave them on and annoy other people, like me.

When I missed the turnoff that would have taken me back to the Virginia side of the river that same set of headlamps was behind me. I did not think anything of it at first, flowing with the rest of the traffic around into Independence Avenue. But then I exited onto the lonely spit of land separating the Tidal Basin from the river, looking for a quiet place to turn around. The only other vehicle to exit was the Chrysler.

There is not much down there, just park land dotted with occasional statues and memorials, the way park land is in D.C. There was no other traffic. The Jefferson Memorial loomed ahead, the marble rotunda gleaming in the sunlight, a few sightseers wandering about. There was a parking lot beside it, with a scattering of cars. If I was being followed, then I guessed it would be better to turn in an area where people were around.

I pulled in. Behind me, the high beams pulled in, too.

I came to a stop. The Chrysler halted about fifty yards away. For the first time I could see something of the vehicle other than the glare from those discharge beams. It was a big sedan, black. The windows were tinted, but I could make out the shadows of two people sitting inside.

I was driving my old pickup, a vehicle I was happy to have left in long-term parking at Dulles for the duration of the Belize trip because no one would want to steal it, and any incidental dings and scratches would just blend in with all the others. It had the power to pull tree stumps from the ground, but it was all torque and no action:

there was no chance of using it to outrun a car with a big Hemi V-8 under the hood.

I had the rifle, but it was locked in the backpack currently stowed in the cargo bed. Ammunition was in a separate compartment, also locked. To access and assemble the weapon would take several minutes, an operation that would be impossible to disguise. In the end I figured that I did not really need it. I was at the wheel of five thousand pounds of Detroit steel, grade-A kinetic material: my pickup was all the weapon I needed for now. I parked so that if required there was sufficient room for me to quickly swing the truck around and use it to effect.

It turned out to be unnecessary. No one got out of the other vehicle.

I looked up at Jefferson looking away from me. It had largely been on his advice—acquired in a prison cell and delivered across two centuries in the form of his *Notes on the State of Virginia*—that I had bought my home, a small vineyard on a big bend in the Rappahannock. The advice had been good, but it would have been useful if in that compendium Jefferson had included a warning about the parasitic creatures, like Dortmund, that inhabit the swamps of the Potomac.

I tried to formulate a plan. I had been intending to drive home but that was out of the question now—I was not going to lead these people to my vineyard.

We used to practice rapid operational planning in force recon, doing exercises in which you were suddenly presented with a tactical situation and given a brief set time in which to formulate a solution. Used to do it for real, too, on the battlefield. The key is to make sure from the beginning that you know exactly what it is that you want to achieve. Aims change. Sometimes you still want to destroy the target, just like you had originally planned. Other times the original plans have gone out the window, and all you want to do is get your people out as fast as humanly possible.

I knew right away what my aim was now. I wanted to talk to these guys following me, but I wanted to do it on my own terms. After a few minutes I had a rough plan figured out.

I pulled out of the parking area. The big sedan pulled out behind me.

I drove around the Tidal Basin back toward Independence Avenue. The Chrysler followed, a dozen or so car lengths behind. I rejoined the original route and was soon on the bridge crossing the Potomac.

At the end of the bridge, on the Virginia side, there is a big traffic circle. Most vehicles exit onto either the George Washington Parkway or the Jeff Davis Highway, but if you continue straight ahead as I did you end up on Memorial Drive. There was no traffic here; Memorial Drive is a dead end that goes to just one place. The only other vehicle to take it was the Chrysler behind me.

Ahead rose the wooded hills and stone-speckled lawns of my new destination: Arlington National Cemetery.

I entered the visitors' parking lot, but instead of following me the Chrysler just pulled over to the side of the road. There was only one way in or out and so—perhaps not wanting to risk getting hung up at the cashier when exiting—they had decided to wait outside and resume following when I left. That suited me just fine.

PEOPLE THINK OF ARLINGTON NATIONAL CEMETERY as the burial ground for big shots, but actually it is available to all military of any rank, active duty and retired alike. All except me, that is—dishonorable discharges do not qualify.

If you serve in the military for any length of time the chances are that you will have occasion to come to Arlington. I had been here four times. The least bad of them had been to bury a man who had once commanded me, and for whom I had borne a deep well of respect: Colonel John (Scarlett) O'Hara. It had been a memorable day they laid old Scarlett down. He was long retired by the time he died, and I had been several years out of the service myself, including six months of separation vacation in beautiful Leavenworth, Kansas.

Since Scarlett had been a full colonel he had been entitled to a fine ceremony. It had been a warm summer's day and Arlington had looked its best. We had proceeded by foot from the post chapel to the grave site. A marine marching band led the way; no ordinary band, either: red-coated and white-trousered, they were the President's Own. Behind them had come the artillery caisson on which lay the flag-draped casket. The caisson was drawn by six draft horses, big black English Shires seventeen hands high and each weighing more than a ton, hairy spats over broad hooves, muscular flanks shining with sweat, their progress steady and dignified. They were harnessed in twos, and the left-hand horse of each pair was saddled and bore a rider, incongruous in army dress blues amid the surrounding sea of marine uniforms—the caisson unit is part of the army's 3rd Infantry Regiment, the Old Guard, as they are known. Then tethered behind the caisson had come a lone horse, caparisoned: saddled but riderless, empty boots reversed in the stirrups, symbol of a fallen warrior.

I had smiled at the time, knowing how old Scarlett would have loved it. I could imagine him in his waning years, sitting on the porch and thinking of the day he would go out in style. If there is one thing the marines do well, it's bury you.

Next had come an armed escort, the marine platoon who would fire the rifle volleys at the end of the ceremony. I am sure Scarlett would have preferred the echoing boom of an artillery salute, but to get the big guns you need stars, and O'Hara had retired one rank shy. He had been the kind of guy the marines are happy to have as a colonel but would never consider promoting to general rank. To snare a star you have to play the political game, and old Scarlett had not had it in him.

The other occasions I had been to Arlington were less uplifting. Twice it had been for men who had been killed while under my command. Both times they had buried a casket, although on the second occasion I had known that there could be little inside but the dog tags.

The other time was to bury a woman. Females are not supposed to serve in combat roles but the distinction is not always easy. She was navy; worked intelligence. The helicopter she had been a passenger aboard was shot down south of Samarra, just before the fall of Tikrit. She was twenty-three years old. I flew back for the ceremony. Leafless trees and a bitter March wind, the day she was buried.

I RETRIEVED THE BACKPACK from the cargo bed. Arlington is a huge estate spread over a big broad hill, two hundred acres in all. The parking lot is at the base. I looked up, searching for a suitable piece of high ground. At the top, to the west, is a mansion built in the form of a Greek temple. The house was first occupied by Martha Washington's grandson, then after his death by his daughter, whose husband happened to be Robert E. Lee, so that by a quirk of history Arlington had passed from the family of the man whose army had forged the union to the family of the man whose army had attempted to dissolve it.

Directly below the mansion were the gravesites of JFK and RFK. Lots of visitors there, even during the week. South of the mansion—left as I looked at it—were the amphitheater and the tomb of the unknowns. Good views over the Pentagon; lots of visitors there, too. To the right of the mansion is a ridge line curling around to the northeast, heavily wooded, rising high above the entrance drive. Few memorials or famous graves there. Few tourists, too.

I grabbed a map from the visitors' center and left the parking lot to begin the long walk up the hill. They were probably not tracking me from below but in case they were I kept the pace slow and followed the main path, just another visitor. It was not until I was past the mansion and on the other side of the ridge that I changed direction, veering off in a big flanking curve to the right, out of sight from below.

Arlington National Cemetery is laid out in a series of fields with row after row of standard government-issue grave markers: white stone thirteen inches wide and four inches thick. They are set with military precision, equally spaced and strictly in line—even in death the military requires you to be neat. I reached the northeastern ridge and looked around. There were several patches of brown among the pristine lawns, recent burials where the grass had not yet grown back. More importantly, there were also two open grave sites.

Arlington averages around twenty burials a day, mostly for the military. With military burials come military honors, which include a rifle volley. That makes Arlington unique: it is the one place in Washington where the sound of a rifle shot is not something unusual.

In fact it is common, a sound heard many times a day, something so familiar that it can be safely ignored.

The graves for the day's burials are dug in the morning and a liner placed inside, before the place is opened to the public. Never earlier, in case it rains and floods them. Those two open grave sites meant that there were two more burials due here this afternoon. All I had to do was wait.

I spent the next twenty minutes scouting a suitable location, eventually settling on a site deep in the shade of a group of trees growing along the ridge line, maples and basswoods and a sycamore already in heavy summer foliage. Some roots had come clear of the ground, providing a good rest for the rifle. The section of graves between me and the road far below was a broad shallow dip providing a clear line of sight. I used the binoculars to inspect the Chrysler. It was still closed up and I could see nothing of the people inside, but I could tell by the heat shimmer from the tail pipes that they had left the engine running, probably for the air conditioner.

The day was windless and the target was stationary, so there would be no need for lead or drift adjustments. That left elevation. The map had a scale, and so I was able to accurately assess the range: three hundred and thirty yards, a difficult shot. I only take soft point ammunition with me to Belize, since jungle animals do not have thick hides or body armor, but the lead tips of unjacketed rounds can easily get banged up. I searched through the box for two whose noses were clean and unscratched—I would need the best possible aerodynamics if I was to make the shots.

In the distance a funeral procession approached. They headed for an open grave site in the section behind me, down the back side of the ridge. I would have preferred one in front, since that way I could have followed the movements of the rifle platoon with my peripheral vision. With them behind me, I would have to rely on sound alone, but sound is slow and I would end up slightly out of sync.

There are three seconds between rounds in a rifle volley. The grave site was about four hundred yards away from me. At sea level, sound travels at around 760 miles per hour. That makes nearly 13 miles a minute, but call it 12 to make the math easier: a fifth of a mile a second. The rifle platoon would be about a quarter of a mile away from me, so I would have to fire about a second and a quarter early to have the sound of my rifle shot reach them as they fired. But my timing cue—the sound of their first volley—would itself have taken a second and a quarter to reach me, and so my timing would already be slow. Therefore I had to fire about half a second after hearing their first volley for the sound of my first rifle shot to reach them as they fired their second volley. A fraction late would be okay: it could be attributed to echo.

It was important to get two shots off; one would not be enough. But there are only three rounds in a rifle volley. The first would initiate the timing, and so I had to get the second two exactly right—there would be no opportunity for another attempt.

I removed the two sections of the rifle from the backpack and began to reassemble it. The weapon I take to Belize is a Remington 700 model. The Remington 700 is a simple design half a century old, but which has been continually refined over its long life to produce a weapon that is not the fanciest or most expensive, but which is nevertheless a benchmark by which others are judged. It is available in many variations upon the central classic theme. The one I own is the titanium model, optimized for light weight. When you spend five days at a stretch trekking through the jungle, carrying not just your own gear but a share of the guests' supplies, weight becomes an issue—especially when you have to scale a 1,500-foot waterfall. The entire receiver of the rifle is machined from solid titanium. This not only saves weight; titanium also resists corrosion better than steel, an obvious advantage in the humidity of Central America. The barrel is only twenty-two inches long—about the shortest you can have in a hunting rifle. This is for weight-saving too, but has an unintended benefit: in the jungle there is never much room to maneuver—the shorter the barrel, the less chance of getting caught up. The buttstock is molded in a single slender piece of carbon-reinforced composite, which is lighter than wood and more weather resistant, too.

Simple, elegant, reliable, lightweight: perfect for Belize. Unfortunately, less than perfect for long-distance precision work. The two big shortcomings were the short barrel and low magnification scope, both of which reduce accuracy.

At least it was chambered for .308: a good long-range round. If the biggest threat in the jungle had been jaguars I would have chambered down to something with lighter cartridges, .243 Winchester or .223 Remington. But the proximity of Guatemala and its criminal gangs—uniformed and otherwise—was always in the back of my mind. I had run through various encounter scenarios, like the way we used to in force recon, developing a preplanned response strategy. Most of these imagined scenarios ended with the guides escorting my party out of the jungle while I covered the retreat. So when ordering the weapon I had selected .308 because it is the same ammunition as in the 7.62mm-caliber carbines we use for sniper work in the marines, and therefore a round I knew to be suitable for picking off elements of a superior force from a distance, should the need ever arise.

I finished assembling the weapon, used the J-key to unlock the open bolt, and tested the action. It was smooth and easy, no worse for wear during the journey. I cleaned the scope and adjusted the elevation for a 330-yard shot.

Behind me, the burial proceeded. A moderate group of mourners, perhaps thirty. A mixture of dark civilian clothing and military uniforms, mostly marine, including the cleric; the family had opted for a service chaplain. The honor guard wore white covers and Dress Blue A's. The officers' uniforms had red stripes running down the trouser seams, a uniform I had once worn myself.

The pallbearers carried the flag-draped casket to the grave. Next would come the committal service. I turned back around and examined the Chrysler through the scope.

No change. I rehearsed the sequence of movements I would follow from the moment I heard that first volley, softly counting the timing while working the bolt and practicing the drill. Behind me I could hear the chaplain's clear voice echoing across the field, uttering not a prayer but a poem, a fine one that I had heard before on occasions like this:

> *They shall not grow old,*
> *As we that are left grow old;*
> *Age shall not weary them,*
> *Nor the years condemn.*
> *At the going down of the sun*
> *And in the morning*
> *We will remember them.*

I loaded the magazine, closed the bolt, and settled in. Body prone but relaxed, rifle on the rest, sights steady on the target.

The chaplain fell silent. The NCO's parade ground voice took over, preparing for the rifle volley. When he ordered "Aim!" I put my finger on the trigger and took a deep breath.

First volley. I fired. The sound of the second volley reached me two-and-a-half Mississippis later, meaning that the timing had been good so far. I fired again and continued counting until the sound of the honor guard's next volley—the third and final—followed.

I put the rifle aside and used the binoculars to study the target. The wheels had wide rims and the tires were low profile, so it was hard to tell whether I had flattened them or not. The doors to the Chrysler flew open. Two men emerged, dressed as if they were going to a funeral themselves—dark suits, white shirts, muted ties. They looked around in confusion, not yet certain what had happened but wondering what those two sharp thumps to their vehicle had been. One of them had a long-barreled automatic pistol in hand.

I could imagine how it went. They had been sitting inside with the engine on and the air-conditioning running. Perhaps they had been listening to the radio or playing music while waiting for me to return. If it was on loud enough they might not have heard the impact, but they would certainly have felt it: even at that range the rounds would have lost less than half of their initial kinetic energy, arriving at the vehicle with around 2,000 foot-pounds of force—a hefty whack that no one would miss.

One of them suddenly stopped, his eyes fixed on the front wheel. He slowly knelt and inspected the tire. He called to his companion, who came and knelt beside him. After a while the second guy stood and moved to the rear wheel. He crouched down and was soon poking at the tire wall with a finger, shaking his head in disbelief. The other guy joined him, and I could see them talking. They both turned around and looked up at the tree-covered ridge line where I currently lay, too well concealed for them to see. They were starting to get it now.

I took a deep breath of satisfaction. Difficult or not, it had been essential to hit both of those tires. Just one, and they could have used the spare. But two meant that they would not be able to fix it themselves. Two meant that they would have to call a repair service, which would then send out a flatbed to pick up the vehicle and take it back to the shop. Now all I had to do was wait until the flatbed showed up. The name and phone number would be painted on the side, same as on all tow trucks. I would call the number and ask the dispatcher where they took the Chrysler. They would give me an address, and I would go and wait. Most likely it would be a long wait; this late in the day they probably would not fix it until tomorrow morning. But I was used to long waits. Eventually, someone would show up at the shop to retrieve the repaired vehicle. That was when I would intervene.

A conversation would ensue, on my own terms. That was the plan.

Behind me I could hear the bugler begin playing "Taps." They would be folding the flag now, twelve times in total. The chaplain would then present it to the next of kin with the words that he must know by heart: *On behalf of the President of the United States and a grateful nation, please accept this flag as a token of the honorable and faithful service of your loved one.*

I rolled onto my back to check, expecting to see the committal service reaching its conclusion. Instead I saw a woman standing just twenty feet away, staring straight down at me.

VII

S HE WAS A YOUNG WOMAN BUT had a solemn air that made
her seem older. Dark dress, dark hair, fair skin. Fine round face
with a mouth open slightly in surprise. Full lips painted bright
vermilion—it was the one slash of color on her and therefore a
natural focus, although I suspect that my gaze would have lingered
on that mouth with or without the lipstick. Her hair was up, probably
because of the heat of the day. Black slip dress, silk. Black stockings,
one knee slightly bent. Black pumps, patent leather. Little balled
fists, one of which held a white handkerchief. Eyes wide with
amazement, but the combination of a single raised eyebrow and an
upward tilt of the chin gave her more an appearance of vague
disapproval than outright alarm. She had the bearing of a Gilded Age
aristocrat having suddenly come across something ghastly in the
garden.

She was not amused. She was not crying, but her face was
streaked with tears, and I understood what must have happened: she
had begun to weep at the funeral and—perhaps a woman who did

not like her emotions to be on display—she had come to the trees for solitude. Instead of solitude, she had found me.

We stared at each other in silence for what seemed a long time, although it was probably just a few seconds.

"You're shooting people," she said eventually.

Calm, not accusatory, as if she were stating a simple and incontestable fact.

"No, I'm shooting a car."

"You're shooting cars?"

"No, a car. Singular."

"Why?"

"It was following me."

"This is...a traffic dispute?"

"No."

A short silence.

"I'm going to report you to those armed men over there," she stated with authority. "If you shoot me, they will shoot you."

She turned and began to stride back toward the burial party.

"Excuse me."

She stopped and reluctantly looked back over her shoulder.

"Yes?"

"They use blanks."

"What?"

"Blanks. Cartridges without bullets. The honor guard is just here to make noise, so they use blanks instead of live rounds because it's safer. So even if they wanted to, they couldn't actually shoot me."

The news that she could not have me conveniently shot visibly disappointed her. She spent a moment considering an alternative course of action.

"I could scream," she said eventually. "And I could run in a zigzag so that you couldn't shoot me."

"I just flattened two tires at over three hundred yards range. You are point-blank."

She thought about this for a while, then gave a little shrug of her shoulders.

"I could promise that I wouldn't report you, but it wouldn't be true."

"Why don't you take this?" I held out the rifle, butt-first. "You can keep it on me while I explain. If you're not fully satisfied then you can shoot me yourself."

She did nothing for perhaps half a minute. Then without speaking she came back to where I lay. Same determined stride—I got the feeling that this was a girl who always got to where she was going on time.

She snatched the rifle from my grasp.

"You think that I'm just an upset female who wouldn't use this," she said. "You made a mistake." She shouldered the weapon and pointed it steadily at my chest. "Start talking."

"Like I said, they were following me."

"And so you decided to shoot them?"

"Not them. I shot the tires."

"For which you happened to have a rifle handy?"

"I just came in from the jungle."

"The jungle? In Washington?"

"In Central America. I flew back this morning: the miracle of modern air travel."

"And these people followed you from the airport?"

"No, they followed me from the Watergate."

"What were you doing at the Watergate?"

"Breaking in."

I realized from the look on her face that this was the wrong response.

"Now, or during the Nixon administration?"

"Now."

"So after touchdown, you just had this sudden urge to break into the Watergate?"

"I had a job to do."

"Armed robbery?"

"Government investigation."

"What government?"

"Ours."

"Show me some ID."

"Not me. I'm doing it on behalf of a government person."

"Oh, please."

"No, really."

"A government person whom you met in the jungle, perhaps?"

"Actually, he had me abducted from a remote Mayan ruin and taken out to an aircraft carrier in the Caribbean. That was where I was given the job."

I am not good with interviews at any time, but I could tell from the long silence following my last response that, even by my own modest standards, this one was faring poorly.

"You should have tried aliens," she said at last. "That would have been more believable."

I stood and walked toward her. She pulled the trigger unhesitatingly.

I took the rifle from her grasp and handed her the binoculars.

"Go look for yourself," I said. "There is a big Chrysler sedan with blacked-out windows and two flat tires parked down there. There are two guys in suits. One of them is probably still holding a pistol. They're waiting for me."

She accepted the binoculars and stepped forward to look over the ridge. She must have had trouble finding the car because she kept moving around as if searching. Eventually she stepped back.

"There's nothing there," she said.

I stepped over and looked for myself. She was right, there was nothing there. I walked out from the cover, opening the field of vision in case for some reason they had pushed the vehicle further down the roadway. But there was no sign of them; they had disappeared.

I lowered the binoculars.

Run-flats. For a while now they have been making these tires that you can drive on even when they are flat. Not fast, not far, but you can drive. They are designed so that if you suddenly have a puncture they will still get you home, or at least off the freeway and to safety. I had not thought of run-flats, although in retrospect I should have guessed that professionals like this pair would naturally have them. Especially when those same professionals have already shown a liking for expensive options, like high-intensity discharge beams. This is what happens when you make on-the-run tactical plans, you miss important details. It looked like I would not be talking to these guys on my own terms after all.

I came back under the tree cover and stood face to face with a pair of fearless and penetrating eyes.

"Why didn't the rifle fire when I pulled the trigger?"

"No rounds," I said. "The magazine was empty."

She slapped me. It was not the first time that a woman has slapped me, but usually they pull up a little, giving it just enough to convey discontent. This one hit me like she wanted to send my jaw into orbit.

"You lied to me," she said.

She turned and walked away with the determined stride of a woman who has decided to put something distasteful behind her. Technically, I had never represented the weapon as being loaded. And since she had tried to shoot me, I thought that having given her an unloaded rifle was in retrospect a wise thing to have done, having saved me my life, and her what would at minimum have been a lengthy and expensive legal burden. But I could tell that she would never see it that way. For her, to be deceived was unforgivable, and the reasons were irrelevant.

I watched her walk away, past the long rows of white headstones, growing smaller in perspective. She did not look back, not once, not even after having rejoined the others.

I broke down the rifle and put the two parts into the backpack. Stowed the binoculars, too. I found the expended brass cartridge cases and packed them away as well—not for forensic purposes, I just did not want to litter Arlington cemetery.

It was time to move out. A last glance toward the funeral party. No one coming my way, no one even looking over here. She had obviously said nothing to them about me, and I wondered why. I turned and headed down from the ridge, away from the woman with the intrepid eyes.

VIII

W HEN I RETURNED TO MY TRUCK I found that one of the
tires was flat.

At first I thought they must have patiently held the valve open to
let the air out, but then I saw the torn tread around the puncture.
Then I recalled the long barrel of the automatic pistol that Thug #2
had been holding when he first emerged from the Chrysler.

A silencer. So they had shot out a tire before leaving.

A payback? But if so, why not shoot out two, tit for tat? Or all
four, if you really wanted to get the message across. There was
something not right about shooting out just the one.

I thought about it for a minute and soon had a working theory.
The men who had followed me were professionals, and
professionals do not waste time with childish gestures like paybacks.
No doubt they expected me to assume that's what it was, but there
had to be a better reason for them to risk being seen shooting out a
tire, silencer or no silencer. My guess was that it had been to keep
me busy until someone else got in a position to take over from them.

That was why it had been just the one tire, something I could fix myself with the spare. Two or more would have meant a long delay, probably for a flatbed, same as I had wanted to do to them. Worse, I might have simply left it there and taken a cab. So they had done just enough to slow me up, but not enough to make me ditch the truck.

Although they could not have guessed at the time, in fact it had been unnecessary. On the way back down from the northeastern ridge I had stopped by one of those four graves—not for long but long enough. There was probably another vehicle outside by now, waiting for me to exit. If I was running the operation I would have had the replacement car continuously drive around the big traffic circle at the end of Memorial Drive, a junction that I could not avoid, and in the confusion of cars there I would have been unable to pick out a vehicle waiting to follow from all the others.

It was a simple plan but effective. These guys were good. It is hard to think of simple but effective plans when someone is shooting at you.

I walked away from my truck and returned to the visitors' center, intending to call a cab. But then I saw the intrepid-eyed girl enter the parking lot. She was with some other people. Several were smiling and talking animatedly, a good ending to a funeral—it is right to remember the dead, but then you move on. Not the intrepid-eyed girl, however; too much had happened today for her to smile.

She said her goodbyes and struck off alone, presumably toward her car. It occurred to me that a private car would be better than a cab. They might be thinking of a cab, especially if they saw an empty one go in. No way they would expect me to leave in someone else's car. I left the visitors' center to intercept her.

She came to an abrupt halt when she saw me. A glance over her shoulder toward her companions, then eyes back on me. She looked at me squarely. If the woman had any fear of confrontation she refused to display it.

I stopped well short, not wanting to make her any more nervous than she probably already was.

"Sorry to bother you," I said. "I need a ride."

No response.

"Not very far. You could drop me anywhere once we get past the traffic circle."

I gave her a long time, not wanting to rush her, but she remained silent.

"They shot out one of my tires," I explained. "It was to force me to change it, which would slow me down enough for them to get someone else in place before I left."

Again no response.

I decided to shut up—no amount of further explanation would have any effect. She just continued to study me in cautious, evaluative silence. I returned her stare. I had never seen eyes quite that color before, a striking mixture of green and gold, like copper with a faint sheen of verdigris. She was younger than I had originally thought, probably not yet thirty, but her calm self-assurance made her seem older. She held herself with natural gracefulness, erect but not stiff, without any trace of that weighed-down slovenly slouch currently fashionable. As a child I had not been allowed to lean on walls or stand around with my hands in my pockets, which turned out to have been excellent preparation for the marines, an organization that shared my parents' views regarding posture. Perhaps she had had strict parents, too. Eventually, she spoke.

"Which aircraft carrier?"

"What?"

"The aircraft carrier you were supposedly taken to. What was its name?"

"*Theodore Roosevelt*."

"And this was somewhere in the Caribbean?"

"Yes, off the coast of Belize."

"When?"

"Yesterday."

"Wait here."

She turned and walked fifty yards across the parking lot to a car where her companions were gathered, still in conversation. She pulled one of them aside, a man in naval officer's uniform. He wore the twin gold stripes of a lieutenant, naval equivalent of a marine captain, the rank that I had held before it had been removed from me at the conclusion of my court-martial. At one point he looked up and carefully checked me out before reverting to the woman with the intrepid eyes.

Their conversation went on for some time. Eventually she came striding back across the asphalt to me.

"My cousin's husband is in the navy," she explained. "I was going to ask him to make a call to find out where the *Theodore Roosevelt* is currently located, but he already knew. He said that a week ago the carrier's battle group was returning home from the Persian Gulf when it was suddenly diverted to the Caribbean. The decision came from somewhere high up, higher than headquarters at Norfolk, which is where the carrier's orders usually originate. Everyone has been wondering what's up. His guess was Cuba. He was pretty surprised when I told him that they had apparently been diverted to fetch you."

No wonder the lieutenant had checked me out so carefully. Now I knew why Gandry and the PFC had been wearing desert cammies: they would have had no use for woodland pattern in the Middle East.

"Does that mean you'll give me a ride now?"

She stared at me for a long time before responding, a look of frank disapproval on her face.

"You reek of trouble," she said.

"Just till we get past the traffic circle and out of sight. Then you'll be rid of me forever."

Another long pause, then she nodded her head in reluctant assent.

HER CAR TURNED OUT TO BE an Aston Martin. It was a sleek hardtop, very low, voluptuously curved, and painted a deep racing green. The interior was luxurious, upholstered in supple tan leather, and fitted with instruments that looked like precision chronometers machined from precious metal. It had the pristine smell of a new car. There was not a mark on the carpet, so I took out my handkerchief and unfolded it onto the floor before putting my greasy old combat boots on it. I kept the backpack on my lap so that it would not touch anything and tried to sit forward to prevent the shirt from leaving grass stains on the back. My fingers still had gun oil and black powder residue, so I left the seat belt untouched and made no adjustments to the seat itself, although it was way too far forward for me. My knees bumped up against the dash. It was awkward, but at least it would not be for long.

I scanned outside, looking for anything that did not fit.

After a while, I became aware that there had been a long period of inactivity in the seat beside me. I turned to find that the girl with the intrepid eyes was once again staring at me, except this time she was smiling.

"Comfortable?" she asked.

"I don't want to mess up your car."

"So I gathered. It's okay, you can sit like a normal person."

"No, I'm fine. I can tell that it's new."

"Used, actually, but well cared for," she admitted. "I recently got laid off, and after my grandfather died I was so depressed I just decided to go and blow the entire severance package."

"Laid off from what?"

"An airline."

"They must pay flight attendants pretty well."

"Pilot, actually."

She hit the big starter button mounted on the center of the dash. The engine burst into life. It was loud and curiously high-pitched, sounding less like a car than a World War II dive-bomber.

I noticed a small winged metal badge lying in the center console.

"Yours?"

"Yes."

"Can I look?"

"Sure."

I studied it as she pulled out of the parking lot. There were two broad wings spread on either side of a central shield. Three inches wide. It was similar to the parachute wings I used to wear on my Service Dress As, except those had been gold, and these were pewter-colored. There was a clasp on the back to pin it to the shirt. The shield in the center bore the airline's logo, coincidentally the same airline that I had flown in on this morning, and I vaguely recalled the headlines from when they had announced layoffs a while back.

"How did they pick you?" I asked.

"Last in, first out. I'd only been with them a year."

She stopped at the cashier booth.

There was a second badge in the console, which I picked up. It was her name tag.

She closed the window after giving the money to the cashier and made ready to move on, but then stopped when she noticed me with the second badge in hand. Her brow furrowed. I realized that she did not like the idea of someone she suspected of being a homicidal maniac knowing her name.

She jerked out her arm, at first I thought to snatch back the name tag, but it turned out to be only to offer her hand.

"Miranda Grey," she said.

"Lysander Dalton." We shook hands. "Most people call me Lee."

"How's your cheek, Lee?"

"It'll be a while before I eat solid food again."

She seemed pleased to hear it. I returned the name tag to the console. She worked the stick shift. Six speeds. Most women dislike sticks, but I could tell from the way she snapped off the gear changes that she had deliberately wanted a manual transmission.

We negotiated the Arlington Bridge without incident. I kept an eye in the wing mirror after we crossed the river, looking for cars trailing us, but we took the Georgetown exit without anyone following. After she dropped me I found a cab and had it take me to the auto rental lots down by Union Station.

On the way I kept reviewing the conversation with Miranda Grey. Something about it was not right, but no matter how many times I went over it I just could not put a finger on exactly what it was that bothered me.

IX

I AWOKE AT FIRST LIGHT, UNRESTED. It had been one of those nights when you sense that the gods are gathering, and they mean to cause trouble.

I dressed and went outside. The long rolling rows of post and wire stretched out across the fields, still mostly naked. I did a walk-through as I had on a thousand dawns in various places around the world, although now I was looking not for breaches in perimeter security but simply checking on the vines.

The grafts were in good shape. The vines had slowly extended themselves during my absence in Belize, reaching along the proffered wires with ever-strengthening promise. Many leaves now, and here and there even the initial bud of what would one day become a plump bunch of grapes.

There is hope in the fruits of cultivation, an antidote to the miseries of men.

I opened the drip system. The ground at the base of the vines had buried in it polyurethane piping with holes drilled for irrigation. In summer I give the vines water in the early morning, something with which to face the heat of the coming day.

I returned to the house and had breakfast on the terrace. I rarely dine inside, never during summer. It was not until I was finished, sitting back with coffee and studying yet again the photograph of Hanna Moran, that I figured out what the fifth key was for.

I had been wondering how Moran spent her days while the senator was in session on the Hill. According to Stolper she had gone to the museums or shopping or the gym. I could not verify the first two but from that photograph of her I could tell that she must have spent serious time working out. The Watergate has a health club; Moran almost certainly used that. She had probably changed into her gym gear at home and walked over. Late morning most likely, when it would be the quietest.

Then I focused on her shoulders. They were relatively broad and muscular, the shoulders of a gymnast. Or a swimmer. I looked up the health club on the internet. Sure enough, they had a lap pool.

A lap pool made a difference. If Moran only worked out on the machines, then she would change at home. But if she also swam, then she would have had to change at the health club. That would mean a locker.

It would be natural to keep the locker key with the house keys since she would always be out of the apartment when using it. When she had a set cut for Stolper she would have likely given the entire key ring to the locksmith. Perhaps she went shopping while he cut them. By the time she returned he would have made copies of all five and placed them together on a new ring for her. She would have handed the entire set over to Stolper, not thinking that he had no use for the locker key. Or perhaps she had left it on there deliberately, knowing that if she ever lost her own key then she could always get the spare from him. And so, if my guess was right, Stolper had ended up with a key to Hanna Moran's gym locker.

The question was how to get into the women's change room at the Watergate health club to check. It was obviously not something that I could do myself.

I went inside and looked up 201 area code listings under "Grey."

"I PRESUME YOU'RE CALLING TO ASK ME OUT."

These were the first words that Miranda Grey said after I had identified myself over the phone. It seemed that she had little patience for people who failed to come to the point promptly, or perhaps she just liked to take charge. I almost said no, but caught myself in time.

"Yes."

"Go ahead."

"Would you like to go out?"

"Where?"

"I might be able to get a table at Le Diplomate since it's a weeknight."

"No, that's too expensive."

"I owe you."

"It was just a ride. Least I could do after hitting you."

"It wouldn't be for the ride. It would be for something else."

"What?"

"Something that you haven't actually done yet."

IT WAS A NINETY-MINUTE DRIVE from my vineyard at the foothills of the Blue Ridge Mountains back into D.C. We arranged to meet in the grounds of the Watergate. I looked around for the Chrysler while waiting but saw no sign of it. Maybe it was still in the shop.

I took a seat in the garden. A melancholy willow provided shade. One of the flower beds was planted with roses, mostly tea roses, but also a couple of climbing varieties on a small trellis. Beyond those were hydrangeas, bright pink—swamp soil is obviously acidic.

I heard Miranda Grey before I saw her, the high-pitched wail of the Aston Martin loud enough to be audible above the surrounding traffic. The car appeared on Virginia Avenue. She found a parking spot and emerged wearing slim jeans and a collared cotton shirt that was too big for her, a man's shirt perhaps. It was buttoned low but there was a tank top beneath. Running shoes. Her hair was tied in a ponytail. Sunglasses. No makeup. No smile, either.

She opened the trunk and withdrew a gym bag, for which I was grateful. I had been afraid that she might have decided not to go through with it.

It had been difficult to persuade her. My proposal that she go into the gym alone was frankly rejected. She would only do it if I went with her, and then only if I did all the talking. I had suggested we go during the day but Miranda had insisted on early evening, when the gym would be at its fullest—if a place is crowded, she said, you are more likely to be ignored. At 6:00 P.M. we entered the Watergate Health & Fitness Club and approached the front desk.

I had intended to purchase two memberships on the spot, but when I explained that we had never been to the gym before the woman behind the front desk said we could give the place a try for free. I signed the visitors' log as Lee & Miranda Smith, and gave as the home address that of Hanna Moran's apartment.

We entered the gym. The only other gym I had been to in D.C. was an old boxers' hangout in the eastern quadrants run by a pugnacious Irishman called Mick Shanahan, a man who smoked unfiltered Camels while on duty and kept a snub-nosed .38 in the drawer. The other patrons had been tattooed ex-cons.

The Watergate Health & Fitness Club was the polar opposite. For a start, it was clean. It was also carpeted. No boxing ring. Instead of speed bags and free weights the floor was populated with cardiovascular machines that the clientele used to support magazines, cell phones, and their own heft. There was much sound and fury but little actual sweat.

All in all, I preferred Mick's.

We split up and went to the locker rooms. I changed into swim gear and then located the pool. There was a handful of people splashing about, dressed for the beach rather than serious swimming; I was the only person in Speedos. There was a single lane reserved for doing laps, currently unoccupied, and delineated from the rest of the pool by a float line. I put on the goggles and began swimming up and down, watching the calm passage of the long black line below, pounding out laps just as Hanna Moran must often have done.

At lap twenty-four someone came by the other way. This time I stopped instead of tumble-turning at the deep end and waited for the other swimmer to approach.

She came to a halt by me. It was Miranda. She wore a sleek racer-back one-piece, black with neon-pink piping. It was zippered down the front, not a genuine racing suit. Swim cap and goggles. She raised the goggles and crossed her arms on the float line to talk.

"Nothing so far."

"How many did you try?"

"All the ones around the locker I'm using. Twenty or thirty. A lot of them are combination locks, so I didn't need to try the key. And now I can recognize by sight some models that I know the key doesn't fit, so I should be able to get through them all okay."

Since the key had been a copy instead of an original there had been no manufacturer's name on it to help limit the potential candidates, and she had feared having to physically check every single padlock.

"Did anyone notice you?"

"I don't think so. I'll try some more when I return, then some more after I shower, then some more after I dress. Break it up, so that the same people aren't always around."

Miranda was smiling and I realized that, far from being fearful, she was enjoying herself. She swam for twenty minutes more— enough time for whoever had initially been in the locker room to have left. She swam slowly but well, with the easy even strokes of a long-distance swimmer. I overtook her a few times, but on the last approach she suddenly sped up, turning the final twenty meters into an impromptu race. We hit the wall almost simultaneously, ending up floating next to each other at the deep end, holding onto the side while regaining breath.

"You let me win," she said, still breathing heavily.

"Who says you won?"

She laughed. Our elbows touched where we rested by the edge of the pool. I was as close to her as I had been. Her skin was smooth and fair and slightly translucent, like a child's, the blue of the blood vessels beneath visible. This, together with the fact that her hair was hidden under the swim cap, gave her face a sort of sculptural purity, as if hewn from white marble that was lightly veined. She returned my gaze without expression, a Praxiteles come to life, regarding the world with cool reserve.

"Time for the next round," she said, and hauled herself from the pool.

MIRANDA RETURNED TEN MINUTES later, transformed. During that time she had showered, changed, and dried her hair—a record for the fairer sex. She wore high-heeled sandals and a short sleeveless dress, emphasizing her slender taut form. Once again her hair was up and a slash of red lipstick was the sole point of color on that otherwise marble-hued face.

But above all, she radiated eager tension. I knew before she nodded that she had found Hanna Moran's locker.

THE BAR AT THE HAY-ADAMS IS CALLED the Off the Record Bar, a discreet room that advertises itself as the place in Washington to be seen but not heard. The tables are well separated, each occupying a space slightly inset into the wall—a small alcove—so as to ensure that conversation cannot be overheard. The furniture and walls are covered in plush red upholstery, and the floor is thickly carpeted, a combination perhaps intended to absorb any rogue sound waves.

We settled in at a table. It was an appropriate place to have a drink before dinner while examining the contents of Hanna Moran's gym locker.

Miranda placed the bag on the seat between us. Hanna had squeezed a lot into her locker. There were several changes of workout gear: shorts, tops, socks, plus a single pair of gym shoes. Swimsuit. Goggles and a swim cap. Basic toiletries like deodorant and shampoo and even her soap in a plastic container—presumably she did not like the generic stuff provided by the gym. Money; not just spare change but some crumpled notes as well, about twenty dollars' worth. A pen that had originally belonged to the Peninsula chain of hotels, although unfortunately it did not say which particular Peninsula the pen had come from. A handkerchief. Some matches. Crumpled tissues. Gum wrapper. A hairbrush, but no comb.

"No makeup," I said. "Isn't that odd?"

"Maybe she didn't bother with it."

"I think appearances were important to her."

"Then she probably always carried the basics in her purse."

That made sense. Our martinis arrived.

I could tell that Miranda was disappointed by what we had found: it was unremarkable—workout gear and toiletries and a scattering of detritus of the type emptied from pockets while changing clothes—exactly the sort of stuff you would expect to find in someone's gym locker.

"It doesn't tell us much, does it?" she said.

"No, it tells us quite a lot."

"Really?" Her eyes returned expectantly to the bag. "Which bit?"

"All of it," I said. She looked back up in puzzlement. "Hanna Moran's apartment was completely empty," I continued. "Not a thing left behind. Utilities disconnected, mail stopped, even her dry cleaning had been picked up. Why didn't she clean out her gym locker, too?"

"Maybe she just forgot."

"I don't think so. Her disappearance was not rushed; it was well planned."

"Then why?"

"Because she didn't make the arrangements to move out. Someone else arranged it for her. Whoever they were, they were thorough—the entire place was scrubbed clean. Every surface had been wiped down, probably to erase fingerprints. They even flushed out the drains, perhaps so that there would be no hairs that could ever be used for DNA sampling. But they didn't think of a gym locker."

"Are you saying that she was abducted?"

"I'm saying that she did not arrange the details of her departure. There are several possibilities as to why that would be. And yes, one of those possibilities is abduction."

We were silent for a while.

"Are you going to tell me why you're trying to find this woman now?"

"No."

Miranda had naturally wanted to know what it was all about, and I had told her as much as I could, but I had refused to reveal anything about the missing notebook.

"Has she done something wrong?"

"Yes, she has. And she apparently means to do a lot worse."

"What will you do when you find her?"

I shrugged my shoulders. It was an inadequate response, and I expected a negative reaction, but instead Miranda just nodded quietly to herself. I think she approved because it meant that I was not going to give her dressed-up answers. No more deception.

"Are you really with the good guys?"

"I'm really working on behalf of a government person," I said. "I'm not sure that I would characterize him as good."

"What next?"

In response, I showed her the matchbook we had found inside Hanna Moran's locker. It came from a place called Oblivion, presumably a bar or a nightclub, with an address on the East Side of Manhattan. She inspected it.

"A matchbook isn't much of a basis to go on."

"No," I agreed.

I could not tell her that I had already decided on New York, even before we found the matches. The city is unique in that it hosts foreign embassies, even though not the national capital, because it is the home of the UN. Although we have no diplomatic relations with Iran, in New York there would be an Iranian mission to the United Nations. If you want to make contact with representatives of the Iranian government, New York City is the only place in America you will find them. All that matchbook had done was confirm what I already knew: NYC was the obvious place to go.

She returned the matchbook to me.

"So you're going to New York?"

"We are, if you'll come."

"Me?"

"I could use your help."

I have never before had to track down a woman, but I had already figured out that doing so would be best accomplished by another woman. Not just in the obvious ways, as with Hanna Moran's locker. People generally would likely be more helpful to a woman asking questions about another woman than they would with a man. Especially a man like me.

Miranda took a thoughtful sip of her martini before responding.

"Two hundred dollars a day, plus expenses."

"Two hundred?"

"That's what Jim Rockford charged."

"He was a full-service guy. You would be just an assistant."

"It was a 'Seventies show—call it inflation."

Once again I wondered what the limit was on that credit card Dortmund had provided. I hoped there was not a separate limit for cash advances.

"Okay, two hundred dollars a day it is."

"Plus expenses," she insisted. "And if those expenses involve nice clothes or shoes, I get to keep them."

A true female.

"Agreed," I said.

"Good." She smiled broadly and took a celebratory sip of her martini, perhaps pleased with having found a new job, even if only temporary. "Let's drive up first thing tomorrow morning."

"I was planning on taking the shuttle," I replied cautiously.

"No, I'll drive," she announced. "The Aston needs a long run, and since you'll be paying for the gas this is the ideal opportunity."

She withdrew the pick and ate her olive, perfectly content and apparently indifferent to my reaction. Obviously my consent was not required.

I drained my glass.

I thought I was hiring an assistant, but it seemed that I had acquired a partner.

X

W E DROVE DOWN PAST CENTRAL PARK and Grand Army Plaza into the man-made canyons of Midtown. The city's immense verticality hits you here, where the buildings first begin to obliterate the sky. There is a certain insolence to it all, to this architectural assumption that man's place is to live not upon the earth but in the heavens high above. Manhattan is Caracol as it might have been but for the vicissitudes of history. Or perhaps Caracol is Manhattan as it is destined to become.

The sidewalks were crowded, and on Fifth Avenue the Aston Martin was just a small dab of dark green amid the moving field of sunflower-yellow taxi cabs. But even in the cacophony of New York the engine was clearly audible, one pitch and many decibels above everything else. I could not help but think of the howler monkeys.

The Peninsula Hotel occupies a twenty-three-story Beaux-Arts building at 700 Fifth Avenue, originally the Gotham Hotel and at the time of its completion in 1905 the tallest building in New York City. The main entrance is around the corner on West 55th Street, presumably because there is less traffic than on the avenue. We turned at the light and pulled up to the curb.

On the sidewalk a small crowd of spectators, perhaps alerted by the car's noise, stopped to stare. Tourists mainly, clutching maps and cameras and bags bearing the logos of MoMA or Saks, but among the sea of shorts were some suits, office workers pausing to see what all the fuss was about. A uniformed doorman rushed to the car, parking valet and porter in tow. He opened the driver's side door. When Miranda emerged from the vehicle several people started taking photographs, as if she might be a movie actress just in from the Coast, someone whose precise identity could be determined later.

Nobody opened my door, and when I got out nobody took my picture. I was probably just the bodyguard, and not worth wasting time over.

I had checked the hotel chain's website before leaving Washington. They have only eight properties worldwide, just three in the United States. The one in New York is the U.S. flagship, and it has something unusual for even the most luxurious of Manhattan hotels: a rooftop swimming pool, glass-enclosed, a place from which bathers can enjoy views over the city while taking a dip.

I wondered if it was the rooftop pool that had attracted Hanna Moran.

It was a relief to emerge from the confines of the car, in more ways than one. I had expected that we would take the Interstate up to New York, but Miranda decided instead to go via country backroads across rural Maryland and Pennsylvania. There was too much traffic on the northeast corridor, she said. Too many state troopers as well. It had not taken me long to see why the absence of state troopers was important to her. She pushed the Aston Martin hard, braking late on entry into corners, heel-and-toeing as she changed down, then pouring on power through the apex and exiting the turn on the verge of oversteer. She whipped past other vehicles as if they were stationary. The car was equal to it, the chassis transitioning with aplomb, the V-12 singing along joyfully. The only thing that was not equal to it was me.

Miranda handed the keys to the valet and asked him to have the car washed and waxed—the front fenders were caked in a slaughter of bugs. We went inside and the spectators moved on.

I had booked two suites. Since it was a luxury establishment right on Fifth Avenue the rates were astronomical, but Dortmund's credit card took care of it. Once again, I wondered what the limit was.

"What now?" Miranda asked.

"Can you go to the pool? While you're there, ask the staff if they remember Hanna Moran, casually, as if you know her. Perhaps tell them she recommended the hotel to you, something like that. Describe what she looks like—if she was here, they'll remember her. We'll meet tonight in the cocktail lounge at six. After dinner, we'll go to Oblivion."

"What are you going to do in the meantime?"

"I'm going to follow another lead."

IF YOU STROLL AROUND THE QUIET tree-lined streets of Manhattan's Upper East Side, nestled among the many fine townhouses you will occasionally come across one with a colorful flag flying outside and a discreet brass plaque by the front door announcing it as an embassy to the United Nations. These plaques can make for illuminating reading. When you discover that some of the world's most expensive real estate has been purchased by some of the world's most impoverished nations (for the pleasure of their diplomatic staff, who are no doubt relatives of the strongman *du jour*), then you begin to understand how it is that no matter how much aid is poured in nothing ever seems to change.

I had assumed that the headquarters of the Iranian permanent mission would be much the same, but when I arrived at the address—630 Third Avenue—it turned out not to be a quiet townhouse but a towering office block. I checked the directory inside the lobby. The Permanent Mission of the Islamic Republic of Iran was listed as occupying offices on the thirty-fourth floor.

There was a security desk, and guards who checked the passes of everyone coming and going to the elevators. There was no way anyone going up could avoid them.

I left the lobby and walked over to nearby Bryant Park, a small oasis of quiet green amid the steel and concrete of the city. There was a scattering of street carts. I bought an Italian sausage smothered in onions and took a seat to consume it while thinking about what I had discovered.

The location of the Iranian mission in an office building with controlled access changed things. If it had been a townhouse I could have imagined Hanna Moran stepping up the stoop and knocking on the door. After a brief explanation she would have been admitted. Perhaps she would have brought along a sample: a photocopied page or two, suitably redacted, but retaining enough detail to whet the appetite. A conversation would have ensued with a hastily summoned representative of the Iranian intelligence services. He would have quickly realized that this was his chance to make a big name for himself back in Tehran. Negotiations for the notebook would have soon begun.

But there was no way she could get to the thirty-fourth floor of that office building without an appointment and a visitor's pass. Arranging the appointment would be risky enough—a woman who had read the diary of the chairman of the senate select committee on intelligence would surely know that making a telephone call to the Iranian mission would be certain to bring her to the attention of the authorities. And even if she was able to fabricate a story good enough to gain access, obtaining a visitor's pass would require her to hand over a photo ID, thus leaving a trail that could never be erased. I knew little about Hanna Moran but enough to suspect that she had too much cunning to make such an obvious mistake.

My best lead had turned into a dead end.

The sausage was done. I put a straw into the egg cream. Egg cream is a soda pop unique to New York City, and which in true Madison Avenue fashion contains neither eggs nor cream. I sat back while drinking it, deciding what to try next.

The only unexplored lead was the nightclub. I had little hope of finding anything at Oblivion that would help in tracking down Hanna Moran—most likely she had simply gone there one evening when in town, probably as some lively relief from the dull company of William Stolper. No one would remember her, or if they did it would mean little. Nevertheless, if they could recall the day then at least it would help to pin down the timing, and so the place was worth a visit.

There was a clock visible on a spire rising above the buildings to the left: 1:30 P.M. No need for a watch here; in Manhattan you are never far from the time. The city measures it out relentlessly, as if it is a commodity whose precise value must be continually tracked. The clocks are like cosmic stock tickers, endlessly declaring the irredeemable value of each passing moment.

There were hours to go before I was due to meet Miranda. I would have liked to use some of that time doing online research. I had no computer with me but there was an alternative close at hand: Bryant Park shares its block of land with the New York Public Library. I walked around to the Fifth Avenue side, up the broad staircase, and into Astor Hall, the grand barrel-vaulted lobby built in the form of a Roman basilica and named for the man whose checkbook had paid for it.

The New York Public Library is actually dozens of buildings located throughout the city—this most famous of them is technically the Humanities and Social Sciences Research Library. Research only, no lending. That meant professional librarians. I located the readers' services desk and explained what I wanted. The woman there quickly identified the best resources, scribbled some notes for me on a scrap of paper, and directed me to the main reading room on the third floor.

To enter for the first time the main reading room of the New York Public Library is a memorable experience. It is a huge high-ceilinged space spectacularly stretching the entire width of the building, hundreds of feet across, and is occupied by row after row of great long tables with reading lamps perched upon them. Not that the lamps were necessary, for the long wall in the back is pierced by huge arched windows, nine in all, each one the size of a typical Manhattan apartment's floorplan, vast expanses of glass through which on a bright day like today light flooded into the room. Below them was a mezzanine in which thousands of periodicals were stacked, bound into volumes with identical cloth covers, and below the mezzanine the walls were covered in bookcases filled with every conceivable reference work. It was a room in which you could not help but feel the living weight of intellectual history, that patient building of knowledge, brick upon brick, from the Ancients through to the present day, a magnificent edifice often threatened but miraculously never lost.

Some of the reading tables had set upon them computer terminals, which is where I went. I took a seat and followed the directions the librarian had given me to access the online newspaper archives. I used "Oblivion," "night," "club," and "Manhattan" as the keywords, and initiated a search of the *New York Times*.

A dozen articles were returned, stretching back several years. The earliest was an account in the City Section of attempts by the local residents' board to block the granting of the nightclub's license. The next several articles were all on the same theme—the owner's commitments about controlling noise and after-hours activity in the neighborhood, the progress of the licensing panel's hearings, and eventually, despite some questions raised about both the sources of financing and the candidate's background, the granting of the license and subsequent opening of the club.

Among the later articles was an interview with the owner that had appeared in the Sunday edition magazine, declaring him and his new club to be part of a "neo-Glam" fashion wave. His name was Felix Zane. He had been born and raised on Long Island. At eighteen he had moved to France, imagining himself, as he put it, to be an artist. He settled in the south and spent five years there, seeking to capture the same light that had inspired Cézanne, Van Gogh, Picasso, and Matisse. Following in the footsteps of this last artist he had even tried Tangier for a time, but eventually Zane had been forced to accept that his name was not destined to be mentioned among their successors, and he came back home, deciding to invest what artistic talent he had into the outfitting of a new Manhattan nightclub that would go beyond anything that had come before.

There was a picture of him: a slight man wearing snakeskin jeans and a tailored jacket over a dark turtleneck, leaning on a table in his club, facing the photographer with a look of negligent disinterest.

Oblivion occupied a building that had once been the city morgue. Rather than suppress what would presumably be a discouragement to custom, Zane had decided to play it up, naming the place to reflect the immediate destiny of the original clients. This had been the theme for the opening party, a ghoulish Grand Guignol bacchanal in which guests had been encouraged to wear appropriate costumes. New York's demimonde had responded enthusiastically, and judging from the accompanying photographs the editors of the Style section must have had difficulty in finding shots suitable for publication in a family paper.

That party must have set a precedent: over the years the place had been shut down several times for brief intervals due to the various excesses—behavioral, sexual, and pharmaceutical—of the club's clientele.

The last article was unlike the others: it appeared in the National section, a place for real news. It revealed that several months ago Felix Zane had briefly been the object of a federal grand jury investigation, and the charges against him were startling: he had been accused of supplying women to a global white-slave trade. This ring was supposedly centered in the Middle East. Zane had readily admitted that from time to time he recruited women to work at various nightclubs in the Persian Gulf but that it was entirely benign. In petrodollar-fueled boomtowns like Dubai and Bahrain and

Kuwait City there were many new nightclubs, but the seclusion of women in the Middle East meant that there were few females to populate them. Zane would occasionally approach club-goers at his own premises, explain the situation, and invite them to take an all-expenses-paid vacation to the Gulf in which the days were their own to do with as they pleased, and the evenings would be spent partying in the latest nightclubs. For each girl that accepted he earned a commission.

According to the prosecutors, several of the women so recruited had subsequently disappeared without a trace. And, not by coincidence, most of the women who disappeared had been blonds—it seemed that blonds fetched a premium on the white-slave market. The prosecutors claimed that Zane had tried to recruit women without close family or friends, women who would not be much missed. Despite these precautions there had been complaints made to the authorities, the end result of which was that one of the women he recruited had been an FBI informant.

Her story was an ugly one. On arrival at the airport in Dubai she had been met, as expected. But as soon as the car was out on the road the men on either side of her had hooded and drugged her. She had been taken not to the hotel as promised but instead whisked away to the waterfront. She had awoken at sea, apparently already destined for delivery to her new owner, when she managed to steal one of the rubber dinghies and escape.

She made her way to the embassy and briefed the local FBI representative. Afterward, she had been escorted to a hotel before taking a flight back home the next day. It was not to be.

She failed to show up for the flight. A week later her body, bloated and rotting, was found floating in the waters of the Persian Gulf.

With the primary witness dead the grand jury investigation had stalled. The testimony, as with all grand jury investigations that do not result in charges, had been sealed. But someone had obviously not felt right about it: they had made photocopies and passed them to a reporter at the *New York Times*.

The investigation of Zane's background revealed some details that had not been included in the earlier puff piece. It seemed that one of the reasons he had been unable to capture that southern light was because he spent part of his French sojourn inside a Marseilles prison doing six months on an assault conviction. When he was released the French deported him. It turned out that the financing for the nightclub, whose exact nature had never been clear to the licensing board, had come from offshore investment companies that were just shells whose beneficial parties remained hidden behind banking secrecy laws.

If the accusations were true, then Felix Zane had been at the bottom of the pyramid—just a recruiter. The prosecutors had told the grand jury that they believed the principal was Balthazar Kadri, a billionaire commodities trader who lived in the south of France— perhaps that was where Zane had met him. Kadri held dual citizenship: French and Lebanese. He was a frequent visitor to the Middle East, where he conducted much of his business. This was the point at which the *New York Times*' reporter earned his money, for according to the encapsulated biography accompanying the article Balthazar Kadri had gotten his start in the import-export business during Iran-Contra, when still just a teenager he had been a minor go-between in handling the negotiations between the Americans and the Iranians.

That meant he had Iranian contacts. Not just any contacts, but contacts in the Iranian intelligence services.

I checked the internet for Felix Zane's address, but the search engines returned nothing. They use telephone directories; if they did not have an address for Zane it meant that his number was unlisted. The only way to find him would be through the nightclub.

As soon as I was out of the library I called Miranda. I gave her a quick summary of what I had discovered. There was no choice now but to explain that Hanna Moran intended to sell something of immense value to the Iranians, although I did not reveal what it was or how she had obtained it.

"So we'll go to Oblivion and try to find him?" she asked when I was finished.

"Yes, but there's one thing we need to do first."

"What?"

"We need to make you blond."

XI

I KNEW BEFORE LOOKING THAT Miranda Grey had entered the room. There was a sudden drop in the level of conversation—not loud to begin with but noticeably quieter now—and I could sense around me the subtle measured alertness of people pausing to take in an interesting new arrival. Her presence went through the place like a ripple across a pond.

I stood.

Miranda was at the entrance. It took me a moment to be sure that it was really her. The change in hair color I had expected, but the transformation that accompanied it I had not. Her hair was much shorter, off the shoulders, and styled in a series of smooth waves like a screen siren from the days when movies were black and white. She wore an elegant cocktail dress whose cut emphasized her long slender neck and the delicate tracery of bones at the base of her throat.

She saw me and gave a brief wave of acknowledgment. Her walk as she strode across the room retained its customary purposefulness, but to it had been added a new quality, a long-legged willowy languor that had not been there before.

The cocktail lounge at the Peninsula is situated on a mezzanine perched above the lobby and is reached by a grand staircase. There is a small bar at one end and along the length of the room two rows of plushly upholstered sofas and chairs grouped around low tables. This arrangement allows for good sightlines along the passage between, and as Miranda negotiated it many pairs of eyes unabashedly followed.

She came to the table. This was the first time I had seen her with any makeup besides lipstick. I caught a trace of perfume.

"Hi."

"Hello, Miranda." I found it hard not to stare, and I was not alone. "Perhaps we should sit."

She settled back into the chair and crossed her legs. She wore high-heeled sandals and carried a matching clutch bag. The soles of her sandals were unscuffed, and I realized that not all of her time this afternoon had been spent inside a hair salon.

A waiter came to the table.

"What are you drinking?" she asked me.

"A Manhattan."

She ordered the same. After the waiter left she leaned forward and spoke quietly.

"I have something to tell you."

"Okay."

"I went to the pool today, as you suggested. The pool is part of the spa. To use it you have to first sign in at the front desk, name and room number. When I signed in I checked through the back sheets."

"And?"

"I found Hanna Moran's name."

"Are you sure?"

"Certain. A lot of them were illegible scribble, but Hanna Moran's name was printed clearly. She signed into the spa on Saturday. She was staying in Room 605."

"Well done," I said, genuinely impressed. But she waved her hand dismissively.

"There's more," she explained. "I talked with the pool guy. I asked him if he remembered her. I didn't even need to give him a description, he recognized her by name. He told me that she had been very friendly and they had talked for a while. She wanted to know about the nightspots in New York, he said. Specifically, she asked him what he knew about Oblivion."

This was more than I had hoped for. It was positive confirmation of something important: in the time between Stolper misplacing the notebook and Hanna Moran's disappearance, she had come to New York City. Her interest in the nightclub was more than just casual—and why would that be, if not to use Felix Zane's connections in finding a buyer for the book.

The drink arrived. We raised our glasses in a toast.

"Congratulations, Miranda. I think that now we know what Hanna Moran was doing in New York."

"No," she corrected. "*You* know what she was doing in New York." She put down her glass. "I think the time has come for you to tell me exactly what all this is about."

She was right: the time had come—especially if she was to do what I was next going to ask of her.

OBLIVION OCCUPIED AN ORNATE three-story brick building on First Avenue, not far from Bellevue, perhaps located so that in its original incarnation as a morgue mistakes at the nearby hospital could be quickly disposed of. The architects had been the famous firm of McKim, Mead & White. I wondered if, with the humor of history, Stanford White himself had been brought here following his murder by the enraged husband of the actress who had been his mistress. The husband had shot him to death in public during a performance at Madison Square Garden—ironically, another building that Stanford White had designed: the architect's version of dying with your boots on.

I looked up at the nightclub. In the day when this building had been designed the dignity of the deceased, even adulterers, had warranted pilasters and cornices. Today, it would be just a plain cinder-block box with a roll-up door for the meat wagons to come and go.

It was little changed on the outside: elegant brick and stone in shadowed repose; the original inhabitants would have found it familiar. There were no flashing lights or neon signs: in New York City, true hip advertises itself by other means, and external glitter attracts tourists alone. A modern awning had been added, suitably black, stretching down from the entrance and underneath it was a red carpet with brass posts and velvet ropes for crowd control. Presumably in its previous role there had never been a rush to get inside.

There were a lot of people milling around outside, despite it being one A.M. on a weeknight. We sat in the car for ten minutes, watching. Miranda had found a parking spot across the avenue and slightly down from the club, a place with a good view of the entrance. More importantly, the space ahead was next to a fire hydrant and so there was no chance of getting parked in, always a risk on the streets of Manhattan.

The aim tonight was to flush out Felix Zane. Miranda was the reluctant bait.

Zane would be more likely to bite if she were alone, and so I had been able to persuade her of the need for us to separate for the evening. I would go in first to check things out and be on hand if needed when Miranda arrived. She would come in half an hour later. Between us, we would hopefully identify Felix Zane. Later, when Zane left for the evening, we would follow him. If he took a cab, Miranda would follow in the car. If he took the subway or walked, I would follow him on foot. Either way, by the end of the evening, we would have discovered where Felix Zane lived.

ENTERING OBLIVION WAS LIKE stumbling onto a Hollywood sound stage during the filming of a hallucinogenic horror movie: part glamorous fantasy, part gothic fairy tale, part acid trip gone bad—a production in which all the sets were the result of a design collaboration between Lewis Carroll, Edgar Allan Poe, and the Marquis de Sade.

The main room was large and windowless, like a cistern or a dungeon. There were wide areas of ill-lit space, interspersed here and there with shafts of vivid, shifting light. The place was cool, as befitted a morgue, and the floor was covered in a thin layer of fog. The music was heavy psychedelic funk on a hard metal base, laden with feedback and distortion. There were half a dozen go-go girls dancing inside individual cages hanging from chains attached to the ceiling high overhead. They were dressed not in miniskirts but fetish gear: polished metal collars, studded leather bustiers, spike-heeled boots. One of them was blindfolded and her wrists were secured by rope to the bars. Another wore nothing but thigh-high boots, patent leather hot pants, and an abundance of black eyeshadow

It was a phantasmagoria; a dizzying chiaroscuro of light and sound that enveloped the newcomer—a space designed to disorient. To enter was to step through the looking glass and leave reality behind.

The wall to the immediate left of the entrance was fitted with a stack of large metal drawers of the type used to store dead bodies, presumably original equipment. One of the higher drawers was open and it was occupied. Upon it lay a long slender woman wearing a red leather catsuit. The zip was open low, revealing a gently undulating expanse of shiny black skin beneath. She had rolled onto her side and was resting her head on her right hand as she stared down at me. Huge afro and a wide smile—she was Oblivion's version of the Cheshire Cat.

"Hi," she said.

I stepped over and inspected her toe tag.

"Hello, Draghixa."

"First time?"

"For everything."

Her smile broadened. She had brilliant white teeth.

"I'm the hostess," she said.

"Of course."

"Table?"

"Please."

Draghixa slid down from the drawer with the fluid swiftness of a tree snake descending upon an unlucky ground squirrel. Her stomach tensed while doing so, revealing a series of taut smooth moguls upon an otherwise flat plain; she could probably do more ab-crunches than me. She came and stood close. She was tall; although her feet were bare we were almost eye to eye. I could smell her—musk with a touch of jasmine. Bath oil, I assumed, which would account for the fabulous shine. Or perhaps it was a body lubricant applied to help her slip into that ultratight cat suit.

She put a hand on my waist and leaned forward, wet blood-red lips by my left ear.

"Welcome to Oblivion," she whispered.

At that moment I felt a brief touch of metal on my right wrist and heard the sound of a ratchet clicking shut. I looked down. She had handcuffed me. The cuffs were bright chromed metal and the chain linking them was at least two feet long: not genuine law enforcement hardware. She attached the other end to her own wrist.

"So you don't go wandering off," she explained.

"I wouldn't want to get lost," I said agreeably.

"Follow me?"

"Wherever you lead."

Draghixa smiled, a hostess who appreciated obedience in her guests. She led me across the room, a sleek panther moving confidently through the nocturnal jungle. Perhaps that was why she wore no shoes, so as to approach her victims in silence.

There were strobe lights and lasers and roving spotlights that must have had revolving kaleidoscopic lenses fitted to them, fracturing the light into a craze of constantly changing fragments. They jitteringly revealed a strange crowd as we crossed the room. The men were mostly downtown types with a scattering of Eurotrash thrown in—swarthy dark-complexioned Mediterraneans with hair gel and carefully tended stubble; or Nordic variants, body-builders with shaved heads and aviator sunglasses. More interesting and more varied were the women, a wild amalgam of New York's female demimonde. There was an elegant vampire smoking from a foot-long cigarette holder; several anorexic models; a girl in a baby doll with bee-stung lips and belladonna-glazed eyes. One woman wore a transparent body stocking. In the dark it took me a moment to figure out that the glowing patches beneath it were fluorescent tattoos. Another had been wrapped, or wrapped herself, entirely in bands of flexible neon tubing. They were on, glowing bright pink, and she gave off a faint buzz. A third was wearing a man's dinner suit but without the shirt, just trousers and jacket and cumberbund. In passing I could not help glancing at the landscape thus revealed: two breasts whose only effective coverage were the straps of her suspenders. She noticed me noticing her, and so I gave a nod of appreciation. In response she took from her breast pocket the monocle that was hanging on a cord around her neck, secured the lens to her left eye, and did some inspecting of her own. She snapped a suspender with her free hand, although whether this indicated approval or otherwise I could not tell.

Halfway across the room, Draghixa came to a halt.

"This is the bar," she explained.

At first I thought it was an old-fashioned zinc bar, but then I realized that the metal top was actually composed of autopsy tables. They had been laid end to end, forming a series of stainless steel surfaces, each sloping gently down to a drain. It occurred to me that autopsy tables were a pretty good idea for a bar top, not a bad example of urban resource recycling.

"Charming," I said.

We proceeded to the table.

Oblivion was not laid out like a normal nightclub. There were no tables in the traditional sense, just groupings of sofas and lounge chairs around coffee tables, scattered in a score or more of random clusters across the broad floor. The walls were fitted with built-in tables and stools where people who wanted to sit up could do so, but most patrons opted for the big comfortable seats. This encouraged a collegial atmosphere, with people moving from group to group and sitting down to talk or share a drink with whoever else happened to be there. There was no dance floor; if people wished to dance—and many did—they simply stood and did so, wherever there was space. The other patrons were theater enough, and the go-go dancers provided a continuous spectacle for those who wished to be further entertained, but for the hopelessly dull there was a twenty-foot video screen mounted on one wall, and on which an old black and white silent film was currently playing. I recognized it: the original *Nosferatu*.

Draghixa led me to a long sofa. I discovered that the low wooden platforms I had assumed to be coffee tables were in fact coffins, something that until now I had not noticed in all the mist. Votive candles sat on top, failing to dispel the gloom.

We sat. Actually I sat, and Draghixa lay stretched out comfortably across the sofa, her left arm along the back and my right arm of necessity doing the same. She put one foot up behind my head and the other into my lap. Her toenails were painted bright red, matching the lipstick and catsuit. The piece of string tying the tag to her big toe had been secured with a neat double bow.

A cocktail waitress came by. She wore a top hat, an expressionless white Venetian carnival mask, black fishnet stockings, stiletto-heeled shoes and Lycra boy-shorts; otherwise she was naked, but from the neck down her body was covered in a layer of high gloss black—liquid latex perhaps—upon which in white had been stenciled the outline of a skeleton. All that was missing was the scythe.

"As it's your first time and all," Draghixa said, "why don't I get you one on the house?"

It is an old interrogation technique: put the detainee under a subtle obligation. We used to do the same thing, although in very different circumstances. For us it had been a cigarette or some water or treatment for a wound, not cocktails. Draghixa may or may not have been the hostess, but her primary function was obviously to identify newcomers who did not fit in and check them out. That FBI informant must have really rattled Felix Zane.

I wondered who they would use on Miranda when she showed up.

"My treat," I insisted, "since you've miraculously arisen from the dead."

"In that case I'll have a Corpse Reviver, Number Two," she said. "That's the one with the absinthe," she added with a wink.

I ordered the same.

"Have you ever drunk absinthe?" she asked after the waitress left.

"From time to time."

"They say that it drives you insane."

"I wouldn't like to vouch for it, Draghixa, either way."

She raised her foot and hit me on the nose with her toe tag in a gentle gesture of admonition. "You know my name," she said, "but you haven't told me yours."

"Benjamin Braddock."

"And what are you into, Benjamin Braddock?"

"Plastics."

She burst out laughing. "I prefer leather," she eventually admitted.

Our cocktails arrived. We raised our glasses in cheers and drank. One taste and I could tell how the cocktail had gotten its name.

"How are we ever going to get apart?" I asked, indicating the handcuffs.

"With the key."

"You mean that you have a key on you?"

"I do."

"I wouldn't have thought there would be room in that outfit."

"Well now," Draghixa declared, "I'm just full of interesting little nooks and crannies." She replaced her cocktail glass upon the coffin. "Why don't we see if you can find it?"

I took a generous slug before putting my own glass down and spent a long moment in contemplation of the lithe body laid out before me, wondering where a key could be concealed. The cat suit was absolutely skin tight over her arms and legs; hard to imagine even something as small as a key hidden in there. I thought of a ring but her fingers were unadorned, as were her toes, apart from the tag. Huge hoop earrings, but no key hanging from them. Eventually I decided on the particular cranny whose inspection it seemed to me could most acceptably be performed in public.

"I think you have a navel ring."

"Do you?"

"And my guess is that the key is on it."

"Really?"

"Unfortunately the zipper is not quite open that far."

"Yes, I believe you're right."

"In order to check, I would therefore have to open it some more."

"You've got to do what you've got to do."

She raised her hips to help with the maneuver, and once again her abdominal muscles tightened, hard as concrete. I grabbed the zipper and slowly lowered it. A cute little belly button was soon revealed, and sure enough there was a ring through it. But no key.

"Guess I was wrong," I said.

She put a pinky to the corner of her mouth. "I wonder where you'll try next."

I suddenly realized the most obvious hiding place: that mass of hair. It probably was not even real hair but a wig; no one wears afros anymore.

I leaned forward and tapped her lightly at the hairline.

"It's hidden in there, I'll bet."

"We'll see," she said.

I carefully ran my hand through her hair, and since I had to feel with the tips of my fingers it turned into an impromptu scalp massage. Draghixa enjoyed it, the way all cats do. The afro turned out to be genuine but there was no key in it that I could find.

"Would you like some help?" she said after a while.

"Yes, I would."

"Cold."

I ran my hand down past her ear to her neck.

"Cool."

To the base of her throat.

"Getting warmer."

Along the side of her chest.

"Very warm."

To her hip.

"Cooler."

Back up to her chest.

"Warm again."

I was starting to get it now. I put my hand on her left breast.

"Getting hot."

I put my hand on her right breast.

"Boiling."

I slid my hand under the cat suit. Her breasts were naturally small and her current posture flattened them further, but the change in texture was unmistakable. Soon my palm slid across her right breast and then brushed up against metal. Since I had lowered the zipper there was sufficient give in the cat suit for me to be able to tug it clear, revealing a dark nipple pierced by a thin golden ring identical to that in her belly button, and from which dangled a small silver key.

"Well, well," I said. "Look what I found."

"I hope you know what to do with it."

I brought my arm down and, twisting the wrist rather than the key so as to not risk hurting Draghixa, unlocked the cuffs. With both hands now free I carefully extracted the key from the lock.

"I've always enjoyed hide and seek," I said.

She put an arm around my neck and used it to pull herself up so that her face was six inches from mine. Her breath was cool and moist and reminded me of the jungle in the evening.

"I should have hidden it better," she whispered.

She finished her cocktail in a single long mouthful, then stood.

"Perhaps we'll run into each other again."

"I would certainly like to see more of you," I admitted.

She laughed a genuine laugh, gave a little wave, and then headed back to her post at the entrance. Perhaps when she got there she would do an internet search on "Benjamin Braddock." If so she was going to get several thousand results, all of them related to *The Graduate*.

I sat back and reviewed the conversation while finishing the Corpse Reviver. I concluded that, as interrogations go, this one had been pretty enjoyable.

MIRANDA GREY ENTERED THE NIGHTCLUB ten minutes later. Even among the neo-Glam crowd of Oblivion she stood out, an island of cool composure in a sea of strained affectation. She took a seat at the bar, as we had planned, and ordered a drink. I stayed where I was and maintained a cautious watch. Her martini arrived just as her interrogator did.

It turned out to be Felix Zane himself, recognizable from the photograph I had seen in the newspaper archives. I had not expected Miranda's presence to flush him out until later in the evening, but in retrospect I should have guessed that Zane would personally check out any new woman who entered his domain, thus combining a security check with a potential recruiting interview. Especially any new woman who looked like Miranda. And more especially if she were blond.

Zane was wearing a dark suit and tie, but the cut was exaggerated and the fabric bore a sheen; the sort of stuff often seen in advertisements in glossy magazines but rarely on real men in real life. He was accompanied by a long-legged woman in a short backless dress, the top of which was a halter style composed not of fabric but many thin metal chains. She stood slightly to the side and behind him, an accessory rather than a companion.

After a few minutes Zane and Miranda were laughing like old friends. Miranda especially, head thrown back, long neck exposed. The plan had been for her to disengage as soon as we had identified Zane sufficiently to be sure of following the right man when he left the nightclub, but Miranda gave no sign of doing so. At one point Zane gestured to the bartender and soon a fresh round of drinks was served, although only Miranda had finished her first. When they arrived Zane spiked her drink—not surreptitiously but quite openly, removing a little pill case from his pocket and plopping one into Miranda's glass as casually as if dropping in an olive.

He put a second into his girlfriend's. The pills briefly fizzed, then dissolved.

They continued to chat, laughing frequently, all three getting along nicely now. This was not the reserved Miranda I knew, or thought I knew. During the course of the conversation Zane's girlfriend gradually moved closer to Miranda and rarely took her eyes from her. Eventually Zane leaned forward and asked a question that ended with a jerk of his head toward the rear, apparently suggesting that they go somewhere else. Miranda nodded in consent.

She quaffed the remainder of her drink and stood, a little unsteady but smiling broadly. The other girl ran her arm through Miranda's and all three disappeared into the gloom at the back of the room.

I stood and followed.

There turned out to be a discreet spiral staircase at the rear wall which led up to a platform raised high above, presumably the owner's private suite. Probably there had originally been a whole floor up there—why would a building whose original purpose was a morgue have needed such high ceilings?—but most of it had been knocked down in the redesign. The remainder was therefore open to the main floor, forming a sort of mezzanine, a good spot from which the privileged could relax in privacy while gazing out upon the scene below.

The bottom of the stairs was guarded by a tattooed bouncer wearing a black T-shirt from which the sleeves had been torn off to better expose his biceps. He was grinning to himself, perhaps pleased to be out of prison and successfully reintegrating into society.

I decided to give Miranda ten minutes to extract. If she did not come back down in that time, I would go in and extract her myself.

YEARS AGO, I HAD BEEN TAUGHT how to perform the "Liverpool Kiss." The Liverpool Kiss is not a form of osculation, it is a form of head butt. Like a real kiss it is necessarily applied at very close range, and to ensure that the target does not balk the approach is best made with an open smile and a hand extended in a gesture of friendship. Your opponent, disarmed by the grin and no doubt relieved that the threat of violence has apparently receded, willingly accepts. At the moment you have his hand you grab tight, go toe to toe, and whip your forehead into your opponent's face. The neck muscles are amazingly strong—if you get it right you can inflict a dizzying blow.

The man who introduced me to the Liverpool Kiss was an officer in the British Army by the name of Jock MacGregor. He was Glaswegian rather than Liverpudlian, but the Scots are ardent head butters, too. MacGregor was on temporary assignment to my unit and he taught by example, applying one smack into the face of the insurgent fighter who had just shot him. We were in Mujahideen-controlled Anbar at the time, doing some battlefield prep, back during the buildup before the second battle of Ramadi. MacGregor was on the ground, unarmed, the jagged shaft of his shattered tibia poking through his cammies, in extreme pain and clearly no threat. The Muj leaned over him, perhaps intending to finish him off, more likely to search for anything of value that he could loot. A second later he too was on the ground, also in extreme pain, blood gushing from his newly remodeled nose.

I was out of ammunition by then—we all were—but the Ali Baba's confusion following that Liverpool Kiss was sufficient for me to get to him with my knife, as MacGregor had intended. I had my young lance corporal, the only other survivor, cover us with our newly acquired AK-47 while I used the Muj's belt for a tourniquet. I ended up humping MacGregor across my shoulders in a fireman's lift all the way back to the LZ.

I CHECKED MY WATCH. Ten minutes were up.

The bouncer returned my smile as I approached; prison had taught him nothing. I did not offer to shake until the last moment, so he held out his own hand in instinctive response before really thinking about it. I grabbed it and stepped forward, whipping my forehead smack into his face. He did not immediately go down—I was not as good at this as Jock MacGregor—but he leaned forward, blood pouring from his nose or mouth. I brought my knee up into his head and this time it was lights out.

I looked around but no one had noticed—back here in the shadows it was hard to see anything at all, and the bouncer's two quick grunts would not have been audible above the music.

I began the ascent.

I moved cautiously in case Zane was armed and aware of the ruckus below. I need not have bothered.

Felix Zane's private suite was the size of a small apartment and luxuriously if strangely furnished. In the corner to the right was a bar composed of a curved facing in brushed aluminum topped with a lucite counter and backed by lucite shelves holding the glassware.

There was an ice bucket on top with a bottle of champagne sitting in it. The rear wall—which was the only complete wall—was covered by a curtain of mother of pearl: hundreds of shiny shards hanging on strings close together, forming a surface of subtle ever-shifting light. On the left was a sand-blasted plate-glass wall, pierced by a door, presumably leading to a bathroom.

In the main space there were sofas arranged in a U-pattern around the perimeter, with the open side facing forward so that people could look out over the view below. The sofas were low and upholstered in a strange white fabric that had the same sheen as the mother of pearl, a sort of soft holographic plastic. The place was lit by votive candles like the ones downstairs, a score or more occupying various horizontal surfaces around the room. There were several tables, lucite tops on aluminum frames. One was occupied by champagne glasses, already mostly empty. The floor was carpeted and further covered in thick animal fur rugs. But the room was dominated by the feature at its center: a sunken rectangular pool, about eight feet by twelve, composed of gradually reducing rectangles of shallow marble laid one on top of the other, like the interior of an inverted pyramid. It was lit from underwater and heated; a little steam rose from the surface.

Sitting on the sofa to the left were Miranda and the other girl. They were embraced, kissing with passion, and did not notice me. The girl's dress lay draped over the arm; she retained only her shoes and a little underwear. Miranda was still technically clothed, but her zipper was undone, the bottom of her dress had been pulled up over her hips, and the other girl was exploring her with abandon.

Felix Zane was on the middle sofa, back to me. His eyes were fixed on the two girls. There was a sudden flash, and I realized that he had more than his eyes fixed on the scene: he was photographing them with a small camera.

I went over to the bar and picked up the champagne bottle. From the distinctive shield-shaped label I recognized it as Dom Pérignon—Zane was not a cheap seducer. The bottle was solid and empty. A quick flip to get the grip right. I stepped over behind Zane, who was still madly photographing the performance. At the last moment he must have sensed me behind him; he turned around, but by then it was too late. I brought the bottle down on his head. Just a tap; I did not want to kill him. The bottle did not break but the blow was enough for him to have entered the twilight zone.

I quickly pocketed the camera then stepped over to the sofa and untangled Miranda from her new friend.

"Time to extract," I said.

I got her to her feet, zipped up the dress, and hustled her downstairs. The bodyguard was still lying in undisturbed slumber at the base. We left the nightclub without incident and returned to the Aston Martin. I put Miranda into the passenger seat and got in behind the wheel.

"What were you thinking?" Miranda demanded after I had closed the door. They were the first words she had spoken since I had gone upstairs. Her diction was surprisingly clear.

"Rescuing you, of course."

"Rescuing me? I had them right where I wanted them."

"Zane spiked your drink."

"I know. He asked me if I would like a little something and I said yes."

"Your virtue was in danger of being compromised."

"Don't be ridiculous. I was just showing them I was a good sport so that we'd go back to his place and find out where he lived."

"What do you think would happen back at his place?"

"I would have immediately thrown up on the carpet and then no doubt have been kicked out."

I did not reply right away, and we sat in silence for several minutes. Obviously I had underestimated this intrepid-eyed woman. Indeed, it was clear that she had done exactly what we most value in special forces: adapt to shifting circumstances in order to achieve the mission objective. I had blown it for her. Nevertheless I was not sorry to have done so: her plan was good and it might well have worked, but Felix Zane was a very dangerous person. I preferred to try following him, a feeling that was reinforced by Miranda's next remark.

"I'm having such a good time," she said.

She closed her eyes and curled up in the seat. By the time I had secured her seat belt she had fallen asleep.

Zane came out of the nightclub twenty minutes later. He was alone and he did not look happy. Probably he had a headache. He stepped off the curb and hailed a cab. I pressed the starter and the Aston Martin sprang into life. Soon I was following him uptown on First Avenue.

It was easy: the cab made just a single turn, onto 79th Street, before stopping outside a luxury apartment building. I pulled over to the curb and kept watch. It was nearly three A.M. now and apart from the lobby there were no other lights on in the building. I waited, and eventually some of the windows high above lit up. Zane had entered his apartment.

Thirtieth floor, the penthouse. Just my lousy luck.

I refired the Aston and drove downtown to the meatpacking district. In Manhattan you can always get a good meal, any time, day or night. We stopped at a gritty French joint. I figured that I should feed Miranda to dilute whatever was in her stomach, and I was pretty hungry myself. I ordered steak-frites and an omelet for Miranda. She was semi-comatose but at three A.M. so was much of the restaurant's clientele, and we did not particularly stand out. I wiped the other girl's lipstick from her face and convinced her to drink some coffee, which perked her up a little.

I studied Miranda while waiting for the food to arrive. A little the worse for wear, but still beguiling. Those intrepid eyes remained crystal clear, notwithstanding the drinks and drugs. Intelligent. Resolute and courageous, that much was certain, but at bottom she was probably unknowable. A woman I would have liked to have spent more time with, but it was not to be: there would be no further endangerment of her by me, no matter how valuable that notebook was.

After returning to the hotel I left a note under her door.

Miranda,

Not sure how much you will remember this morning, but the bottom line is that last night we accomplished what we set out to do. You have more than earned your $200 a day plus expenses: I would never have gotten this far alone.

I'll take care of things from here and will let you know how it turns out.

Lysander Dalton

P.S. I settled the hotel bill.

P.P.S. The Aston is back in the hotel garage, and I've enclosed the ticket in the envelope.

XII

I WAS SITTING ON THE STEPS of the church across the street from Felix Zane's building. The lights in his apartment had gone out long ago and he had emerged from the lobby shortly afterward, presumably on his way to Oblivion for the evening. If last night was typical then he would not return until the early hours of the morning. I remained where I was for another thirty minutes, watching, waiting for things to settle down. The doormen changed shifts at midnight— it was a building with twenty-four-hour security. There was no way to get past unseen, and even if it were possible to somehow circumvent the doorman and make it to the elevators unnoticed, I did not possess the lock-picking skills to enter Zane's apartment when I got there.

I had no intention of going in through the front door. A brick apartment building is just a big man-made rock. Rocks can be climbed. There was no need to find a way past the lobby staff and through the front door—all I had to do was scale the outside of the building.

I had spent the afternoon inside a sporting goods store that stocked climbing gear. Technically, I would be performing a roped solo ascent—"roped" meaning that I would climb with a safety rope, so that any fall would hopefully terminate before making contact with the sidewalk. The technique is to climb a little, place the protection, then run the rope through it. The ends of the rope are secured to you, one to the harness, the other to an ascender which allows you to ease out more line as you climb. If you fall, hopefully the protection takes your weight.

I made some variations on the usual equipment. Climbers today normally use removable protection—cams and hexes and the like, things that can be jammed into cracks in the rocks and recovered once the next higher piece is in place. But I would have no natural cracks into which to place removable protection, just the narrow space in between bricks, most of which would be filled with mortar. And even after securing a cam into the remaining gap I was not confident of a brick's ability to support the force of a fall without the edge breaking away. So, in addition to removable protection, I carried some old-fashioned fixed: pitons—large metal pins that could be hammered right into the mortar. They were certain to be secure but placing them would be noisy. I had bought a rubber-covered mallet that I hoped would prevent me from attracting the unwanted attention of residents on the way up.

Instead of climbing shoes I decided to stick with my combat boots. Climbing shoes are flexible, designed for the uneven surfaces of a genuine rock face. But I would be scaling a sheer vertical wall and so my boots, with their good stiff welts that could be jammed into the narrow space between bricks, were more suitable.

I bought two sixty-meter lengths of climbing rope, ascender, harness, and quickdraws with which to attach the rope to the protection. I also bought a lightweight backpack, although I was not planning on taking much up with me. The last stop was a hardware store where I purchased a crowbar. Windows on modern apartment buildings are fitted in sliding aluminum frames. They have simple catches, not at all burglar proof—no one anticipates a break-and-entry three hundred feet up in the air.

I checked the time. I had wanted to wait until moonrise, another thirty minutes from now, but decided that it was unnecessary: there was already sufficient light to climb by; the ambient glow of Manhattan needed no celestial aid.

I stood and crossed the street. The entrance to the building consisted of a revolving door with a regular door beside it. Both were glass-paneled and so I made sure to keep clear of the doorman's line of sight. Above the entrance was a broad fixed platform projecting from the building—a portico—and then attached to this was an awning leading across the sidewalk to the curb. The exterior was faced in marble. At the base of the wall to the left there was a built-in flower bed rising about three feet from the level of the pavement.

I went twenty paces down from the entrance and made a last check of the sidewalk. There was no one coming from either direction, and no one across the street that I could see. I took a deep breath and began to sprint. At the flower bed I put one foot on the ledge and, losing as little as possible of forward momentum, used it to propel myself upward. I went briefly sailing through the air before catching the edge of the portico with a loud thump. I remained dangling a moment, waiting for the swinging to subside, then quickly hauled myself up and out of sight from below.

I crouched low and remained absolutely still. Soon I heard the door below me open, followed by hesitant footsteps—the doorman had come out to investigate the noise.

I could imagine him looking around, wondering what the strange sound had been. He could not see me now, but if he was willing to walk far enough down the sidewalk and then look back he would notice me. But doormen do not stray far from their station. I heard him go back inside and close the door.

I opened the backpack and removed the climbing gear. Harness first, then rope, then hardware and mallet, the latter secured with a tether. When all the equipment was checked and ready I began the ascent.

Three hundred feet does not sound far. Just a hundred yards, a distance that the fastest human beings can cover in less than ten seconds. But being vertical rather than horizontal makes a big difference, and climbing the thirty floors to Felix Zane's apartment that night became for me a monumental test of physical endurance. The main problem was finding adequate handholds and footholds— the spaces between the bricks were fine for short bursts of climbing, but I could not risk releasing a hand to tap in the pitons. I relied on window ledges, choosing those whose curtains were closed or blinds drawn, supporting my weight on the three-inch-wide ledge while quietly placing new protection in the adjacent brickwork, and hoping that any occupants did not choose this moment to get out of bed and inspect the view. The higher I climbed the longer became the periods of rest and the shorter the distances covered between them.

Eventually I made it, exhausted. My forearms and wrists ached, my fingers were cut and bleeding. I withdrew the crowbar and went to work. The latch was a simple tongue-and-groove mechanism. I intended to use the crowbar to sufficiently bend the frame so that the tongue came free, but it proved unnecessary: as soon as I applied pressure the latch just popped right off.

I slid the window open and entered Felix Zane's apartment.

XIII

T HE FIRST THING I DID AFTER ENTERING Felix Zane's
apartment was to take the gloves from the backpack and put
them on. Then I pulled out the cloth I had packed for the purpose
and wiped away my bloodstained fingerprints from the window and
frame. Given Zane's relationship with the law, he was probably not
the kind of person who would willingly invite the police into his
apartment—break-in or no break-in—but if I was mistaken I had no
intention of leaving evidence.

I found a light switch and turned it on.

I was inside a large living room. It had a hardwood floor and was
furnished minimally but luxuriously: sleek leather sofa and chairs,
large flat-screen television, a low sideboard in brushed aluminum.
There was a coffee table with a green glass top. It was lit by little
spotlights dangling on silver wires hanging from the ceiling. The
interior walls were off-white and occupied by a series of paintings,
also lit by little spotlights, as if in a picture gallery. I briefly
examined one of them, an incoherent smearing of unrelated color.

There was evidence of brushstrokes, but the accumulation of dried paint was thick enough to be impasto—it was as if the artist, using the brush like a dagger, had repeatedly attacked the canvas, pounding paint upon paint in a crazed frenzy.

It was signed in the lower right-hand corner: *Zane*. So he hung his own works here; no wonder the room felt like a gallery.

The spaces of blank wall between the paintings turned out not to be blank—on closer inspection they revealed inscriptions rendered in soft gray, barely distinguishable from the background. They were quotations and, in contrast to the artworks they presumably sought to elucidate, had been done with the precision of a sign painter. I read a few.

The first duty of a revolutionary is to get away with it.
-Abbie Hoffman

Money is human happiness in the abstract.
-Arthur Schopenhauer

Being born is like being kidnapped and then sold into slavery.
-Andy Warhol

Zane was obviously a man with a good ear for a quotation, although their use amid the abundant display of his own failures suggested a man with too much pent-up frustration to have fully appreciated their ironies.

No photographs, no books. No decoration or display of any sort— Zane wanted nothing to detract from the appreciation of his own artworks.

There were several small ceramic bowls sitting on the coffee table. They were filled with candy. I helped myself to a handful, thinking that after the climb I could use some sugar. Luckily, I inspected the wrappers before ingesting the contents. One was labeled as "Speed Demon." Another was called "Galaxy Acid," and promised a trip to the stars. A third came without covering, the M&M-like candies simply stamped "XTC." I was thinking that perhaps the paintings looked better after a handful when I heard the sound of keys.

I picked up the crowbar, snapped off the light, and moved quietly into position behind the front door.

The noise had come from the corridor outside. It had not been the rattle of a key entering the lock but rather the jangle of keys on a ring, as if someone had just pulled them out prior to entering the apartment.

I tried the spy hole but could see no sign of whoever was outside. I put my ear to the door and listened instead. Nothing, for a moment. Then I heard the electronic ding of an elevator arriving, followed by the sound of the doors opening. So it was not someone coming but someone going, obviously from one of the other top-floor apartments, and probably the noise had been the sound as they put away their keys while waiting for the elevator to arrive.

I resumed the search.

The kitchen was a small space off the entrance hall. There were the usual appliances but the faint coating of dust on the stovetop suggested that cooking was rarely performed here. The refrigerator contained mostly mineral water in the bottom and vodka in the freezer.

I tried the bedroom next. The bed was king-sized and the sheets were silk. The closet was neater and fuller than you might expect of a man living alone—at least in comparison to my own sparse stock of clothing back at the vineyard, mostly working clothes: khaki twill trousers and stiff cotton workshirts with secure chest pockets, the civilian equivalents of the uniform I had once worn every day, and in which I still felt most comfortable.

The last room was more interesting. There was a large desk, a printer on a separate stand, and a big bookcase brimming with volumes on art, architecture, design, photography, and poetry. No doubt this was originally a second bedroom, but Zane had converted it to use as a study.

I searched the desk. There was a laptop, which I turned on. While waiting for it to boot up, I examined the contents of the drawers. There were just stationery items in the first drawer, but the second revealed paperwork. Zane was surprisingly well organized. Anyone running their own business needs to be, but in his case it extended to his private life as well. All the outstanding bills were bound together with a large clip. They consisted of the predicable and mundane: ConEd, telephone, common charges for the condo, a mortgage statement, a medical bill, a credit card account. None of them showed any amounts past due. I noted down the number from the phone bill. Most of the credit card charges were for fashionable restaurants; Zane must have made it a habit to eat out before going to the club, something already suggested by the meager contents of the kitchen. The largest charge was from Air France and the ticket price was several thousand dollars—Zane must travel first class. I wondered where he had traveled to.

I examined the medical bill, which came from a group called New York East Medical Associates. Usually such bills are quite detailed, as the insurers demand, but this one specified the service rendered only as "consultation." It was almost as expensive as the plane ticket—a reflection of the astronomical costs of health care in America.

The laptop finished booting up but a window had opened demanding a password before continuing. The logo revealed it as proprietary software—not the routine security feature built into the operating system, which an expert might be able to circumvent, but special software designed to ensure no unauthorized access. I tried a few obvious choices but after the third attempt the system announced that it was freezing the computer due to too many failed logins. I closed the screen and turned it off.

There was little else of interest in the desk drawers: no check books, no bank statements, no IRS filings. Felix Zane was a modern man, someone at ease in the electronic age. No doubt all his financial statements existed in digital form on some distant server and were accessible via the machine that I had just shut down, if you knew the correct passwords and so on. I thought of my own home and the boxes full of statements filed away in the attic with secret embarrassment. I was an anachronism, and probably in more ways than just this.

I checked the closet. There were more clothes here, a vacuum cleaner, some sporting goods (Zane was a tennis player), and a set of expensive luggage—if you travel first class, you might as well have the bags to go with it.

In the corner, sitting on the floor, was a safe. It was a solidly-built metal box the size of a bar fridge, painted green, and despite the modest size it probably weighed a hundred pounds. The manufacturer's name, Sargent & Greenleaf, was stenciled on the door in old-fashioned script that was chipped and faded with age. There was both a combination lock and a key lock, and a large stainless steel handle. There was a key in the keyhole, a big brass one of the type you imagine jail cells being locked with (but are not, at least not at Leavenworth—they are electronic instead).

I knelt in front of the safe and gently tried the handle. Nothing.

I turned the key until hearing it click, then tried again. This time the handle turned and the door swung free.

Possibly Zane had left the safe unlocked by mistake, but more likely he always kept it that way, closing it only via the key and never using the combination lock. The safe was an antique, something purchased for its aesthetic value and that Zane probably used to protect the contents against not theft, which is unlikely in a doorman building, but against fire.

I opened the safe. There were several bundles of abstract human happiness inside. Not all of it was U.S.-denominated—along with five piles of bills bearing Benjamin Franklin's disapproving portrait there were several bundles of euros. The latter were mostly of the purple-hued variety with Bauhaus-themed architectural renderings: five-hundreds. Like the world's central banks, Felix Zane apparently chose to maintain a portion of his cash reserves in the European currency.

I made a quick inventory. About a hundred and fifty thousand dollars' worth, give or take. Now I understood why he flew first class, but the fact that it was not in an account earning interest suggested that the method of its acquisition would not have withstood close scrutiny.

Next to the piles of banknotes was a little black velvet pouch with a tie at the top. I opened it and poured the contents into my palm. Diamonds. They sparkled prettily, several dozen in various sizes and cuts, some of them quite large. I had no way of assessing what they were worth, but it would not have surprised me to learn that they had more value than the dollars and euros combined.

Under the pouch were two other objects. The first was a passport, a little larger than normal, and instead of the usual dark blue this one had a thick green cover on which was imprinted a coat of arms at whose center was a pentagram, a five-pointed star. The country's name was in Arabic script but there was a French translation below: *Royaume du Maroc*: the Kingdom of Morocco. The passport opened backward with the binding on the right-hand side, in the Arabic fashion. On the main page I found a younger version of Zane's unsmiling face staring back at me. The name was printed in both Arabic and Latin forms, in the latter as Farhan Al Zanah; presumably an Arabicized version of Felix Zane. The *place de naissance* was specified as *New York, Etats Unis*: apparently neither foreign birth nor foreign citizenship prevented the holding of a Moroccan passport.

I went through all the pages but none of them had been stamped.

The second object was a white index card, folded in two, and held flat by the passport and diamonds that had been lying on top of it. Inside was an American Express Platinum Card of the same type that Dortmund had once given me until becoming disenchanted with my spending habits. It was shiny and unscratched, a credit card rarely used.

The index card was not blank, as I had originally thought. In the upper left-hand corner was the strange phrase: "Let us go then."

I recognized it. It comes from the opening line of 'Prufrock':

Let us go then, you and I,
When the evening is spread out against the sky
Like a patient etherised upon a table;

But poetry was not the purpose: the 'O' had been printed as 'Ø,' which meant that it would be typed using the zero key, a common substitution to meet the usual demand of financial institutions that their customers' passwords include a combination of letters and numbers.

I realized what it was that I had discovered: this was Felix Zane's getaway kit. The passport was unused because it was his means of escape if and when the occasion ever arose—immigration control might be on the alert for a Felix Zane traveling on a U.S. passport, but Farhan El Zanah on a Moroccan passport would likely pass through unmolested. The passport may have been a forgery, or if genuine then it was likely obtained illegally—something for emergency use only. The diamonds were the ultimate in portable wealth: just swallow the contents before fleeing the country and then retrieve them again when you have safely negotiated border control. The choice of credit card also made sense: Platinum American Express Cards have no limits and are therefore suitable for the exigencies of escape. Zane had made sure to set up online access to his account so that he could make financial arrangements from wherever circumstances took him. *Letusg0then* was the password. When presented with the demand to create a password Zane had probably grabbed the nearest book at hand, in this case a volume of T.S. Eliot, and opened it to the first page, which would have been Prufrock, Eliot's first published poem. That opening phrase must have struck him as particularly appropriate since he would be on the run, perhaps a lucky find, and so he had chosen it. But no one can remember the password of an account they never use, and so Zane had written it down on the index card. His last act before fleeing would be to memorize the password then tear up the card and flush it down the toilet.

On the shelf below the money was a blue plastic carrying case, about the size of a large book. I opened it and withdrew the contents: a SIG Sauer P232 automatic—compact and lightweight; a gun designed for concealed carry. The barrel extended from the end of the slide and was threaded. Also in the case was the attachment that screwed onto that thread: a short cylindrical sound suppressor.

There were two magazines, both of which were loaded with .380 ACP. A bad idea: storing loaded magazines causes the springs, now permanently compressed, to gradually lose their effectiveness. The tips of the rounds were copper-sheathed but with a deep conical crater an eighth of an inch wide sunk into the top: jacketed hollow-point ammunition—bullets designed to expand and flatten on impact, maximizing damage to soft tissue and bone.

So this was part of the getaway kit, too. If necessary, Zane would use it to shoot his way out of trouble, relying on the silencer to avoid attracting attention. He would dispose of the weapon in a trash can at the airport terminal before passing through security.

The gun had no trigger lock attached. On the right-hand side of the frame, ahead of the trigger guard, was a shallow groove left by a circular grinder that had been used to remove the weapon's serial number.

Well now, that was illegal. Being a good citizen, I confiscated the weapon. The silencer, too. I also noted down the details of the passport and credit card.

I had seen enough. The next step was to talk to Zane. I decided to wait downstairs until he returned to the building. I would give him a minute or so after the apartment lights went on to fully grasp that the place had been tossed, then call. With the shock of realizing how easily I could get to him, he would likely be in a cooperative frame of mind when he answered the telephone.

I packed up and left. I took the elevator this time; doormen announce people coming in but ignore people going out. I walked back across the street and was about to climb the church steps to my previous position when I realized that I was no longer alone.

Three men were behind me, having apparently been waiting in the shadows by the side of Zane's apartment building. Two of them had baseball bats; the third carried a knife. Zane's weapon was in my backpack, and I had no chance of getting to it in time. This was not going to be pretty.

I recognized one of them: the bouncer to whom I had applied the Liverpool Kiss the previous evening. He had a plaster across his nose and he looked very pleased to see me.

So it had been Zane's keys that I had heard in the passageway after all. When approaching the apartment he must have noticed the light under the door and the shadow of someone moving about inside. Or perhaps he simply heard me, as I had him, after which he had done an immediate about-face and returned to the elevator. In any case, he had obviously called in some of his people; probably their instructions were to bring me back to the club for an extended Q & A session.

An automobile engine started nearby. The car was in shadow and the driver did not turn on the headlights, but the engine was loud and high pitched; I recognized it immediately. I backed up the steps a little, guessing what was to come.

The Aston Martin blasted out of a parking space a little way down, rubber squealing under hard acceleration. It fishtailed out into the street in a sea of tire smoke, then curved back in toward the sidewalk, still under full power. The other three turned around in time to see it mount the curb toward them. The car slammed into the two men to my left. One of them, my friend with the broken nose, was propelled twenty feet through the air; this was just not his week. The second was laid out on the sidewalk, unconscious or dead. The third guy, unhurt, took to his heels and disappeared around the corner.

I walked over to the Aston Martin as Miranda emerged from the driver's side.

"So you'll *take care of things from here*?" she said, quoting my own words to me.

"*I had them right where I wanted them*," I replied, returning the favor.

Miranda smiled and she knelt by the front of the car to inspect for damage.

"What about these two?" I asked.

"What about them?"

"They might be dead."

"They had better be, if they dented my fender."

I walked over to my buddy. He was conscious. The bandage was soaked in blood and he was in tears of pain. Reconstructing that nose was going to pay for the college tuition of some plastic surgeon's offspring.

"I take it that you decided not to go back to D.C.," I said over my shoulder.

"Just as well for you, I think."

"And you were awake last night when I followed Zane?"

"I woke up when you started the car."

Not even Rip van Winkle could sleep through the sound of that V-12. I walked over to my other would-be assailant and gave him a little interrogatory kick. He was alive, but his tap-dancing days were over.

"Well, they'll probably both survive," I told Miranda.

"Wonderful," she replied in the flat tone of someone not bothering to disguise their complete indifference.

MIRANDA AND I went back to the hotel. We had an early breakfast after which I returned to my room and composed a short note to Felix Zane.

Mr. Zane,

My apologies for the damage to your associates last night, and the necessity of having entered your apartment uninvited.

I would like some information from you: the whereabouts of a mutual friend whose location I think you know. After learning that, I will have no further interest in you.

There is a small Vermeer at the Met, a domestic interior depicting a woman pouring water from a pitcher—I will be there at 4:00 this afternoon, should you wish to settle this without further disruption.

It seemed reasonable enough to me. Zane would surely realize by now that I had enough on him to make life difficult, should I choose to do so. It would be much easier to just give up Moran than deal with me. But when I went to the front desk of Zane's apartment building later that day, intending to ask them to deliver the note, the doorman told me that Zane was gone.

"He left for the airport early this morning," the doorman explained. "I have no idea when he'll be back."

Zane had fled, and I had lost my only lead.

XIV

I STOOD ON THE HOTEL BALCONY looking out over the city below, a sparkling sun-drenched necklace draped around the throat of the lustrous deep-blue sea. There were palm trees and cypresses nearby plus an enormous Norfolk Island pine, its towering trunk rising dead straight like the mast of some great sailing ship—an incongruous tree to find here in a place that must be at a point on the globe more or less directly opposite its native habitat. But it was nevertheless a popular tree, serving as a roost for a changing variety of birds: white egrets bouncing from branch to branch on bright yellow feet, occasional doves and ravens, and for several minutes a Barbary falcon: a noble creature with distinctive bands of white and brown across its breast, a bird whose menacing presence caused the others to very gingerly depart.

Beyond the trees lay Tangier itself, tiers of whitewashed buildings tumbling all the way down to the harbor. The city occupies a natural amphitheater with the wide semicircular sweep of the bay as the stage and Spain, visible in the distance across the Strait of Gibraltar, as the backdrop. Through the binoculars I could make out the lighthouse at Tarifa and on the hills above it wind farms: dozens of tall white towers, their long slender arms revolving in slow deliberate time. Back on the African side, to the east, rose the Atlas Mountains, obdurate brown peaks bereft of vegetation, immense and unyielding. They were miles away but the air was clear here, desert-pure, and from the hotel balcony it seemed as if you could almost reach out and touch them.

It was an active town. Vessels constantly came and went in the harbor, occasionally freighters, more often ferries like the one that had brought Felix Zane here. The narrow streets and alleyways were a hive of noise. Despite being perched high above the city at the El Minzah I could smell cooking from a restaurant, obviously nearby but invisible among the warren of alleys below. Grilled fish and spices; I realized that I had not eaten since taking the flight last night.

Miranda, back on the payroll, was in the adjoining room. I checked my watch, longing for her to hurry up so that we could eat, but this has been the futile lament of men from time immemorial.

Instead, I went back inside and set up the laptop.

Felix Zane had made a single mistake—he had used the credit card—and it had been this machine, hastily purchased in New York, that had enabled me to take advantage of it.

Since discovering that he was gone I had monitored his American Express account. A single charge had come up that same evening, less than twenty-four hours after Zane had fled. The transaction had been made at Tarifa in Spain. The payee was listed as "FRS," which when I looked it up had turned out to be an operator of high-speed ferries crossing the Strait of Gibraltar to North Africa. There was only one destination: Tangier. The €52.20 charged to the card corresponded exactly to the fare listed on their website.

Zane was a careful man, probably especially so since his grand jury appearance. Most eastbound transatlantic flights are red-eyes, evening departures from the Atlantic seaboard that get to Europe early the next morning. The exception is London, to which there are early morning departures that arrive the same evening London time. After what happened to the hired help, Zane had elected not to wait around for an evening flight taking him directly to Morocco. Instead, he had chosen to get out of town on the first available transatlantic flight, and that meant London.

Or perhaps, being naturally cautious, he always took a circuitous route to his final destination—something that a man who keeps a getaway kit in his closet might do as a matter of course. After arriving in London he must have spent the night making his way south, most likely by train, starting with the one that goes through the Channel Tunnel and then eventually arriving at Tarifa the next morning in time to make the final leg by ferry, crossing the Strait to Morocco. No credit card record for those trains: he must have paid cash. By now he was somewhere here in Tangier, hidden in a city that he knew well while waiting out whatever was going on in New York, safe from me and in a country where he was also safe from extradition, too, should the law get involved back home.

Except for that one mistake: he paid for the ferry by credit card—perhaps the ferry only accepted cards, something reasonable if the company did not want their cashiers to have to keep on hand change in both euros and dirhams, or maybe Zane simply got careless.

In any case, it is true what they say: you should never write down your password.

WE WENT FOR AN AFTERNOON STROLL, getting our bearings while there was still plenty of light. Tangier is really two towns, the

Ville Nouvelle and the Medina, the latter being the old walled city, a jumbled maze of narrow steps and serpentine alleyways, the city of the Moors. The El Minzah is located where the Medina meets the new town, a Europeanized area of broad avenues and sidewalk cafes. We walked along the Avenue de la Liberté down to the Grand Socco, then back up around to the Place de France, past the French Consulate—a magnificent villa in a luxuriant garden, the best place in town—chatting as we went.

Miranda had called the main hotels as I had asked her to (I had hoped that the front desk would be more helpful to a female voice). She had used her cell phone so that the calls would appear as international, should they have such a thing as Caller ID here. There were not many big hotels in Tangier: in town there were only the Continental and the El Minzah, where we were staying, and on the outskirts a handful of luxury hotels clustered by the beaches to the city's east. On each call Miranda had asked to be put through to Felix Zane, and on being told that they had no Felix Zane staying there she had said that he must have registered under his Arabic name, Farhan El Zanah. Each time they had rechecked, and each time they had again reported that there was no such guest.

It had been a long shot—a man laying low does not stay in such places; more likely he would be deep inside the Medina, holed up in one of the cheap hotels or hostels around the Petit Socco; maybe he still had friends here from his days as a budding artist, or perhaps he had simply paid someone to put him up for a while and keep quiet.

I was going to need help in finding him.

I left Miranda back at the hotel after having explained what I intended to do.

"Shouldn't I come with you?" she asked.

"No."

"Why not?"

"Did you notice the sidewalk cafes as we walked past them?"

"Of course."

"Were there many?"

"Certainly. A dozen a least."

"And were the tables occupied?"

"Some were. Perhaps most."

"Were there any women at any of the tables?"

That stopped her short. She thought about it for a moment, surprise slowly registering on her face, then discontent as she realized the answer.

"No," she admitted at last. "I didn't see any women at all."

"Because there were none to see," I explained. We must have passed at least a hundred people sitting at the outdoor tables. Not a single one of them had been female. "And that's why I should go alone."

I ENTERED THE MEDINA VIA an arched portal—the Bab Fahs—forty-feet high and shaped in that ornate horseshoe style favored in Moorish architecture. Going through it was to pass from a city unchanged for fifty years into a city unchanged for five hundred.

I had entered the marketplace. There was a crowded mass of pedestrian traffic, mostly human, occasionally ungulate. Goods were transported by pushcarts whose handlers made little accommodation for the crowd as they barged through. The buildings looming on either side of the narrow street were three or four stories tall, whitewashed stucco crumbling away here and there to reveal the brickwork beneath. The higher floors were accommodations, the windows barred with metal grills but the shutters open to catch any breeze. At ground level there were the shops, little stores situated cheek by jowl selling leather goods or prayer mats or silverware worked into intricate arabesque designs. But most vendors simply laid out their wares on the sidewalk, sitting with Oriental patience by richly scented bunches of fresh cilantro and sacks of cumin, jars of saffron, bowls of anise, baskets overflowing with almonds and dates. There were honey-sellers and goatherds and a purveyor of mint tea, his entire apparatus carried upon his back, but somehow not inhibiting the precise ritual of tea-making, something in which the Moroccans are second only to the Japanese.

As varied and fragrant as the goods were the people. Many of the market stalls were tended by women in huge straw hats with strange pompoms the size of baseballs hanging from them, their dresses drawn up between their legs to form makeshift pantaloons—farmers' wives presumably; women used to keeping their clothes clear of the mud. There were sharp-eyed Syrian merchants and dark-clad Shiite matrons, some of these latter so completely covered as to include a little veil across the one opening in their clothing: the slit for the eyes. Many men were dressed in djellabas, others wore smocks and loose trousers, some had little white skullcaps of crocheted material. Most commanding were the occasional Berbers, old men in long desert robes, turbaned, usually carrying a tall stick, their weather-beaten faces deeply tanned and set into that stoic expressionless long-looking gaze of men inured to endless space and endless hardship. They walked with slow dignity, never bent, and always alone—men not given to keeping company.

I came to a prosperous-looking rug store. The most expensive goods sold in the market were probably carpets and the majority of them would originate from outside of Morocco; they likely came from lands as distant as the Caucasus and the Caspian and the Indus. That meant two things. Firstly, the proprietor would probably be comfortably multilingual—an Arab would likely have to use English to negotiate with suppliers whose native language was Urdu or Farsi or Turkmen, and also many of his customers would be tourists. Secondly, he would be somewhat worldly, relatively wealthy, a considerable member of his community—in other words, someone with the wherewithal to do what I needed to get done.

I entered and began to quietly inspect the rugs.

Soon a man appeared from the back room wearing western clothing but also a fez. He descended upon me at about the same speed that the Barbary falcon would descend upon a dove. He was perhaps fifty years of age, beaming, hands extended, exuding the overly familiar bonhomie characteristic of salesmen the world over.

He greeted me in French, then when I replied in that same language he converted to English, apparently unable to tolerate my butchering of what for older Moroccans remains a native tongue.

"You seek a fine carpet, yes?"

"Just looking."

He let go of me and used his arms to gesture at his inventory.

"You will find no better selection in all of Morocco, sir. I invite you to take your time and inspect them. All are the best quality and very inexpensive."

A pause as his eyes followed mine.

"Ah, so you like this one," he said, moving to a three-by-six rug lying on top of a nearby pile. It had a rust-red field with a series of distinctive medallions. "You have a very good eye, sir." He stepped up to it and spent a moment inspecting the underside. "This carpet has 288 knots per square inch, a very fine quality. I really should not allow this beauty to leave me for less than 12,000 dirhams, but for you, sir, a discount, so let us say 10,000."

About $1,200. I joined him and briefly inspected the rug.

"I think perhaps you are mistaken," I said. "You appear to have double-counted the knots. This is a Bokhara, and therefore the warp is quite flat."

He adopted a look of the deepest concern, withdrew a set of spectacles, and with them placed upon his nose he bent down and made a great show of carefully inspecting the back of the carpet. Finally he stood up straight, removed the glasses, and regarded me with what would have passed for deep and sincere contrition, had he been able to keep the smile from his face.

"You are absolutely right, I find. How clumsy of me."

It was not believable, nor meant to be believed. And even had it been a 288-knot count, the rug itself was worth perhaps 6,000 dirhams. This was a game, a gentlemanly sport, something to be enjoyed as such, even relished. We passed on to the next round.

"Perhaps you would like an antique," he said, moving to a carpet hanging on the wall. "Like this one, a beautiful example from the 1920s. It has 360 knots per square inch: very fine, very fine."

I stepped over to it and lifted the bottom right-hand corner, once again inspecting the back. I did not bother estimating the knots this time; that particular card had already been played, and the trick was mine. But I quickly saw that the thread at the back was lighter than the thread on the front, which gave the game away: washing and painting is an old and venerable method of artificially aging rugs—washing ages the texture, and the painting reapplies the dye to the pattern. But it necessarily leaves the back lighter than the front, the reverse of the usual process in which the upper surface, being permanently exposed to light, fades first.

An easy win for me, or so I thought.

"This rug is lighter in the back than in the front," I said.

But instead of admitting defeat as I had expected him to, he merely shrugged his shoulders.

"Perhaps it was stored upside down," he coyly suggested, as if he still held a trump that I had yet to flush out.

So there was something else for me to find. I returned to inspection of the front. It took me a while, but eventually I located it. Carpets occasionally have the year of their manufacture woven into them, usually on the border, and among the intricate scrollwork on this rug I found one:

١٣٧٤

The rug had been manufactured in the year 1374, the date of course being from the Islamic calendar. Islamic dates can be difficult, because some countries, like Afghanistan, where I guessed this rug was from, use solar years while others, like Iraq, use the shorter lunar year—something that always confused us when we moved between theaters in the Sandbox. But all of them count the Hegira as the year one—that is, the date of Mohammad's flight from Mecca to Medina, 622 A.D. in the Gregorian calendar—and so, either way, in western terms this carpet had been made sometime in the second half of the Twentieth Century, decades later than the date he had suggested.

This time I said nothing, merely looking closely at the date, then at the merchant. He was beaming with pleasure, enjoying a game well played. He opened his arms in a gesture of defeat.

"So tell me, sir, which carpet is it that you desire?"

"The azure Persian in the corner," I said. "From Isfahan, I would guess."

"It is indeed," he replied, genuinely pleased.

I accompanied him to the corner where the rug lay, loosely rolled, a foot or so of it visible. He picked it up and with a practiced sweep flipped it open upon the floor, allowing full appreciation of its beauty. There were minor borders of vine scrollwork surrounding the main border, an intricate design highly geometrical but also somewhat architectural, suggesting caliphal arches perhaps. But it was the primary pattern that captivated the eye, a single central medallion exploding like a supernova upon a field of fabulously pure blue.

The merchant stood back, chin cupped in his left hand, elbow supported in his right. No smile now but instead the serious look of a connoisseur contemplating a masterpiece. "As you say, it is an Isfahan. Four hundred and eighty-eight. Not quite perfection, you understand, but in the human realm perfection is not for us to behold. Yet that color! Surely heaven is that color, do you not believe?"

I did not, but now was not the time to say so. He introduced himself as Aziz and I gave him my name in return. We shook hands, the way men do after a good hard game of tennis or racquetball.

"Let us go to the back room," he suggested. "We will sit upon this rug and drink tea."

I agreed. He rolled it back up and went to a doorway curtained with hanging strings of beads, which he held aside for me to pass through.

THE BACK ROOM HAD NO ARTIFICIAL LIGHTING, just what came in from outside through the small arched windows located high on the wall. The shafts of sunlight lit the dust in the air, and the gratings cast crisscross trapezoidal patterns across the floor. There was a desk on one side of the room, old and battered, a jumble of paperwork lying on top. A shelf with a few books, mostly in Arabic or French, but I noticed an English-Arabic dictionary. The wall above the desk bore an old-fashioned office clock—Patrice Cheval & Fils, Paris. The dial, once white, had yellowed with age and the hands were steady at 10:26; it got the time exactly right twice a day.

In the opposite wall was a small alcove with a low built-in bench, not very large, but cushioned and with a blanket and pillow as well— presumably the merchant took naps there when business was slow, although he would have to curl himself up to fit in the space. There was a sink and a shelf with the apparatus for making tea on the back wall. In the middle of the floor sat a low table on which stood a large hookah, filled with water but not alight. The pipe fabrics were frayed with age and the nickel tips had worn through to reveal the brass beneath: a hookah that had seen much use. Beyond the table were several wooden crates—the room served as both office and warehouse. I could smell the timber, or perhaps the odor carried by the timber: a combination of salt and cloves and old cordage, something probably acquired during the course of long ocean voyages in the holds of tramp steamers working the Arabian and North African routes.

The merchant laid out the rug next to the table with the hookah. We sat on it at either end, cross-legged and facing each other. He showed no inclination to use the hookah. Perhaps it was reserved for tourists, a little local flavoring to help open the wallet, something that he thought would be wasted on me.

The merchant barked out a quick command in Arabic. In response a third person tentatively emerged from behind the crates, where she had been hiding. A young girl, about ten, big-eyed and barefoot, skinny as a greyhound.

She looked at me with cautious curiosity until the merchant issued another quick command, at which she retired to the back of the room and began tearing a bunch of fresh mint to make tea.

"Your daughter?" I asked.

"No, the daughter of a distant cousin, now deceased. Zoraya is an orphan, and I have taken her in."

Now I knew who slept in that alcove.

We spent a few minutes in general discussion about carpets. He carefully plied me in an attempt to discover where I had learned about them, but I deflected his questions: the truth was that I knew very little about Oriental carpets, just remembering a few things from having researched the topic before purchasing one of my own, way back before shipping home after a tour of duty.

The girl soon brought a tray with the tea set upon it and placed it on the low table next to us. The tray and teapot were of highly polished silver, ornately etched. The glasses sat in little silver holders so that they could be picked up without burning the fingers.

The merchant dismissed the girl, who disappeared out the back door. He poured, using the technique of starting low then rapidly drawing the pot skyward, so that the stream of tea was several feet long. We drank ceremoniously. It was very fine, sweet without being cloying, bursting with fresh mint.

"And so to this rug, Mr. Dalton." He rubbed his hand across it with genuine appreciation. "Twenty thousand dirhams, I think you will agree, is not an unreasonable sum."

Twenty thousand dirhams is about 2,400 dollars—around what the rug would have cost in the United States, perhaps a little higher. It should be cheaper here, but Aziz was just raising the price for me to bargain him down the traditional twenty percent. The right price was sixteen thousand dirhams, about 1,900 dollars.

"Five thousand dollars," I said.

A long pause.

"I beg your pardon?"

"Five thousand," I repeated.

"U.S. dollars?"

"Yes."

He lifted his fez and briefly scratched the bald pate thus revealed, the existence of which was no doubt the reason he wore the hat in the first place. He settled his hands back into his lap.

"Excuse me, Mr. Dalton, but I believe you are making an arithmetical error."

"Five thousand dollars," I repeated. "Take it or leave it."

I pulled out the wad of bills with which I had come prepared and counted them out: fifty one-hundred-dollar notes. I placed the pile on the rug between us.

He looked at it longingly, then back up at me. Eventually his hand slowly moved toward the pile of notes. Just before it got there, I put a single finger on top.

"There would be one other thing," I said.

He could not suppress a sigh. He knew that it had been too good to be true.

"There is a man I am looking for," I explained. "An American. He came to Tangier two days ago. He is hiding here somewhere, probably in the Medina. I wish this man to be found. I also wish him to remain unaware of having been found."

Aziz said nothing. I pulled out a sheet of notepaper and slid it across the rug.

"This man."

Aziz looked at it without picking it up, as if it might be poisonous.

"Two men," he said.

"One man," I explained. "Two names."

I pulled out the photograph of Felix Zane and pushed that across, too.

"This is what he looks like. As I say, he is American, but he might be traveling as a Moroccan. He speaks French as well as English; perhaps other languages, too."

"Arabic?"

"I doubt it."

"Then he can be found," Aziz stated.

"Do you accept?"

His eyes continued to go from me to the money. Every time he looked at me he wanted to decline, but 5,000 dollars is a lot of money in Tangier.

"How long would I have?"

"Three days."

"I will do it," he said. "You must pay me half now, half later."

"You can have it all now." I released my finger.

He looked at me in happy astonishment, then scooped up the money. At first his face betrayed pleasure in having received full payment without the fulfillment of his obligation. I stared at him steadily, without expression, until he understood what I needed him to understand. His look slowly changed as it came to him: if I was paying in full now, it was because I did not need to rely on money as an incentive. I would rely on fear.

His head began to shake, the unconscious gesture of a man realizing that he has made a bad bargain.

I stood.

"When you have found this man, have the carpet delivered to me at the El Minzah. The next morning, have a guide waiting for me at sunrise at the Porte de la Kasbah."

He nodded, but I made him repeat the instructions, not just to check that he had the details straight, but also to ensure that the new nature of our relationship was clear to him. It was important that Aziz not make any errors of judgment, such as exploring the possibility of a counteroffer with Felix Zane. That was why I had chosen fear instead of money as the motivator.

We completed the transaction and I left the Medina.

The rug was delivered to the hotel the same evening.

XV

I KEPT WATCH ON THE PORTE DE LA KASBAH, waiting for my guide to arrive.

The Kasbah is a fortified area within the walled city, very old, originally built to protect the Dar el Makhzen: the former sultan's palace. It occupies the highest part of the old quarter. I was standing on the ramparts to the immediate west of the gate, up and out of sight of casual observers, a place from which I could safely inspect whoever showed up. On the other side of the ramparts and far below was the sea, this morning covered in a layer of vaporous fog that left the sky clear but obscured the view of Spain across the Strait, a mist that would soon burn off once the sun had fully risen above the Atlas Mountains. The first rays were already illuminating the octagonal minaret of the Kasbah mosque, the highest thing in the city.

The quiet of the coming day was suddenly broken by the amplified wail of a muezzin summoning the faithful to prayer. He was soon joined by those at the other mosques scattered across the bay, and in the still air their cries carried over the water. It was a surreal scene: mournful chants echoing across an empty city set upon the mist-shrouded sea.

Not quite empty, despite the early hour. My guide emerged through the Porte. I recognized her: Zoraya, the little girl who had served us tea.

I had not expected this. I sheathed the knife, a fine Berber dagger of the Koummya tribe, a weapon that I had bought yesterday before leaving the souk. It had a horn handle and the traditional gently curving blade of damascened steel, etched with scrolling flower-like arabesques, and double-edged to be effective when slashing in either direction. The dagger came with a silver scabbard which I wore not in the traditional way, lying at the left hip and slung on a long woolen baldric across the right shoulder, but instead tucked into the waist of my trousers and concealed by the shirt.

I came down off the ramparts, allowing Zoraya to see me. She approached without slackening her pace, strangely unhesitant for a child alone with a stranger.

"I am to take you," she said.

Without further ado she turned and proceeded back up the shallow steps to the Porte, then down through to the Medina. I followed, observing this fearless little girl before me whose bold stride led us along. She wore sandals now, but the dress was the same one that she was wearing yesterday. Perhaps it was her only clothing. Aziz obviously treated his orphan cousin as unpaid labor, a slave in all but name. He gave her sufficient food and clothing for subsistence, but no more, and no doubt locked her in the back room at night, leaving her there alone to perform the function of a guard dog.

I wondered how she had learned English. Perhaps with the linguistic facility of the very young she had picked it up from overhearing her keeper talking with his customers.

We walked in silence through the Kasbah. The paths were narrow and cobblestoned, often reverting to steps on the steep inclines as we descended deeper into the old city. The Medina is less than a square mile in area but contains over eight hundred streets, none of them straight and few bearing street signs. I realized what a very good place it was to hide out in: difficult enough to navigate by day, it would be impossible for a stranger to find his way by night. But my guide negotiated the shadowed and anonymous twists and turns with ease—I wondered if she had found a way to get out of the shop after Aziz had left for the day and was given to wandering the Medina of an evening, lonely and alone. It would help explain the fearlessness, for the Medina was not a safe place after dark.

We came to a flatter section and the path was wide enough for us to walk side by side. She looked up at me.

"What is *bling*?" she asked.

"Bling?"

"Yes."

I was not too sure myself.

"I believe that it has to do with jewelry."

"Jewelry?"

"Yes. Gold chains, I think. Lots of them, worn around the neck to show off."

She thought about this for a moment.

"Is that not vulgar?"

"Yes, I suppose it is."

Perhaps her late-night ramblings had included the surreptitious watching of MTV on someone's satellite dish. No doubt she had tried to look up the word in that English-Arabic dictionary I had seen by the desk, but without success. A curious child. She made no further comment, and we pressed on.

Eventually we emerged from the close shadows of the narrow alleyways into a small open space with views over the harbor. Long slanting sunlight streamed across it. The commanding position had been used in the past for the mounting of shore batteries; two cannons remained, rusted beyond repair. Zoraya went straight to the low fence at the perimeter and sat upon a post there with easy familiarity; she must have spent much time in this spot, perhaps gazing out at the ferries taking people across to Europe, to another continent and another way of life.

I stood by her. She looked at me with the earnest intensity peculiar to little girls.

"Is it true that Italian shoes are the most desirable?" she asked.

She was entirely serious. It took me a moment to compose a reply.

"Yes, I believe that is the general opinion. At least as far as women's shoes are concerned."

She withdrew a folded piece of paper from her pocket and offered it to me.

"Are these such shoes?"

It was an advertisement from a glossy fashion magazine, a full-page ad that had been carefully torn out. The photograph showed a leggy model emerging from a sports car, shot from low down, emphasizing the shoes that it advertised. The paper had been neatly folded to fit into the pocket of Zoraya's pinafore, and the wear and tear at the edges indicated that she had carried it about with her for a long time. The advertisement was obviously a highly valued possession.

"Yes," I said, "these are such shoes."

"How does one receive the training required to wear them?"

"Training?"

"You will observe the heel," she said. I dutifully observed the heel. "It is clearly impossible to walk in such a shoe, unless one is trained." She leaned forward and whispered confidentially, "I have tried."

"I understand that women simply wear the things until they get the hang of it," I explained. "Like learning to ride a bicycle."

She looked doubtful.

We continued to discuss shoes for a while—were sandals acceptable of an evening? was it a *faux pas* to wear stockings with open-toed shoes? must the color of the handbag match that of the footwear? and other such issues. I answered to the best of my ability, but I could tell that on the whole she was disappointed with my ignorance of women's fashions (and the training required to master them, for despite my assertion she obviously did not believe that they could be worn without prior instruction).

She looked again at the advertisement.

"Is Gucci considered to be a reputable cobbler?" she asked.

"Yes, I believe so. And I understand that it is pronounced GOO-chee." She had rhymed it with lucky.

Her eyes lit up. Here at last was something I knew, something useful: how to pronounce the names of Italian fashion houses.

"Are you certain?"

"I am."

"GOO-chee," she said quietly. She repeated it several times, getting a feel for this fine new word.

"Purse your lips on the first syllable," I advised, demonstrating how.

She puckered into a perfect O, saying the word over and over, savoring it now and smiling widely. A few minutes of contemplative silence, and then she jumped down from her perch on the post.

"When I grow up I think that I shall be beautiful," she declared. "I should not like to wear Mr. Gucci's shoes if I were ugly."

She carefully refolded the paper and put it away. We resumed the journey.

There were a few people around now: an early morning street sweeper, farmers coming in with carts of fresh produce, pious insomniacs returning from morning prayer. We went up through the Petit Socco—a square of cafes and flophouses that had been the center of social life back when Tangier was an international city, a town of licensed abandonment. Up a narrow lane, then a few swift turns later Zoraya came to a halt.

She pointed mutely to a fourth-floor side window, east facing and therefore shuttered against the morning light, but it was not grated.

"How many rooms?"

"I have not been inside. One room, I should think."

"Is he alone?"

"He lives alone." Her English usage was more precise than my own.

"How long has he been staying there?"

"Four days."

The adjoining building was three stories tall, ending just below where Zane's window began, and like all buildings in Tangier it was flat-roofed. The shutters I could easily kick in, so that if there was a way up to that adjoining roof I could practically walk into Zane's room. I stepped around the side and found a drainpipe that would work well enough. It seemed too easy to be true.

"You have done very well, Zoraya. This is for you."

I gave her a hundred-dirham note, which she accepted with polite thanks.

"Your cousin will expect that I will give you something for your trouble. When you return to the shop he might ask you for it. If so, you will give him the hundred-dirham note." I opened my wallet and took out all the U.S.-denominated cash it contained, several hundred dollars' worth, and then handed it over. "However, this money is not for your services. This money is for Italian shoes. Therefore, since it is not for your services, when your cousin asks you will not show him this money. You will keep it, hidden from thieves, and when you are older and your feet have stopped growing you can use it to buy a pair of Mr. Gucci's shoes."

This time she did not thank me, did not speak at all, just stared in silence at the wad of banknotes in her hand. What life had this child led, I wondered, to be struck dumb by such an offhand gesture? A child unused to any kindness; a child whose best friend was a piece of paper.

I convinced her to put the money away in her pocket: carrying any sum in the open in the Medina was foolish, but hundreds of dollars in broad daylight was begging for trouble.

"I have one more thing to ask of you."

She nodded, still speechless.

"If you can do so without getting into trouble, I would like you to keep watch here this evening. When the man who occupies that room returns for the night, I want you to scratch a cross on the wall and then leave."

I indicated a suitable spot by the corner, low enough for her to reach, and used a pebble to show how the scratch could be made on the whitewashed stucco. "Like that," I explained. "Place it next to mine, but wait until you are sure he is staying, until the lights have gone out."

She nodded, a little girl who picked things up quickly.

"Are you coming back?" she asked.

"Yes, I must visit this man. But I will be very late, and I would like to know if he is in before I go up."

She nodded again.

"Thank you, Zoraya. Now, off you go."

And off she went.

XVI

I CHECKED THE TIME. My watch, old and battered, had been mine since I had graduated from OCS. It had shared with me the hardships of countless operations during many years of service: not just explosions and firefights but swamps and sandstorms and snowdrifts and all the other hazards to which a marine is naturally subject. It had been immersed in mud, in water, in blood, and it had never once faltered. At the end of my career I had worn this watch at my court-martial, but like my honor and rank it had been removed from me at the conclusion. When they released me from Leavenworth six months later it had been the only familiar face there to greet me. It was the one thing in my life that was constant.

Two A.M. I looked up at the window above. The shutters were closed and the lights were off, but on the wall next to mine I had found no mark left by Zoraya. Perhaps she had grown tired of waiting for Zane to return; more likely she had not been able to leave the shop and keep watch in the first place.

A last equipment check, then I put on the gloves. The drainpipe was old but it had been made back in the days when things were built to last and was solidly attached to the wall. The neoprene gloves provided good grip and I was soon up on the roof of the building adjoining Zane's. I went across to the window and crouched by the shutters.

I listened for several minutes. There was no sound from inside.

I wore boots to kick my way in, but before doing so I decided to try the latch. I withdrew the dagger and inserted the blade into the bottom of the gap between the two shutters, then very gently raised it. It came to a stop halfway up. A little more pressure, then a sharp metallic pop as the latch came free.

I hoped Zane was not a light sleeper.

But my good luck was running out: the shutters still failed to open. By applying gentle pressure around the frame I could tell that in addition to the latch both sides had been bolted, top and bottom, to the frame—the latch was probably only meant for use during the day, sufficient to keep them from swinging but easy to open when the occupant wanted to look out or let in more air. For security at night it had been fitted with bolts.

I took a deep breath, kicked open the shutters, and dived into the room.

I went straight to the bed, intending to pin Zane with a knee to the chest and the knife to his throat before he was wide enough awake to get a weapon in hand. But whatever was in the bed, it was not Felix Zane.

No sound, no movement. I found the light switch and turned it on.

It took me a moment to figure out what I was looking at.

I walked over to the window and swung the remains of the shutters closed.

There was no need to check Zoraya; she was unquestionably dead. The sheets and pillow and floor beneath were all soaked in blood, very sticky and already turning that peculiar rust-black color that blood acquires as it dries. I was covered in blood, too, from having jumped onto the bed—who would have thought so small a body could contain so much.

She was secured by strips of bed sheet and gagged with one, too. But the gag had obviously not been enough: on the floor beneath the bed was the wet towel that Zane had used to further muffle her screams.

The little pinafore she had been wearing this morning was in the trash can under the table. Ripped and frayed: it had not been cut from her body but simply torn off. The magazine advertisement was still in the pocket, still neatly folded.

Torture, much torture. In the end Zane had drawn her: the body had been slit open from sternum to abdomen. He had removed the intestine and hung it from the light fixture—a tin shade and low wattage bulb on a cord dangling from the ceiling—so that the last thing Zoraya would have seen was the content of her viscera displayed above her. But it was her expression that was worst, lips pulled back and twisted, bloodied not from the beating but from her own teeth biting through them as she had died in the utmost extremity of pain.

Rapid footsteps on the cobblestones. I switched off the light and went to the window.

There were several people in the alleyway below. Uniformed, and I understood at once.

The excessive brutality was not for Zoraya, nor even for me; it was for the police down there. Zane had spotted Zoraya keeping watch on his place. He had lured her into his room and tortured her.

After Zoraya had revealed all she knew Zane had butchered her, making as much of a mess of it as possible. Then he had left the room and installed himself somewhere in the shadows outside, waiting for me to show up. When I arrived he made an anonymous call to the police, then walked away.

The setup with Zoraya had been to ensure that there would be no chance of a trial, probably no chance of me even surviving the night. Once they got me back to the police station I would never come out alive.

I hit the roof. I made my way not back toward the hotel but the other way, toward the harbor. I stuck to rooftops, always opting for the highest I could get up to, even if it was not in a direct line to the destination, because the more height I had the less likely it was that I would be cornered. Down in the alleyways of the Medina, deserted at this hour, they would soon have had me, but up here on the rooftops the narrowness of the streets worked to my advantage: I was able to cross them by taking running leaps.

Behind me I could hear the crashing as they entered the room, then louder as they emerged onto the roof. Flashlights and much shouting, but I doubted they could see me; I had acted with speed and was at least a hundred yards distant now.

I came to that same open area where less than twenty-four hours ago I had stood with Zoraya discussing Italian shoes. I came down off the rooftops and climbed over the embrasures housing the old canons, then clear of the Medina and into the harbor. I ran out along the breakwater. The only illumination came from the light at the end of it, signaling to ships out at sea.

To be an officer in Marine Corps Force Reconnaissance you must first undergo the same induction course that every force recon recruit endures—officer or enlisted—which is formally called the Reconnaissance Indoctrination Program, but which in the corps is universally referred to by its initials: R.I.P. An appropriate term, because this is the course that nearly kills you: eight weeks of intense physical hardship. If you survive it, as I barely did, then you get another ten weeks of pain at Amphibious Recon School—R.I.P. was just to get you into shape. Altogether, four months of hell.

The names have changed now and they say that the deliberate torture (politely termed *hazing*) has stopped. But the dropout rate for the combined courses still hovers at around 85%.

If you survive it all, then you have earned that precious MOS: 0321—you are officially a force recon marine, and no one can ever take that away from you (except a court-martial, which took it away from me). You then go on to the many specialist schools: jump school, combat diver, assault climber, demolitions, and the like. Most of these are for officer and enlisted, too; rank more or less goes by the board in force recon—the teams are small, and many operations are led by NCOs without any officer in the field. To an outsider, we would appear to be a band of unmilitary thugs with little respect for rank or protocol. But the usual spit and polish of the Marine Corps is not so much discarded as replaced by something that in its own way is much tougher: intense and unbending self-discipline. If there is no more parade-ground barking—special ops troops speak softly—it is because there is no longer any need for it.

Nevertheless there is some officer-only training, conducted back at Quantico, where you learn the logistics and staff work required to conduct operations of the type peculiar to special ops. Most of this is classroom time, a luxury vacation after the rigors of R.I.P.

When I arrived at Quantico, the opening lesson was conducted by the commandant himself. It was not a welcoming address. The commandant did not normally teach classes but he did this first one because he said that it was the one that counted most, the one that if you did not learn the lesson you would end up killing yourself and all the men under you.

He wrote the letter P on the whiteboard six times, in a column, with blanks after the Ps to indicate missing letters. Then he told us to figure out the lesson for ourselves. After much guessing we finally had it: *Prior Preparation & Planning Prevents Poor Performance.*

The Six Ps, he called it, and he told us never to forget.

I never did.

In blackside work, one of the things that you always plan—always—is an alternate extraction route. Why? Because if you rely on just a single way out then, as sure as the sun is coming up tomorrow, one day you will find that the primary extraction route is denied—mined, patrolled, occupied, destroyed or perhaps the map was simply wrong—and there will not be time to figure another way out.

I had known that when I kicked in those shutters tonight the chances of violence were pretty high: I would get to Zane, or Zane would get to his weapon first. Either way, I had no intention of explaining the circumstances to the Moroccan authorities. Miranda was already extracted: I had sent her and our luggage across to Spain on an afternoon ferry. All that was left to get out was me.

The primary extraction route was the same one I had taken on the way in—on foot, through the Medina—and then catching the first fast ferry out the next morning. But remembering the commandant's lesson all these years later, I had planned a secondary extraction route, should the violence get too messy to risk going through passport control.

I began stripping off my clothes.

Tangier is thirty-four thousand meters from Tarifa, Spain. That is about twenty miles. It sounds like a long way to swim but is not really so far. More than a thousand people have swum the English Channel, twenty-two miles across, and through water subject to the same tidal race that I would be battling in crossing the Strait of Gibraltar, but very much colder. Every year New York City hosts a swimming race around the island of Manhattan, more than twenty-eight miles, much longer than my twenty. And even a poet can swim between continents, as Byron demonstrated.

Besides, I would cheat.

From the balcony of my room at the El Minzah, the view over the harbor had included the yacht club, a modest facility in which through the binoculars I had identified a dive boat. This morning I had gone down and asked the crew where I could find a dive shop. It turned out to be an hour out of town, a long cab ride but the place was well equipped.

Now, hidden carefully among the huge boulders of the breakwater, I extracted my purchases. Firstly the wetsuit, a full-body wetsuit whose gloves I had already worn for the insertion into Felix Zane's room. Wetsuits are banned in any officially recognized long-distance swim events—they add buoyancy—but I would not be chasing any records tonight. I shifted into the wetsuit. Fins. Face mask—although I would not be diving the eight hours or so of salt water exposure I was expecting would irritate unprotected eyes. Waterproof pack in which I stowed my passport, wallet, and Zoraya's shoe advertisement.

The last item had also been the most expensive. The diving scooter was perhaps three feet long, the torpedo-shaped body housing a battery and a shrouded propeller in the back. They are designed for underwater use but are neutrally buoyant and so would work just as well with me on the surface and the device held just below. It lacked the endurance to take me all the way across the Strait, but any shortening of that long stretch of water would be welcome.

Shouts from behind. Someone must have seen me entering the breakwater, nominally a restricted area. I could hear footsteps running down the long concrete quay. So the extraction would be underwater after all, but free diving, without scuba gear. I went down the rocks and entered the water. I was fast but not fast enough: the sea above me was suddenly churned with gunfire, and even underwater I could hear the loud staccato discharge of automatic weapons.

I had already noticed that police in Morocco carry short-barreled machine pistols, presumably nines. The ones following me decided to give it everything they had, emptying their magazines into the sea. But I dived deep and would have had to be desperately unlucky to get hit.

I had been intending to run the scooter on the lowest setting, thus maximizing endurance. Now I set it to high. This propelled me at three knots, about a hundred yards a minute. I held my breath for as long as possible before surfacing briefly for air. The scooter pulled me swiftly but without a weight belt I had to use my legs as well, kicking to ensure that my body's buoyancy did not pull us prematurely to the surface.

No one shot at me when I came up for air, and I thought that I had probably made it clear. But a few minutes later I heard the deep rumble of marine engines and recalled that on the wharf next to the yacht club there had been several gray-painted vessels: patrol craft belonging to the Moroccan navy. Soon they approached and reduced speed. On the surface above I could see the play of searchlights on the water.

But the patrol boat was inshore of me and concentrating their search toward the coast—they were looking for what they believed to be an unassisted swimmer, not knowing that I had a diving scooter. After a dozen or so further stints underwater I was clear enough to remain on the surface and reduce the setting to the endurance mode. Eventually I could no longer even hear them: either they were too far away or had given up and returned to harbor.

After two hours the diving scooter's battery was expended. By now I was well out into the Strait and riding the big Atlantic swells that were rolling in, slowly rising aloft then abruptly dropping back down into the deep saltwater canyons separating them, an endless liquid roller coaster. At the crests I was able to check my navigation marks: ahead was the light at Tarifa, flashing three-in-ten, and astern the massive tower on the cape beyond Tangier—Phare du Cap Spartel—flashing four-in-twenty, visible for dozens of miles out to sea and marking the extreme northwestern tip of the African continent.

I took my first meal, liquid carbohydrate in a foil pack, purchased at the dive store.

There are two things that will kill you in a long-distance wet extraction: exhaustion and hypothermia. The wetsuit was good insulation against hypothermia, but without food it will get you eventually, even in relatively warm water. I had been taught the drill for surviving long saltwater immersion on four separate occasions: the combat diver course; the diving supervisor course; the survival, evasion, resistance, and escape course; and lastly while undergoing GOPLATS training (gas and oil platform assault)—if there is one thing the marines know well, it is how to drum stuff into you. Food is key: an initial meal after two hours, thence once every hour. In extremes you should monitor body heat—hypothermia begins when body temperature drops below 95°F, leading to unconsciousness at 86°F and cardiac arrest at 75°F—but I had no thermometer since there was nothing I could do about it so far from land.

I was entering the traffic lanes. You would think that in a twenty-mile-wide expanse of water the odds of a swimmer intersecting course with a ship would be remote, but somehow I seemed to keep attracting them. In the dark they could not see me, and I was far too small a target to be picked up on radar—twice I had to sprint to avoid getting run down and sucked into the screws. I watched them as they passed by, thousands of tons of thundering might, reverberating deeply. Oil tankers mostly, a statement in sea trade of the world's number-one problem.

Eventually the sky lightened and I had less need to worry about getting run down. By the time the sun had fully risen I was about halfway across, and it was slack water so I no longer had to swim at an angle to the target. Long-distance swimming can be surprisingly peaceful, a good way to think, and it gave me time to evaluate the situation.

It was obvious that I had made the classic error: I had underestimated my enemy. The charge to the credit card was not a mistake at all; it had been a well-planned feint. Zane must have realized that during the search of his apartment I would have found that American Express card and likely noticed the password as well. He had deliberately used it to make the transaction at Tarifa. If I was not monitoring the account, then no harm was done. But if I was, then he knew that it would lure me to Tangier, a place to which he was accustomed but somewhere that I would be sure to stand out. With neither contacts nor the language my search for him would necessarily be clumsy, giving a cautious man plenty of warning. There, in an Arab country without links to western law enforcement, he could deal with me in his own way. Like any savvy commander, he had chosen the battlefield with care. It was a good plan, and it had very nearly succeeded.

As I kept swimming I began developing a plan of my own, something to take my mind off the unending pain in my arms. By the time it was complete I was closer to Spain than Africa.

But then exhaustion hit. I had known it would come, that critical point where—notwithstanding all the high-carb food—the body begins to burn fat reserves. This was earlier than I had expected and for the first time I realized that physically I was no longer the same man who had survived R.I.P.

There was only one thing to do: fight through it. I switched to breaststroke for a while. It is slower but I wanted to use more leg and less arm for a break.

I never reverted to freestyle. I was struggling.

A fishing boat spotted me and came by to investigate. Algeciras registration: they were Spanish. The nets were hauled. No one spoke English but with a series of gestures I was laughingly offered a ride, which I gratefully accepted. Once onboard I was given coffee heavily laced with Pedro Ximénez—not something made specially for me; they all drank it. They were returning to the Mediterranean after a morning spent fishing the Atlantic. By pointing to the chart I was able to make the captain understand that he might choose to run inshore a little further than usual: there is a fine deserted stretch of coastline between Tarifa and Algeciras.

He got the message and laughingly agreed. When we were less than half a mile off he slowed the engines and gave me a nod. I shook hands all round, then dived back into the sea.

Twenty minutes later, I stepped ashore in Spain.

XVII

W E DROVE ALONG THE MIDDLE CORNICHE, hugging the twisting roadway hewn precariously into the steep hillside. The top was down and overhead the sky was a bright unsullied expanse. I could smell the thyme that grew wild on the slopes. Ahead rose the Alpes-Maritimes, a great spur of rugged mountain range whose peaks were still snowcapped, despite the season. Far below lay the Riviera and beyond was the Mediterranean itself, deep blue and ageless.

I took the turnoff to our destination—Monaco—and began the long descent to the coast. The car negotiated the endless progression of hairpin turns with little speed but much dignity, for it was a Bentley Azure, a car from the era before the brand had become the favorite of basketball players and hip-hop artists, from back when they were built big.

We rented the car in Nice from a firm specializing in luxury automobiles. Miranda had picked the Azure from the company's selection because, despite the massive avoirdupois, it was a two-door convertible, appropriate in both name and body style for cruising the Côte d'Azur. It had the weight, engine capacity, and maneuvering characteristics of an ocean liner—we wallowed through every hairpin—but the car had not been chosen for its handling. It had been chosen to make an impression.

The center of social life in Monaco is the place du Casino, a square onto which face two fine Beaux-Arts buildings: the casino itself, and the principality's finest hotel, the Hôtel de Paris. There is a sprinkling of sidewalk cafes surrounding the square from which people can sit and watch the passing parade. It is a human theater where the square is the stage, the cafes accommodate the audience, and the rich are the actors.

I pulled the Bentley up to the hotel's entrance.

A valet came to my side, the doorman to Miranda's. As she exited the vehicle several occupants of the hotel's terrace cafe, who until now had observed our arrival with the studied indifference with which the wealthy regard each other, put down their coffee cups and openly stared. Miranda was dressed in a very short skirt with very high heels: her debarkation from the Bentley garnered the complete attention of everyone with a view. Her silk shirt was unbuttoned to the solar plexus and she was obviously wearing nothing beneath it, but what Miranda lacked in clothing was made up for in jewelry: bracelets and necklaces and earrings all aglitter in the sunshine. She ignored the attention, aloof behind big sunglasses, striding long-legged around the car and up the front steps into the hotel.

"Are you checking in, sir?" the doorman asked.

"Yes. The luggage is in the trunk, and we'll need those shopping bags, too." The back seat was crowded with our purchases from this morning's expedition to Cannes and the high-end boutiques lining La Croisette. Most of the purchases were Miranda's, but I had endured an hour or so of fussing and fittings in the Brioni store—at least now I would finally have garments fit to match Dortmund's impeccable priest-cloth suits.

The doorman surveyed the pile with a practiced eye and then signaled to a bellhop for additional carts. I entered the hotel.

The lobby was a huge high-ceiling space, all marble and mirrors and gilt. A vast flower arrangement on a tall console dominated the central area, perfuming the air. There was a scattering of plush chairs and sofas, on one of which was Miranda, leaning back, legs crossed, and flicking through a fashion magazine with negligent disinterest.

The reception was at the rear, a small desk literally for receiving: the actual business was transacted elsewhere. I was escorted into an elegant private sitting room where the details of check-in were discreetly handled by one of the managers. This was conducted with the polite and efficient formality that most guests would be used to from dealings with their private bankers. When we were done the manager asked if there would be anything else that I required.

"A safe deposit box," I said. "A large one."

"Certainly."

He made a brief note on his pad.

"And I understand that the casino is closed to the public today."

"I regret so, sir. It is being prepared for a private function this evening."

"What sort of function?"

"A charity event hosted by Mr. Balthazar Kadri, the famous entrepreneur."

"Which charity?"

"Société du Dauphin Commun de la Méditerranée: an organization chaired by Mr. Kadri and dedicated to saving the

Mediterranean short-beaked common dolphin—an endangered species, I believe."

"Well, I am most concerned for the fate of the Mediterranean short-beaked common dolphin. I wonder if I might obtain tickets."

"I would be happy to arrange it. The affair is 25,000 euros a plate."

"Two tickets then. I will have my people deliver a cashier's check this afternoon."

"Very good, sir."

Another brief note on the pad, and our business was done.

EVENTUALLY MIRANDA AND I WERE ALONE IN OUR ROOM. It was a two-bedroom suite. Before I made the reservation Miranda had suggested what I was already thinking but for fear of misinterpretation had been reluctant to articulate: separate rooms might seem strange. I finished pouring and took our glasses out onto the balcony where she stood looking over Monte-Carlo and the sea beyond.

"So far so good, I think."

Miranda turned. Somehow between our arrival in the suite and my mixing the drinks that silk blouse was buttoned higher now. The material was still thin, however, and somewhat translucent under the bright Mediterranean sun.

"I tried to be haughty," she said. "I hope I didn't overdo it."

"Ah, so you were acting?"

She laughed and accepted the champagne. We said cheers and drank.

"Shopping exhausts me," she said. "Odd for a female; I must lack the gene. Shoes excepted, of course."

The remark made me think of Zoraya. After swimming to Spain I had told Miranda everything that had happened except for Zoraya, allowing her to instead believe that I had found Zane's room empty—Zane having fled—and the police on the way for the break-and-entry only. I was already stuck with the image of what I had found in that room; there was no need to burden someone else with it, too.

There was a table and chairs on the terrace. Miranda sat down.

"It's the fuss gene," I said.

"The fuss gene?"

"Yes, I think so. That thing that causes so many women to fuss; the preoccupation with trivialities, I mean."

"Trivialities such as shopping?"

"Exactly. Shoes excepted, of course."

"Of course."

We sat in silence for a while.

"I think I'll go to the pool this afternoon," Miranda said, "and work on my character. Are you going to come?"

"No, I've had enough swimming for a while. I'm going to use the laptop to find out what I can about the woes of the small-beaked common dolphin."

She finished her drink and stood. "I better go unpack."

"Save the smaller boxes," I told her. "I need something to put in the safe deposit box that might conceivably be thought of as containing jewelry."

BUT AFTER MIRANDA LEFT FOR THE POOL, instead of researching the small-beaked common dolphin I reviewed again all that we had found out about Balthazar Kadri, the man who according to the prosecutors back in New York had financed Felix Zane's recruiting operation. In force recon we had done endless KYE/KYF—know your enemy, know your friend—and the habit had stayed with me. Since Felix Zane was now out of the picture, Kadri was the only lead we had, and I did not want to blow it.

Kadri was a French citizen of Lebanese birth, fifty-eight years old. He was very rich, having made his fortune running import-export businesses operating between Europe and the Middle East: clothing, textiles, foodstuffs, tobacco, and if the various sins attributed to him were to be believed, weapons and women.

Certainly weapons: in the few interviews he had granted Kadri made no secret of his involvement as a youth in the Iran-Contra affair—being a then Lebanese citizen operating outside of the United States, he was not subject to the American sanctions that had existed at the time and so professed to have acted entirely within such laws as were applicable to him. But Iran-Contra was just a starting point: although never convicted of arms trafficking, nor indeed ever even charged, it was common knowledge that he continued to play an active role in the sale of French weaponry and nuclear technologies to places where such sales were illegal, or if not strictly illegal then at least transactions that the vendors would prefer remain unremarked. Since the French armaments and nuclear industries were in bed with, indeed usually owned by, the French government, then it was clear that Kadri was a protected citizen, a man with sufficient pull in high places to make him all but immune to legal intervention.

There was less on the women: just a newswire piece repeated in several sites that contained the same information I had already seen in the *New York Times* article: that Kadri had been mentioned in leaked grand jury testimony as being a principal in a ring of white-slave traders.

He was not a recluse, but there was little detail about his private life. He made the usual public philanthropic obeisances that the rich perform to pass the time or to protect themselves against accusations of avarice—perhaps the small-beaked common dolphin was one such case. He was unmarried, but in the photographs I found of him smiling for the cameras at various social and charitable functions there was usually a woman on his arm. All young and attractive, but rarely the same girl.

He maintained a residence in Beirut but his primary home was located in France, a luxurious villa high in the hills above Monaco, close by the Italian border. Perhaps the location had been chosen to allow an easy exit from France, should his enemies on the Quai d'Orsay ever come to power.

We had driven past it this morning but had gotten no closer than the front gate: a steel grill piercing the high brick wall that surrounded the property. All we had seen of the estate beyond the gate was the cobbled driveway disappearing into groves of olive and lemon trees.

But we had found another way to get to Kadri: he was hosting a *fête* at the casino for the organization that he chaired. This was an annual event, well attended by the well-heeled of Monaco, apparently not so much for their love of cetaceans as for the fact that Kadri knew how to throw a really good party. Thus Miranda and I had ended up in a suite at the Hôtel de Paris with a closet full of haute couture and a convertible Bentley in the parking lot.

The phone rang. I answered, and there was an interval of tense silence before the caller spoke, a period punctuated with the sharp inhalation of deep dissatisfaction.

"I have just had a most unpleasant telephone call from the administration department," Dortmund said, apparently feeling no need to identify himself.

"Is that so?"

"He said that you have already exceeded the limit of the credit card, Captain Dalton. Less than a week, and you have completely used up the entire credit line. First-class ticket from Belize to Dulles. *Two* first-class tickets to Morocco—I won't even ask who this female is that you are now hauling around with you, apparently at our expense. Suites at the Peninsula and again in Monte-Carlo. Huge cash advances. Thousands in clothing. And what on earth are you doing renting an automobile for five hundred dollars a day?"

"Did you have anyone else watching the apartment?"

"Whose apartment?"

"The person you sent me to find."

"You mean Hanna Moran? No, of course we're not watching her apartment: Hanna Moran fled long ago. And don't change the subject."

Dortmund must have been really annoyed about the credit card, to be using names over an unsecured line like that.

"Well someone was watching it," I said.

"How do you know?"

I explained about the car following me, and how I had shot out the tires.

"You shot out the tires? In Washington, D.C.?" Dortmund's voice had raised an octave. "Captain Dalton, are you quite sane? Please do not go around shooting things in the future: it will only draw attention to yourself and annoy other people. Especially me. Now, about this spending—"

"I'm glad that you brought it up. You have to clear the credit card bill immediately, Mr. Dortmund, and have the limit expanded. Double it. And I need a cashier's check for fifty thousand euros made out to the Société du Dauphin Commun de la Méditerranée, delivered to the hotel before the close of banking today." I spelled out the name of the payee so that there would be no clerical errors.

"Anything else?" he asked, in a tone of incredulity.

"Yes, I also need a line of credit established for me at the casino for this evening. A hundred thousand dollars ought to be enough."

"Don't be ridiculous."

"Do you want the notebook or not?"

"Of course."

"Then just get it done, Mr. Dortmund, or I walk."

A long silence. Dortmund did not know me well, but well enough to know that I was not bluffing.

"Very well, Captain Dalton. I will see to it." He spoke softly now, Dortmund at his most dangerous. "But you had better find Hanna Moran. And you had better recover that notebook before the Iranians get their grubby hands on it. If not, don't bother coming back."

"To you?"

"To America."

He hung up, a man who had said all he had to say.

Forty minutes later I got a call from the front desk letting me know that the cashier's check had been delivered and that my name was on the guest list at the casino this evening.

XVIII

I T TOOK ME A MOMENT TO REALIZE that the woman who had just entered the bar was Miranda Grey. I had not seen her since she had left for the pool, although I had heard her enter the suite while I was changing into the dinner suit. Eventually I had knocked and suggested through her closed door that we fortify ourselves with a drink downstairs before walking over to the casino.

Now, sitting at a table for two on the terrace, I saw that Miranda had not spent all of her time by the pool this afternoon. Her hair was up, not casually as at Arlington, but in a smooth formal style that could only have been achieved in a salon, an arrangement that emphasized her long neck and the gently undulating hills and valleys of the bones at its base.

I stood. Miranda saw me and came over to the table. She wore a long gown of champagne-colored cloth finished in a dull metallic luster, as if a fabric for use in space. There were vertical folds running its length, like the drapery of an ancient Greek statue, and as she walked the dress flowed voluptuously around her body. There were bands behind, leaving her back mostly bare, and the front was cut to suggest the array of subtle curvature beneath. It was a dress designed to emphasize that which it pretended to conceal.

There were slits in the sides, apparent only as she walked, and I could see that she was wearing sandals. I felt a brief stab of pleasure in having correctly guessed that sandals were just fine of an evening, until realizing the stupidity of such a thought now.

Miranda came to the table.

"Dortmund's money well spent, I think."

"It's a Valentino," she said. "Absurdly expensive; I hope your mysterious Mr. Dortmund doesn't object."

"Not at all. I spoke to him this afternoon and he is perfectly content."

We sat and I studied this new woman: Miranda, version 3.0. As at the Peninsula it was the abrupt change in hairstyle that had the most immediate impact, but the difference was more than just superficial. Previously she had been remote and disengaged, a cool distant presence in a room. Now she seemed newly invigorated, smiling broadly, full of life: a girl who was enjoying herself. Perhaps this was in part a reaction to climate. The smooth skin that was ghostly fair, almost translucent, had with just a few hours in the sun acquired a healthy golden glow: probably the apparent colorlessness had come from spending too many hours enclosed in airplane cockpits or air-conditioned terminals—artificial environments without sunshine or fresh air. Miranda was solar-powered.

The waiter came to the table.

"Two martinis," I said. "Very dry."

THE CASINO AT MONTE-CARLO WAS DESIGNED BY Charles Garnier, architect of the Paris Opera. It is a palatial Belle Époque building, Palladian in basic form, but Garnier had been unable to restrain himself, or perhaps his patrons, from garlanding the place with baroque niches and pediments and cupolas. Too ornate for the modern eye, but lit up with floodlights and silhouetted against the violet dusk as we walked toward it that evening the place looked like an emperor's pleasure dome.

The open square in front of it was crowded with onlookers held back behind barriers by Monegasque policemen wearing starched white uniforms and tall pith helmets. The staircase leading up to the entrance was lined with red carpet and manned by attendants whose primary function was to keep back the paparazzi, a mass of flashbulb-popping humanity jostling for position from which to photograph people as they arrived. Several limousines were discharging their guests at the foot of the steps. I had obviously underestimated the size of the event, although in retrospect anything that takes over the entire casino for an evening is likely to be a big show.

We reached the steps and began the climb. Halfway up Miranda stopped and turned smilingly to the paparazzi, striking a pose. The flash bulbs exploded. She changed pose; they went off again. This happy symbiosis of photographers and photographee continued for half a minute, Miranda obligingly turning first one way and then the other so that no one would miss out.

"*Qui est-elle?*" I heard one of them ask, but his colleague just shrugged his shoulders with a smile of happy indifference as to her identity and continued to snap away.

Miranda turned and again took my arm.

"I've always wanted to do that," she whispered as we continued the ascent.

We passed into an entrance hall styled as a magnificent domed atrium: marble floor, columned mezzanine, and high above were big windows through which the day's last purple light poured in.

There was a receiving line of a dozen or so men and women, probably officials of the Société du Dauphin Commun de la Méditerranée; some perhaps representing the Société des Bains de Mer, the organization that operates the casino. At the head of the line, in the prime position as both president of the charity and host of the event, was Balthazar Kadri. He was deeply tanned, a little older than in the few photos I had found on the internet, and somewhat shorter than I had expected. But he had a patrician air of natural authority, the demeanor of a man used to taking charge, and I could tell that all the others deferred to him.

We gave our names to a steward. No ticket or identification was required, but before announcing us the steward passed our names to the man sitting at a small secretaire upon which was a laptop. He typed rapidly on the keyboard then gave a nod of assent—we were on the guest list.

Despite this apparent lack of formal security I had already identified several men who, although dressed in evening wear like everyone else, were standing by themselves and inspecting the guests with deliberation: obviously security personnel. No earpieces, but they maintained visual contact with each other, communicating with gestures alone, nothing more than a nod of the head.

One of these nods was directed toward me. Two of them immediately closed in. Not threateningly, they just came and stood discreetly ten feet away on either side and slightly behind me, positioned so that they could see my hands. I understood this in part: they would have known many of the guests by sight—either residents of the principality or people famous enough to be recognizable anywhere—and for all the others they would have run security checks before the event. But I was someone unknown, someone who had shown up at the last minute, purchased tickets too late for a background check, and was therefore worth a little extra attention. Nevertheless, it seemed like overkill: how much trouble could I cause?

Then a cheer from outside. A long black Rolls-Royce pulled up at the curb. Two flags flew from the fenders: the national flag of Monaco on one side and the personal blazon of the ruling family on the other. Many more policemen now. The rear door was opened and a man emerged who from the eruption of flash bulbs and applause from the crowd I guessed must be the current prince.

Now I understood the security guys on either side of me. Not only was I an unknown; from their point of view I had timed my arrival to be just before that of the head of state.

I made sure that both my hands were clasped in front of me as the prince came up the stairs. He wore an ordinary dinner suit but underneath the jacket there was a broad sash across his chest on which was pinned a glorious-looking medal. A reluctant concession to protocol, no doubt, for the man looked uncomfortable with all the fuss, someone on his way to the dentist instead of a party, but he was putting on his best face and trying to be affable under all the attention. At the top of the stairs he briefly turned and waved to the crowd, then entered the atrium. He was announced with appropriate regality and made his way along the reception line. One of the women attempted a curtsey, which he curtly cut short. He seemed impatient with such ceremony, and I could see that he was annoyed that they had not been briefed properly.

My timing was bad not just for the security people; it was bad for me. The reception line was the ideal opportunity to meet Kadri, but after greeting the prince Kadri accompanied him down the line, performing introductions, and when the formalities were completed they walked off together, chatting amiably, and for the first time the prince looked relaxed. Obviously he and Kadri were well acquainted.

After they left, the remainder of the reception line melted away, and the steward did not announce us after all.

We took a stroll around the interior. In the reception and public rooms the floors were intricately inlaid with variegated marbles—travertine, porphyry, malachite, and the like—arranged in complex geometric roundels at the center then expanding like starbursts across the room. In the gaming areas there was carpet instead, suitable for the hushed composure with which the gambling was conducted in Monte-Carlo, a world away from the raucous hubbub of a Las Vegas casino. There were sculptures and bas-reliefs and elegant crystal chandeliers. Everywhere the walls were paneled and gilded in rich rococo profusion. One room had a series of engaging frescoes in which nymphs, naked apart from the cigarettes on which they cheekily smoked, gamboled upon a sylvan landscape. It was like having stumbled into some gloriously decorated maze full of little niches and hidden alcoves, a place in which around any corner something new and wondrous might suddenly appear.

One such alcove in the Salle Renaissance revealed a small bar. We sat and ordered oysters and champagne.

"What now?" Miranda asked.

"I want to meet Kadri," I admitted, "but I don't want to initiate it. In the receiving line it would have been perfect—just part of the protocol of the evening—but now if I went and sought him out it would seem strange. Yet it has to be done, one way or the other."

"And what will you say to him? 'Got any nice blonds for sale, Mr. Kadri?'"

"Something like that. Not in those words, of course."

Our food arrived: two enormous silver platters covered in ice, each bearing a dozen oysters which, according to the little sign on the counter, were from a once-polluted area that with the Society's help had been returned to a healthy marine habitat. Conversation was more or less put on hold as we consumed these, Miranda with her fork, me slurping them down directly from the half shell. They were small, plump, tart, and had that distant fresh saltiness, like a good manzanilla, that makes the oyster such a noble dish.

Miranda sat back after finishing the champagne, smiling with pleasure.

"Should we seek out Kadri now?"

"No. We'll wait an hour, and I'll see if I can attract his attention first."

"How?"

I emptied my glass and put it down on the counter.

"If Dortmund did what I asked him to do, I should now have a hundred-thousand-dollar line of credit at the casino."

THE ATTENDANT BEHIND THE BARS OF THE *CAISSE* confirmed that I did indeed have a hundred-thousand-dollar line of credit. I gave her my passport for identification and was in return given the gaming chips, which were denominated in euros. I had expected that this would amount to an impressive pile but there were only ten of them, eight denominated at ten thousand euros apiece, and two of a hundred euros each, it apparently being assumed that no gentleman would gamble in denominations of less than a hundred. The hundreds were conventional circular chips but the ten-thousands were squarish objects, hefty and tactile, made of what felt like a semiprecious stone—jade or jasper or the like—and embedded in the center with an intricately engraved medallion.

Thus armed, we entered the gaming rooms. A sign at the entrance to each salon reminded players that all proceeds from tonight's gambling would go to support the small-beaked common dolphin. There were many gaming rooms: Le Salon de L'Europe, occupied entirely by roulette tables in both forms of the game, English and European; La Salle des Amériques, with slot machines; Les Salles Touzet with craps and blackjack; La Salle Médecin, with chemin-de-fer and punto banco; and a number of *salons privés* hosting various games, usually with higher table limits. I found no sign of Kadri in any of the rooms.

We ended up in a high-stakes area called Le Club Anglais, where I took a seat at one of the blackjack tables, Miranda standing behind to watch and hopefully attract Kadri's attention should he happen into the room. I had intended to break the ten-thousands into something more manageable but the man sitting beside me, a gruff cigar-smoking Russian with a big square Slavic head, was gambling in chips of the same denomination. Not only had I underestimated the size of the guest list, I had also underestimated the size of the guests' wallets.

Not wishing to appear puny, I put out the first of my precious ten-thousand-euro pieces, and immediately lost. The Russian won, and as he pointedly looked at my busted hand his face assumed a broad smile of serene *schadenfreude*.

He continued to win; I continued to lose.

I made sure to do so without comment and with as much indifference as I could muster, but it must have been too much for Miranda to bear: when I was down to just two of the big chips left I could feel her slide from behind me and heard the rustle of her dress as she walked away.

I had already noticed that, despite his winning, my neighbor played blackjack badly. He pressed the deck needlessly, hitting on twelve with the dealer showing a five, and again on fourteen with the dealer showing a two. He doubled-down on ten despite the dealer showing an ace, but split fives against a dealer's seven instead of doubling down then as he should have. When dealt a soft eighteen he elected to take another card, always the wrong choice, but especially egregious with the dealer showing a six.

Inevitably, the odds caught up with him. When his fortunes changed, so did mine. I was dealt two blackjacks in a row and given royalty after doubling down on an eleven in the very next hand. Soon I had won back the eighty thousand euros I had lost and was up another fifty thousand or more.

The shoe came to the blank and the dealer began reshuffling. My neighbor took advantage of the pause to leave the table with a few gruff Russian phrases and no tip. I checked my watch: fifty minutes had passed; by the time the shoe was restacked the hour would be up. I gave the dealer one of the hundred euro chips and went in search of Miranda.

It took me a while to find her. She was way down the other end of the building, in a richly gilded room called La Salle Garnier: a small theater that is the home of the Monte-Carlo Opera, but which tonight was staging a different event: an auction.

The objects being auctioned were women. One of them was Miranda.

According to the sign at the entrance it was technically a kiss that was up for sale. The proceeds from the event, like those from the gambling, would go to support efforts to save the small-beaked common dolphin.

An audience of thirty or forty men occupied the orchestra seats, bidding on the merchandise. I took a seat several rows behind them. The mood was congenial but high-spirited, with genuine competition among the bidders. A number of the female guests had been persuaded to offer themselves for auction. They were sitting at the side, awaiting their turn. Miranda was second in line. There was a woman on the block now, standing center-stage upon a small platform with stewards on either side. She looked shy and self-conscious but from the good-natured enthusiasm of the bidding she might have been forgiven for believing herself to be a goddess. The auctioneer conducted the proceedings primarily in French but with English and Italian thrown in from time to time. When the gavel came down, the Société du Dauphin Commun de la Méditerranée was fourteen thousand euros richer. The winner came up to the side of the stage as the blushing prize was handed down. He escorted her away to the side then up a small staircase to one of the opera house's boxes: a plush velvet-lined little spot in which the winner could enjoy his purchased kiss in comfort and privacy.

The next woman was a tall brunette in a revealing dress: the bidding was suitably spirited, and when the gavel came down she had been sold for twenty-five thousand euros. The smiling winner came up to claim possession.

Miranda was next. The auctioneer introduced her; she smiled and dipped in a small curtsey toward the crowd. After mounting the platform she adopted a pose I recognized as one the paparazzi had particularly liked on the steps earlier this evening.

This was not the cool reserved Miranda I knew, or thought I knew.

Bidding began, starting at one thousand and going up in intervals of five hundred as before. But at two thousand, five hundred a loud voice came from the back of the room, crushing the previous bid.

"Ten thousand."

Even the auctioneer was shocked into silence. The audience turned.

A small round red glow, the tip of a cigar as someone drew on it, then Kadri emerged from the shadows, walking slowly down the aisle. He had been sitting back there all along, quietly watching, awaiting the one he wanted.

I was the first person to turn back toward the stage.

"Twenty thousand," I said, as matter-of-factly as I could.

"Thirty," said Kadri, continuing to stroll down toward the rest of us.

"Forty," I countered, not turning.

No response, and no one else dared bid.

In the silence I could hear the squeak of his patent-leather shoes as he approached. He came to a halt beside me. I continued to look ahead, ignoring him, and I could tell that he too had not taken his eyes from Miranda.

A long pause. I could smell the cigar smoke.

"How strange," he said at last, *sotte voce*, "that a man should be so eager to purchase that which he already possesses." He turned toward me at last. "Or perhaps I mistake the nature of your relationship, Mr. Dalton?"

I turned to face him.

"You forget who gets the money, Mr. Kadri. My love of the dolphin knows no bounds."

He smiled, a man who enjoys a little joust now and again. Kadri turned back toward the stage and pointed at the auctioneer with his cigar.

"Fifty thousand."

"One hundred," I said without pause.

Kadri laughed, the way an elephant might laugh at a charging rabbit.

"Two hundred," he said, in the easy manner of a man whose bank account is indefatigable.

The astonished auctioneer looked at me in long-eyed hope that the contest might continue, but I shook my head. He reluctantly called for last bids, and the gavel came down. The audience burst into applause but Kadri ignored them and they soon subsided into excited chatter, twisting between the two of us and the woman coming down from the stage who had been the common object of our desire.

Kadri turned to me.

"The dolphin is a stupid animal, Mr. Dalton."

"You surprise me."

"They allow themselves to be kept in captivity. They perform for their supper."

"A little prison time never hurt anyone."

"But even in the wild they exhibit what is an immensely foolish trait: they are not panmictic. As a man who loves these creatures, you are of course familiar with the term?"

"Of course," I said. "Panmictic animals mate freely or randomly. But as you correctly point out dolphins, in common with most of their fellow cetaceans, form pairs for life."

"Quite so," Kadri nodded, satisfied that I had passed the test. "As I am sure you know, much of the decline in the Mediterranean population is due to accidental mortality: that is, to dolphins drowning in the nets of fishermen. Since the animals are not panmictic, the surviving mates often fail to further reproduce."

"As in humankind."

"Man is certainly the stupidest of all creatures."

"Yet surely successful."

"That is only because we are also the most vicious."

Miranda joined us. Kadri introduced himself with a gracious deference that failed to disguise the hardness beneath.

"I fear that you have overpaid," she said, "and will be disappointed in the goods, Mr. Kadri."

"That would be impossible for any man with a pulse, Miss Grey. But if you would choose to entertain the whim of a man entranced, I ask you to consider a substitution: I invite you to lunch aboard my yacht tomorrow. A kiss would be beautiful but so very brief; long could I savor the memories of an afternoon spent in your company." He turned to me. "And I invite Mr. Dalton, also. We share a common interest in dolphins, I find, and I hope that tomorrow I might be able to show him some of them at close range."

This sounded suspiciously like an invitation to a drowning, but Miranda accepted with pleasure—as well she might: it was better than we could have hoped for.

"And Mr. Dalton?"

"I look forward to it, Mr. Kadri."

We shook hands.

"My yacht is the *Speed Graphic*," Kadri said. "She is berthed alongside in the harbor. Shall we say noon?"

"Certainly, but how will we recognize her?"

"Very easily, Mr. Dalton: she is the biggest."

XIX

T HE *SPEED GRAPHIC* WAS NOT ONLY the biggest yacht in the harbor, it was also the most distinctive. The other vessels were variations on the traditional theme: white-painted hull, superstructure above, bridge forward, funnel amidships.

The *Speed Graphic* was nothing like that. To begin with she had not one hull but two, like a catamaran. They were very long and quite narrow. The bows were sharply raked, not forward in the usual way but the reverse: they jutted out underwater, like an ancient trireme with a ram, and sloped steeply backward as they rose from the waterline.

Between them was perched a third hull, much bigger than the other two, very broad-beamed but suspended so that it was mostly clear of the water, a remarkable design. The forward third of this main hull was formed in a massive aerodynamic body, pointed at the tip, then slowly broadening as it came aft: a sleek shape as if designed for maximum performance inside a wind tunnel.

Where the curvature ended the bridge emerged as a crease in the superstructure: a broad series of windows running across the entire width, but very low, like the windshield of an armored car. At this point the third hull merged at the sides with the other two, forming a unified whole, a great swathe of ship completely uninterrupted with decks or boats or anything else. Behind the bridge was a mast with an imposing array of antennae and radar aerials and a single large dome. Much of the equipment was familiar to me from my time aboard warships, but it seemed like overkill on a private yacht, as if intoxicated with joy during her construction Kadri had opted to adorn her with every gadget in the catalog. Aft of the mast the high deck continued in a long broad sweep three-quarters of the way to the stern. This extension served two functions: a helicopter pad and also a permanent awning for the main deck below.

The ship's sides were too tall for me to see onto that main deck, but it was obviously very large, not just longer and wider than is usual aboard a yacht, but also much taller, almost atrium-like, with great flying buttresses along the side, supporting the helo deck high above. I had the sense that the main deck would be the center of shipboard life, partially enclosed to protect against the wind, but sufficiently open to allow sun and air to flood in.

The most startling feature was not her structure but her color. She was gray. Not battleship gray but something darker: graphite almost, a hard metallic color, deeply lustrous, not paint but a color embedded into the structural material itself, as if the whole yacht had been carved from some massive billet of yet to be discovered metal, one that when it was found would end up located way down at the bottom of the periodic table. It gave the vessel a sinister brooding air, a spaceship that had alit upon the surface of the sea and within which aliens were now quietly observing and planning, patiently awaiting their moment to pounce.

I walked over to the edge of the wharf and ran my hand along the side. Miranda joined me, a long-legged presence in a Cavalli print dress, tied at the front with leather laces that were just sufficient to hold the garment closed.

"Carbon fiber," I said. "This thing has more in common with a stealth fighter than a motor yacht."

I stood back. On careful inspection I could make out windows. Not portholes but regular windows, very large, but which were fitted seamlessly into the side and were coated in a film that had been carefully matched to the carbon fiber, making the vessel's structure appear to be a smooth uninterrupted continuum.

There was one part of the vessel which was not carbon fiber. The first fifteen or twenty feet of the main hull, from the pointed tip back to where the curvature began to broaden and flatten, was composed entirely of glass. Not a frame with glass paneling, but one enormous and singly-made piece of crystal-clear glass, perfectly shaped, fitting snugly like a cap upon the hull. It was something akin to the big glass nose of a World War II bomber, designed to give the aircrew an unobstructed view of the approaching target. Perhaps the aliens within intended it for a similar purpose.

Some things were missing. No funnel, for a start, nor any type of exhaust venting for the main propulsion that I could see. No visible anchor—I later discovered that the anchors were brought up completely within the hull to maintain her smooth lines. There were no cranes or davits for heavy lifting—most vessels have at least something to help with getting bulk stores aboard. Nor were there any boats that I could see.

I looked aloft. Ships fly the flag of their country of registration from the stern. As an act of courtesy they may additionally fly the flag of the country they are visiting from the yardarm on the mainmast, if having completed customs and quarantine, or the plain-yellow flag Quebec if still awaiting free practique. Most vessels in the harbor displaying anything at all from their yardarms were simply flying the French tricolor—clearing French customs was sufficient for Monaco since there is no border control between the two—but with vexillological exactitude the *Speed Graphic* flew from her starboard shrouds the red and white national flag of Monaco.

I looked aft to see where she was registered. The flag there was much larger, white with red horizontal bands on top and bottom and a tree in the middle, a flag that was familiar but which I could not immediately place.

We walked down to the stern. The transom was a single vast flat surface, apparently hinged. The name *Speed Graphic* was painted across it. The port of registration was below: Beirut. So the tree had been a cedar, and the flag was one all too familiar to the Marine Corps: the flag of Lebanon.

The landing pad was occupied. The *Speed Graphic* was not the only yacht in the harbor with its own helicopter, but those few on the other vessels were small utility aircraft, basically a motor and rotor atop a perspex bubble, a latticework boom to support the tail, fixed skids instead of landing gear, and with room for one or two passengers only. The *Speed Graphic*'s helicopter was nothing like them—it was a big black bird with twin turbines and retractable landing gear, capable of carrying a squad if it had to. The tail assembly was unusual, with the tail rotor shrouded within the fuselage. Not American; it was a design I was unfamiliar with.

There was a gangway aft, connecting the ship to shore. We caught an occasional glimpse of a crewman in uniform on duty at the top.

"Shall we?"

"Lead on."

We began to make our way on board.

OUR PRESENCE ON THE WHARF MUST have been noted, for by the time we made it to the top of the gangway Kadri was already approaching. He was wearing slacks and deck shoes, a short-sleeved shirt, and a broad smile of welcome. The crewman saluted as we stepped aboard. Kadri held out his arm.

"Welcome aboard, Captain Dalton."

We shook hands. I could tell by his expression—a penetrating gaze softened by a wry smile—that the salutation had not been accidental. I had not told him that I was an ex-marine, let alone my former rank. Slipping in the *Captain* had been deliberate: his way of making it clear that he had already checked up on me. I was not to take it personally, his smile seemed to say: a man in his position was naturally obliged to be cautious. I wondered how much he had discovered about the circumstances of my discharge.

He let go of my hand and turned to Miranda.

"*Madame*, delighted." He took Miranda's hand and brought it to his lips while making a polite little bow, superficially a gesture of formal courtesy, but performed with a slight pause as he looked at her, an underlying sexual suggestion.

He let go of her and checked his watch, a platinum chronograph with nautical pennants engraved upon the bezel—a sailor's watch, if the sailor happens to be a millionaire.

"I'm pleased to say that we still have time before lunch. May I give you the tour?"

"I was hoping you would," I admitted. "A remarkable vessel."

"She is of an interesting construction, is she not? The hull form is called wave-piercing. Have you come across it before?"

"I have not."

"It is a recent innovation in marine architecture, intended for sustained high speed in the open ocean. As I am sure you know there are many high-speed designs—hydrofoils and hovercraft and the like—but they all suffer from a common drawback: when the sea becomes choppy they can no longer perform at speed. This makes them unreliable for open ocean work; they depend too much on fine weather and fair seas. But in choppy conditions these wave-piercing hulls literally do pierce the waves, breaking them up so to speak, so that by the time the main hull drives into the wave it has been changed from solid water—what they call green water—into a turbulent foaming mass, or even just spray. This makes it much easier to penetrate, so that instead of being tossed and slowed by the wave, the hull simply plows right through."

"It must take considerable power."

"It does indeed, and I propose to show you her propulsion. Shall we begin with the engines?"

"Yes, certainly."

Kadri took us along a passageway and then through a clipped aluminum door to a steep metal stairway leading below. We rattled down and down again, descending deep into the starboard-side hull. Eventually we went through another watertight door and entered what was an engineering compartment. We stood on a narrow metal gantry overlooking the long space into which had been squeezed a large gas turbine, a marine version of a jet engine. Unlike aircraft, on which the engines are hidden behind fairings, here the thing was out in the open: an extended series of cylinders, tapering or broadening either side of the combustion chamber, and surrounded by a maze of fine precision plumbing. There were auxiliary units: pumps and probes and control boxes, plus masses of electrical harness.

"Engine Number One," Kadri said. "A Pratt & Whitney MFT8 gas turbine."

"Twenty thousand pounds of static thrust," Miranda said, looking at the engine with nodding familiarity. "That must equate to..." She paused, making a mental estimation. "...something like thirty thousand shaft horsepower in a marine version?"

Kadri looked at her in amazement.

"Madam, I thought that I had reached an age at which it was no longer possible for a woman to astonish me. How happy I am to be proved wrong."

Miranda shrugged her shoulders. "Same as on a Boeing 737," she said. "Until four weeks ago I was a first officer flying Fat Alberts, and so I am well acquainted with these engines, Mr. Kadri. In aviation we call them JT8s."

"I had no idea. You are a woman of accomplishments, Miss Grey."

Obviously the security check had been restricted to me alone.

Kadri pointed aft. "You will see that whereas in your Fat Albert the thrust is directed into the atmosphere, here it is used to turn a shaft. But this shaft does not lead to a propeller in the usual way. Instead it powers a second turbine, a water turbine, so that the actual propulsion for the *Speed Graphic* is by water jets from aft, much like a water scooter, although on a much grander scale. And not only do we have no propellers, we also have no rudder: the jets themselves are directable. This is a very much more robust arrangement."

"Where does the exhaust go?" I asked.

"Exhaust?"

"I saw no funnel outside. No exhaust vents at all."

"How very observant you are, Captain Dalton. No, there is no funnel. In fact all the exhaust gases are vented underwater."

"Underwater?"

"Yes. In that way there is never any risk of me or my guests having to smell it."

Underwater exhaust venting is usually employed to reduce a vessel's heat signature, to make it more stealthy. I had never heard of it being used commercially on so large a vessel.

"I am very impressed, Mr. Kadri."

"I hope that I may impress you some more. Shall we continue?"

We went up to another internal deck, this one running the entire width of the vessel and therefore within the main hull. It was a vehicle deck. Now I understood the reason that the transom was hinged: it performed the function of a ramp. I also understood the absence of cranes now: there was no need to lift goods on board; they could simply be driven in on a truck.

There were several vehicles. To the side were half a dozen motor scooters, little Vespas with baskets fitted in front, presumably the preferred mode of transport for guests and crew in places like Capri and St. Tropez. There were two four-wheel drives. One was a Jeep in which the back seats had been taken out and replaced with a cargo bed—obviously the boat's workhorse. The other was a Hummer, gun metal gray to match the ship, windows blacked out, probably armored and fitted with bulletproof glass: this would be the vehicle Kadri used during his visits to the Middle East.

There was another vehicle, very long, but it was concealed under a cover.

Kadri noticed me looking at it.

"Shall I show you?"

He pulled aside the cover to reveal a huge hunk of metal, a car from Detroit's chrome age, massive and finned.

"A 1959 Cadillac Biarritz," he announced.

It was a two-door convertible. Over half a century old, but the vehicle was in pristine condition. The chrome was untarnished and the black paint gleamed. The tires were whitewalls and looked brand new, but I could see from the cross-ply pattern that they must have predated the age of radials. The interior was in similar condition, the dashboard gleamed, and the white leather seats were unmarked. Even the carpet looked untrodden upon. I checked the odometer.

"Only eight hundred miles. Is that possible?"

"Genuine, I assure you. This car originally belonged to the Shah of Iran. It was purchased for parades—a convertible so that the top could be lowered and he could sit up on the deck lid, visible to his people and basking in their admiration. It went with him during his exile. By then he had no need of it, there being no admiration in which to bask, and so the car was never again driven." He shook his head. "Power not only corrupts, it also deceives, does it not, Captain Dalton?"

"It certainly deceived him."

"Just so." He replaced the cover. "I purchased it at an auction last year. Not so much to use, you understand, but to serve as a reminder to myself—I am humble by origin, and I intend to never let paid obeisance be mistaken for genuine admiration."

We left the vehicle deck.

The next stop was the bridge, arrived at not by a ladderway but an elevator. It looked fit for a spaceship, full of equipment, and as clean and quiet as the control room of a nuclear reactor. In the warships I had been aboard pretty much everyone except the captain stood, but here there were seats for all the bridge staff: huge plush armchairs mounted high on poles so that they had a good view through the narrow windows, and with circular rails underneath so that there was somewhere to rest the feet. There were communications panels embedded into the armrests of each seat. The captain's and helmsman's chairs had something extra: at the end of each armrest projected a control arm, like the stick of a fighter jet, and shaped to be held in the hand. Kadri showed them to me.

"These work in two ways," he explained. "In engine-control mode they operate as throttles, the left hand for the port engine, the right hand for the starboard. Pull back for astern propulsion, push forward for ahead propulsion, as you would expect. This makes the *Speed Graphic* extremely maneuverable: by setting one throttle forward and the other astern, she can be completely turned around in her own length. This is what we normally use in harbor or close quarters. In the other mode—helm-control mode—their functions change: the right-hand stick becomes the rudder, and the left-hand stick becomes the throttle for both engines: forward for more speed, back for less. This is for use in open seas, although in cruising we are normally on autopilot."

My attention was caught by a black control box on the bulkhead. "IFF?"

"We operate a helicopter, Captain Dalton. We therefore carry a number of air navigation aides."

But IFF—Information Friend or Foe—is something more than just a navigational aid. Aircraft have transponders which, when hit by an air search radar, emit a specific programmed response telling the interrogating radar their identity and sometimes other data like course, speed and altitude. To use it you need to have an air search radar, something rare in non-military vessels, whether or not they operate helicopters. Air search radars are much bigger than those little surface-navigation radars that all ships carry. Now I knew what was under that large dome on the mast.

"Perhaps we should see the rest of the yacht," Kadri said. I had the impression that he was not pleased with my having identified the IFF.

We took the elevator back down, this time stopping at the level labeled Main Deck.

The interior of a ship is normally composed of many small compartments opening into a long central passageway that runs the length of the vessel. They are by necessity cramped, sometimes with a porthole but often having no natural light at all, and with the fittings built-in to maximize the limited space. The main deck of the *Speed Graphic* was the complete opposite of this arrangement. The compartment onto which the elevator doors opened was one single vast space stretching from side to side, much wider than a normal vessel because of the *Speed Graphic*'s unique construction, which gave her an exceedingly broad beam. No mere portholes here, but great plate-glass windows through which light flooded in, giving the space an open airy feeling, something rare inside a ship.

"The main salon," Kadri announced. He led us through it.

The room served several functions. In front, where we were, there was a library on the starboard side. The forward bulkhead was fitted with shelves stacked with books and magazines. There was a writing desk with racks holding notepaper and envelopes bearing the ship's crest, and a pair of comfortable armchairs for sitting back and reading. On the port side the forward bulkhead was fitted with a large flat screen, perhaps twelve feet wide, and facing it were two broad sofas placed to watch whatever was playing. Various cabinets held expensive-looking audiovisual equipment. Aft of these was a formal dining table stretching athwartships, polished to a high shine and large enough to accommodate a banquet. There was a big vase in the middle, a Grecian urn full of fresh flowers. The compartment had several such arrangements, rushes and lilies on a console, roses by the secretaire, a spray of lavender further aft—flowers were used to provide separation between the various areas without interrupting the sight lines. Further aft was a broad sitting area, low leather sofas and chairs surrounding a travertine coffee table, all in modern Italian fashion. On the other side was a bar in the same style, an ellipsoid in which the part facing forward was more formal, with a carpeted deck and stools upholstered in leather matching the chairs, but more casual in the part facing aft, with wooden stools and decking.

In the center, between the bar on one side and the sitting area on the other, was a spiral staircase leading up.

"To my private quarters," Kadri explained.

The rear bulkhead was composed of double doors in the middle, currently latched open, and on either side of them plate-glass panels stretching across the remainder of the ship, giving an uninterrupted view over the deck beyond. Kadri went to a control panel and with a showman's flourish pulled a small lever. The glass panels began sliding open, automatically folding behind one another, until they stood stacked on either side, completely opening up the rear of the compartment.

"My aim was to create a unified space," Kadri explained. "I wanted there to be no abrupt difference between inside and outside, but instead a transition which begins with the change in decking, then continues beyond the interior into the shaded area, and which is complete when the overhead deck ends, leaving the aftermost deck fully exposed. This is how one should live in the Mediterranean, I think, always close to sea and sun."

We stepped outside. The shaded part of the deck, under the overhang of the helicopter deck above, contained a table and chairs for dining on one side and lounging chairs on the other. Two stewards were putting finishing touches on the table.

It was set for four.

I looked up. The level above, Kadri's living quarters, ended in glass panels coated in that same carbon fiber-like film that prevented anyone from looking in, but from inside of which he would no doubt have a broad view over the main deck and the sea beyond.

The immense flying buttresses reaching all the way up to the helicopter deck served as windbreaks, but these ended before the overhang, so that there was further space where you could have both shade and breeze if you chose, then a final fifty feet or so completely open. Here was the pool, quite large, and more deckchairs.

We walked all the way aft.

"She is most impressive Mr. Kadri. I've never seen anything like her."

"In fact I suspect that you have, in a way. You have no doubt served on those landing ships in which the rear is opened and somewhat flooded, allowing amphibious craft to enter and leave?"

I nodded. Amphibious Transport Dock is the technical term. Late in my career one of them—USS *Shreveport*, LPD-12—had been my temporary home for an extended period during Gulf Two.

"The *Speed Graphic* has the same capability: she can be ballasted with sea water to sink several feet by the stern, which causes the area below the vehicle deck to flood. That's where we keep all of our small craft: water scooters and so on." Now I understood why I had seen no boats. Kadri continued. "There is also an extension that can be deployed out twenty-five feet from the stern, at water level, but unfortunately I cannot show you this while we are alongside. It forms a temporary dock, allowing direct access to the sea for my guests to enjoy water sports and so on."

"Do you have any guests now, Mr. Kadri?" Miranda asked. She had noted those four places at the table, too.

"Yes, Miss Grey, a single guest whom you will soon meet. Now, a drink before lunch?"

Kadri signaled to one of the stewards, who came and took our orders: Camparis all round. We moved back to the main salon.

"How did you come to call her *Speed Graphic*?" I asked.

"It is the name of a famous camera," Kadri replied. "Shall I show you?"

He went to a console up by the library and returned with a large square camera on the side of which was mounted an old-fashioned flash with a big metal reflector, a unit of the type whose bulb has to be replaced after each photograph. Kadri passed it to me. The camera was surprisingly heavy, five pounds or so.

"A Speed Graphic," he announced. "From the 1920s through the 1960s, this was the standard press camera." It looked like the sort of thing that Jimmy Olsen might have carried when working with Clark Kent. "Many of the images that are now part of the collective public consciousness were shot with Speed Graphics: the crash of the Hindenburg, raising the flag on Iwo Jima, Marilyn Monroe's dress billowing above a New York subway grating. During one stretch, every Pulitzer prizewinning photograph for fifteen straight years was shot with a Speed Graphic. They were manufactured by the Graflex Corporation of Rochester, New York, from 1912 until 1973:

a remarkably long production run for a modern piece of technical apparatus, an achievement unlikely ever to be matched. At the time of its introduction it was highly advanced, but also very robust, hence its use by newspaper reporters. It had two shutters; the focal plane shutter was capable of exposures down to one one-thousandth of a second, hence the word *speed* in Speed Graphic. I like to think of my ship in the same way: a vessel that is technologically advanced, and certainly very fast, but also robust: something that works reliably under difficult conditions. Heavy seas in particular, as the wave-piercing hull form is designed to do."

He showed me some of the camera's features: a bellows which could be stretched out a foot or so in length, accommodating a great variety of lens sizes; three separate rangefinders—optical, wire frame, and ground glass—whose flexibility and redundancy helped make the model a favorite; the "graflok" back which had been introduced on the Speed Graphic and that he assured me remained the standard for large-format cameras.

I was looking through it, focusing on the nearby spiral staircase as he coaxed me in the use of a rangefinder, when two shapely calves suddenly came into view.

I put the camera aside.

The guest, I assumed, slowly descending the staircase, making her entrance. I realized that Kadri had planned it like this, seating us here deliberately, the best place from which to view her arrival.

She emerged from the bottom up: platform espadrilles tied at the ankle, long legs and short skirt, a loose cotton blouse revealing a tank top underneath. Her straight blond hair framed a face that, as with many women, looked better in the flesh than it did in photographs.

It was Hanna Moran.

XX

I STOOD AND TRIED NOT TO SHOW any sign of having recognized Hanna Moran. She came to the table. Kadri introduced her and we shook hands.

Hanna and Miranda regarded each other with a cool half-smiling appraisal. A steward arrived with a silver tray bearing a single long-stemmed flute, which Hanna wordlessly took. The champagne had arrived without having been asked for, confirming what her descent from the spiral staircase had already suggested: Moran was more than just a casual lunch guest.

We resumed our seats. Hanna sat back and crossed her legs.

"Has Balthazar given you the tour?" she asked.

"Yes, he has. A remarkable vessel."

"Are you familiar with the sea, Captain Dalton? I presume that with such a title you must be."

"I was in the marines, Miss Moran. A captain is a much lower rank in the marines than it is in the navy, barely worth saluting; a naval captain is the equivalent of our full colonel. But I am familiar with ships, marines by nature spending so much of their time at sea. However, none of them was like the *Speed Graphic*, and we were almost never served cocktails."

She laughed and turned her attention to Miranda.

"Are you familiar with the sea too, Miss Grey?"

"Miranda, please. And no, I've never been to sea in my life."

"Then today will be a first for you."

"Today?"

"Yes, certainly; we're putting to sea soon. Didn't Balthazar tell you?"

Miranda and I turned inquiringly to Kadri, who seemed surprised by our reaction.

"But, of course: we will soon be casting off," he said. "Otherwise, how am I to show you those dolphins, Captain Dalton?"

I was saved from the need to reply by the steward announcing that lunch was served. We went outside to the table. As we took our seats the ship's engines rumbled into life. Soon the lines were let go and the *Speed Graphic* put to sea.

It was no millionaire's feast that day but instead simple Mediterranean peasant fare; a meal that could not have been improved upon. We started with seafood antipasto: little slices of smoked white fish, big caper buds in brine, Spanish *boquerones* on roasted red peppers, octopus in oil and vinegar with finely chopped garlic and parsley, mussels and periwinkles, a salad of artichokes and watercress, and to follow little grilled fish served whole, three to a plate. The bread was a single round loaf from which we all tore chunks, and there were shallow side bowls filled with olive oil— green and grass-pungent—in which to dip it.

For wine we had a crisp Ravello white poured into the pitcher straight from the demijohn.

"I had hoped to serve some of your own wine at today's lunch, Captain Dalton. Unfortunately, my steward was unable to locate any when he went ashore this morning. You have vineyards, I believe?"

"Yes, I do," I admitted. I was fortunate that my profession revealed nothing about my income, for winemakers run the full gamut of wealth, from the Rothschilds at one end to me at the other. "I'll send you a case, if you like."

"I would be most pleased."

We tucked into the food without further conversation.

"I once used to hate seafood," Kadri said after a while, pushing back a plate now empty apart from the skeletons. "I swore that if I was ever in a position to do so I would eat nothing but meat."

"What caused you to dislike fish?" Miranda asked.

"Poverty. As a child I was very poor. My father was a fisherman, you see, and so I naturally associated seafood with want. We lived at Al Mina then, a small port near the town of Tripoli in the north of Lebanon. My father owned a wooden fishing boat, completely open to the elements. He called it a *caïque*, but even that modest term was too grand; it was just a simple felucca, although it had a long bowsprit and was quite high-prowed, as is common in those parts. Single mast with a lateen-rigged sail on it. My father painted the hull turquoise green, so as not to scare the fish, he said. I was often required to accompany him to help haul in the nets. We got underway before dawn and made the fishing areas by sunrise. We would cast the nets for several hours and then return. The boat was fitted with an old engine but fuel was expensive, so whenever wind and tide were favorable my father would shut it down and hoist the sail instead. This slowed us a good deal and it took hours to get back in, waiting for the land to sufficiently heat up so that the sea breeze would begin blowing onshore, bringing us back to harbor. This frustrated me greatly because by then the other fishing boats would already be in, having returned under engine, and they had sold their catch. Thus there were fewer potential purchasers remaining for whatever we had, which naturally lowered the price. I tried explaining this to my father, showing him how saving the fuel was a false economy, but he never listened, or perhaps he listened but did not understand, and so we would continue to creep in every day, watching the other boats beat us to the buyers."

I understood a little better now why Kadri had spared no expense when building his own vessel, especially with the engines.

"I was expected to become a fisherman in turn; to inherit the boat. It was not to be."

"What happened?"

"The civil war. A disaster for Lebanon, but an opportunity for a young man with ambitions. The country broke up into factions. I left home and went to Beirut. 'The Paris of the Middle East' it used to be called, but by the time I got there it had largely been reduced to rubble. Druze versus Maronite versus Sunni versus Shi'ite versus Palestinian, all hating one another and their internecine rivals even more: the Phalangists despised the Marada, the Alawites despised Hezbollah—all this notwithstanding that an objective outsider would have been hard-pressed to distinguish any difference between them. Beirut became a wasteland with a highly permeable 'Green Line' separating, or rather failing to separate, the warring factions."

"What did you do there?"

"Made my way as best I could; bought goods on credit and sold to those who could pay; kept my head down. I was just a simple fisherman's son from the north: no one had any interest in me and I was able to cross the lines quite freely. I made a little money but hardly enough to compensate for the risk. Then in 1982 came the big break: the American invasion. Until then it had been just neighbor against neighbor, but when the marines arrived suddenly everyone had someone new to shoot at: a foreigner, an invader. Demand for the sort of goods that I could provide skyrocketed, and I prospered. But perhaps this is indelicate of me, and I apologize if I cause offense, Captain Dalton."

"Before my time."

"Nevertheless excuse me for having brought it up. All this was just to explain that by then I had left the humble world of my youth far behind. Yet now I find myself longing to return to the sea, hence the *Speed Graphic*. Perhaps it is in the blood: the Lebanese people are as you perhaps know the descendants of the ancient Phoenicians: a sea-faring people, founders of Carthage and sons of Dido. After so many years of indulgence I once again crave the simple seafood of my childhood, although now at least I do not have to participate in its capture. As for my work with the Société de Dauphin Commun, you will understand that it is not for that animal alone. The dolphin is at the top of the food chain: dolphins eat fish, who eat smaller fish, who eat yet smaller fish, and so on down to the humble protozoa. Protect the dolphin and you must necessarily protect the entire ecological system, but the dolphin—being a well-loved animal, smiling and intelligent—is a creature for whose preservation it is much easier to persuade potential contributors to write a check than a single-celled organism of no charm whatsoever. If fish played fetch we wouldn't eat them. Yet when you consider the matter, it is the very bottom of the food chain—protozoa, and the ecological system which allows the protozoa to thrive—that must really be saved. So in short my aim is to help preserve the world of my youth, an imagined world I suppose, in which the simple joys of the sea are remembered but the long hours and backbreaking toil are conveniently forgotten."

"Especially in Monaco."

"Yes, indeed. But you must not underestimate the Monegasques. Monaco has two things essential to success. Firstly, political will. Rainier worked tirelessly to preserve the marine environment while he was alive; indeed he established a marine reserve off Larvotto Beach way back in 1975, long before such things had become fashionable. That tradition has continued: Monaco sponsors the Grand Prix de l'Océanographie, hosts the International Hydrographic Office, and the prince acted as the patron for the UN's Year of the Dolphin activities. Also, Monaco remains the state which presses hardest for a full Ligurian Basin reserve, something so necessary if the Mediterranean is to be brought back from the brink." .

"You said there were two things?"

"The other is money, of course. Nothing happens without money, and nowhere in the world is there a greater concentration of it than in Monaco."

As he talked, I thought about Hanna Moran. Obviously she had sought out Kadri to use his connections in finding a buyer for the book. Perhaps Felix Zane had unwittingly provided the introduction, thinking that she would be an amusement for his master. Instead, she had presented Kadri with a business proposition. No doubt he had invited her to remain as his guest until the transaction was consummated. I wondered if the relationship was strictly commercial, or whether she had found in Kadri not just a business partner but a replacement for the senator as well. She remained mostly silent through the meal—if she was his mistress, then she was one too new to have transitioned into the function of hostess.

Whatever her role, Hanna showed no sign of discomfort: she sat up straight, looked people in the eye, ate with relish, and smiled with genuine good humor. I wondered if she had physically handed over the notebook. Probably not; certainly not if she was wise, for Kadri could not conceal beneath the courtly manners and touching childhood stories his ruthlessness. Hanna Moran was not a fool: the notebook would still be in her possession.

By the time we finished the meal the *Speed Graphic* was well out to sea, a deeply inviting blue of the sort that makes you want to dive right over the side. Gulls soared behind, riding the wind, eager for scraps. Monaco and the rest of the Riviera lay astern, a great sweep of mountain-backed coastline tumbling down into the sea, with the narrow strip where the two met forming one of the world's finest playgrounds. It was worth preserving, and I could not help feeling a little admiration for our host.

Kadri turned to Miranda.

"I hope you brought your swimsuit, Miss Grey"

"I'm already wearing it, under my clothes."

"Very good. I invite you to join Hanna and make use of the pool. Such a perfect day for a swim."

It was a polite dismissal. Hanna and Miranda stood and left the table. The steward brought us two tiny cups of espresso, two shot glasses, and a long-necked bottle of grappa. Kadri added sugar cubes to his coffee and poured the grappa, a fluid that smelled not unlike the jet exhaust that had wafted across the deck of the *Theodore Roosevelt*. We sat back, glasses in hand, gazing aft to where the two women had selected deckchairs around the pool. Hanna had gone back upstairs, presumably to change.

Now as we watched Miranda casually unzipped her dress and let it fall to the deck. Underneath she was wearing little bikini bottoms but no top.

She stood unselfconsciously atop her high heels, apparently unaware that we were watching her, or uncaring if we did. Her breasts were already brown, the same golden glow shared by the rest of her skin, and I realized that she must have been sunbathing topless yesterday, maybe to ensure that there were no tan lines revealed by the low-cut gown she had worn the previous evening. I now regretted not having accompanied her to the hotel pool.

Kadri wordlessly drank off his grappa in a single mouthful. I did the same. He replaced the glass on the table and looked at me with a wry smile.

"Perhaps we should check on those dolphins now?"

Kadri and I returned to the elevator and descended to the vehicle deck. This time we went forward beyond where the cars were parked, through a metal passageway lined with watertight doors, probably leading to equipment rooms and auxiliary engineering spaces, before finally emerging into a single broad compartment right at the front of the main hull.

The forward two-thirds of the space was enclosed by that single big glass cap that I had seen from the wharf, and which allowed a remarkable view outside. High above was the unbroken azure that gave the coast its name. Ahead was the sea stretching to the horizon, but because we were lower here the sense of speed was much greater, as if we were flying just above the wave tops. On either side the great trireme hulls jutted forward, the spume and foam of their bow waves flying along the sides. The bottom few feet of the glass were below the water line. Despite the deep blue color that it had appeared from above the water was green here, aquamarine liquid rushing along the sides. Underneath you could see as far as the light allowed, down and down, disappearing into the endless depths below.

But the main treat was ahead and to the sides. Here the two hulls projected far forward below the waterline, revealing not rams but long cigar-shaped bulbs at the tips: the structures designed to actually pierce the waves. And playing among these bulbs were dolphins, matching us for speed, diving in and out, sometimes crossing from one side to the other, tremendously fast and agile but powerful too, as any creature which plays chicken with a thousand-ton ship must necessarily be.

"The nose cone is very strong, Captain Dalton. You may walk on it if you wish."

I stepped onto the glass, surrounded on all sides now by a swirling mass of sea and sky as the vessel hurtled forward through the waves. We were much closer to the engines down here: the hull vibrated with the power and their deep insistent tone contributed to the enormous sense of speed. Whatever money it had taken to build the *Speed Graphic*, this experience alone was worth the cost of construction.

"What do you think?"

"It's like skin-diving at thirty knots," I said.

But it was better than that: it was like being a dolphin yourself, able to see both above and below the water, all the while moving at tremendous speed, senses filled with the joyful rush. No wonder they smile so much.

We stood there for ten minutes or maybe twenty, silent, staring at the mesmerizing ever-shifting scene.

"Isn't there a risk of the glass shattering?"

"It is toughened and laminated, stronger than the glass in an airliner's windshield, stronger even than bulletproof glass, and so there is little risk of breakage. The hard part was achieving not strength but optical purity. I wanted there to be a minimum of distortion so that I could see exactly what was out there. In the end I had to have the thing designed by a firm specializing in lenses for the large optical telescopes used in observatories, although the actual manufacture was subcontracted out."

"You must spend many hours here," I said.

"Yes, I never tire of it."

Yet there were no chairs, no furnishings of any kind: just plain metal deck covered with non-skid paint, interrupted with occasional ringbolts that could be used to chain down bulky cargo. There were marks on the deck where something had recently been secured here, something large and heavy. As we headed back to the elevator I looked more closely at the compartments we passed to see what it might have been, but they were shut tight.

We returned to the main salon. The two women were down by the pool. Miranda was lying on her side, apparently sound asleep. Hanna was prone on an adjoining chaise, reading a magazine and wearing no more than Miranda, but it may have been that she had just undone the strap while sunning her back.

By unspoken agreement Kadri and I took seats facing aft. A steward brought a pair of Camparis with lots of ice and slices of orange. We raised our glasses in cheers and sipped quietly, looking at the scene astern, naked sea and sky, two near-naked women. We sat in silence for a while, enjoying the rush of sea and air astern of us. Eventually Kadri spoke up.

"What do you think it is that makes a woman beautiful?" he asked.

"Courage," I replied without hesitation.

He turned to face me, surprised by the answer, or perhaps the speed with which I had delivered it. But he did not immediately respond, instead turning back aft to gaze upon the pair who had presumably been the inspiration for the question.

"Yes, now that I think about it you may well be right. You have of course hit upon the heart of the matter: that female beauty is not merely physical attractiveness. Not even primarily, for that matter."

Miranda moved slightly, her hand brushing her mouth; she was dribbling in her sleep.

"What is it that you think makes a woman beautiful, Mr. Kadri?"

"For want of a better word, I would have said *style*. But that is a poor term, sullied by Hollywood and the fashion media into false bravado, an affected behavior that is the exact opposite of what I mean, and deeply unattractive. True style is genuine. It derives entirely from character; it cannot be put on like a cosmetic."

I could not help thinking of Zoraya and the seriousness with which she had decided to be beautiful when she grew up, as if such a thing was electable. Perhaps she had been right.

"Some would say that character and beauty are distinct."

"As they nominally are, but one infests the other. Take facial expression, for example. A shrew will often have a cast of shrewishness about her: pinched mouth, narrowed suspicious eyes. Or the peevish, always looking ready to break into a long nasal whine. And think how frequently vacancy within is perfectly expressed in vacancy without."

"Poor character makes an otherwise beautiful woman less beautiful?"

"I think so. Certainly fussiness uglifies. Posture, too: a self-confident woman stands in a certain way, quite unconsciously, while the meek stands in another, equally unconsciously. One is attractive, the other is not. Movement, too. Gracefulness is generally not given to the stupid: the lumpishly minded move like lumps."

"Body language?"

"No, there is no hidden meaning, just the physical reality. And it is more subtle than body language. Take for example the narrow gap between pride and self-conceit. A woman with pride will look after her appearance, but the self-conceited will preen. What is the difference? I do not know how to define it, yet I know it instantly when I see it. There are some people who on hearing just a single bar of music, even if they have never heard that particular piece before, can categorize it precisely: period, style, sometimes even composer. In the same way I believe that I can instantly tell the character of a woman just by looking at her. Nine times out of ten, at least."

A useful trait in the white-slave trade, I realized.

An officer came down a ladderway from the deck above, white uniform with four gold stripes on his epaulets: the captain. He came to Kadri's side and bent low to speak quietly. Kadri checked his watch.

"I didn't realize that it was so late." He turned to me. "I must apologize for being a poor host, Captain Dalton. I regret that it is time for the helicopter to take you and Miss Grey back to shore."

"The *Speed Graphic* isn't returning to Monaco?"

"Not for months. It is my habit to spend the summer at sea, and today we commenced this season's cruise, which is why I invited you to lunch on the yacht rather than at my villa. I do regret the inconvenience, but at least the helicopter flight should be scenic."

We stood and shook hands. A steward brought bottled water to the women, an excuse to rouse them.

This changed things. Ever since Hanna Moran had come down that spiral staircase I had been silently planning the operation to retrieve Stolper's notebook. I had identified two insertion routes: over the stern was easiest, or a tougher route via the bow if activity on the main deck precluded entry from aft. The door leading out to the main deck had a lock but no visible alarm, and I had not seen any security control panel nearby. If the area was occupied I would enter via the accommodation deck instead, swinging down from the helicopter pad. Identifying Hanna's quarters would be easy: she was the only female on board. I would take insulation tape for the smoke detector and an oxy-acetylene shoulder pack in case there was a wall safe. But I had counted on the *Speed Graphic* being secured alongside in Monaco.

"Where are you headed?"

"Italy, tonight. There's a little place down by Portofino that does a wonderful asparagus and truffle oil risotto; I've booked the corner table on the terrace."

"And afterward?"

"Oh, all over. We'll go from place to place, staying until we feel like moving on."

I asked no more; further inquiry would have risked arousing his suspicion.

THE HELICOPTER TURNED OUT TO BE FRENCH, built by Aérospatiale. The version was technically an AS365, but perhaps Kadri had selected the model because of its commercial name: Dauphin. I had the passenger compartment to myself—since Miranda was an aviatrix she had been invited to sit up front with the pilot. I was used to helicopters like the HH-60H that had picked me up in Caracol: unpainted metal decks, webbing instead of real seats, enough noise to make conversation impossible except by shouting. The interior of the Dauphin was the opposite: a little insulated enclave in which the passenger was cosseted in soft leather armchairs surrounding a small table fixed in the center of the space. The table had indentations designed to hold glasses so as not to spill cocktails in flight. There was a tiny bathroom aft and a huge entertainment center on the forward bulkhead that separated the cabin from the cockpit.

I checked the refrigerator. Peroni, a good beer. I opened a bottle and sat back to enjoy the ride.

It was a bumpy one. We were not flying very high, less than a thousand feet, and I supposed that the turbulence from the onshore breeze was causing the helicopter to bounce around. Down below I saw many pleasure craft—sailboats and some private yachts—but nothing to compare to the *Speed Graphic*. As we approached shore there were speedboats, too: lovely varnished wooden craft with sparkling chrome fittings carving wide V's across the water. Some of them towed water skiers.

Eventually we came to the harbor and the pilot put us down on a helo pad on the western side of town. When I debarked Miranda was already standing on the concrete, barefoot with sandals dangling from her fingers and smiling broadly. We waved as the helicopter lifted off and disappeared back out to sea.

"New shoes hurt?" I asked.

"Never fly in high heels."

"You flew?"

"For a while," she admitted. "I've never flown a helicopter before. Strange things, unnatural really: wings should be fixed."

I suddenly understood why the ride had been so bumpy.

"Well, I guess we now know where the notebook is. But Kadri told me that he's going cruising for the rest of the summer. He might be tough to find."

"Not really." She opened her purse and handed me an envelope. "The pilot was instructed to give me this."

Heavy, high-quality paper. The *Speed Graphic*'s crest was on the upper left-hand corner. Inside was a single sheet of matching notepaper, again embossed with the ship's crest. On it was scribbled a short note in an elegant flowing hand—a hand used to Arabic script, I realized.

My Dear Miss Grey,

What a pleasure it was to see you today. My sole regret is that it was so short.

I will be cruising aboard the Speed Graphic *for the remainder of the summer; perhaps if you have the opportunity you might choose to join me. I find that life at sea in this season is immensely pleasurable: fresh cooling breezes by day, spectacular sunsets, and long warm summer evenings. There is much to do—apart from all the water activities you may wish to play with the helicopter, too—and going from port to port as one chooses allows for interesting trips ashore, not to mention an endless variety of good wines & fine dining.*

Should the idea appeal to you I can be contacted at any time on the above satellite number. If you are nearby, I will have the helicopter come to collect you; otherwise, I will send a private jet. I do so very hope to see more of you in the near future.

I remain, madam, your humble and obedient servant,

Balthazar Kadri

I put the note back in the envelope and returned it to Miranda. At least I now knew why we had been asked to lunch: it had been to provide an opportunity for Kadri to invite Miranda to become his mistress.

XXI

W E SAT QUIETLY FOR A WHILE, recovering from the climb. There were no trees but it was cooler up here and despite the high sun we had no need of shade. In the valley far below the winding road rose in precipitous switchbacks to the outlook where the cab had dropped us—we had taken a taxi because the road was too narrow to have parked our own car, and in any case the Bentley would have been conspicuous. From there we hiked for an hour, higher and ever higher.

The view was worth the climb. Monaco was far away, a city in miniature, and beyond it the sea stretched to the horizon, an unbroken plain of lapis-lazuli blue. In the distance to the right was Cap Ferrat, about eight miles away, and far beyond that was Cap d'Antibes, more than twenty miles away, but the air was so clear that even at that range I could make out the lighthouse without binoculars.

The famous white villages perched high in the hills above the coast were lower than us now: we looked down upon Roquebrune to the east, la Turbie and Eze to the west: little collections of whitewashed houses clinging to the peaks.

Apart from the distant snow-capped Alps, the only thing above us now was a lonely raptor soaring the rising thermals, searching for unlucky rodents below. White head, pale gray-brown body and wings, thick black band on the trailing edges: it was a Griffon vulture. Huge wingspan, at least twelve feet. I watched it through the binoculars for a while, gliding and rising and turning, a perfect flying machine, apparently moving not a muscle for minutes on end, able to completely control its flight by faint adjustments to the upward-curving primaries alone.

I could smell lavender growing somewhere nearby and eucalyptus rising from the trees lining the ravine below.

Across that ravine lay Balthazar Kadri's villa.

Once again I checked the map. When yesterday I had gone in search of large-scale local maps I had expected to find nothing better than a hiking guide, but instead the woman at the *librairie* had directed me to a rack at the back of the store in which there was a series of good folding maps. They were marked IGN: Institut Géographique National: the French government equivalent of the U.S. Geological Survey maps that I was used to working with from the marines. I selected #3742OT from the Series Bleu, a walking map covering the country above the coast.

Very detailed; 1:25,000 scale. Individual buildings were often marked, fire trails, power lines, streams and dry beds, sometimes even conspicuous trees. There were contours from which I could tell that Kadri's villa was around 150 meters below us—about 500 feet.

I pulled out the notebook I had bought with the map—a fine quadrille-ruled Moleskine—and began drawing a detailed diagram of the compound.

Fifteen or twenty acres, walled all around. Quite steep, and the olive groves that occupied much of the estate were terraced. A single driveway beginning at the southern side where the wall ran by the roadway, the lowest point on the property. A small gatekeeper's lodge but probably no gatekeeper these days: I could see an electronic control panel on a steel pole by the side, and no doubt the gates were opened and closed by remote control. The driveway wound up through groves of olive and lemon trees until reaching the forecourt of the house, where it swung around a central fountain. The villa itself was built of undressed stone with a red-tile roof. It would have begun life as a *mas*, a country manor more substantial than a mere farmhouse but less grand than a château. Kadri or his predecessors had added to it, but the additions were in keeping with the character of the original building, indeed would have been indistinguishable from it had not the red roof tiles been brighter and less weathered than the original.

A bell tower to the side. Wide front steps, mossy with age. A broad, shale-tiled terrace running off the west wing, balustraded, and with a large pool sunk into the middle, tiled in dark stone rather than the usual garish bright blue. At the far end was a little projection under a vine-covered trellis. I could see a table and chairs, and guessed that most meals were eaten there, in the fresh air and while gazing out over the magnificent view below.

In the back of the terrace was a little colonnaded cloister, sunny but protected from the wind, no doubt a favorite spot in winter when the Mistral blew.

There were two other buildings of note. One was a long structure of the same undressed stone as the house but fitted with a series of wide wooden doors—originally a stable and carriage house but now a combination garage and equipment shed. Two of the doors were open, and I could see a small tractor poking out of one, and the back of a low-slung bright-yellow sports car was visible inside the other.

On the eastern side of the property, perhaps a hundred yards away from the *mas*, was what had probably once been a barn, but which had been converted into living quarters. A Citroën was parked outside, one of the old ones with the sharply sloping hoods. Directly behind the house and shielded from view were the clotheslines. A woman was hanging out laundry now.

About sixty years old, I guessed, perhaps older. She was hanging sheets, too many to be hers alone: the housekeeper, I supposed, doing the master's bed linens now that he had left for the summer. Out of habit I designated her as Enemy Combatant Number One and wrote a rough physical description in the notebook. I would record her movements during the day—activity and time—gathering as much intelligence as I could.

That completed the initial survey. I put down the binoculars. Miranda was behind me, laying everything out.

I saw the rose in her hair and could not help smiling. She glanced up and smiled back, apparently reading my mind.

CULTIVATION OF THE VINE IS SATISFYING; any man worth his salt must live a life of production, and the slow season-compelled work of making wine from soil and vine is production not just visible but tangible, tastable, and even smellable: a process that addresses four of the five senses. But in addition to vines I also cultivate roses.

Not for sale; I grow them for my own pleasure alone, and those that are not cut for inside the house are allowed to expire on the bush.

Right next door to the heliport, in the Fontvieille section of Monaco, is the Princess Grace Rose Garden. After Kadri's helicopter dropped us off yesterday we had wandered through it: ten acres and thousands of plants. Since it was June most of the roses were in full bloom, and the air was thick with their perfume. There was one that particularly caught Miranda's eye: a large well-formed blossom with voluptuous velvet petals of a striking reddish-orange hue. We read the label: it was a Cary Grant rose, a hybrid originally commissioned by the actor's wife. The only place they could be found outside of America was in this garden, planted here because the then Grace Kelly had first met Rainier while filming *To Catch A Thief* with Grant while on location in the Riviera.

After leaving the garden we had separated: Miranda returning to the hotel, me in search of a bookstore and hiking maps. It was late afternoon by the time I had gotten everything I wanted and returned to the hotel. I entered the suite to find the sitting room full of roses, hundreds of them.

My room was occupied by them too—and something else. Miranda was lying in the bed, covered by a sheet and wearing nothing but a look of mischief. I came and sat beside her. There was a vase on the side table. Unlike the others, which bore big bunches of flowers, this one was a slender vase occupied by a single reddish-orange rose whose stem had not been cut but torn. I picked it up. There was no doubting what it was and where it must have come from.

"I assume this one was stolen."

"It's all the fresh air and sunshine," Miranda said. "It makes me behave badly."

NOW, THE NEXT DAY, SHE WAS STILL GLOWING. I looked at the picnic hamper she had laid out. Crusty peasant bread, still warm from the oven. Niçoise olives. Avocado salad. A cold saddle of rabbit cooked in honey and lavender. Fresh figs for desert.

We also had energy bars and bottled water, which I put aside for later tonight, along with the rope, knife, grapnel, compass, gloves, flashlight, crowbar, and hacksaw.

I uncorked the rosé, a Provençal wine made by the bucketful and this particular bottle of which had cost us less than a dollar. It tasted just fine for a hilltop picnic at three thousand feet. All in all I thought this was a good way to conduct a recon mission, much better than the way we used to do it in the marines.

I ate ravenously. Apart from the oysters and bottle of '93 Dom Pérignon I had had sent up around midnight, we skipped dinner entirely last night.

Miranda slept for much of the afternoon. I kept watch on the villa below. A man emerged from the house a little before three. He was dressed for a climate ten degrees cooler: baggy woolen trousers, a sweater, even a beret. He trudged to the equipment shed with the gait of an old man, slow and slightly bowlegged, then emerged with a barrow and tools. He spent the remainder of the afternoon weeding the flower beds—the housekeeper's husband, no doubt, who did duty as the gardener.

There were no other people and no visitors. I guessed that in Kadri's absence the elderly couple looked after the villa by themselves, and the rest of his staff—valet, chef, maids—accompanied their master on the yacht.

The security was adequate, although not impressive. Two live-in people, but they were old and they lived in a barn up by the back of the property, not down near the gate, which was the obvious access point. The wall surrounding the estate was high enough for privacy but not so high that it could not be scaled without difficulty. No embedded glass or wire on top. No dogs. But Kadri was not a fool: if the estate lacked perimeter security then the house probably had an electronic system of its own.

At six o'clock the old man wheeled his barrow back to the shed and closed the door. He shut the garage door as well but locked neither, then trudged back toward the barn. He suddenly stopped while passing by the front of the villa itself, as if having remembered something left behind. A surreptitious look around, then he moved with newfound agility to a terracotta pot by the wall from under which he retrieved a key. He bounded up the steps and let himself into the main house.

I could see little inside. I tried to tell if he went to an alarm panel, but it seemed to me that he disappeared directly into the interior without pause. He emerged five minutes later and locked the front door carefully but without rush, the way a man would if he did not want his wife to hear him, but not with the speed of someone who had to get it locked within the timeframe required by a resetting alarm system.

He replaced the key, wiped his mouth with a ragged handkerchief, then continued the journey back to the barn, having now resumed his habitual slow pace. My best guess was that he had gone inside for a quick slug of the boss's liquor, perhaps his only opportunity to enjoy a quiet aperitif at the end of the day without his drinking habits coming under the disapproving scrutiny of the stern creature whom we no doubt both thought of as Enemy Combatant Number One.

It looked too easy. Yet I could imagine why Kadri might not have an alarm system installed. The sheer isolation of the place served as security: way up here in the hills any vehicle approaching by night would be heard and the headlamps seen long before it made it to the gate. There was nowhere to park inconspicuously, no place to park safely at all. There was also no way to escape in an emergency: a call to the authorities from alerted occupants would have police on the road long before any getaway car could have made it to the bottom. And being permanently occupied meant that it was an unlikely place for thieves to target.

Or it could be that there was a security system but it was habitually left off— maybe as a result of too many false alarms, something inevitable in a house full of staff, or perhaps the caretaker himself left it unset when the boss was away, the better to sample Kadri's cellar without accidentally alerting his wife.

One way or another, I was soon going to find out.

XXII

T HE FIRST THING I DID AFTER breaking into Balthazar
Kadri's house was take off my boots.

It was four in the morning. Cool now; at three thousand feet it gets cold at night, even in the middle of summer. The last lights in the barn had been extinguished by eleven and the people who lived there must have gone to sleep long ago, but since it was a cloudless night I decided to wait until moonrise so that we could see where we were going without the need of a flashlight. It was a good fat moon; yellow at rising when we had commenced the insertion but a high bright silver now. It illuminated a startling interior.

I had expected a rustic look matching the outside of the building—exposed beams blackened with age, bare stone walls not quite plumb, sturdy country furniture on rough tile floors. But the interior was just the opposite: a vast stark expanse, composed and rectilinear. Most abundantly there was space. The foyer opened onto a single broad room occupying most of the first floor, several thousand square feet, and presumably the primary room in the house. Not the original configuration: Kadri must have removed many of the internal walls and the effect, as with the main deck of the *Speed Graphic*, was a brilliant airy spaciousness, even by moonlight. Perhaps those days of his youth in an open fishing boat with no interruption between himself and the horizon had given Kadri a disinclination for enclosure; a man who despised walls.

The main deck of the *Speed Graphic* had been designed for living well, but whatever function this room served homeyness was not among its virtues. There were many large windows, each perhaps five feet across and eight feet high, all of them frameless. The walls between them were smooth and white, but the paint must have been embedded with mica or metal shavings that glittered softly in the moonlight. At frequent intervals there were shallow insets in the walls; these were fitted with mirrors whose dimensions exactly matched those of the windows, so that you could never be sure whether you were looking at a direct view or a reflection. I could see half a dozen moons without moving. An occasional long slash of chromed metal ran across the walls or floor or ceiling at an abrupt angle like an igneous intrusion, perhaps something intended to further disorient. There were dozens of pillars, probably an architectural necessity to bear the load that had once been supported by the internal walls, but these pillars were completely made of glass. They were not the rounded columns of the classical orders: instead, they were polygonal in cross-section and looked like giant quartz crystals.

The floor was composed of white marble tiles polished to a high shine. No rugs. My boots would have echoed walking across a room like this, and on something so well polished they would probably have left prints as well, which is why I removed them. When I was down to socks I could feel warmth beneath my feet. There were hot water pipes embedded under the tiles, no doubt connected to a thermostat so that whenever the temperature dropped the system would automatically turn on, something designed to ensure that the occupants would never tread upon cold stone. But this was a room that would have been cool at any temperature.

There was no security system—or at least no visible alarm panel, which is not quite the same thing.

There was a staircase leading to the second floor. The steps were long slabs of marble individually anchored at one end to an internal wall but otherwise unattached, which gave them the effect of floating free in space. There was no rail or banister.

I left the crystalline room and began searching through the rest of the house. There was a study located in the far end of the east wing. The door was very heavy and fitted snugly into a sealed frame. The windows in this room were the regular-sized ones of the original dwelling and they had shutters that fitted into seals, too. I realized that a businessman like Kadri would occasionally require absolute privacy in his study so that he could be certain that whatever he had to say would not be overheard by any curious staff. The door and shutters were designed so that no sound could escape, but they would also serve to keep in light. I closed them all, then turned on the desk lamp.

The room continued the modernist theme: the desk was spare and sleek, and the various items on top of it were of minimalist European design. The bookcases were fitted with sandblasted glass doors, and office items like filing cabinets and printers and the photocopier were all hidden away in a wall closet behind sliding doors. Another closet was occupied by a safe, big enough to fit a man inside.

In the corner stood a high stool in front of a broad draughtsman's table. Laid on top of the table was a nautical chart.

The last was what I had come for: some way of figuring out the *Speed Graphic*'s itinerary. Kadri had said that he would sail from place to place as the mood struck him, which is fine as long as you are willing to lie at anchor. But occasionally the *Speed Graphic* would need to come alongside a wharf: certainly for fuel, or indeed to conduct maintenance of any kind. If she did not have an evaporator she would also have to dock for fresh water; even if she did have one it might not keep up with consumption, in which case they would need to top up from time to time, especially after laundry day. Storing the ship could theoretically be accomplished by a combination of boat and helicopter, but would be far less arduous if done while docked. And to take the vehicles ashore they would also need a wharf, so in any place they intended to stay for a while and explore the hinterland they would likely not remain at anchor. But finding dock space would be difficult enough for any vessel during the cruising season; for something the size of the *Speed Graphic* it would be next to impossible. So my guess was that although there might be long intervals with no particular destination in mind, somewhere in the sailing plan there would be specific dates and places where they had reserved facilities alongside. That would be where I would find the *Speed Graphic* and retrieve the senator's notebook.

It turned out that there were several charts, one laid upon the other: golfe du Lion, the entire Eastern Basin, Adriatic and Ionian Seas, Aegean, Levantine Coast. But there were no tracks on any of the charts or any other markings to indicate where they were headed. Perhaps these charts had nothing to do with the present cruise, and

Kadri just kept them on the draughtsman's table to refer to as needed.

The study yielded nothing else of interest; everything was locked away. I left the room and continued searching the house. The rear wing had been completely sealed off: staff quarters, I assumed, shut down since they had accompanied Kadri onboard the yacht.

Upstairs, the austerity of the main room was replicated in what was obviously the master bedroom: a broad marble-and-glass space, filled with moonlight. Here too there were many mirrors, but unlike the room below the blank spaces of wall between them were occupied. At first I thought they were paintings but on second look decided were photographs. I was wrong both times; they turned out to be mosaics. There were eight of them. The tiles were not the traditional tiles of colored ceramic. There were only two types of tile here: one of black stone, onyx perhaps, the other chromed metal. They were tiny squares, each about a sixteenth of an inch a side. Thousands of them had been embedded with what must have been painstaking precision to form an image resembling a blown-up black-and-white photograph in which the tiles simulated enlarged pixels.

All of them were of women, but never the same one. They were full-length shots, life-size, mostly naked, but the poses were not at all suggestive or coy. The women simply stood, their expressions disengaged and difficult to decipher.

Conceivably they could have been the results of a series of photoshoots, but I wondered if what I was looking at was something else entirely: not models in a studio but merchandise on the auction block. There seemed to be a common underlying theme to their expressions, a sense of fatalistic inevitability, something that would have been difficult to fake. If I had guessed correctly, then there was an audacity to these mosaics, an open declaration of Kadri's trade. Perhaps they were intended to be instructive to the women who shared this room with him. I wondered if Hanna Moran had seen them.

I returned downstairs, disappointed. We would have to start calling dock offices at random across the Mediterranean. I began making a mental list of the most obvious ones to try first: St. Tropez, Marbella, Capri, Santorini. But while walking through the least likely of rooms, the kitchen, I at last found what I had been looking for.

The kitchen occupied a corner of the first floor. The equipment was industrial-sized and made of stainless steel; it was the sort of kitchen in which a professional chef would have felt at home. There were long granite counters around the perimeter and a central island topped with big butcher's blocks. On the counter to the left, where it opened onto a casual dining area, I found a shallow bowl with various sets of keys, and a large padded envelope, unsealed. I upended this last and a dozen or so letters slid out onto the counter. They were all addressed to Kadri, and I realized that this was the most obvious of ways to track down the yacht: the address to which the mail was forwarded. With Kadri away the housekeeper was no doubt sorting through the mail each day, putting aside anything that was obviously junk and keeping the rest to be sent on. This big padded mailer was the package in which she would forward it all. I turned it over to reveal the address:

MV Speed Graphic,
C/- Dockmaster's Office,
Emirates International Marina,
Dubai,
United Arab Emirates

Now I knew where to find Kadri. I had assumed that the cruise would be confined to the Mediterranean, but instead he was heading for the Persian Gulf. I recalled my own time there: endless windless days on the blue-green water, waiting and waiting, decks too hot to walk on, the *Shreveport*'s air-conditioning unable to cope with the combination of extreme heat and a battalion of marines living in close quarters. We even experienced a sandstorm: where else in the world would you have a sandstorm out at sea?

I was replacing the mail, trying to put it back the way I found it, when I recognized the sender's name on one of the envelopes. Manila-colored and square-shaped, made of cardboard rather than regular paper. The sender was printed in the upper left-hand corner: New York East Medical Associates, the same outfit whose bill for consultations I had seen in Felix Zane's credit card account. But the stamps were French and the envelope was postmarked today— yesterday now, since it was the early hours of the morning.

I would have liked to know what was inside, but it was sealed tight and there was no way for me to open the envelope without it showing. I decided to open it anyway and just keep the thing, hoping that since the housekeeper had already put it in the mailbag she would not notice its absence later.

I found a paring knife and slit open the envelope. Inside was a disc: a DVD or CD-ROM. On it was stuck a square yellow note:

I just missed you in Monaco, so sending this now in case it gets to you before I can (I dare not use the satellite phone, for obvious reasons). The disc is self-explanatory: Moran is not what she seems. Suggest that you just keep her amused—I will fly on ahead to Dubai and take care of matters permanently when you arrive. /Z

"Z": presumably Felix Zane. It was not hard to guess why he had missed Kadri: unlike me, he had not taken the expedient exit from Morocco, and the business in Tangier must have held him up. I presumed that the "obvious reasons" preventing him from using the satellite phone was the possibility of an FBI wiretap. I wondered what was on the disc, that it should make him want to permanently dispose of Hanna Moran.

On the bottom of the note he had scribbled his hotel and flight details. He was booked into the Burj Al Arab in Dubai and traveling on Emirates flight 906. The arrival date was today, at 5:25 P.M.

I did a quick mental approximation. Taking into account time-zone changes and the length of the flight, if he was arriving in the Gulf this evening then the plane must leave France early this morning. I looked up Emirates Airlines on my phone and punched through the menu to flight information.

Emirates flight 906 was on time, scheduled to depart Nice airport at 7:45 A.M.

I booked two tickets on the same flight, using the pause while the system verified the credit card details to search through the keys in the bowl. I found the set that I wanted, distinguished on their fobs by an upward-pointing trident symbol. On the same ring with the keys was a small remote control.

I pocketed the keys and completed the transaction. Nice airport was about thirty miles away. By the time we got through security and customs, I figured we would only have around ten minutes to spare. It was going to be a near thing.

XXIII

I LOCKED THE DOOR TO THE VILLA and replaced the key. The sky was already lightening to the east, obliterating the stars above Italy; only Venus remained visible, hanging low over the land. I went through the olive trees up to where Miranda lay hidden behind a terrace, keeping watch on the barn, ready to alert me at any sign of activity within so that we could quickly extract.

I quietly explained the urgency of the situation.

We made our way back past the villa to the carriage house. I unbolted the double doors at the end, opening them to reveal that same low sports car that I had glimpsed from the hill yesterday afternoon. A Maserati, as I had guessed from the symbol embossed on the keys, but an old one: a Ghibli SS, a car out of production for at least thirty years. I hoped the thing worked; there was no time to return to Monaco for the Bentley.

I circled the car in rapid inspection. If it was a restoration project then the bodywork had been completed: from the outside the car looked brand new. The bright yellow paint was unmarked and the chrome wire wheels gleamed. It was very low and wide, a fast-backed two-seat coupe, sleek shark nose with the famous trident symbol rising in the center of the grill, long side gills to cool the big engine within, four huge tailpipes to allow it to breathe.

I opened the door and got in behind the wheel. The car was too old to have come with an alarm but I inserted the key and quickly turned on the ignition in case an after-market version had been fitted. The gauges sprang into life and I heard the ticking of a fuel pump from astern. The steering wheel was wood-rimmed and had three drilled aluminum spokes. The dash had a big tachometer on the left and a speedometer on the right. Redline 5,500. The fuel gauge between them showed a full tank. Five-speed stick shift. Above the center console was a series of engine gauges, including oil pressure, which registered correctly. You can never be certain until the motor is running, but by now I was pretty sure that this vehicle was fully functional. I released the handbrake and got out of the car.

"Let's push."

I shoved from the B-pillar so that I could also steer the thing. Miranda pushed from the front. Between us we backed it out. When there was sufficient momentum I turned the wheel, swinging the Maserati around so that the nose was pointing somewhat downhill. I applied the hand brake and returned to the stable to close the doors. I was not sure how long it would take the housekeepers to realize that the Maserati was missing, but I did not intend to make it obvious. I rejoined Miranda.

"Get in," I whispered. "But open the door quietly and don't close it."

When we were both aboard I released the brake and allowed the car to roll gently down the driveway. You would think that a rolling car with the engine off would be all but silent, but in the quiet still air every pebble seemed to crunch and explode under the wheels. Worse, the brakes squeaked.

We rolled down through the citrus groves toward the front of the property. I pointed the remote control at the gates and pressed the top button. They sprang into automated life, opening to allow our passage through. The car bounced down onto the asphalt of the public road. I hit the second button on the remote and the gates swung shut behind us.

I allowed the car to continue to roll for another hundred yards or so, wanting to get as far away as possible before firing the engine. It was just as well, for when I engaged the starter and the motor sprang into life it was not with the sound of an ordinary street engine but the uneven rev-reaching rumble of a racing powerplant, all but unmuffled, a sound that must have echoed along the valley walls for miles.

We finally closed the doors. I took the stick through the gate, getting a feel for the transmission. Long throws and a heavy clutch, but in a thirty-year-old car with this much power a heavy clutch was a foregone conclusion. By now it was light enough outside not to need the headlamps but I turned them on anyway: a warning to other traffic, since I intended to drive in an unsafe manner. I engaged first and released the clutch. The Maserati surged forward, a horse having spent too long in the stables, eager to canter. As I came onto the gas the engine note rose in both pitch and volume, transforming from a deep basso thump to a sharp metallic bark.

I checked my watch. Leaving the estate had taken longer than I had anticipated; it would be touch-and-go getting to the airport in time. On the plus side the road was all but empty at this early hour, and we were already familiar with the route. This time I drove the

Corniche at twice the best speed the Bentley could have managed, taking the Maserati deep into the corners, braking heavily, swooping through the apex after changing down, then exiting with as much power as was possible without losing the rear end. The car handled it well: mild understeer on entry caused by the mass of the engine up front, then the chassis transitioned smoothly to progressive oversteer as the gas came back on, with sufficient tire wail to warn you when it was becoming unhappy before actually letting go. High-speed mountain driving is the purpose for which the Italians build such vehicles; the Maserati could have done this all day. On the short straightaways we flashed past the few other vehicles we came upon; one even pulled over before we got to him, apparently alarmed by the sight of the Maserati approaching in his mirror, or more likely the tremendous noise.

We made good time on the Corniche but eventually the road dropped down into Nice. There is always traffic on the promenade des Anglais, the wide avenue running along the waterfront, and I had to thread the Maserati through it as best I could, surging and braking, until finally reaching the exit for the airport.

Nice airport is situated on a spit of land stretching into the baie des Anges. I left the car in short-term parking. We sprinted to Terminal One, checked in, and then swiftly passed through security and passport control.

It was 7:10. Plenty of time for the flight but that was not the point. I needed to find Zane before he boarded.

I had booked into first class to ensure that we would have access to the lounge, but it turned out to be unnecessary: Zane was at the departure gate, sitting by himself on a row of seats by the windows, looking out over the runway and the water beyond. There was a fair-sized crowd, between fifty and a hundred people, mostly in western clothing but a few wore robes and headdress. Boarding had not yet commenced. A score or so of the more anxious were crowding around the entrance to the airbridge like dairy cows with full udders, eager for the milking shed. A pair of uniformed Emirates officials fussed at the podium. A few children were running about noisily. I could smell coffee from a nearby stall.

I pulled Miranda aside, out of sight should Zane happen to turn around, and told her precisely what it was that I wanted her to do. She was obviously unhappy but did what few women would have done on hearing what I had to say: she just nodded and said nothing more.

We split up. Miranda joined the line at the coffee stall. I went first to the *tabac* where I shoplifted a ballpoint pen—a fine-pointed Bic—then to the men's room, where I flushed the packaging and wrapped my right hand in a handkerchief. When I emerged I kept both hands hidden in my jacket pockets and took up a position by the monitors, as if checking flight information but situated so that I had a good view over both the concourse and the gate.

Zane was still seated but the agitation at a departure gate when boarding is overdue was affecting him: he was punctuating his gaze outside with occasional glances at the podium now. One of the Emirates' officials had picked up a microphone in her left hand, obviously about to call for boarding, but she was still searching for something under the counter with her other hand. There was little time left: if Zane stood and joined the line my plan was finished.

Miranda finally got her coffee. She looked around and saw that I was in position but made no acknowledgment. She started walking down the concourse. I gripped the Bic tightly in my pocket and began walking toward Zane.

The timing had to be right but I was too early: I found myself standing behind him, waiting. Zane was still looking outside, but in the reflection of the plate-glass windows our eyes suddenly met. His face betrayed a brief moment of confused recognition followed by a flash of understanding, but by then it was too late. I heard Miranda scream behind me. I grabbed Zane's head with my hand over his mouth and jammed the Bic into his ear canal. There was a split second of resistance as it met the cartilage and those many little bones, but then I rammed it home, upward-pointing, all the way through the temporal lobe and on into the brain stem.

He died instantly, a better death than he deserved.

I walked out of the gate area and along the concourse, head down, making eye contact with no one, but in my peripheral vision I could see Miranda sprawled amid the puddle of spilled coffee, cursing loudly while being helped to her feet by a couple of passengers, still ensuring that all eyes in the departure lounge were on her.

I ignored the scene, continuing down the concourse and out of the terminal.

"HE WAS STILL SITTING UPRIGHT WHEN I LEFT," Miranda said quietly.

They were the first real words she had spoken since the airport. She had still not looked me in the face.

Miranda had extracted on foot as I had insisted she do. There might have been a security camera at the parking lot exit, and I had not wanted her recorded on surveillance tape leaving with me. Instead, I had picked her up by a closed ice cream stall on the promenade des Anglais. We had driven in silence back toward Monaco where I had eventually pulled into an outlook high above the still slumbering principality.

We would dump the Maserati here.

My hands had stopped shaking. It had started in the car and I had needed all of my concentration to keep driving. Adrenaline surge? Age, perhaps. I was getting older, weaker, softer. Zane was far from the first man I had killed; he was not even the first I had killed out of uniform. And he had certainly deserved it; I felt no regret. Yet I had gotten the shakes; how strange.

We were leaning on the hood and gazing out over the Mediterranean, a panorama familiar to us by now. After leaving the terminal I had collected the car and left the airport. No cost: the cashier told me that for the lot I had parked in, P2, there is no charge for less than twenty minutes. I was still astonished that to have entered an airport, acquired a murder weapon, killed a man in broad daylight under the eyes of a hundred people, and then safely gotten back out again could have taken less than twenty minutes.

"You looked at him?"

"Not obviously, just glancing around in the way a woman who has just covered herself in coffee might, wondering what she should do next."

"Had anyone noticed him?"

"No, they were all looking at me. There was no blood or anything; he's probably still sitting there," Miranda said. "He might be there for days."

There would not have been much blood. The pen would have killed him instantly, and as soon as his heart stopped all the blood would have drained down internally. But the body would not remain there for days: airport security would notice him soon enough.

Miranda turned to face me at last.

"I didn't realize that you were so good at this stuff," she said. There was no admiration in the remark.

The time had come to explain about Zoraya.

I had not killed Zane because of what he did to Zoraya; I had killed him because of what he might do to Hanna Moran. One was sentiment, the other was practical, and only fools kill out of sentiment. Yet I knew that hearing the story would make it easier for Miranda to reconcile having helped me, and so I told it slowly and evenly, keeping to the facts but not sparing the detail.

After I finished, Miranda leaned over the rail and vomited.

When she was done I gave her my handkerchief, realizing too late that it was the same one I had used to ensure that there would be no fingerprints left on the pen. I hoped it was clean; I had not checked after killing Zane. Finding foreign matter on it would really ruin what for Miranda had already gotten off to a pretty bad day.

I wiped down the car in the places where either of us had touched it and left the keys in the ignition. With a little luck someone would resteal it, complicating any investigation once the vehicle was recovered.

We began the long walk back down to Monaco. The computer disc was still in my coat pocket.

XXIV

T HE WATER ALTERNATED IN BANDS of warm and cold, or more accurately cold and colder, for it was all snowmelt from the surrounding Alps and none of it would have qualified as warm. I wondered how such bands formed—not from wave action: Lake Lugarno was as still as a painting and the only thing moving on it was a duck and her brood paddling past me toward the shore, off to find their breakfast.

I looked up at the hotel: a classic Italian villa sitting on the shoreline, vine-covered and reposing in quiet decay, the morning sun revealing its age but not necessarily to disadvantage. Behind it and all around loomed the great peaks that fed the lake.

Three things had dictated coming to Italy's lake country. Firstly, we had to leave France: the authorities would soon examine the manifest for Zane's flight and find the names of two passengers who had checked in but failed to board. That did not necessarily make us suspects, but they would want to interview us. I had called Emirates Airlines and told them that a sudden family emergency had caused us to miss the plane, then rebooked for the same flight in a week's time—a flight that we had no intention of taking, but the fact of the reservation might make the French police think there was no urgency in finding us. Secondly, I wanted to be near a major international hub so that when the time came to move we could move rapidly, without the complication of connecting flights. Milan's Malpensa airport was less than an hour away. Thirdly, I wanted to be near a border that we could escape across if the Carabinieri suddenly showed up at the hotel. Lake Lugarno was perfect: a body of water whose shores are shared by Italy and Switzerland. If the Carabinieri came to the front door, Miranda and I would extract via the lake-facing terrace, go down to the water and simply swim the half-mile to Switzerland and freedom, much like Hemingway's Frederic and Catherine in *A Farewell to Arms*. That was the reason I was in the water so early in the morning. I had swum far out to where there was a long view of the shoreline, a place where I could pick out the navigational markers that we would use if needed.

The doors to our terrace opened and out stepped Miranda. She had obviously just woken up: unselfconsciously naked, head held high, hair all in sleepy disarray. She stood with her hands on the rail and bathed in the warmth of the morning sun. I waved but she did not notice me; probably her eyes were closed against the light.

I began swimming for the shore.

Miranda must have seen me returning. By the time I got back to the room she had already ordered breakfast to be brought up. She wore a robe now.

We ate on the terrace—croissants and rolls, pitchers of coffee and milk. We wolfed down everything; last night after checking in we had skipped dinner and gone straight to bed—apart from the few hours Miranda had snatched on the slopes above Kadri's villa neither of us had slept in two days.

When breakfast was done it was time to see what was on that computer disc.

I had an adapter sent up from the front desk. When the laptop was ready I inserted the disc and checked the contents. There was a single file labeled "Hanna_Moran.mpg." The operating system offered a choice of programs with which to open it. I selected one and hit Play.

It was a video file. The picture quality was poor: grainy, as if taken by a security camera and further distorted by having been shot through a wide-angle lens.

It showed what I assumed was a doctor's office. The camera was obviously mounted in the ceiling. There was a medical examination table to the right, a small stool on castors beside it, and a long bench to the left with various boxes and pieces of medical apparatus on top.

For the first minute there was no action. Then the door opened and two people walked in. One was Hanna Moran. The other was wearing a white lab coat, hair secured in a ponytail, a stethoscope hanging around her neck, a clipboard held in her hand: presumably the physician.

"First of all we'll take a blood sample," she said. "Just sit on the table and roll up your left sleeve."

The sound was tinny and echoing. Hanna did as instructed. The doctor took the blood sample swiftly and with no visible discomfort on Hanna's part. After she was done the doctor released the rubber hose and applied a band-aid with little cartoon characters on it.

"Why don't you get undressed now, Hanna? There are some coat hangers behind the door."

"Okay."

"I'll be back in a few minutes."

The physician left the room, taking the blood sample with her. Hanna Moran stripped down and hung her clothes behind the door. She placed her shoes neatly to the side and sat down on the examination table. The paper covering it crunched under her weight.

Hanna rubbed her arms the way someone does when they are cold, and despite the poor quality of the video I could make out the goosebumps on her flesh. She looked around the room while waiting but never once at the camera; it was probably hidden. Eventually the physician returned.

"Okay, let's have a look, shall we?"

She made a routine medical examination of the type the marines are so fond of, except that Hanna did not have to do the part where you cough. The doctor listened to her chest and back with the stethoscope, inspected her eyes and ears with an otoscope, and tested her reflexes with a tiny hammer.

"Okay, that looks fine. Lie down, Hanna, and I'll connect you up."

Hanna lay down on the table, supine. Her breasts flattened but the nipples were taught, another sign that the room was too cold. I wondered why the physician did not seem to notice. Instead she maintained a professional patter as she went through the process of hooking Hanna up to what was presumably an EKG.

"Did you apply any body moisturizer this morning?"

"No."

"Good—sometimes the electrodes don't stick if there's moisturizer. Now for the fingers."

She put little caps on the ends of Hanna's fingers, each connected to an individual wire. Next she applied a sphygmometer sleeve, which automatically inflated and deflated, measuring Hanna's blood pressure.

"We call this the Frankenstein machine," the physician quipped. "Lots of wires, but it measures absolutely everything and so makes the whole checkup much faster."

The machine was hooked into a laptop. The physician began tapping keys. Suddenly a graph appeared on the video, and the image of Hanna and the doctor automatically reduced in size to accommodate it. A number of readouts began ticking across the graph. We were no longer just witnessing the examination but also seeing the results as the machine monitored Hanna. The physician sat on the stool by her, crossing her legs with the clipboard on her lap and pen in hand.

"While the machine does its thing, why don't we finish the paperwork?"

"Okay."

"Are you comfortable, Hanna?"

"Yes," she said, although I could see that she was not.

"So, your full name is Hanna Moran? No middle name?"

"Yes."

"And you're getting the checkup as a requirement for foreign work?"

"Yes."

"You're going to be working in Dubai?

"Yes."

"How interesting. What work do you do?"

"I'm a model."

"I'm not surprised; I thought you must be when I saw you. Will you be modeling in Dubai?"

"Yes."

"Will you be over there long?

"Six months."

"How lucky. I've always wanted to go to the Middle East. Have you been to the area before?"

"No, it's a first time for me."

"You must go to some great places. Have you always been a model?"

"Yes, ever since I left school."

"Fashion?"

"Yes, mainly."

The conversation became more medical after that, with the doctor questioning Hanna about her diet and sleep and the other sorts of things you might expect a female patient to be quizzed about. Moran's answers were routine.

Finally the physician stood and put the clipboard aside. She went to the machine and flipped a switch. The readouts next to the video disappeared, and the screen went back to full size.

The doctor examined the results on her computer.

"This all looks good," she said after a while. "You're in fine physical shape, Hanna; absolutely no problems at all."

"Great."

"So you can get dressed now and come out. We'll get the blood work back tomorrow and let you know the results."

"Okay, fine."

They shook hands and the doctor left. Hanna dressed, obviously grateful to put on her clothes again. She soon left.

The video remained on for several more minutes until the physician returned to the room. She again sat by the computer and began tapping at the keyboard. Then she stopped, pushed back the stool, and turned around. She looked directly up at the camera. The screen went blank: it was the end of the file.

"A medical checkup," I said.

I could see that Miranda was as disappointed as I was. Puzzled, too.

"Why would it have been filmed?" she asked after a while.

"Required by their medical malpractice insurer, perhaps? The ultimate defense in a lawsuit: proof of what actually went on, what the results were, what was said by whom."

"They would have to get a patient's consent, wouldn't you think?"

"I guess."

"But Hanna didn't look at the camera once."

"Perhaps she didn't care."

"Being filmed while undressing and undergoing a medical examination?"

"Maybe the camera was concealed."

"But she would have looked for it. Any woman would."

"Let's watch it again."

This time I paid more attention to the readouts. There were five in total. I could figure out pulse and blood pressure easily enough, but the other three I did not understand: Upper Pneumo, Lower Pneumo, and GSR. The scale for this last was in "μmho," units of measurement I had never heard of. The program was doing more than just recording the results, it was analyzing them: as the graphs ticked by across the screen an occasional symbol would appear: little green triangles marked "NDI", occasional red dots marked "PDI" and twice there was a vertical red band running across all the readouts, marked "EDI."

On the bar at the bottom of the graph was the name of the maker of the medical device: Technotronika. I decided to look them up on the internet; with any luck they might have downloadable user guides for the equipment.

Our hotel was not the sort of place with high-speed internet access. After a long slow process, we eventually got to the website of the Technotronika Corporation.

It turned out to be a company based in Forth Worth, Texas. It was not in the medical equipment business. The Technotronika Corp. manufactured only one type of product: polygraph machines. They built lie detectors.

So it had not been a genuine medical examination after all. It had been the administration of a lie detector test, disguised as a medical examination.

I realized what must have prompted it: after nearly getting burned by an FBI plant, Zane had decided to polygraph all his recruits for the Middle East. How easy it would be to do. On the face of it the requirement for a medical examination was believable: the girls would be told that it was a government prerequisite for the granting of a work permit, or better still something that the employer required, in case one of them decided to check on the official regulations for herself. It was conducted in professional offices by a genuine physician—female, so they would feel more comfortable— and included the attributes of a regular checkup, like the blood work, that were irrelevant to the actual purpose. And all of the wiring was more or less what you would require for a genuine EKG.

We watched the video again several times.

Now that we knew what we were looking at, the conversation that before had seemed to be just routine bedside manner was now revealed to be a carefully planned interrogation process. Early on had come the control question, something intended to deliberately generate a dishonest response: *Are you comfortable?* Clearly Hanna had not been comfortable but as most people would have done she had said that she was fine, despite the air-conditioning on too low— a combination of politeness and just wanting to get on with it. It was not much of a lie but it was a lie, and the machine would register the response, using it as a baseline for comparing responses to future questions.

I learned much through the web search. The upper and lower pneumo readings were measures of respiratory rate. GSR stood for Galvanic Skin Response: essentially a measure of perspiration. And "mhos" are units of electrical conductivity: the machine measured very fine changes in the skin's conductivity—calibrated in μmho, that is, micro-mhos—in order to capture the tiny variations caused by the increased sweating of a subject telling a lie.

The abbreviation NDI meant No Deception Indicated. PDI meant Potential Deception Indicated. EDI meant Extreme Deception Indicated. Hanna had gotten a PDI when asked her name—Hanna Moran was the name she chose to go by, but as Dortmund had already surmised it was probably not the one she was born with, and that had been enough for the machine to pick up the uncertainty. A second PDI had come to the question *What do you do for a living?* But the big reactions had come in response to the questions *Will you be modeling in Dubai?* and *Will you be over there long?* The machine had drawn a wide red bar through her answers and marked them Extreme Deception Indicated. Coming after the uncertainty with her name and profession, those responses would have been the ones that had worried Zane.

I sat back and considered what we had discovered. The more I thought about it, the more likely that Kadri rather than Zane had come up with this clever scheme for polygraphing recruits: there was a combination of bold originality and elegant simplicity to the thing, a subtle audacity that was beyond the scope of the younger man. The deception was particularly well-conceived: polygraphs can be easily fooled—the spy Aldrich Ames had done so on multiple occasions with minimal training from his Soviet handlers—but if the subjects are not aware that they are being tested then they cannot gird themselves to beat it.

Certainly this one had worked: it had identified Hanna Moran as someone other than the woman that she represented herself to be.

It was enough to have made Zane want to dispose of her, but I had disposed of Zane first.

XXV

D UBAI LIES ON THE NORTHERN COAST of the Arabian Peninsula, where the desert meets the sea. The flight from Europe comes in across the fretful waters of the Gulf, shimmering and saline-green. No clouds, but the horizon is blurred by salt haze. Oil tankers the size of football fields pass below, making their ponderous passage through the water with the steady inevitability of a tectonic movement. The first sign of Dubai's approach is a strange one: housing estates on the water—broad collections of man-made islets arranged in fanciful patterns: the fronds of a palm tree, the continents of the world. Then the city itself appears, narrow and humpbacked, a listless heat-drugged lizard stretching lazily along the shore. As you come closer the horny scales resolve themselves into a frenzy of construction cranes.

From time to time, all the world's construction cranes seem to gather in one place. In the 1990s it had been Berlin, reunited after half a century and madly rebuilding as if to make up for lost time. Before that it had been Las Vegas, and before that Hong Kong. In the Jazz Age it had been Manhattan, erecting skyscrapers like exclamation points to proclaim the American Century. And now, as the plane flew in low across the coast, it seemed that the world's cranes had flocked to Dubai.

We emerged through customs. I had ordered a car, and a uniformed driver was standing on the other side holding a sign with my name on it. He was a long-faced man of about forty who solemnly introduced himself as Wahid. He bowed politely to Miranda before grabbing the luggage and leading us outside.

I have done a fair amount of time in desert environments: urban ops training at the Twenty-Nine Palms base camp in the Mojave, HALO jumps over the Army's Yuma Proving Ground in the Sonora, and of course we fought Gulf Two in the desert. But none of that prepared me for what hit us as we emerged from that airport terminal. It was not just the heat, although there was plenty of that, but the accompanying humidity. Desert air is usually dry, which renders the heat bearable, but the proximity of the sea made stepping outside in Dubai seem like walking into a steam bath. It lacked the quality of genuine air, was almost unbreathable, as if all the heat and humidity had somehow deoxygenated it.

The driver turned out to be an Egyptian from Cairo who worked in Dubai for ten months of the year and spent the other two back home with his family. He gave us an impromptu tour of the city on the way to the hotel. Wahid must have assumed that shopping would be our principal activity, perhaps because fifty percent of us were female. We went to various places that he called souks, but in reality they were just shopping malls—modern and enclosed—nothing like the real thing in Tangier. One of them had a large sign out front with a combination clock and thermometer. It registered 43 degrees Celsius. I did a quick mental conversion: about 110 degrees

Fahrenheit. All the malls were air-conditioned, one apparently to the point where you could ski: Wahid told us that they had constructed a ski slope inside and covered it in machine-made snow. You rented equipment at the bottom and took an elevator to the top.

He showed us mosques and amusement parks and even a racetrack; I had nothing but sympathy for any horse required to gallop in this climate. Little we saw was more than thirty years in age; the only place that looked old, a small complex of low stucco buildings down near the mouth of the creek, turned out to be new, too—a recreation of what Dubai had supposedly once been like, not so long ago, when the main industry was not oil drilling but pearl diving.

The last thing Wahid showed us was a towering skyscraper.

"The Burj Khalifa," he announced. "It is the world's tallest building."

"How high?"

"Eight hundred meters."

Another mental conversion; it was about half a mile high, twice the height of the Empire State Building. There was a construction site on the other side of the road, chain-link fence surrounding a lot that had been deeply excavated.

"Another tower?"

"No doubt," Wahid said. "Construction never stops in Dubai."

I noticed that the workers were darker skinned than most Arabs and slighter in physique.

"Who are the people building it?"

"Pakistanis. In Dubai, all manual labor is performed by foreigners. The Pakistanis work in construction and oil rigs. Filipinos work in domestic service. Jordanians or North Africans or

Egyptians such as myself work in the service industries, where the Arabic language is required."

"What do the locals do?"

But he just shrugged his shoulders in reply: it was not the sort of question that a guest worker who values his job would willingly answer. A group of Pakistanis on the other side of the fence had removed their construction helmets—lunch break perhaps—and were busy setting up equipment in the dusty lot for some sort of game.

Wahid noticed me looking at them.

"Have you ever seen the game of cricket?" he asked.

"No."

"It is immensely stupid." He tapped the side of his head, the universal gesture indicating idiocy. "Who in their right mind would go outside in the middle of the day in the desert to bowl a ball at a bat?"

I had to admit that he had a good point. Wahid drove on and soon we were heading west on the coast road along Jumeirah Beach, with the desert to our left and the water to our right. The distinctive shape of our hotel became visible in the distance ahead.

The Burj Al Arab occupies its own private island a quarter-mile offshore, sitting like a great yacht poised upon the waters of the Gulf. The landward side of the skyscraper is built in the form of a giant parabolic section so that the hotel mimics the shape of a sail as seen from the side—a frozen sloop forever tacking out to sea. It is the tallest hotel in the world and very likely the most expensive.

In any new operational environment the thing to do is get oriented early. Firstly, study the maps, as I had done during the flight. Then get a local to show you the lay of the land, which is why I had booked a limousine rather than relying on a cab: taxis are always in a hurry, but limo drivers have the time to take you around. Lastly, get up as high as you can to a point where you can look down on the entire area and match the physical reality with the maps in your head, noting topography, landmarks, navigational points, extraction routes, and so on. This was the reason I had chosen the Burj al Arab: from our suite two-thirds of the way up—a duplex the cost of which was certain to send Dortmund into a fit—we had a good view of not just Dubai in general but the Emirates International Marina in particular. I could keep watch from there and see when the *Speed Graphic* showed up.

But the best view of all was from the bar located on the top floor, so that was where we went as soon as we had settled in.

We took a sofa and chair by the windows and ordered. I looked out over the coastline to the northeast. There was another hotel nearby but far below us, this one built in the form of a wave. Perhaps being surrounded by so much flat land had led to a local reaction against rectilinearity. Like the Burj Al Arab it had its own private dock facilities, and like ours there were several large motor yachts secured alongside, as if there was a billionaires' convention taking place. I used the binoculars to scan them. No one on deck, unsurprising in the heat. Most flags hung limp in the stagnant air. The few whose registrations I could make out were all from Gulf states: Bahrain, Qatar, Saudi Arabia. Past the hotel was more coastline and more beach, but the city beyond was mostly obscured in heat haze. I could just make out what I knew to be the Emirates International Marina. No sign of the *Speed Graphic*, which was unsurprising: it was a 4,000-mile cruise through Suez, and she would take another day at least.

Our gin and tonics arrived, and I put the binoculars aside. We drank deeply, the way you do with the first drink after a long journey. Miranda sat back on the sofa, glass cupped in her hands, looking at me.

"What do you think?" I asked.

"I think you're agitated."

It was true. The steady beat that is always there had become irregular as soon as we landed. It is not a heartbeat; I do not know what it is. Something atavistic. Occasionally I would find myself unconsciously working in time with it, walking at the same pace or tapping my finger against the trigger guard or even grinding my teeth—not gnashing, just a gentle rhythmical movement that matched the time. I had noticed this last years ago because when taking deliberate aim with an M-16 your jaw rests against the stock, and I had wondered what was making my sights jitter slightly. The beat speeds up and slows down, according to circumstance. You would think that action would cause irregularity, but not so. Faster, yes; but if you are fully prepped then going into action is just fine, even pleasurable. Fighting an action is a balancing act: a set of continuously shifting circumstances that you must assess and react to fast enough and accurately enough to emerge unscathed on the other side. Surfers understand: it is like riding a wave.

Irregularity is just the opposite: an unsettling loss of mental acuity; a condition I usually associate with inaction. Something is not right but you are missing it, and the beat acts as a warning, an alert system built into the genes perhaps. I was feeling it now, that lack of clarity: jumpy, insistent, awkward, irritating—a bad song that keeps playing in your head.

I had not been aware that variations in the beat were visible, and Miranda's comment caught me by surprise.

"I meant what do you think about Dubai?"

She shrugged her shoulders in acceptance and then looked around, as if deciding to judge the place from the bar decor.

"Immense wealth, obviously. But vulgar and fake."

"Vulgar and fake?"

"Snow in the Persian Gulf?"

"I get your point."

"Not to mention the restaurant."

We had decided to dine this evening at the hotel's seafood restaurant, located underwater and accessed by the hotel's "submarine," which was another fake: just a dressed-up elevator ride.

"There is a little of Las Vegas in Dubai," I admitted.

"But I mean more than that. Take that new tower, for example. If the world's tallest building was in New York or Tokyo or Hong Kong you would understand: land is at a premium, and the obvious way to go is up. But here? Dubai is a small city surrounded by vast tracts of land, all but unoccupied. There is no rationale behind building the world's tallest building here, just hubris."

"The architectural equivalent of a jewel-encrusted Rolex?"

"Yes, exactly. Very *nouveaux riches*. The 'souks' too: they're nothing but shopping malls. And did you see the women going in and out of them?"

"There was nothing to see: they were all buttoned up in black robes."

"Which is precisely what I mean: women are still chattel here. Well-cared-for chattel perhaps, but chattel just the same. All this modernity is fake: the Middle East is medieval. And in Dubai they even import their own peasantry."

One of the peasants came to our table and asked if we would like a second round. I declined; it was time to go catch our submarine.

THE EMIRATES INTERNATIONAL MARINA was busy. As with the smaller hotel marinas we had seen earlier, there were many large private vessels alongside: megayachts, in the terminology of the wealthy. The dockmaster's office was a polyglot frenzy, awash with crew members and shore workers organizing berthing arrangements or fueling times or potable water and so on. I checked the noticeboard while waiting for someone to free up: there was a weather forecast (hot and humid, cloudless and windless: it was probably unchanged for weeks), tidal information, times of sunrise and sunset. A few Notices to Mariners warning of navigation buoys undergoing repair or lights temporarily out of service. Advertisements for providores and chandlers and maintenance facilities. A dive shop's business card was tucked into one corner.

A woman behind the counter asked me what I wanted. She wore a lapel pin with the Greek flag, another with the Union Jack: symbols of the languages she spoke, a useful thing here. She was harassed, which was good: she would give me what I wanted quickly, without questions.

"When is the *Speed Graphic* due in?"

Her brow furrowed. "*Speed Graphic?*"

"Yes."

She quickly checked a clipboard.

"She's not due in again."

"Again?"

"She left early yesterday."

"Are you telling me that she has already been and gone?"

"Yes, certainly."

"You're sure you have the right yacht: *Speed Graphic*?"

"Of course. She's a most distinctive vessel; I have never seen anything like it."

"How long was she here?"

"Just long enough to take on fuel and stores. In one day, out the next morning."

"Do you have her next port of call?"

The question irritated her—she wanted to get to the other people waiting—but she must have realized that it would be faster to get rid of me by just going and looking it up. She went to a computer and quickly tapped a few keys.

"I do not have her next port. We have been told to forward everything to the home address of her owner, but I cannot give it to you."

I thanked her and left the office.

I had underestimated the *Speed Graphic*'s rate of advance: she must have made seven hundred miles a day. In the cab on the way back to the hotel I did the mental calculation: thirty knots at least; maybe thirty-five, taking into account what would have been the restricted speed of the Suez passage. That is more than most ships can go flat out, let alone cruise at, but given that I knew the *Speed Graphic* had been built specifically to go fast. failing to guess that she could sustain an unusually high cruising speed was not good. She must have left Dubai as we were flying across the Gulf toward it.

Dumb error, very dumb.

I had lost the edge. You have to stay in training to remain sharp; I was out of practice. In force recon they would have recognized me for what I was now: an operational liability. I would have been sent me back to a regular unit. Or worse, a staff job.

After returning to the hotel, I found Miranda by the pool. I explained the facts to her. After all the effort and risk we had taken, I expected Miranda to be at least frustrated, if not outright annoyed. But I should have known by now how unpredictable she was.

"No problem," she said evenly. "I can find the *Speed Graphic*."

"No."

I had already made it clear that taking up Kadri's invitation was not an option, but she shook her head with a smile.

"I don't mean me."

"Then what?"

She took off her sunglasses, put aside her book, and stood.

"I'm going for a swim," she said. "Meanwhile, why don't you see if you can find me a helicopter?"

XXVI

G ULF & DESERT AERIAL SERVICES normally operate their
helicopter tours out of Dubai Airport, but when I revealed that
we were staying at the Burj Al Arab they offered to pick us up
directly from the hotel.

The helipad at the Burj Al Arab is a large spaceport-like disk
projecting from the building about six hundred feet aloft, a sort of
oversized crow's nest on the hotel's mast-and-sail structure. The
helicopter arrived on time. It was one of the many variants on the
basic Bell JetRanger design: light and nimble, single-engined, skids
instead of landing gear. There was seating for six including the pilot,
which meant that Miranda and I could have sat together, but as with
the *Speed Graphic*'s helicopter she rode up front with the pilot
instead.

The seating arrangements had been agreed to ahead of time and
so the pilot showed no surprise at her getting in beside him, but he
looked her over carefully, the way someone does when they are on
their guard.

After booking the helicopter I had asked the operator to have the pilot call back to arrange the details of the itinerary. When he did so thirty minutes later, I had put him on hold and gone down to the pool.

"We have a helicopter for two hours this afternoon," I told Miranda. "Here is the pilot."

She had taken the handset and put it on speakerphone. *My name is Miranda Grey*, she had informed him. *What sort of navigational equipment do you carry?* A long silence had followed this first question: it was not something that customers normally asked. At that point the pilot must have realized that it was going to be something other than a routine tourist charter.

Miranda strapped herself into the harness with the ease of someone used to the task. The pilot handed her a headset. When they had communications he passed her an aeronautical chart and what looked like a thigh holster. This turned out to be pretty much what it was: Miranda folded the chart to fit the plastic holder and then secured the straps around her leg, so that the map was on top, face up, and more or less flat.

All I got were binoculars, more powerful than my own pair. The pilot throttled up and we lifted off. Normally the tours take in the desert and the coastline; we headed straight out to sea instead. Soon the land was far behind us. Miranda and the pilot conversed over the intercom, and after a while Miranda began fiddling with the cockpit controls.

I assumed that the device she was manipulating was the "Collins 60 Alpha" that had been the pilot's bemused answer to her second question *What sort of ADF?* This was how Miranda thought we would find the *Speed Graphic*. Before the flight she had explained to me that—notwithstanding the advent of GPS—commercial air traffic continues to navigate by radio beacons. There are two basic types of beacon: VOR and the older NDB. The V in VOR stands for Very High Frequency, which as I already knew was line-of-sight only. This is fine for jetliners at 35,000 feet, where the line of sight extends for hundreds of miles, but helicopters operate at far lower altitudes, typically not much above 1,000 feet. Navigating over land is difficult enough, but for a helicopter trying to locate a moving ship in the middle of the featureless sea some longer-range beacon is required. Thus NDBs—non-directional beacons—which operate at Low Frequency, where the radio waves bounce off the ionosphere and so have much longer range.

The *Speed Graphic* was fitted with an NDB. Miranda had discovered this on the flight back to Monaco during which the pilot had tuned his ADF—automatic direction finding—to the yacht's NDB beacon so that he could find his way back. At the time, Miranda had noted the two features necessary for finding an NDB: the frequency and the three-letter Morse identification code. She guessed that the *Speed Graphic* probably never turned the beacon off because of the potentially catastrophic consequences of forgetting to turn it back on again when the aircraft was away. She probably transmitted on it twenty-four hours a day. Miranda was betting that we could pick it up.

The helicopter's ADF was a long black box on whose small square face were dials and a digital readout. Miranda tuned to the frequency: 307.5 kHz. Then she turned up the audio volume, and soon we heard a beacon's Morse transmission:

short-short-short long-long-short long-short-short-long

I knew Morse and did not need the decoder to figure it out—Sierra-Golf-Xray: the *Speed Graphic*'s call sign. A yellow needle on the compass card came alive, pointing to the yacht's position somewhere out way beyond our line of sight. Miranda had found her.

Not quite. Miranda had found the *Speed Graphic*'s direction but not her precise location—for that both direction and range were required. There is a navigational technique for achieving this, a sort of on-the-run triangulation whose math Miranda had explained to me on one of the hotel's notepads while we were waiting for the helicopter to arrive. The pilot turned beam-on to the signal and then transited at a steady 110 knots across the track. Miranda carefully noted elapsed time while the pilot monitored the angular change in the beacon's bearing. When this last had changed ten degrees they did the calculation:

$$\textit{Distance = Ground speed/60 x (Elapsed time in seconds)/ Angular change in degrees}$$

It took ninety-eight seconds. The *Speed Graphic* was therefore eighteen nautical miles away—a little over twenty statute miles. Miranda quickly applied the fix to the chart. She and the pilot discussed it. I could tell by the way the pilot shook his head that something was up. Eventually Miranda removed her headset and turned to face me.

"The *Speed Graphic* is near an island," she said. "The island is owned by some Arab bigshots, and the airspace above it is restricted. The pilot won't go there. He won't even ask for clearance because he knows that there's no chance of getting it."

"Ask him to keep doing these traversing runs so that at least we can fix her position as accurately as possible. And if the position doesn't change then we'll know that she is probably at anchor or secured alongside."

Miranda nodded and reverted to the headset. The pilot must have agreed: we did several more runs, extending more than just ten degrees so that we could get more accurate fixes. Eventually the fuel remaining was down to the point where we had to return.

The helicopter dropped us back at the hotel. Dortmund was not going to like the charter bill, but it was money well spent: now we not only knew where the *Speed Graphic* was, we also knew that she was not moving.

XXVII

S EAL DIVING WAS THE NAME OF the outfit on the business card that I had seen tucked into the dock office's noticeboard. *Seal* is a reasonable name for a dive shop, since those animals are so at home in the water. But I had noted at the time that all the letters in the word SEAL were capitalized, but not so in *Diving*, and had guessed that the name had nothing to do with marine mammals.

The shop was over on the Deira side of the city, in a district known as Al Rass, located on a spit of land formed by a sharp bend in the Dubai Creek. This must have been the original part of town, probably first settled because the narrow neck of the spit was easily defensible against marauding desert nomads. The area retained its original character: whitewashed stucco buildings, narrow winding alleys, arched arcades and linen canopies to allay the relentless sun: a tiny piece of real Arabia hidden away amid the towers of modern Dubai. And here at last was a genuine souk: the spice market, an open-air collection of robed vendors sitting cross-legged on carpets or low stools, smoking quietly, some chatting or drinking coffee.

They were surrounded by burlap sacks of spices whose sides had been carefully rolled down to reveal the contents. I recognized some by sight, some by smell—ground cumin, tamarind pods, yellow-orange turmeric so bright that it almost glowed—but most of them were a mystery to me and would remain so since all the signs were in Arabic.

No street numbers, no street names even. I had to ask the merchants, making diving and breaststroking gestures to indicate what I sought. This raised a few laughs, but it got the message across: they gave me voluble directions, not a word of which I could understand, but I followed the way they pointed.

Eventually, I found it. Handpainted sign. There was a wetsuit hanging out front to dry, still dripping. I pushed past it into SEAL Diving.

It took me a moment to adjust to the sudden transition from sunlight into shade. There was no artificial lighting; the place relied on what filtered through from outside. No air-conditioning, either. The room was large but low. No counter, nor the cash register that you would expect in a real shop, but there was a lot of equipment laid out in an orderly fashion: wetsuits, fins, masks, weight belts, bottles, regulators, and so on.

The place was unoccupied but there was an archway leading to a back room from inside of which I could hear activity. I went on through.

The second room was smaller than the first. It was also darker, despite the presence of a genie-style oil lamp burning away on a small pedestal. The floor was laid with an Oriental rug. There was a wooden desk to one side, covered in paperwork. A telephone. One of those old credit card machines for making an impression on a preprinted form. The wall to the right was fitted with a whiteboard.

Spearguns stacked in the corner. A bunk bed in the rear. Some framed photographs and certificates on the far wall, but too deep in the shadows for me to make out any detail. A door leading out to the back.

There were two people in the room. In the middle, sitting on a low divan, was a man I took to be the proprietor: a lanky white guy, long hair pushed back and, like the wetsuit outside, still damp from the morning dive. He was wearing nothing but camouflage pants and dog tags. On the floor by him was a young bikini-clad girl. Beside her was a wide silver bowl filled with cool water, which she was using to wash the man's feet. The legs of his cammies had been rolled up to accommodate her.

Both of them looked up at me when I walked in, but neither showed much interest in what they saw. The guy was smoking a huge roll-your-own from whose pungent odor I took to be hashish, and so his indifference was probably pharmaceutically induced. But I was surprised by the girl: she was an Arab—black glossy hair, smooth olive skin; to be seen by strangers as she was dressed would be a cause for trouble.

"We're closed," the guy said.

"Not when I walked in."

"Front door's that way." He pointed languidly. "May Allah go with you."

"Allah and I haven't been on speaking terms for some time now."

"I never ask a third time."

Clear diction, no wavering—hashish or not, he was fully with it.

I ignored him and walked over to the whiteboard. Until then I had my doubts; anyone can use the word SEAL—it is not as if the navy has it trademarked, and so far this guy had not seemed the type—but when I saw what was written on that whiteboard I could not help smiling.

"Magruder," I said, remembering the name.

"What?"

"The person who taught you how to make a dive plan: Chief Petty Officer Magruder."

Magruder had been my instructor at the Combat Diver Supervisor's course. He was a stickler for pre-dive preps, insisting that we do it precisely his way, and no variations. The plan on the whiteboard was laid out in exactly the format he demanded, a complex arrangement that could not have been a coincidence.

I turned around. His free hand was still hidden from me on the blindside.

"KA-BAR?"

He smiled and shook his head, but that hand stayed where it was. He took a big draw on the hashish and let out a slow stream of smoke. The stuff smelled like the spice market might have if someone napalmed it.

"You were never in the team," he said after a while.

"Not yours."

It took him a while to figure it out.

"Jarhead," he said at last. "Recon jarhead."

I nodded.

"I hate marines." No inflection, just a bald statement of plain truth, but that hand was still hidden from me. "Don't tell me you were an officer."

"I was an officer."

"I hate officers, too."

Well, we were just not hitting it off.

"How do you feel about money?"

He paused before answering, as if giving the matter thoughtful consideration.

"According to the Prophet, riches come not from an abundance of worldly goods but a contented mind." He inhaled some contentment, then let the smoke out slowly, as if still thinking on it. "However, Confucius urged men to make their way in the world, and even Gandhi admitted that capital is not in itself evil."

Lucky for me this guy was so ecumenical. He said something in Arabic to the girl, who quietly took her bowl and left through the back door.

"What exactly is it that you want?"

"Gear for a dive."

"A dive where?"

"Dar Al Jawan."

"Can't dive there," he said flatly. "It's restricted."

"Yes," I agreed. "Hence the necessity of an underwater arrival."

He leaned forward, and for the first time his face showed something other than indifference.

"And so I take it that this would be something other than a recreational dive?"

"Definitely not recreational."

"More in the line of a *tactical* dive?"

"I think *tactical* would be an apt description."

He leaped up from the divan and came over, smiling with pleasure now. I had thought that revealing the nature of the dive would be the toughest part, the point at which he would likely refuse to have anything more to do with me, but it proved to be just the opposite. I should have guessed from the dog tags: he was a guy who could not let it go. Once some people get the taste, they just cannot get rid of it.

He put the hashish in an ashtray and offered his hand.

"Gulliver Hoyle," he said. "Everyone calls me Gus."

"Lysander Dalton," I responded. "Dalton will do."

We shook. I looked at the knife that had been hidden from me, and which Hoyle was still holding in his other hand. Fixed blade, clip point, partially serrated edge. The blade was powder coated, perhaps to make the surface non-reflective or maybe for protection against corrosion. I wished he would put the thing away. He noticed me eyeballing it.

"SOG knife," he explained. "Only you marines use KA-BARs."

He offered it to me for inspection. It was a fine weapon, well balanced, beautifully made. I handed it back.

"How long have you been out?"

"Four years," he said. "Left after doing my twenty. By that stage I was back in the real navy; too old for the team. Didn't like it much, was glad to go."

We have the same issue in force recon: there is no career path, and if you re-up for your twenty then eventually you have to go back to a regular unit. Lot of guys find it tough to do. Since my career path took a detour to Leavenworth I never had to face that particular problem.

"How did you end up in Dubai?"

"I like warm water."

"You serious?"

"I am. I did an SR into Petropavlovsk once." SR: special reconnaissance; that is, dives into opposition territory in which the aim is to gather intelligence while avoiding direct contact. For a SEAL doing an SR into the Russian's Pacific missile-submarine base, that probably meant getting up close to their big boomers, taking measurements and photographs, collecting small samples of their sound-absorbing anechoic surface coating, maybe putting a nick or two into the leading edge of a propeller blade, enough to make the submarine's acoustic signature individually identifiable. "It was a new year's eve. They chose new year's eve because all the Borises would be out celebrating. Even the duty crews get drunk in Russia on new year's eve. Good idea, right? But do you have any idea how cold the water is in Petropavlovsk on December 31st? That night, I decided that when I got out and started my own business, it would be someplace warm. Doesn't get much warmer than here in Dubai."

That much was certainly true; at the Burj Al Arab they refrigerated the pool water.

We went to the whiteboard. Hoyle erased it, then picked up a marker.

"Ready to begin?"

"Ready."

"Dive date?"

"Tonight." He gave me a look that meant *Why are you leaving the planning so late?* but he knew better than to ask outright. He wrote down the date, then beneath it the headings for high tide and low tide, moonrise and moonset, just the way Chief Petty Officer Magruder liked it.

"Number in the team?"

"Three," I said. "One in the boat, two on the dive."

"Okay, divers first. Who is the team leader?"

"Me." He wrote down my name. Last name only, no first names, no nicknames, no rank—Magruder would have been pleased.

"Weight?"

I told him.

"Height?"

I told him.

"Flipper size?"

"*Flipper* size?" Magruder would no longer have been pleased. If you call them *flippers* in combat diving school they send you on a two-mile beach run with full wetsuit and air bottles. But Hoyle just shrugged his shoulders.

"The tourists don't get it if I say fins. Masks, too: got to call them goggles."

I told him my fin size.

"Name of the other diver?"

"Grey."

"Weight?"

I told him. This time he paused before writing it down. "Midget?"

"Female."

"She tactically trained?"

"Not exactly."

A long pause, and then a slow look of understanding came to his face.

"She certified at all?

"Not exactly."

"She ever even dived?"

"No."

"This is crazy."

I shrugged my shoulders. "The lady insists."

"So stand up and say no."

"You haven't met this woman."

I could tell from his expression that my response had not improved his opinion of either marines or officers. He reluctantly wrote down Miranda's weight on the whiteboard.

"Equipment?"

"Closed-circuit."

But he shook his head in response. "Sorry, no rebreathers."

I had wanted closed-circuit apparatus not so much because they extend the dive time, which they do, but because rebreathers do not release bubbles and so are less likely to give away the presence of someone underwater. Rebreathers are standard in tactical work but not common in recreational diving, so I was not surprised that he did not have any.

"Okay, then: open circuit, mixed gas."

"One or two?" He meant Nitrox I or Nitrox II, the standard mixes.

"Neither," I said. "Forty-five percent oxygen."

Again he stopped writing, marker poised above the whiteboard. The more detail I was giving him, the less he was liking this dive.

Everyone has heard of decompression sickness—the bends—a condition due to nitrogen bubbles forming in the blood from spending too long underwater, or diving too deep, or returning too fast to the surface. Increasing the percentage of oxygen, and so reducing the percentage of nitrogen, lessens the likelihood of decompression sickness, and means you can dive for longer without the need for decompression stops. That is why I wanted Nitrox. But nothing is free in this life. it turns out that oxygen can be a problem as well. Too much in the central nervous system causes oxygen toxicity, a sudden onset of convulsions that unlike the bends comes without warning and is extremely dangerous. Standard air is 21% oxygen, the same as we breathe every day. Nitrox I is 32% oxygen, Nitrox II is 36%. Forty-five is very high. Increased oxygen increases the length of the dive, which was why I was opting for such a rich mixture, but it makes the risk of oxygen toxicity much greater.

Hoyle wrote EAN/45 on the board: Enriched Air Nitrox, 45% Oxygen.

"Max. actual depth?"

"Whatever the mixture dictates."

He nodded in understanding. Normally you work backward from the depth to get your mixture, but I was not diving down to anything, I just wanted to go a long way underwater. The maximum depth was a function of how much partial pressure of oxygen I was willing to take.

"So what's the max. PO2?"

"One four."

"I meant for the female."

"One four."

Far too high for a first dive, but he wrote it down without comment: 1.4 Bar, actually a measure of pressure rather than depth, but for a given mixture they are effectively the same.

"Contingency depth?"

"One six."

Contingency depth is for emergencies only. He shook his head in silent disapproval. We went through the calculations, working with the numerous variables—PO2: the partial pressure of oxygen; OTUs: oxygen tolerance units; CNS%: percentage of oxygen in the central nervous system; EAD: equivalent air depth—to develop a profile of the dive.

Increasing the percentage of oxygen increases the duration of a dive but reduces the depth, since more pressure means more oxygen seeping into your central nervous system. We calculated that the maximum actual depth on this dive would be seventy feet. Not especially deep, but that was fine: it was range I needed, not depth. But untrained divers have difficulty maintaining a steady depth, even in daylight. Miranda would be doing it for the first time in the dark. If she slipped below seventy feet, she was at risk of oxygen toxicity.

"You'll need oversized cylinders," he said.

Normal cylinders have ten-liters capacity; two were enough for a little over an hour only. It would not make sense to use a mixture designed for a longer dive without taking larger capacity tanks.

"What sort of blending do you have?"

"Partial pressure."

"Wait till I've gone," I said.

Mixed gases need special handling. There are several ways to do it, of which partial-pressure blending is the worst. Hoyle would have to mix the EAN/45 himself: start with a clean tank, then partially fill it with pure oxygen before adding the nitrogen. Pure oxygen is about as explosive as nitroglycerin; filling the tanks would likely be more dangerous than the dive itself.

We went through the rest of the equipment: wetsuits, dive boots, fins, masks, compensators, weights, knives, compass boards, combined watch and dive computers. At the bottom he wrote down the location of the primary and secondary decompression chambers, same as on any plan, but we both knew that it was for completeness only: if there was a problem, neither Miranda nor I would ever make it to a medical facility in time.

Finally, he asked what we wanted to use for a dive boat.

"I have a thirty-foot RHIB," he said. Rigid hull inflatable boats are pretty standard for dive work, but I wanted something with as small a profile as possible, something unlikely to be detected by radar.

"Got a Zodiac?" A Zodiac is a fifteen-foot inflatable fitted with an outboard that scoots over the surface of the sea. Combat Rubber

Raiding Craft is the formal title, but everyone knows them by the manufacturer's name.

"Sure. You'll need an extra gas can with the dive point out so far."

I nodded in agreement.

"Who's your boat guy?" he asked.

"You are," I replied.

A long pause.

He inserted the now extinguished roll-your-own into the side of his mouth and considered my response for an extended period in thoughtful silence, staring into space. Finally he removed the hashish and slowly nodded to himself.

"Hooyah," he said quietly.

"Hooyah," I agreed.

XXVIII

D AR AL JAWAN IS A PRIVATE ISLAND lying in the waters of the Persian Gulf, twenty miles north-northwest of Dubai. It is not large, just several dozen acres in total. Many charts do not show it, not because it is small but because until recently it did not exist—like the housing estates off the coast, the island is entirely manmade.

It has for its neighbors to the north three natural islands situated at the western end of the Strait of Hormuz: Tonb Al Kubra, Tonb Al Sughra, and Abu Musa. Their location makes them strategically important: they not only sit astride an oil field in their own right, their position also means that whoever possesses them can close shipping through the Strait at will. Twenty percent of the planet's oil production passes through the Strait of Hormuz every day. The islands are like the fingers of a gigantic handheld around the throat of the world, ready to choke at leisure.

Ownership of these three islands is disputed between Iran and the United Arab Emirates. Iran settled the matter to its own satisfaction by militarily occupying them. They then went one step better, declaring a twelve-mile territorial limit around the islands, thus claiming for themselves almost the entire waterway. No one but the Iranians recognizes this.

To register their disagreement the UAE allowed the island of Dar Al Jawan to be built, nominally under their sovereignty and not far from Abu Musa, the southernmost of the islands occupied by Iran. The Persian Gulf is shallow, but even so construction of the island was a significant civil engineering achievement. It is not big, but it is big enough to make the point. Nevertheless, the sheiks did not want to unnecessarily antagonize the ayatollahs and so they made it clear from the start that there would be no military base on the new island, just private security personnel. They set a restricted zone over the surrounding water and in the airspace above to reduce the chances of an accidental provocation—in any hot war the heavily armed and aggressive Iran would likely overwhelm the Emirates' defenses.

"What do they do there?" I asked.

We were in the Zodiac, running down the Dubai Creek toward the open waters of the gulf. There is a speed restriction on the creek, so we were going slowly with the motor barely above idle, and conversation was still possible.

"Part of the arrangement is that the investment group who built the island occupies it tax-free. They have to provide all the services themselves: infrastructure, utilities, security. Fresh water, too: they supposedly make it with big evaporators. In return, they are allowed to nominate the island, which has a special legal status, as the headquarters of their investment operations. No taxes and no oversight either—they are exempted from all legal requirements for inspection of their books and banking records, including those under international treaty obligations."

"Who are the investors?"

"No one really knows. The sheiks for sure: they would not have allowed it to be built without having a finger in the pie. Strange to say, it's rumored to include Iranian money, too. Seems weird at first, but it makes sense when you think about it: the Iranians are always looking for ways to invest all those petrodollars without international scrutiny, since technically the U.S. capital markets are closed to them. And from the Emirates' point of view, including Iranian investors is a good way of keeping the peace. Iran and the Emirates already share revenue from the Mubarak oil field up there, so there's a precedent for cooperation, despite the territorial dispute."

The sun had just dipped below the horizon and the city was beginning to light up. Dubai comes alive at night, when the heat subsides.

"What do they actually do on the island?"

"They supposedly built a palace."

"A palace for whom?"

"Themselves. Their friends. It's a sort of private club, a retreat for megarich Arabs to go and let their hair down. Since it's restricted there's no chance of the public getting a glimpse. No offending Islamic sensibilities; no arousing a resentful populace. No paparazzi either—they can do whatever they want without any kind of scrutiny."

"What's it like?"

"I have no idea. There are no reliable maps of the island. As far as I know it has never been photographed. There's a lot of foliage, they say. The rooftops are all gardened and the pathways are covered in canopies of trees so that even the satellites can't see what's going on."

"Any rumors?"

"Plenty. Too many, really—you don't know what to believe."

"Does the name mean anything?"

"*Dar* means a gathering place, like a market or a fair. *Jawan* means a pearl. Around here they have as many words for pearls as Eskimos have for snow—*juman, hasbah, lulu, dana, gumashah, hussah.* Each means something subtly different; for example, *khardil* means a black pearl, but a really good black pearl is called *sinjabaasi.*"

"What sort of pearl is a *jawan*?"

"That's reserved for the finest of all. Perfectly round, young and unblemished. The color must be white but with a faint rose tint, pure and full of luster."

We emerged from the Creek. Either side of us rose towering oil rigs, appropriate symbols for the seaward entrance to Dubai. Miranda stripped off her shirt and jeans to the more practical bikini she wore underneath. Cooler for her, more scenic for Hoyle, who could not help looking, or perhaps he was just trying to figure out how someone so tall could weigh so little. I made sure she had a tight grip with both hands on the ropes secured to the inflatable's sides, then gave a nod to Hoyle. He opened up the throttle and the Zodiac leaped up onto the plane.

Traveling at full throttle in a Zodiac across open ocean is like riding a bronco at a rodeo: in both cases the aim is to not get tossed off. The Gulf that night was not particularly rough but the breeze that comes in every evening as the land begins to cool was enough to set up a good chop. We went bouncing across the disturbed water, soon soaked in spray, holding on hard, all conversation at an end.

Apart from a red band low to the west it was dark now; sunsets are rapid in these latitudes. No navigation lights; no light at all apart from the glow of Dubai behind us and the illuminated screen of the handheld GPS with which I was navigating us to the dive point.

We reached the position. Dubai was below the horizon now; we could not see the lights themselves but the loom from the nocturnal city lit up the sky above it. Hoyle cut the motor. We drifted to a stop, listening. No sound of any patrol craft, and nothing at all visible in the direction of the island, although it was not far away. I undid the cargo netting which had secured our dive gear during the ride and also served to camouflage the equipment from any curious eyes on shore during the run down the Creek.

We suited up in the soft green glow of a chemical light stick: a flashlight would have been visible from miles away, but the faint illumination from a light stick lying in the bottom of the boat was unlikely to be seen beyond a hundred yards. It took a long time to fully suit up: Miranda was still unused to the gear, despite the quick instructional dive that I had taken her on at the hotel's beach while Hoyle was mixing the Nitrox. We had used normal air this afternoon, black tanks. Now the bottles were bright yellow with a thick green band near the top: Nitrox. They were larger, too: twin 15-liter, 300-bar cylinders which if all went well would be enough to get us out and back again. Surprisingly, the tanks were not much heavier than our 10-liter tanks this afternoon; they were made from an aluminum composite rather than steel, expensive technical gear.

I applied face black to both Miranda and myself then took a last fix with the GPS, giving us an updated range and bearing of the island. Unchanged, we were not drifting much—tide and current are weak in the Persian Gulf. I applied the variation correction, converting the GPS's true heading to the magnetic course that we would follow underwater, and marked it with a grease pencil on the compass board. Fins over the booties, and a last clean of the masks with spit and seawater.

We went onto the Nitrox. I made Miranda turn around and carefully checked her valves and buoyancy compensator. All clear. I turned her back to face me and checked the rest of her equipment: mouthpiece and regulator, diving light, a waterproof pack like mine, one of which would hopefully soon contain Senator Stolper's notebook. Lastly I attached the tether, fifteen feet of webbing running from my equipment belt to hers, then initialized the wrist computer.

We set ourselves on the side of the Zodiac, backs to the water. I gave her an interrogatory thumbs-up and received a confirming thumbs-up in return. I began the timing signal with three fingers, two, one, and on zero we both rolled backward into the sea.

Usually entering seawater is refreshing but rolling into the Persian Gulf was like falling into a warm bath. Inky blackness, absolutely no visibility at all. I was used to it, but I had warned Miranda that the first time it would be alarmingly disorienting—she was to ignore it and follow the plan. We both had compass boards: flat surfaces that you hold in front of you with both hands while propelling with the legs, much like small children use when learning to swim, except that compass boards are less buoyant. They have built-in instruments with luminescent markings, including a compass rose and a depth gauge: the two essential elements in a night dive.

I oriented myself to face the correct compass heading and switched on the diving light, pointing directly astern. A small wait while Miranda got herself into position, then her answering flash from behind me: we were ready to go. I turned off the light and began swimming slowly, allowing the tether to stretch and the weight to come on. The strain released: she was following.

We were at fifteen feet, quite shallow, but there was no need for us to go deeper. I maintained the heading and worked on keeping the depth as constant as possible, but I could tell from the periodic down pull on the tether that Miranda tended to sink. I wondered if it was disorientation, or if I had just put in too much weight, making her negatively buoyant. It did not matter: as long as I kept her on that tether there was no risk of her going too deep.

We had gone for half an hour or so when I first heard the engine. I had anticipated it and briefed Miranda that we would likely come across a patrol boat conducting a security sweep. The engine noise was deeper than I had expected, diesel rather than outboard: the patrol boat must have been a fair-sized vessel. It was too bad that we did not have rebreathing apparatus, but in the surface chop there was little chance of them noticing our bubbles. For good order I slowly dropped us down to forty feet, hopefully beyond the penetration of any hull-mounted lights they might have.

The sound grew louder and deeper as the boat approached. Water distorts sound, and so what on top was probably just a loud rumble sounded to us down here like the earth was opening up. The direction of the sound was unchanging, meaning that the vessel was headed right for us. Soon it seemed as if the sound was everywhere, a deep ethereal bass all around us. It was incredibly loud, unnaturally so, and I briefly wondered if I was undergoing some sort of diving narcosis. Then I figured it out.

It was no patrol boat; it was a sea-going ship. And in the Persian Gulf what would that be but an oiler? We were about to be run down by a supertanker.

It was a stupid mistake. I had discounted the possibility of commercial traffic because of the restricted zone. A restricted zone would be effective in keeping out sightseers and recreational traffic, but supertankers play by their own rules: they are the largest things afloat, and if one wanted to steam through a restricted zone it would simply do so. To stop it would be impossible: supertankers take miles just to turn and half an hour to stop—the ship would be through before it could ever come to a halt.

The mistake was doubly bad: I had not briefed Miranda. Her second-ever dive, and first night dive: what would be her reaction when several hundred thousand tons of supertanker came barreling down upon us? Panic, I presumed, and there was no way to reassure her. If I had figured it out sooner there might have been time to surface and use her navigation lights to swim out of the path, but now with her almost upon us there was no way to judge the precise course and no time to swim away even if we could. There was no practical place to go but down.

I began the descent, formulating a plan on the way. If we were lucky she would be a Panamax—that is, a vessel built to transit the Panama Canal. I tried to recall the dimensions: maximum deadweight something like 100,000 tons, I thought, and maximum draught of forty feet: around the same size as the *Theodore Roosevelt*. If she was a Panamax we could get under her: at seventy feet she would pass far enough above us that we might not get sucked into the screw. If we were less lucky she would be a Suezmax: too big to transit the Panama Canal but small enough to pass through Suez: 150,000 tons. Fifty-something feet draught—I could not remember exactly. Ninety feet was our contingency depth—the depth you can go down to briefly in an emergency. Being run down by a supertanker qualified as an emergency.

But if we were unlucky she would be a Capemax: too big to transit either canal, a vessel condemned to roam the world's oceans via Cape Horn and the Cape of Good Hope. She could be any size then: a VLCC, very large crude carrier, or worse still a ULCC: ultra-large crude carrier: a ship greater than 300,000 tons deadweight. ULCCs run up and down the Gulf regularly. The largest of them all, the *Knock Nevis*, was moored not far away in Qatar doing duty as a transshipment station. She displaced more than five *Theodore Roosevelt*s and had a draught approaching a hundred feet.

Simple choice then: die in the screw or die of oxygen toxicity trying to avoid it.

But a Capemax would be unlikely to pick this patch of water to transit through: it was too shallow. They would go through the regular shipping channel, north of Abu Musa, where the water was deeper. So she was likely either a Suezmax or a Panamax. I decided to go to the contingency depth.

The sound became all-consuming now, no longer just noise but a palpable physical presence. The pressure grew as we descended and the steady thudding of her propulsion became ever heavier. I was aiming for seventy feet, but we never made it.

All vessels making way have a pressure wave in front of them, caused by the fact of the hull pushing a gap into the sea. I had seen the effect of this back in my marine days, during endless replenishments from supply ships steaming alongside our LPH or LPD, and the great difficulty the two vessels had in steering a steady course with their twin pressure waves trying to push their bows apart. But I had never guessed what it was like underwater.

It hit us like a breaker crashing upon the shore. We lost all control, flung down and further down, twisting and turning in the turbulent water as the huge hull came overhead, the tether threatening to become an entangling snare. We hit the bottom of the Gulf, a soft thud into the sandy seafloor. Then we were immediately sucked back up again: behind any pressure wave there must be a corresponding rarefaction—a lowering of pressure—and as the great ship passed blindly above the low pressure amidships drew us back up, less turbulent but still impossible to fight against, and threatening to suck us into the screw. Then a noise far greater than before, not just noise but a singing sound, for the faint resonant note of the individual propeller blades was briefly audible to me, pure and music-like. It passed by overhead. How far? Fifteen feet? Five inches? I had no idea. The churning water caught us and we were engulfed in a mass of conflicting vortices and currents, tossed around and totally disoriented.

Slowly, it died away. We surfaced. I ripped off the mask and regulator, sucking in air and gazing upward, hoping to get an identification, but all I saw was the vast anonymous bulk of the supertanker rising high above, rapidly retreating, leaving behind her the long wake in which we now floated. She was definitely an oil tanker: I could smell the characteristic sour sulfur odor of her cargo. I swam over to Miranda, expecting her to be the worse for wear, but when I turned on the flashlight I found that not only was her mask still secure, she was still breathing Nitrox, apparently prepared to continue the dive. I gently removed her mouthpiece, and she breathed freely.

I asked her if she was okay but she could only nod, grateful to be sucking in big lungfuls of now blissfully unrestricted air.

"What was that?" she finally gasped.

"Supertanker trying to make up time."

"Make up time?"

"She cut the corner of the restricted zone and was heading directly up to the Strait instead of taking the shipping lanes further north. And she was steaming very fast, much faster than she would normally transit, hence that massive pressure wave."

"Did we hit bottom?"

"We did."

"Isn't that dangerous?"

"Yes, very."

"I mean, isn't it deeper than we were allowed to go?"

"It is, but I think that we'll be okay. It all happened so fast that the increase in partial pressure was too short for the oxygen that would have poisoned us to transfer into the central nervous system. It's a biological process; it takes a little time. We were down and back in just a few seconds."

"So what now?"

"All my calculations are shot to pieces—we can't dive anymore. Feel like a surface swim?"

It was clear from her reaction that Miranda would rather do just about anything other than dive again: her introduction to the activity had not been a good one. We unstrapped and dumped the gear. Normally you would try to jerry-rig a buoy so that the equipment could be recovered, but if a patrol came across a marker floating out here in the restricted zone they would not ignore it. No matter: Dortmund would pick up the tab.

I found the correct compass heading, and we began swimming.

XXIX

M IRANDA AND I STRUGGLED ASHORE onto a smooth semicircle of beach. We stopped to rest, grateful for solid ground beneath us at last. The soft chalk-white sand was a silver crescent in the moonlight. It was not the coarse brown stuff of the desert; this sand must have been imported. The beachfront was lined with palm trees but these were not the stolid and ubiquitous date palms of the Middle East. They were royal palms, elegant and slender, tall trees of the type that line the regal boulevards of Beverly Hills. Another import, and given the age of the island they must have been purchased fully grown. Whoever built this place had wanted it to be picture-perfect and had possessed the bank balance to make it so.

I checked my watch. Still ticking; it had survived worse than being run down by a supertanker. The luminous hands told me now what they had told me so often in the past: *You are taking too long.* I had expected it—surface swimming is slower than underwater, and it figured that we would be behind schedule by now.

The beach was empty apart from some gulls who knew nothing of restricted zones. They stood one-legged, still asleep, unaware of us or perhaps just uncaring. The only sounds were the soft lapping of the gulf and a little breeze rustling among the fronds high above. I walked up past the tide line to where the sand was dry and easy to dig. Directly seaward of the sixth palm tree, positioned so that we could easily relocate it, I dug a shallow trench with the compass board. I threw my own gear into it and went back down to collect Miranda's. She had discarded the mask and fins, but unlike me she had taken off the wetsuit as well, leaving her barefoot and bikini-clad. The only equipment she retained was her knife, secured in a scabbard strapped to her calf. She made an arresting sight in the moonlight.

"It's hot, and since we don't have the diving gear anymore...," she explained.

True, although she would regret the loss of buoyancy that suit provided if there was no time to put it back on for the extraction. But in the end it did not matter—since we could no longer dive, if it was a hot extraction they would probably shoot us in the water anyway.

I took her gear and buried it with my own.

BEYOND THE PALM TREES WAS a strip of lawn bordered by a tall hedge. We found a gap and passed through. On the other side was a garden, although *garden* is too general a term to describe the luxuriant paradise we had entered. Dar Al Jawan was as Hoyle had heard, an island dense with greenery. The layout was vaguely Moorish, as if the designer had taken inspiration from the Alhambra, but here the plant life was much more abundant: a complex maze of glades and dells, courts and grottoes, each separated from the others by sometimes flora—stands of cypress, hedges of myrtle—and sometimes by masonry: walls and arcades, portals and arches. The architectural elements were in the Arabic style: delicately filigreed grilles, horseshoe-shaped arches, and everywhere were pools and fountains whose gentle burble was a constant and soothing background presence.

The place was lit not with security floodlights but gas lamps whose flickering illumination cast everything in a golden glow. Wherever there is oil there is gas as well, and being right on top of an oil field they probably had more here than they knew what to do with, but it made an unusual choice for lighting. I recognized some of the plants: almond and peach trees, hyacinth, chrysanthemums; many roses. Others were identifiable by smell alone: orange trees and lemon verbena, and the jasmine was obvious, but it took me a moment to figure out what the pungent odor was coming from a sparse tree to which was attached a small bucket, collecting the sap as you might see in Vermont. But this tree was no sugar maple, and as we paused by it the rich licorice-like smell from the bucket was overpowering.

"What is it?" Miranda whispered.

"Myrrh, I think."

We moved slowly, avoiding the paths. I had seen no security cameras but feared they might have infrared detectors. Then I saw movement up ahead. It turned out to be a peacock, or rather an insomniac peahen, poking around with that strange sideways glancing motion they have. No sign of the cock, perhaps they'd had a fight. In any case I was glad to have come across the peahen: it would be hard to calibrate infrared detectors to pick up people but miss a bird that big. It also meant they probably had no dogs. We moved a little faster now, finally emerging through an arched portal onto a small promontory, maybe thirty feet above the sea and clear of the garden.

We had arrived at the harbor. It was *U*-shaped, and we were standing on one side at the outermost point. On the other arm, across the water from us and further down the harbor, lay the *Speed Graphic*, secured alongside, quiet and dark, but somewhere in the shadows of those masts was the small navigational beacon whose forgotten presence had given her location away. There were several other vessels, all smaller than her, including a pair of cruisers painted gray and outfitted with searchlights and hard points for the mounting of machine guns: patrol boats of the type that I had expected us to encounter tonight. Most of the docks were empty.

Dominating the scene was not the *Speed Graphic* but what lay at the end of the harbor. It was the palace, at least I presumed it was, although Hanging Garden of Babylon might have been a better description. Unlike the park the palace was floodlit. It was built in tiers, random rather than symmetrical, some set back, others overhanging those below. Glowing marble everywhere: walls, arches, vaults, columns, and masses of greenery: trees on the terraces, vines climbing the walls, patios with fountains and formal gardens. But the strangest thing of all was at the very center. At the base of the *U* there were broad marble stairs leading directly from the water up to a wide forecourt. It was open on the seaward side but enclosed on the other three by the bulk of the palace so that it formed an oversized niche built into the structure. There, sitting in the middle of this vast space, its diameter not much smaller than that of the plaza itself, was a gigantic pearl.

I counted the stories of the surrounding tiers: fifteen in all, so the pearl was well over a hundred feet in diameter. Presumably it was secured but even so you would not want to be around during an earth tremor: the thing must have weighed hundreds of tons. Now I knew how the island had been named: the sphere emulated not just the shape of a *jawan* but also its color: it was covered in a glossy coating of deeply lustrous, rose-hued white tiles.

The thing sat there icon-like, as if an object of veneration in some ancient and abandoned temple, the worshippers from which had been wiped out long ago. Not quite abandoned: an armed guard suddenly appeared from a door giving onto the plaza. Beside me, Miranda stiffened with apprehension, but I could tell right away that there was nothing to worry about: the guard was alone and he strolled across the forecourt with the bored gait of guards everywhere.

I inspected him through the binoculars. Fair-haired, not an Arab. The uniform was western-style and too warm for this climate. He was armed not with that ubiquitous weapon of the Middle East, the AK-47, but with its replacement, the AK-74: basically an AK-47 rechambered from 7.62 down to 5.45 caliber, and distinguishable by the longer muzzle brake and black plastic furniture (AK-47s use wood). The weapon was adopted by the Russian military in the mid-'Seventies following our own change to smaller caliber assault weapons a decade earlier, and they had taken advantage of the delay: where our M-16s fired 5.56mm rounds, their AK-74s used a slightly larger 5.62mm bullet (notwithstanding the 5.45 caliber designation)—the reason for this was simple: if they overran our stores they could use our ammunition, but if we used Russian ammo our guns would jam.

From the weapon, I guessed that the guard was likely ex-Red Army: soldiers like to stick with what they know. Probably recruited from that vast supply of unemployed soldiers generated by the many conflicts that Putin seemed to so enjoy: Chechnya, Georgia,

Ukraine. Azerbaijan too perhaps, and he might have acquired a smattering of Arabic there. Untrained for anything but war, his pension dwindling to worthlessness, his only practical options were Moscow mafia or foreign security work. This one must have had a special résumé to have landed such a cushy job. He lit a cigarette and spent a minute or two looking lazily around while smoking it. Made visual contact with the crewman on watch on the deck of the *Speed Graphic*, and held it until the latter gave him a wave: all-clear. No conversation: they were too far away, and probably they did not speak the same language anyway. He finished the cigarette but instead of stubbing it out on the ground or throwing it into the water he withdrew a small tin, unscrewed the cap, and stubbed it out in there. Probably house rules—no leaving butts around—but it could have been that the guy was ex-special forces and so, trained not to leave traces, he did it from habit. He walked back across the plaza, footsteps echoing on the marble, and disappeared inside.

He had ignored the pearl the whole time; even the remarkable becomes matter-of-fact with familiarity. I inspected it through the binoculars. Structurally, it would likely be reinforced concrete, but the outside had been tiled with Byzantine excellence, for I could see no joins. In the lower hemisphere I could make out a narrow gap: some sort of doorway or entrance—it was possible to get inside the thing. I wondered what it was they did in there.

There was no time to find out. Our job was to get in and out of the *Speed Graphic* as fast as possible, preferably leaving with Stolper's notebook in hand. I trained the binoculars back on the yacht. As far as I could tell the crewman on duty was just keeping watch on the gangway. There were no screens or laptops I could see, which likely meant that he was not monitoring security cameras—unsurprising: someone who has their own private yacht would probably not want the crew monitoring their every movement. The after deck where he stood watch was well lit, so we would not be going in the easy way, over the stern. The bows were dark but scaling them would require the grappling hook. There was no choice.

I put away the binoculars and checked our gear. A quick briefing, and then we made our way down the bank and slipped quietly into the water.

BECAUSE OF THE VESSEL'S SLEEK design there was not much at the front end for the grappling hook to grapple, but the port bow was connected to the shore by a heavy berthing hawser. This was a better target: easy to catch, and a rope hawser would make no noise when hit with the hook. I threw the grapple over it and slowly pulled back until the hook was fast. I brought my weight onto the line slowly so that the inevitable bending of the hawser would not be sudden enough to be felt aboard the ship that it was securing to shore. I need not have bothered: the *Speed Graphic* was too big to be affected by my weight. I scrambled up the rope and then made my way hand over hand to the end of the hawser. Miranda followed.

We were on the peak of the port bow now. Anyone on the bridge would have seen us plainly, but it was unoccupied, the windows dark. We made our way up the slope and then over the windows and onto the roof of the bridge.

Above us was the mast. In the shadows overhead I could faintly see the navigation radar slowly rotating—like the aeronautical beacon that had allowed us to find her, the *Speed Graphic*'s radar was apparently never turned off, even when in harbor. Astern of us was the helicopter, wheels chocked and body chained to the deck. The tips of the rotor blades were fitted with snug sleeves, each perhaps a foot long, which were themselves secured with long lines to ring bolts in the deck—since the helicopter did not have folding blades this was their method of securing the rotor for sea, and they had obviously neglected to remove the sleeves when they came alongside.

I had intended to move aft and lower myself onto the main deck, but now I saw a better way. Most big vessels have bridge wings: projections of the bridge beyond the sides of the ship, unenclosed, and designed to allow better visibility for close maneuvering, particularly when coming alongside a wharf. When first seeing the *Speed Graphic* in Monaco I had assumed that she had none, having sacrificed their practicality for sleekness of design. Not so, I now saw: the bridge wings on the *Speed Graphic* were folding platforms that could be extended when needed but brought back flush with the superstructure when not in use to maintain the ship's clean lines. The starboard bridge wing was still folded inboard, which was why I had not noticed it when surveying the ship from across the water, but the port bridge wing was extended: it had been used when the ship entered harbor, since she was port-side to, but they had forgotten to bring it back inboard once she was secured.

Bridge wing extended, navigation radar left on, rotors still secured for sea: Kadri's crew were sloppier than they had seemed in Monaco.

It was a great piece of good luck: Miranda and I could simply walk into the ship. We let ourselves down onto the wing and entered the bridge. It was not completely dark: there was a faint green glow coming from one of the pieces of equipment: the radar scope, still with the rubber daytime hood affixed, the only gap was the eyepiece. I went to the chart table and switched on the red light, used in the dark to not ruin night vision, and hopefully not bright enough to be seen outside. There was a single chart titled "Western Approaches to the Strait of Hormuz." It showed the Iranian-occupied islands, the Iranian coast at the top, Emirates' coast at the bottom. Someone had inked in Dar Al Jawan: like most maps, this chart must have been printed before the island existed. I had hoped to find some indication of the *Speed Graphic*'s next port. There was a penciled track heading out of the island but it led nowhere, just ending several miles offshore. A departure track for sure, but not enough to reveal the destination. But it headed north, so probably they would join the shipping channel to exit the Gulf, the beginning of that long voyage back to the Mediterranean.

There was no more to be found here. We exited the bridge and went down the ladderway to the accommodation deck. Until now the ship had been ship-like, but here the interior of the *Speed Graphic* became more palatial: we were leaving the crew area and entering the domain of the owner. The bulkheads were no longer bare but paneled in highly varnished walnut, the decks were covered in soft carpet instead of more practical linoleum tile, and the utilitarian light fixtures had been replaced with sleek Art-Deco-style sconces. We moved aft to a pair of thick wooden doors across the passageway. They were pierced by double-glazed glass panels etched with the ship's crest, the same as the notepaper on which Kadri had invited Miranda to become his mistress. The doors were soundproof, designed to ensure that the master's sleep would not be disturbed by the coming and going of the crew. Somewhere on the other side was Kadri. And Hanna Moran. And Stolper's notebook.

There was a door at the side, which I cautiously opened to reveal a linen closet. Perfect: this would be where Miranda could keep watch, able to duck inside if necessary, and within range to give me an alert on the radio if needed.

I was about to insert my earpiece when the alarm went off.

XXX

I PUSHED MIRANDA INTO THE LINEN CLOSET and squeezed in beside her. There was no light inside, just the faint illumination coming through the gap in the door. The alarm continued. Soon there were footsteps outside, not on the carpet but on the linoleum at the forward end of the passageway, then the metallic rattle as whoever it was took the ladderway to the bridge.

I could smell the salt in Miranda's hair—we were pressed chest to chest in the confined space and her head was right beneath my nose. Lavender, too; whoever ironed Kadri's bed linens used lavender water when doing so.

"Feel these sheets," I whispered. "They must have a heck of a thread count."

In the faint light I saw her smile.

Finally the alarm stopped. More steps outside, several people this time, again heading up to the bridge. Then a sudden vibration, faint but detectable, as the *Speed Graphic* came to life. They had fired up the main engines.

At last I figured out what in retrospect should have been obvious: we were putting to sea. The radar had not been left on by mistake: they had flashed it up this afternoon in preparation for departure. It was probably part of the standard checklist before leaving harbor: confirm the correct functioning of navigational equipment. The rotor tie-down would have been another item in the drill. And that bridge wing was open not from the arrival two days ago but for leaving harbor tonight. With the bridge now manned and the crew at stations for departure, there was no longer any way for us to escape the ship unobserved.

I had failed to think of run-flats in Arlington, been outwitted in Tangier, run down by a supertanker tonight, and we were about to become inadvertent stowaways who if found would likely be shot and disposed of overboard. All in all, my operational skills were not as sharp as they had once been.

A sudden shudder and a slight swaying: we had disconnected from shore. The engine note gradually deepened as more power came on and soon the vessel began that abbreviated flat roll that I had felt off Monaco. The *Speed Graphic* had put to sea.

We could not remain in the linen closet: apart from the discomfort there would likely be someone using it tomorrow morning. I gave the crew forty minutes to settle down after leaving harbor then, on the half-hour to ensure that no watch changes were taking place at the time, exited the linen closet.

We descended into the bowels of the ship, down and down all the way to the vehicle deck. Forward of us were the equipment rooms and the great glass capsule that covered the bows of the main hull. Aft was the vehicle deck itself, lights ablaze. That was where we went.

The Shah of Iran's Cadillac Biarritz was still parked where it had been when Kadri had first shown it to us, still with chocked wheels, still protected by the big canvas car cover. I pulled up the latter sufficiently to open one of the coupe's immense doors and in we slipped. I quietly closed it, and the cover fell back into place.

Miranda went over to the back; I stayed in front in the driver's seat. A fair amount of light filtered through the fabric, enough to read by, but no one outside could see in. The dashboard was an ornate sculpture in chrome and glass. Column-mounted shifter. The odometer was unchanged at just eight hundred miles: the car was over half a century old but had not yet even been run in. I opened my pack, handed Miranda a food bar, and took one for myself. It would not sustain us for long but we needed something.

We ate quietly, too exhausted to talk much.

"This is a good choice," Miranda said after a while, as if we had just checked into a hotel about which she had had some misgivings but was now delighted to find suited her perfectly. "This old leather smells wonderful."

"And no one's going to use the car at sea," I added. "So we're safe in here."

"Got a plan?"

"Working on one."

"Are we still going after the notebook?"

"Yes."

"Then what?"

"Can you fly that helicopter?"

I was facing forward and so could not see Miranda back there, but I could nevertheless sense her slump in response.

"Sorry," she said. "The only time I've ever been at the controls of one was when we were going back to Monaco, and to tell the truth I had trouble just maintaining straight and level flight." No need to convince me; I still bore the bruises. "I'm not qualified, and I would probably kill us."

"It doesn't matter. We would never have had the chance to start the thing unnoticed anyway—I just want to establish the parameters, that's all."

I had not totally ruled it out: we could hide in the helicopter perhaps, hijack it in flight. If the pilot resisted I would kill him and Miranda would have to manage the controls as best she could. But right now a boat was looking like a better idea. The boat deck was below the vehicle deck and we would have no difficulty stealing one, but the problem was getting it into the water. That rear docking door would almost certainly have a lockout on the bridge to prevent unauthorized opening at sea, and I did not possess the engineering skills to get around such a thing.

"Get some sleep," I said.

"What about you?"

"I'm going to have a look around."

UNLIKE THE VEHICLE DECK, the boat well was unlit. I used the flashlight to inspect it. The deck was shorter than the one above, and narrower because of the propulsion plants on either side. The noise of the machinery was much greater here, echoing inside the metal chamber. It smelled dank, as might be expected in a chamber that is regularly immersed in seawater. Astern was the broad transom door. I found the control for its operation on the adjoining bulkhead, and my guess about the bridge lockout was confirmed: there was an indicator on the panel with those exact words and a little indicator light showing that it was engaged—another item on the presailing checklist, no doubt. There was no way to open this door without disengaging the lockout on the bridge. There was a regular people-sized door beside it, enough to allow access without the necessity of opening the entire transom, but it was too small for a boat.

It was not necessary to flood the chamber to use a boat: there was a davit that could be swung out if the transom was open and from which a boat could be lowered into the water without the necessity of ballasting down. The boats themselves were impressive: a half-cabin cruiser, which I guessed was the workhorse, a whaler for foul weather operation, and a beautiful wooden speedboat, highly varnished and finished with sleek chromium strakes: this would be the boat in which Kadri would cruise up and down the beaches of the Riviera, the equivalent on water of the Maserati on land. There were sports craft too: windsurfers, a pair of little sailing dinghies, kayaks, and canoes. These were small enough to fit through that small stern door but were of no use: hand- or wind-driven propulsion would not get us away fast enough, and with her enormous power the *Speed Graphic* would run us down. Then I saw the jet skis.

There were four of these lined up against the forward bulkhead, all the same model, brightly colored and sleek. They would be fast—not as fast as the *Speed Graphic*, but with enough of a head start they might be fast enough. I measured the beam with an oar from one of the kayaks and took it over to the access door. It would fit, with perhaps an inch to spare. I remeasured, more carefully now. Not quite an inch, maybe half an inch, but that was enough.

I would have liked to flash one up to test the operation but that was out of the question. Instead I settled for checking the fuel tank of the closest one. It was full, which is the normal way to store boats at sea, since the gas vapors of a near-empty tank are more explosive than the liquid of a full one. Beside the jet skis was a wheeled cradle for maneuvering the things across the deck. There was a keyboard cabinet fitted to the starboard bulkhead. It was locked but the door had a glass window. I used the paddle to smash it and found among the many keys four identical sets, all embossed with the manufacturer's name and obviously for the jet skis. I tried them in the nearest jet ski until I found the one that fit.

I returned to the Cadillac.

"I have a plan," I said to Miranda when I was safely back inside. She did not seem very impressed when I told her what it was.

"How heavy is a jet ski?"

"Two people can lift it."

"How do we lower it?"

"We don't; we just toss it over the side and dive in after it."

"What if it doesn't land upright?"

"It's self-righting." At least I assumed it would be.

"Okay, when do we go?"

"As soon as we've got that notebook."

XXXI

F OUND SOME," Miranda whispered.

She held up a big roll of silver-colored duct tape. We were in the workshop located off the passageway that ran forward from the vehicle deck to the big glass gallery at the front of the ship. I had been searching for tools and she for the tape. I ran out a strip and used the diving knife to cut a three-foot length. I attached it to the left side of my wetsuit, lightly so that it would come away easily, and turned the last inch upon itself, forming a tab to quickly pull it off. Then I made another strip the same way, this time attaching it to the right side. I answered Miranda's inquiring look.

"The first one is for her mouth," I explained. "The second is for her hands, so that she can't immediately tear the first one off."

We would have to subdue Hanna Moran quickly, before she had the opportunity to alert anyone. Jet ski or no jet ski, our only chance of getting away was with a good head start, and for that I counted on no one being alerted until a steward or the maid discovered Hanna

Moran in the morning, bound with yards of duct tape and secured to some hard point in her cabin, able to breathe but little else.

I continued looking. It did not take long to find the other items I had been searching for: a crowbar, a chisel, a mallet, and a hefty screwdriver: four items that in various combinations should be sufficient to deal with any lock or latch that we encountered when searching through Hanna Moran's cabin.

None of them would deal with a safe. Miranda had not mentioned the possibility of a safe, and I was certainly not going to tell her my intentions if we found one and Moran refused to reveal the combination. I put everything into a canvas toolbag and turned off the light. We stepped cautiously out of the workshop and back into the passageway.

At the same moment as I closed the door the engine note suddenly changed, dropping in revolutions, moving to idle. We could feel the way coming off the *Speed Graphic*. Then a tone began sounding over the ship's broadcast system, identical to the one we had heard before and apparently the yacht's equivalent of a warship's call to maneuvering stations. Given that this had happened just as we emerged from the workshop it instinctively felt as if we must have been the cause, but I knew that was unlikely: there would be no alarm in the workshop, and there were no security cameras in the passageway. We headed back aft toward the safety of the Cadillac but it was too late: I could hear the rattle of people coming down the ladderway from above. When they hit the bottom they would see us. We turned back around.

Miranda went for the workshop, but I pulled her instead toward another door further forward. I had no idea what was behind it, but it seemed to me that if the sudden stop in the middle of the sea was not our fault then it was likely due to a mechanical issue. If so, they would be using that workshop; we needed to find somewhere else to hide.

We entered the compartment immediately astern of the area enclosed by the big glass capsule. I would have thought that nothing on the *Speed Graphic* could have been more remarkable than that crystal-enclosed space, but I was wrong: what Miranda and I found when we entered the new compartment left us speechless.

It was part machine, part robot, part scientific apparatus, part prop from the latest space adventure movie. The thing was about ten feet tall, freestanding in the middle of the compartment. It sat upon a low hand truck like those used to move heavy loads around a warehouse and was chained down to ringbolts in the deck to hold it secure at sea. Whatever it was, it was complex: a mass of components arranged with the detailed precision of a Swiss watch, the many surfaces of metal and glass finely machined or ground or polished, like the parts of a probe destined for deep space. Dominating it was a long tube-like structure suspended in a gimbal ring arrangement, obviously maneuverable. The tube itself had many components, including at one point on its length a surrounding sleeve of smaller tubes, glistening chrome, and from which a small steady stream of white gas or smoke emerged.

The compartment was as unlike the workshop as could be imagined: immaculately clean, all the surfaces lined in stark white tile material. The machine itself hummed, a deep electrical sound, confirming what that smoke or gas had already suggested: the thing was on.

I walked over to inspect it more closely. Fat rubber-coated cables lying on the floor connected the machine to the only other equipment in the room: a series of closet-sized power converters lined up by the after bulkhead. All at once I understood why the *Speed Graphic* had such large engines. Until now I had assumed that it was just Kadri's need for excessive power that had made him decide to fit such extraordinary propulsion to his ship, a reflex from those years in his childhood frustrated with the slow passage back to Tripoli. Diesels would have been sufficient to power the hull as fast as it could hydrodynamically go, and they would have been cheaper. More practical, too: as far as I knew, apart from some extreme racing boats, no other civilian vessel was fitted with gas turbines. Only warships have them, since only warships have use for the surplus of power. Now I realized that there was no surplus: their enormous output was not to drive the *Speed Graphic*; it was to power this device.

I cautiously put a finger in the smoke emanating from the slender steel cylinders surrounding the tube structure. It was water vapor, as I had guessed. Then I touched one of the sleeve cylinders with a quick flick of a finger, just long enough to establish that it was very cold. I followed the steel-braided flexible tubing leading from them down to the base of the device. Here the tubes were connected to a series of gas cylinders not unlike those we had dived with earlier this evening, except these were made of gleaming industrial stainless steel. I read the label: liquid nitrogen.

It was a cooling system. Whatever this machine did, one of the by-products was extreme heat.

The main tube was heavy in the rear and gradually thinned toward the front, like a breech-and-barrel arrangement. There were actually two projections in front: the upper one was longer, the lower one shorter, like the way a grenade launcher is mounted beneath the barrel on an M-4, except in that case the grenade launcher has greater girth, but here the second projection was much thinner than the first. I went to the rear. The gimbal gear was a complex azimuth and elevation control system centering on a series of toothed wheels run by electric servomotors and manufactured from what looked like milled titanium, probably to keep the weight of inertia down and thus the response times up: the machine was designed to react fast. I read the labels on the various control panels and switches and dials, trying to understand what it was that I was looking at.

"Any ideas?" Miranda asked after a while.

"Yes, I think it's a weapon."

"What sort of weapon?"

"A laser weapon." I showed her two readouts which were calibrated in nanometers, the wavelengths in which radiation is measured at the visible end of the electromagnetic spectrum. "Lasers emit pulsed light; this measures the precise wavelengths, or perhaps changes in them, to capture target data. Now look at the front." We stepped to the twin projections at the front of the apparatus. "I think the upper one is the weapon itself: this is the barrel from which the laser beam emerges. It uses tremendous energy, hence the need for these liquid nitrogen cooling bands around it. The second one is much smaller and much lower powered. I think it is the same as the red-light laser scopes we use on our carbines in the marines: it's for targeting. In this case: range, bearing and elevation."

"What is it designed to attack?"

"Aircraft at least, perhaps missiles. The control gear has been manufactured so that it can change direction very rapidly, and that usually means an aerial target."

"Like Star Wars? The defense program, not the movie."

"Yes, like Star Wars. What this stuff is doing on a private yacht I have no idea, but it's no accident: I think the *Speed Graphic* was purpose-built for this machine. That's why she has gas turbines: to provide the energy to power it. And that's why she has a glass capsule: to shoot through."

"What now?"

"We abort. Take the jet ski and extract."

"What about the notebook?"

"We forget the notebook. This is bigger."

I did not understand exactly what the weapon we had found was, but I knew instinctively that it was urgent to let someone else know about it. I had to get ashore and call Dortmund. If he could commandeer a carrier battle group to arrange a meeting with me then he could certainly persuade the navy to stop and search the *Speed Graphic*. They would soon find out what the weapon was and recover the notebook as a bonus. It would put an end to Dortmund's slush fund and Stolper's presidential ambitions, but that was just too bad.

I unsheathed her knife and offered it hilt first.

"Can you kill someone?"

She looked at me in astonishment, then stared at the weapon in my hand for a long moment in contemplative silence. Finally she took it without comment.

"Drive it into the stomach," I said. "It's important not to hesitate, never break stride. Just walk straight up and kill anyone in your way. And hold eye contact; it freezes them."

She nodded. It was not much instruction but it was all there was time for. I took the crowbar in hand: an excellent weapon, probably better than the knife. The adrenaline was coursing through my body now, and I longed to use it.

We moved to the door. I opened it a fraction. The passageway was empty but the moment I cleared the compartment it became obvious that there would be no escape right now. The ship's transom door had been opened. We were much lower in the water: the *Speed Graphic* had ballasted down for small boat operations. It took me a moment to make out in the water astern of us the reason for all the activity. There, silhouetted by the moonlight reflecting off the sea, was a surfaced submarine. She was lying hove-to, several cable lengths away.

I pushed Miranda back inside the weapon room and shut the door.

"New plan," I said. I handed her the keys to the jet ski. "Hide behind those power converters, no one will find you there. If I don't come back stay hidden until everything quiets down again, then take the jet ski like we planned. When you get ashore call the U.S. embassy and tell them everything you know. Make sure they understand that it's urgent they pass it on to Dortmund. He will take care of everything."

"What are you going to do?"

"Identify the submarine."

It was obvious from her reaction that she did not think this was a good idea, but I walked away without giving her the opportunity for debate. People underestimate the need for precise intelligence, from presidents on down. It is one thing to suspect, another to know, as Gulf Two had made clear. From the moment I saw it I knew that I was going to have to identify that submarine out there.

I moved into the passageway. This was exactly the sort of work that I was trained to do. Reconnaissance marines really do perform reconnaissance, battlefield and theater; it is what we are primarily used for. The other stuff is a bonus—since we are so frequently deep in opposition territory it often makes sense to take out a target or two while we are there.

The submarine was still lying dead in the water astern of us. They look sinister enough at any time, doubly so at night. No navigation lights: this rendezvous was not meant to be observed.

Meanwhile, the *Speed Graphic* was alive with activity. I could hear coming from below shouts as the crew prepared to launch a boat. On the vehicle deck there was only one person, a uniformed crewman standing by the Cadillac, back to me and gazing out at the submarine. He wore a sidearm but it was holstered.

I approached from behind at a brisk walk—fast, but not so fast that the innate senses all humans have would alert him—then caved in his head with the crowbar. I tried to moderate the blow, not wanting to make a mess that would give me away, but a spurt of blood sprayed in a long arc across the car cover, and when he collapsed the contents of his skull sloshed out onto the deck. I shoved his body into the Cadillac's front seat, removed the weapon, then scooped up his brains as best I could and dropped them into his lap.

We would not be hiding out in this car anymore.

There was an oily rag on a nearby tool bench which I used to clean up the remains on the deck and wipe off my hands. I closed the car door and set the cover square again. The blood spray was already drying. Hopefully no one would notice it, or realize what it was if they did.

I kept his weapon.

A motor started down in the well, and a moment later the speedboat came surging out from the *Speed Graphic*, headed for the submarine. I moved further aft and crouched down by the Hummer, out of sight of anyone coming up from the boat deck but in a position from which I had a good view of the submarine.

I inspected her through the binoculars. Modern teardrop-hull design; both bow and stern were below the water, invisible to me. She had a long sail without hydroplanes: the maneuverable wing-like control surfaces with which submarines effectively fly underwater. Several of her masts were raised, poking out above the top of the sail. I tried to identify them: one was her search periscope for sure; and nearby was a second, much thinner one: the attack periscope. The third mast had a small rotating antenna on top: a radar mast. The last mast was wider in diameter than the others and was topped with a distinctive valve assembly. I had already concluded that the submarine was not American—too small—but this fourth mast settled it.

There are two types of submarine propulsion: nuclear and diesel. Nukes are fast and go forever, the muscle cars of the underwater world. All U.S. boats are nukes, and they roam the world's oceans as the unseen masters of all they survey.

Diesels are slow and limited in range, but they have a single significant advantage over nukes: when submerged, they operate on battery power alone. On batteries they are quieter than any nuclear boat, and in the war beneath the waves silence is everything. But those batteries must be recharged regularly. For that they need to run the clattering diesels, and worse still the diesels need air. That was what the fourth mast was for: it was basically a big induction tube that gets poked above the surface, sucking down the air for the recharge phase—what submariners call a snorkel.

The Russians never stopped building diesel boats, and I was pretty sure that I was looking at one now: a Soviet-era diesel-powered attack submarine, small and quiet, no match for a U.S. nuke in the open ocean but perfectly suited to the slow, short-range shallow-water work of Gulf operations.

What was a Russian submarine doing down here, thousands of miles from the nearest Russian naval base and nowhere near their sphere of operations? Not for the laser weapon: no way something that big could be stuffed into a submarine, unless they took it apart first.

I memorized estimates of the primary dimensions and recognition features—sail height and length, hull diameter, length at the waterline. Sometime later these might help an intelligence analyst identify her by class.

The speedboat reached the submarine. Until now I had assumed that they were taking something from the yacht out to her, but now I saw that it was just the opposite: they were bringing something back. People—three men scrambled awkwardly down a rope ladder slung from the submarine's deck casing and arcing over the cylindrical bulk of the pressure hull down to where the speedboat lay waiting in the water below. They boarded and the boat got underway, returning fast toward the *Speed Graphic*.

I lay flat on the deck and crawled under the Hummer, positioned so that I would be able to get a good look at whoever came up that ladder from the well deck below. A lot of things happened fast. Before the speedboat had made it back to the *Speed Graphic* the submarine threw up a great plume as she got underway. At first I assumed it was just exhaust from the diesels and that she was anxious to transit away from the clandestine rendezvous. But then her hull suddenly sank beneath the waves and by the time she disappeared out of sight astern all that remained visible above the water was the top of the sail: she was not just steaming away, she was also diving.

While the submarine was ballasting to dive the *Speed Graphic* was doing the reverse: as soon as the speedboat returned she began pumping out in order to get underway, closing the transom door at the same time, as if she too was anxious to get going and not be seen keeping bad company. The whole thing was carried out with smooth efficiency, something that looks deceptively simple on the surface but which I knew from experience requires the careful coordination of a well-trained crew. The visitors came rattling up from below.

A man in naval whites emerged first, four gold stripes gleaming on his epaulets: the captain of the *Speed Graphic*, leading the guests. Next was Kadri. He was dressed in a dark business suit, crisp white shirt, subdued tie, polished black oxfords: his clothing told me that whoever his visitors were, they were big shots. At the top of the stairs he stood deferentially to the side for the first of the guests.

He was about sixty years of age; short, close-cut beard. Like Kadri, he wore a suit but the coat was cut as a tunic that was buttoned to the neck, like the uniform of European military officers about the time of von Moltke (author of the golden rule of warfare: *No battle plan survives contact with the enemy*—a lesson that I was relearning tonight). But this man was no soldier or sailor: there was no rank insignia nor decoration of any kind, and he gazed about with that uncertain curiosity of a civilian in the company of military men.

Following him were the last two visitors. There was no mistaking this pair: scruffy, unshaven, and giving off an acrid odor that reached all the way across the vehicle deck to me—they were submariners. Fresh water is at a premium on any warship, but especially so aboard a diesel submarine that cannot afford to waste precious power running evaporators: submariners shower once a week at most, and then only for the briefest of intervals. For the same reason they rarely shave on patrol, and the pervasive odor of diesel gets into their clothes, their hair, their skin, everywhere.

Even without the smell I would have identified these two: they carried themselves with the easygoing confidence of men used to the sea, perfectly at home living a life of constant and unnatural danger beneath it, and when they reached the vehicle deck they stared around a moment then caught each other's eyes and laughed out loud: space like this was an unimaginable luxury after the confines of their U-boat. I took an instinctive liking to these two: they reminded me of the crews who had taken me and my guys into hotspots from time to time, and we had always looked at each other's professions with headshaking bewilderment, wondering why anyone in their right mind would volunteer for such a job. One of them carried a small pack slung over a shoulder. He made a comment to the other, presumably in Russian and certainly unintelligible to me, but it cracked up his companion and even the civilian raised a sheepish smile: I guessed that the passage aboard the submarine must have been a claustrophobic horror show for him, same as it would have been for any civilian.

Notwithstanding the heat, both submariners wore navy blue sweaters with soft rank insignia on shoulder straps, likely the most formal uniform they took with them to sea. The joker had two stripes, the other guy three. The submarine's captain and another officer, I guessed, but presumably not the XO, who would have remained behind to dive the boat in the boss's absence.

I had expected that the party would next go up the ladder to the main deck, but instead Kadri and the *Speed Graphic*'s captain led the visitors forward along the passageway at the front of the vehicle deck. Several of the yacht's crewmembers joined them. All at once I realized what a bad decision it was to have left Miranda in the compartment with the laser weapon.

New plan. I checked the pistol. It was a Glock, one of those ugly half-plastic handguns that only a mother could love. I presumed it was a nine, but under the Hummer it was too dark to read the slide markings clearly. I ejected the magazine: fifteen double-stacked rounds of hollow-points. They were largish rimless rounds, probably 9mm Parabellum, or perhaps that shortened 10mm Auto round known as .40 S&W, if Glock makes guns chambered for Smith & Wesson ammunition. Either way it would get the job done: the instant I heard the alarm raised when they found Miranda I would walk up, shoot someone before anyone could unholster, take Kadri hostage, force them to ballast down, and then escape in the speedboat. Too easy.

After twenty minutes the remaining crewmen were back up from the boat well, the *Speed Graphic* was unballasted, and we had gotten underway. No alarm from forward; they had not yet found Miranda, and as long as she stayed hidden behind those power converters there was still a chance that we would not have to shoot our way out. From my position under the Hummer I had no view down the passageway and so I could not tell what was going on down there. I heard voices from time to time, and perhaps something else, something vaguely mechanical, but in the vehicle deck the ambient noise from the *Speed Graphic*'s engines was too great for me to make anything out. I was going to have to eyeball it, but that meant breaking cover.

Best thing in these situations is to just go ahead and do it. I chambered a round, rolled out, and ran for the bulkhead at the front of the vehicle deck. Anyone coming down the passageway might still miss me, as long as they did not look behind them when they emerged onto the vehicle deck. I moved to the doorway and peeked cautiously around the corner.

They were all in the glass capsule. Right forward was the laser, its barrel assembly sweeping backward and forward. This confirmed what I had already suspected, the *Speed Graphic* was purpose-built for the machine and that glass capsule was not for people to see out but for the laser to shoot through. In the movies you see laser beams but not in real life. Nevertheless, the noise made it clear that the thing was on: some combination of high power and cooling equipment combined to emit a deep ethereal drone from the thing, a D-minor chord slightly flattened, vaguely elegiac, as if the plaintive wail of some prehistoric creature consumed with regret.

The men surrounding it looked pleased with themselves: Kadri was grinning and the civilian was nodding with quiet satisfaction. I would have thought the submariners would be unflappable, but they were the most amazed of all. Whatever the weapon was doing, it had astonished them.

The demonstration lasted another forty minutes. When it was clear that the show was ending I returned to the hiding spot beneath the Hummer. We were safe: Miranda was well hidden and they would have no reason to look under the Hummer—there was nothing to give us away.

I was pretty sure I knew what was going on now. Kadri had somehow acquired some advanced military technology and was offering it to the Russians, who despite the end of the Cold War had managed through a series of state takeovers and media curbs and opposition poisonings to return themselves to dictatorship while preserving the outward pretense of democracy. Presumably the Kremlin had sent a scientist down to check out the goods. To ensure that the transaction remained secret they had transported him via a submarine. Furthermore, it looked as if Kadri's sales pitch had been a big success.

It was a good theory that fitted the facts nicely. But nothing beats hard intelligence, and when the party emerged from the passageway at the conclusion of the demonstration I gained some new data which immediately blew my theory away. The civilian and the two naval officers were talking among themselves, and for once they were close enough for me to overhear. I am no linguist, but even I could tell that it was not Russian they were speaking. It was Arabic.

XXXII

T HE GROUP CAME TO A HALT IN THE middle of the vehicle
deck, not far from me. Kadri turned his attention to the
civilian, and the two naval officers stood slightly aside, as if they
sensed that their part in the proceeding was done.

"And now, my honored guest," Kadri said to the older visitor, "I
think we have one more piece of business to conclude."

He said it in English and I wondered why Kadri would not have
spoken in what was surely for them both their native language. The
honored guest made a slight bow and opened his right hand palm
outward, inviting Kadri to proceed. Kadri nodded to the *Speed
Graphic*'s captain, who in turn sent a crewman scurrying up the
ladder.

A moment later he came rattling back down, followed at a much
slower pace by a spectacular set of legs slowly emerging from
above. All eyes looked up. I had seen this entrance before and
wondered if Hanna Moran had been secretly practicing it that day
she had come down the spiral staircase to join us for lunch in

Monaco. This time Hanna had gone all out, wearing silver high-heeled sandals of ornate design and a body-hugging metal-hued cocktail dress. Her blond hair was up, perhaps to best display the silver and diamonds hanging around her neck and from her ears.

In her right hand she held a sleek brushed aluminum briefcase, very thin, no bigger than a laptop. It went well with the dress and diamonds, and I wondered if she had selected the ensemble with that in mind.

I had no doubt what was inside that briefcase.

The submariners looked at her as if she were a houri descending from heaven. The civilian showed no reaction whatsoever. Hanna reached the bottom of the ladderway and came across the vehicle deck with a walk made for the runway; she must have been a real model after all.

She joined the men.

"Minister, may I present Miss Hanna Moran, through whose person God has conveyed this wonderful gift to us today."

The older man made a slight bow. "*Enchanté.*"

"The pleasure is mine," Hanna replied.

"Balthazar tells me that you are a most enterprising woman, Miss Moran."

"To both our benefits, I hope."

"Certainly, madam. It is wonderful that you chose to come to us."

"In fact it was Balthazar's idea; he has been an invaluable friend."

"You are most gracious, madam. And so to business."

"Yes, of course—Balthazar warned me that it was important for your party to leave before first light, and I would not like to be the cause of a delay, so please allow me to present this to you now and thank you for the generosity of your kind offer."

She held out the briefcase but the older man made no attempt to take it. Nobody moved for a moment, an awkward pause. Hanna looked at him in increasing confusion, then at Kadri, but he too ignored the proffered briefcase. Instead Kadri turned to the older man.

"Have you any questions of her, Minister?"

"None."

Kadri withdrew an automatic pistol from inside his coat, put it to Hanna Moran's forehead, and pulled the trigger without hesitation. Her body collapsed onto the deck. There was a small red hole, a little ragged from the blast gases but the gun must have been small-caliber because there was no exit wound. Whatever ammunition Kadri was using, it was nothing like the stuff I was used to, which at that range would have blown her head apart. I guessed it was .22, maybe .25 ACP—nevertheless the noise from the gunshot was deafening inside the huge metal soundbox that was the vehicle deck. The briefcase had opened on impact with the deck and a book had come flying out. It landed not far from me, almost close enough to grab. It was octavo, blue-bound, gold-embossed—identical to the one Dortmund had shown me on the flag bridge of the *Theodore Roosevelt*, except this time the pages that fluttered open were filled with the state secrets whose sale had just cost Hanna Moran her life. They were written in an elegant flowing hand, and I supposed that Stolper must have always made his notes with the care of someone imagining them ending up on display in a glass vitrine, an exhibit in his presidential library.

I was not the only one who had been taken by surprise by this turn of events: both naval officers were white-faced now, the older one shaking his head in disbelief, the younger one staring wide-eyed and repeatedly swallowing, the way you do when trying not to heave.

Kadri casually replaced his weapon in the shoulder holster under his jacket.

"As I promised, Minister—no loose ends."

The other man, who had remained totally impassive, took a couple of steps forward so that he was standing directly above Hanna Moran's body. He bent over, as if to more closely inspect the entry wound. Instead, he spat on her face.

He stood back up, removed a folded handkerchief from his pocket, and carefully wiped his lips.

"You have done God's work," he said matter-of-factly. "All western women are whores."

He issued a quick command. The younger of the two naval officers recovered the notebook and then reluctantly walked over to the body. He knelt to take the briefcase, but Hanna's dead fingers maintained their grip on the handle. He had to unfold them one by one.

Kadri glanced at his watch.

"Minister, I deeply regret that the press of time prevents me from giving you a better tour of the vessel, not to mention allowing me to offer my humble hospitality. However, there is one further thing I would like to do before you leave."

The naval officers looked like all they wanted to do was get away from here as soon as possible, but the civilian was completely unperturbed by the slowly increasing pool of blood sloshing on the deck at their feet.

"Certainly," he said.

"As you know, Minister, for many years your nation was trampled under the foot of the western oppressors and their lackeys. You have taken back your land, but you have yet to recover all that belongs to your people. So now I wish to return something that was once stolen from you."

And now at last I got it. Kadri had not spoken Arabic because the civilian would not have understood it. The language in which I had overheard him conversing with the naval officers was not Arabic; it was Farsi, the language of Iran. These three were not Arabs, they were Iranians. The submarine was Russian, but only by construction: she was part of the Iranian navy. I vaguely recalled it from years ago, the Russians selling three of their surplus submarines to Iran, and the outrage that it had caused in the United States at the time. And naturally Kadri would have sought out his old contacts from the Iran-Contra days when Hanna Moran had suddenly landed in his lap, seeking an introduction to a buyer.

Kadri stepped over to the Cadillac.

"When the criminal Shah escaped the revolution," Kadri said, "he took much that did not belong to him. I have recently had the opportunity to acquire one of those stolen items, Minister, and I now present it to you as the representative of the Iranian people, and hope that the Revolutionary Council will take it as a token of my most humble appreciation and esteem."

While delivering this ornate speech he had walked over to the Cadillac, and at its conclusion he whipped off the car cover. Still facing his audience, and so unaware of what occupied the driver's seat, he opened the door with a flourish, grinning at his guests while behind him the body I had hidden there rolled out onto the deck, the brains in his lap sloshing out after him.

This time the lieutenant could not keep his dinner down.

XXXIII

I CHECKED MY WATCH. It was half an hour since the minister and two naval officers had been hastily shuffled back to their submarine following the embarrassing end to what had otherwise been a successful business meeting. The briefcase had gone with them. I remained hidden under the Hummer, unable to break cover because of all the activity on the vehicle deck. One party of seamen had removed their deceased shipmate from the Cadillac, another was cleaning up the car, a third had secured a chain to Hanna Moran prior to her disposal over the side—they had learned their lesson from the recovery of the FBI informant's unweighted body.

Standing in the middle of the vehicle deck, directing it all, was Balthazar Kadri.

The notebook was gone. Short of sinking the submarine, Stolper's political career was at an end, and Dortmund would have to look elsewhere for his slush fund. The operation was blown; all I wanted to do now was find Miranda and jump ship, taking our chances on being near enough to the crowded shipping lanes of the Strait to attract the attention of some passing vessel in the morning.

It was not to be. Kadri had sent out a search party as soon as getting rid of the visitors. Now there was a shout from forward and a moment later three armed crewmen emerged down the passageway. One of them was clutching Miranda. A second was holding her knife, although the scabbard was still strapped around her calf. She was brought before Kadri, who smiled at her with undisguised delight.

"Miss Grey, what an unexpected pleasure to see you again."

"I wish I could say the same."

But the comment just made him smile all the more.

"And I love the outfit: so very Ursula Andress."

"Give me that knife back and I'll show you some tricks."

Kadri laughed out loud. "I should have guessed that you were a spy," he said. "From the first moment that I saw you in the casino, I knew there was something different."

"My people know that I'm here."

"Naturally."

"They'll come for me."

"Perhaps."

"For certain."

"Madam, there was no need for all this drama. Had you wished to come aboard the *Speed Graphic* you need only have called, as you well know." He gestured toward the Cadillac. "And what a mess. What did you use on the poor fellow?"

"A crowbar," she replied. No trace of hesitation. The crewman's body was long gone, but Miranda must have guessed from all the gore what had happened.

"And you are alone?"

"You think I need help?"

Kadri laughed. "No, I do not. But nevertheless I like to be sure of these things."

He walked over to the Cadillac. The crewmen cleaning the car had placed upon the deck the gear that we had left inside. Kadri toed through it, slowly, considering each item in turn, and I realized how fortunate we were that Miranda had stripped off all her equipment on the beach, leaving us with just one of everything.

"This radio unit?"

"What about it?"

"It communicates with whom?"

"The boat that brought me here."

"Where is it now?"

"Somewhere offshore, outside the restricted zone, waiting to pick me up."

"What sort of vessel?"

"I forget."

"Armament?"

"I forget."

"Communications schedule?"

"I forget."

He continued to study the gear, nodding to himself, then eventually walked back to Miranda and took the knife from the crewman. He studied it for a moment in silence.

"Quite a weapon," he said pensively. "Why didn't you kill him with this?"

"I hate it when they gurgle."

"S-O-G," he said, reading aloud the initials etched into the blade. "What does it stand for?"

"Special Operations Group."

Actually, it stands for Studies & Observation Group, a Vietnam-era military unit put together to develop weapons and tactics for a war unlike any we had fought before, and which we were losing. After the war was over it had been spun off to private enterprise, and now manufactured the precision weapons that they had originally designed. But Kadri obviously did not know what the initials stood for, and the speed of her answer seemed to satisfy him that she was the real thing.

He held up the knife between them and casually allowed the tip of the blade to come to rest gently upon her throat.

"You know, I could jog your memory about that boat, Miss Grey."

"You could try."

A long silence. Neither of them moved.

I sighted on Kadri's head. Tough shot; and he was partially occluded by the crewman standing beside him. Hand guns are inaccurate in the best of conditions, but I had never used this weapon and so had no idea if it was sighted in or, if so, to what range, and being unfamiliar with the internal safeties on a Glock I was not even sure that it would fire when I pulled the trigger. The shot was at least thirty feet, which sounds close until you actually try to hit something at that range. In the correct shooter's position you hold the handgun in your right hand, cradle the bottom of the grip in your left, and sight along the barrel with your left eye, but because I was lying prone with an awkward upward shot I could do none of these properly.

I concentrated on making the weapon as steady as possible. From my angle Kadri was in front of Miranda, but 9mm Parabellum is fairly powerful ammo, .40 S&W even more so, so if I pulled the trigger the question of who came first and who came second would not make much of a difference.

But then Kadri smiled and lowered the knife. I breathed again.

"I certainly want no trouble with your people, Miss Grey: you will be returned to them unharmed. But first I have a transaction to complete. We are currently on our way back to Dar Al Jawan. When we get there the *Speed Graphic* will be stripped of fittings and furnishings before being turned over to her new owners. Forty-eight hours from now I will have no further interest in her or any items that she might carry—you can tell the world about it for all I care. But until the money has been wired into my account I am afraid that you will be compelled to remain with me as my guest. You will be installed in a stateroom tonight and at the palace on the island tomorrow. You will have two guards with you at all times, plus a servant at your personal disposal. Miss Moran is presently not with us, but I am sure that she would not object to sharing some of her clothing—I will direct one of the female domestic staff to bring you a selection. Have you any questions?"

"None."

"Good. I am sure that you are exhausted after your little adventure tonight, and I have much to attend to. You will be taken to your stateroom now; let us agree to meet for a leisurely brunch, say at noon."

"I want my knife back."

Kadri laughed out loud.

"And you shall have it, Miss Grey: I promise to return it to you when you leave. But until then I am afraid it's going to be plastic cutlery for you—I can't afford to lose any more crewmembers."

He issued some curt instructions in Arabic, and Miranda was taken away.

I resolved to never tell Dortmund the details of this particular incident: if he knew how skillfully Miranda had handled the situation he would stop at nothing to recruit her for himself.

XXXIV

T HE HARBOR AT DAR AL JAWAN, which had been so quiet
    the previous evening, was bustling with activity when we
returned to it the next day. There was a score or more of luxury
vessels alongside now, everything from oversized offshore
speedboats to long sleek luxury yachts built to roam the world. Some
were more traditional in design, stately prewar vessels whose
original propulsion was probably steam, including the one docked
across from us: single hull painted a dark glossy blue, high straight
cutwater and long curving counter, elegant step-back superstructure
in contrasting white, raked funnels and big forward-facing
ventilation ducts protruding from the deck. She looked like a
miniature *Mauretania*.

Activity in the harbor came to a halt as people stopped whatever
they were doing to witness the entry of the *Speed Graphic*, the alpha
male of the pack, wide and hulking, her huge gas turbines humming
deeply as she came alongside. Many of the other vessels had been
forced through lack of space to secure outboard of others, so that it

would be necessary to cross over the inboard vessels to get ashore, but the *Speed Graphic* had her previous space reserved for her alone: necessary if she was to unload her fittings and furnishings, especially the vehicles.

I returned to my hiding spot, pleased with what I had seen. A man alone stands out but a man in a crowd is invisible: when I got ashore I would be able to keep watch on the *Speed Graphic* more easily than I had imagined.

As soon as all the activity had ended on the vehicle deck last night, and the ship had settled back down into her normal cruising routine, I had gone in search of food and clothing. I had found both at the forward end of the main deck. The laundry had a dozen or so crewman's uniforms, and I had been about to help myself to one when I had spotted something better: Arab robes: a djellaba with tunic and trousers in matching light-colored material; and a *shumagh*, the red and white checkered headcloth made familiar by Arafat. In the corner was a shoeshine box by which stood a single pair of black oxfords. Earlier in the evening from my vantage point on the deck under the Hummer I had gotten a good look at everyone's footwear, and I recognized this pair as the shoes that Kadri had been wearing—whatever footwear he wore during the day was obviously polished that same night. I hoped they would not be missed too much.

The galley was stocked as you might imagine the galley of a billionaire's yacht would be. I could not risk cooking anything so had hastily taken with me only what could be consumed cold: a tin of beluga caviar, a round of camembert, a small box of strawberries, a handful of chocolate truffles, a quart of peach nectar. I had consumed them back beneath the Hummer. As field rations go they were not bad; we hardly ever got caviar or chocolate truffles in the Marine Corps.

Half an hour after docking the transom door had been opened, the vehicle ramp lowered, and longshoremen were constantly coming and going, transferring boxes and furniture down onto the dock. I stood and walked off the *Speed Graphic*. Suntanned and unshaven for days I did not look all that different from the men around me, and I made it ashore unremarked.

It was mid-afternoon. More motor yachts were arriving in the harbor, and in the air above there was a constant coming and going of helicopters; there was a landing pad on top of the palace. Some sort of gathering was going on: a big business meeting perhaps, in which case these yachts and helicopters must belong to the investors in the company that had built the island. I walked along the wharves, looking at the registrations marked on the stern of each vessel: Qatar, Oman, Yemen, the Emirates, Bahrain, Kuwait, Saudi Arabia, Egypt, Jordan, even faraway Tunisia, and Morocco.

I settled myself onto a seat in the garden high over the harbor with a good view of the *Speed Graphic* and waited for Miranda to be escorted ashore. Kadri may or may not be planning to release her as promised, but I had no intention of relying on his goodwill—I was going to release her myself. With two armed guards in close attendance I had little chance of doing so on the yacht, but in the labyrinth of the palace and with strangers all around I was willing to bet that I could get to her. My contingent plan was to disguise myself as a servant to get close, then make my move. As soon as I had secured Miranda we would commandeer a boat and escape, hopefully getting in contact with the U.S. embassy in time for them to organize an interception of the *Speed Graphic* before she made it to Iran.

I was not leaving without Miranda, but to get to her I needed to know exactly where inside the palace she was taken. To do that I had to spot her leaving the yacht and follow not far behind.

Dusk fell. For the first time since returning to the Middle East I had not heard the cry of the muezzins at sunset—at Dar Al Jawan it seemed that religious observance was put on hold. The gas lamps all over the island ignited, and down on the plaza the huge pearl glowed under floodlights. The palace was lit up. Groups of people were out on the balconies and the decks of the yachts, dressed in evening clothes and enjoying sunset cocktails. The whole place took on a strangely festive air, alive with the barely subdued expectation of a big party about to begin.

A group of musicians emerged from the palace and set themselves up on the plaza by the side of the pearl. They sat on rugs and cushions, cross-legged in the Arab fashion, and their instruments were Oriental: small drums played by hand, some woodwinds that I could not identify, a mandolin-shaped stringed instrument that might have been an oud. Strangest of all was a single massive man, old but unbent, dark-skinned, and with a thick gray beard. He was dressed entirely in white: white turban and tunic, breeches ending at the knees. His instrument was a horn in the literal sense, the horn of some unlucky ungulate, twisted and very long. He came forward to where the steps led down to the water, stood in dead center with the mass of the pearl rising behind him, and raised the horn skyward. He played a single note, deep and mournful, that echoed across the water and reverberated around the great bowl of the harbor. It was an announcement of some kind, a signal that the show was about to begin.

He played it thrice, each time holding the note for an amazing length of time. At the conclusion he lowered the horn and the drummer began a fast beat. The other musicians slowly joined in, and the resulting music had a rapid pulsing rhythm such as a belly dancer might dance to, but the use of a scale divided into thirds made the music sound strange to western ears accustomed to half tones only.

A group of security guards, dressed like the one I had seen the previous evening, emerged from the palace. They took positions around the pearl. One of them activated a mechanism located in a control box at the base. A front-facing panel of the pearl slowly opened and lowered, like an alien spaceship arrived on earth. On the inside of this panel, now the upper side, was a set of stairs. Whatever the event was, it would take place inside the pearl.

Groups of people began to go into it, parties emerging from the palace or coming ashore from the yachts. Eventually Kadri came down the *Speed Graphic*'s gangway, dressed in a dinner suit. Behind him, between the two guards, came Miranda, though she was barely recognizable. I inspected her through the binoculars. She was dressed in robes, Middle Eastern-style, but these were not the opaque vestments of purdah. Just the opposite: they were diaphanous silken veils which with the strong arc lights of the wharf behind her revealed the shadowed shape of her body beneath.

Business meeting or not, whatever was happening tonight was a social event, presumably a banquet.

At the bottom of the gangway Kadri turned around and looked back up behind him, at first I assumed at Miranda, but when she had reached the bottom he still stared up, and I realized that he was taking a last look at the *Speed Graphic*. Eventually he turned and offered his arm to Miranda, which she accepted. The guards fell in behind them. They walked down the wharf, onto the plaza, and soon joined the rest of the people streaming into the great pearl.

XXXV

T HE INSIDE OF THE PEARL TURNED OUT to be a theater, but a theater unlike any that I had been in before. The interior shape mirrored that of the exterior: it was spherical. Tiers of seats rose along the sides, shallow at first, steeper as they climbed higher, ending at about the equator and in plan view subtending a broad arc, perhaps 270°. The upper hemisphere was unribbed and uncoffered, a vast sweep of enveloping and uninterrupted curvature. It was completely covered in gold leaf, forming a great gilded dome high overhead.

The stage was below and to the right of the entrance, uncurtained and brightly lit.

I kept my head down—not only to avoid recognition by Kadri but also to not invite any conversation or salutation which would have revealed my ignorance of the Arabic language. I made my way to a staircase and climbed it to the highest tier, furthest from the stage. All the seats up here were unoccupied. I selected one far from the entrance, settled in, and surveyed the scene below.

There were around two hundred people. Most of them were dressed in dinner suits but some, like me, wore Arab dress. A sprinkling of women in jewelry and evening wear, but the majority were men: talking, laughing, greeting friends and acquaintances. Swiss watches and Savile Row—they smelled of money, as the wealthy always do.

I spotted Kadri far below but Miranda and the two guards were not with him. In the center of the stage was a large glass cylinder, ten feet tall and a yard or more in diameter, standing upright. Above and on either side hung three flat screens of a size usually seen in a sports stadium; whatever the show was, it would include video. To the far right was a lectern with a microphone mounted on top; there would be narration as well.

The lights dimmed everywhere except the stage, and an expectant silence fell upon the audience. An actor appeared and made his way across the stage. No applause. He took up a position behind the lectern.

The show began. An actress suddenly appeared inside the glass cylinder. She had come up from below, but it happened so quickly that it seemed as if she had been teleported there. She wore a plain white robe of translucent material but was otherwise without a costume, even shoes. She stood immobile inside the tube, staring out at the audience without expression.

In a moment of intense stupidity, at first I imagined that it must be the beginning of a Greek tragedy, something suggested perhaps by the amphitheater-like arrangement of the place, the spare stage, the woman's robe like an ancient chiton. The sudden appearance of a female protagonist suggested an Iphigenia perhaps, arriving on deck to an airless sea and innocently wondering why she had been so hastily summoned. But then the bidding began.

The woman was no actress, she was an article of merchandise. And this was no theater: it was a white-slave market.

I realized how much sense it made. This was why the island had been built: to provide a place where potential buyers could make their purchases in comfort and security, far from the prying eyes of the public and free from legal jurisdiction. The restricted zone and intense secrecy were explained. And no wonder the Iranian government had made no objection; not only was Dar Al Jawan not a military threat, it had the added advantage of dealing with western women in precisely the way that the ayatollahs thought they should be, a point that the "minister" had made abundantly clear.

I recalled Gus Hoyle's definition of the word *jawan*: a fresh young pearl of perfect rose-white hue—even the island's name fitted.

The video screens came alive with a long close-up of the woman's expressionless face; she could not have been older than twenty-five. The platform on which she stood began to rotate, allowing an all-around inspection of the goods, and the camera roamed slowly down her body. A panel above the stage that I had not noticed before suddenly lit up, showing what was presumably the current bid. Even though we were in the Middle East, the woman was a commodity whose price was—like oil—denominated in U.S. dollars. The bidding proceeded for several frantic minutes and when it was complete the girl on stage had been sold for nearly a quarter million.

Miranda was the fourth item on the block: for the second time in a week, she was auctioned. By now I had guessed why she was no longer in Kadri's company, and seeing her arrive on stage was not a surprise. She still wore the evening gown of multiple veils in which I had seen her leave the *Speed Graphic*, and now the reason for such revealing clothing was clear. I wondered if Kadri had decided to sell her after discovering that she was no spy at all, or whether he had never intended to release her in the first place, and had led her to believe that he would eventually let her go only to keep her quiet until the auction began.

Miranda's expression had not the vacant acceptance of the previous three women; instead her face bore a look of profound annoyance. This was no sacrificial Iphigenia, quietly submitting to Agamemnon. This was Elektra, bent on revenge, or Medea, contemplating murder. The bidding was suitably subdued; most of the people in the audience must have sensed that this was a purchase that would likely come with additional costs beyond the winning bid. But not all of them, and among the incautious men vying for the uncertain merits of Miranda's discontented company was a fat robed Arab whose winning bid—$180,000—was going to buy him more trouble than he could have imagined. His big blubbery lips were shiny with spittle, and his unshaven gray jowls shook with joy. When the gavel came down he clapped his pudgy hands in beringed delight, a fool believing that he had made a bargain.

I almost laughed out loud.

Her purchaser, eager with anticipation, did not stay until the end of the auction; he and his entourage shuffled out of their seats and down the stairs. I followed them. In a vestibule to the side of the entrance there was what at first I had taken to be a box office, but when I passed by on the way out the Fat One was at the window, handing over bundles of greenbacks from a briefcase held open by an attendant—this was apparently where the transactions were completed and delivery of the goods taken. Cash on the nose, as might be expected. He was still grinning a salivary grin. I looked forward to wiping it from his face.

I exited the pearl and took the ramp down to the plaza. There were two guards on duty at the bottom, bored but trying not to look it, quietly speaking some East European tongue, presumably Russian. They ignored me. At the far corner of the plaza was a third guard and as I approached I recognized him: the one from the previous evening. Up close I was left with the same impression: ex-special forces, likely ex-Crimea or ex-Ukraine, probably old enough to have seen service in Chechnya, too. He must have sensed me staring at him. I looked away, but I knew after passing by that he was giving me a long look of sober evaluation, and I could almost feel him thinking *this guy doesn't fit.*

I continued down the wharf. I was on the far side of the harbor from the *Speed Graphic*, heading back to that good observation post by the garden where I had first seen her what seemed infinitely longer ago than the forty-eight hours it was. The guard walked slowly down the wharf behind me, not actually following, just wanting to note which yacht I went onto. If I boarded one without challenge from whoever was on watch he would have been satisfied, but of course I could do no such thing.

Instead I went up the staircase into the garden, trying to look like someone just out for some fresh air, but the guard was not buying it: he increased his pace, more definite now. I entered the garden. I could shoot him, but that would just make matters worse. What I needed to do was dispose of him quietly.

The lamps were gas but the starters were electrical. As soon as I was out of sight in the undergrowth I went to the nearest one, opened the base plate, and ripped out the wiring. Twin flex. I stripped it down to a single six-foot strand. I would have liked to find a suitable branch and fabricate handles, but there was no time. I took a position by the hedge in the shadows at the top of the stairs and waited.

He came up quickly, almost at a trot now. I heard that AK-74 come down off his shoulder and the sound of the bolt being pulled to the rear.

It was unslinging the rifle that made it easy for me. With the gun barrel poking up over his shoulder getting the garrote around his throat would have been tricky. But with the gun in his hands I had a clear target. The wire sliced straight through the cartilage of his trachea, cutting off his cry before it left his throat. The rifle fell from his grasp as his hands went instinctively to his neck. He died ugly, drowning in his own blood. He struggled to the end, but he was likely well enough trained to have known that his life was over the moment the wire went unobstructed around his neck.

I lay back, exhausted, and slowly unwound the wire from my hands. I had made many turns but even so the wire had cut through the skin and embedded itself deep into the flesh of my palms. It was painful, but it beat the alternative. My hands were bleeding profusely and I tried not to get any more on my robes than was already there. I gingerly flexed my fingers: the pressure that comes onto the wire in a garrote can snap a metacarpal bone but all my fingers still functioned, confirming that none were broken. Eventually I picked up the AK-74 and set the fire selector to full auto. It was as well my opponent had actioned the bolt: with the way my hands were now I could not have managed it myself. I hoped the magazine was full. There had better not be any hand-to-hand to follow, for I was sure to lose.

I resumed watch over the harbor below. A few minutes later the fat Arab emerged from the great pearl. Miranda followed, flanked between two of his entourage. I waited to see which vessel they boarded. It was a long two-tone speedboat, silver on black, berthed not far forward of the *Speed Graphic*.

The AK-74 was a better weapon than my handgun. I concealed it beneath my robes and headed back down the stairs, hoping that no one would notice all the blood.

XXXVI

T HERE ARE TWO THINGS THAT LED to the development of the high-speed offshore boats known as cigarettes: racing and rum-running. The original *Cigarette* was one of the latter, a famous rum-runner during Prohibition whose exceptional speed allowed her to avoid the authorities and so help keep America supplied with alcohol under the reign of our own ayatollahs. She was a vessel much admired by the cocktail-starved public of the Jazz Age.

With the Repeal her role ended but her name was revived after the war in a racing boat team. Eventually, Cigarette became a company manufacturing the enormous speedboats but, like Hoover and Xerox, the name came to be applied generically to the product, and small-c *cigarette* now refers to any big powerful offshore speedboat, not just those manufactured by Cigarette.

The boat aboard which Miranda Grey had been taken was such a vessel. Her name was plastered across the transom in large metallic letters: Alcazar. She was very long—at least sixty feet, as long as some of the motor yachts—but lay much lower in the water and looked less like a boat than a sleek rocket ship. She was a Magnum—that is, built by Magnum Marine in Miami. Her uppers were finished in metallic silver, her hull was glossy black. Two-thirds of the way back from the gently convex bows was the only interruption to her smooth lines: the cockpit—low speedster windshield, three heavily padded seats abreast behind the controls, two more on the other side. Between them a forward-facing door led down into the interior. Behind the cockpit the deck continued in a flat sweep over her big inboard engines.

One of the seats was occupied by a uniformed crewman. He stood as I stepped aboard the boat uninvited, and was about to protest when I pulled out the AK-74 from beneath my robes.

I put a finger to my lips in the universal gesture for silence and went cautiously over to the controls. The wheel, two throttles, numerous engine and system gauges, a VHF radio with preprogrammed channels, known as a seaphone. I pointed to the empty ignition. He pulled the keys from his pocket and passed them to me without hesitation—he was a smart guy: never argue with anyone covered in blood holding an automatic assault weapon. I pointed at the door and gestured for him to lead the way below. Down we went.

We entered a salon. It was luxuriously appointed and more spacious than would have been guessed from above. To the left was a sitting area surrounding a table fixed to the floor. To the right was the galley. The other two attendants were in there; one preparing food, the other making finishing touches to the dining table. It was set for two with candles and a bunch of cream-colored roses in a vase—the Fat One was going to try a romantic dinner with Miranda, which was almost worth waiting to see. I was saved from the need to hush the crewmen by the guy from above, who did it for me: he did not want to end up getting caught in any crossfire.

There was a little vestibule forward, with three doors leading off it. I looked inquiringly at my friend. He pointed to the one on the right and made washing gestures with his hands: it was the head. He pointed to the one on the left and traced an hourglass shape with his fingers: Miranda was in there, something I had already assumed from the padlocked latch. Then he pointed to the center and largest door, presumably leading to the master stateroom, and held his hands over an enormous imaginary stomach: that was where the boss was.

I looked at the padlock and made an unlocking gesture. Two of them immediately pointed toward the center door: the master kept the key himself. I would have liked to release Miranda and have her keep watch on them while I secured the boat's owner, but breaking the latch would make too much noise.

I motioned with the barrel and all three of them got down onto the deck. I kept gesturing until they had assumed the position I wanted, lying flat on their stomachs and with hands behind their heads. Then I went forward to the master stateroom and opened the door.

The compartment reeked of cologne. It occupied the full width of the boat. In the center was a double bed, on one side a dresser and the other built-in shelves. The fat guy stood in front of the dresser, combing his hair. When he saw me he put down the comb in a moment of brief confusion, then turned and charged. I put a short burst into his chest, and down he went.

I turned. One of the crewmen was climbing the stairs, trying to escape. I fired a second burst and back he fell into the salon. The other two stayed put. I used the butt of the rifle to smash away the latch and opened the door to Miranda's stateroom. She was sitting on the bunk, legs crossed, looking up at me as I burst into the compartment.

"What took you so long?" she said. "I was about to be ravished."

It occurred to me that any attempt by the Fat One on Miranda's virtue would probably have led to serious personal injury on his part, but there was no time to discuss it now.

"Come with me."

I led her out through the salon and up to the cockpit. If she had any reaction to all the blood and gore she did not show it. On deck I could already hear shouting coming from the end of the wharf: the shots had been loud enough to attract attention, even though all the shooting had been inside.

"Let go all lines."

Miranda hurried forward to begin unsecuring us. I went to the controls, made sure that the throttles were in neutral, then inserted the ignition key. There were two engines, each with its own starter button. I feared they might be diesels, meaning a wait for the glow plugs to get warm, but both of them fired up immediately. The noise was tremendous, not just the normal sound of marine motors but that deep-throated barely muffled gurgle of racing engines, unhappy at idle, longing to be under full throttle. The sound reverberated around the bowl of the harbor.

If the gunshots had alerted people that something was up, then the unexpected sound of those engines confirmed it: the guards came racing down the wharf, weapons unslung, and some idiot on a nearby motor yacht had turned on a searchlight and was directing it toward us.

I went to single-shot mode and fired at the searchlight. I did not hit it, but whoever had turned it on reconsidered the situation and turned it back off again. Miranda went racing aft as I took aim along the wharf. I fired once, but the guards kept running instead of taking cover as they should have. I reverted to full auto and fired an extended burst, which had the intended effect: they hit the deck.

Miranda jumped into the seat beside me.

"All clear."

"Take this," I said, handing her the rifle. "Short bursts, just enough to keep them down. Not too much: if the guys below see that we're out of ammo they might put up a fight."

She nodded in quick comprehension and took aim, letting off a few rounds. They did not return fire: being professionals they would have been wary of firing in the crowded harbor, and with us low in the water on a dark evening they had no clear target to begin with. I cleared us out of the berth and opened up the throttles. The engine note deepened, and the Alcazar swiftly rose onto the plane, carving a long wake out of the harbor and into open water.

Now they fired at us, little high-toned pings barely audible above the engine noise. I weaved a little, enough to disrupt a steady aim. If any of the rounds hit home I was not aware of them. Soon we were out of range. I brought the Alcazar around to a southeasterly course and headed for the coast of the Arabian peninsula.

I called the two surviving crewmen on deck. They were reluctant to come up but when Miranda handed them lifejackets—two apiece—their expressions brightened. I pointed with a thumb at the water and over they went, grateful to be alive. After they were gone I gave Miranda the wheel and went below. Getting the third crewman's body over the side was easy enough, but Miranda's would-be owner was a serious deadweight, and his bulk barely fitted through the door. Eventually I was able to get him up and roll him overboard. The boat felt a little faster after we had disposed of him.

"We made it," Miranda shouted.

I nodded, although I knew that it was probably not going to be that simple. Forty-eight hours ago there had been two patrol boats alongside in Dar Al Jawan; tonight there had been just one.

We soon saw the other boat, fine on our starboard bow, her steaming light and port navigation light visible as she raced to cut us off. We had not put on any lights but it made no difference: she could track us by radar and plot a precise course to intercept. I took the wheel and steered straight for her. A half-empty AK-74 would be no match for whatever she mounted on the forward hard point, probably a .50-caliber heavy machine gun, but I wanted to allow the maximum sea room to get around her: our only advantage was speed, and I intended to use it. When we were what I guessed to be about half a mile away I put the wheel hard over. A moment later she opened fire. We could hear the bursts and see the muzzle flash and even pick up the occasional red streak of a tracer round zinging way beyond the boat. Her fire was wildly inaccurate and fell nowhere near us. We soon left her far astern and once again I was able to come around to the southeast and head for the shore.

XXXVII

THERE WERE SEVEN OTHER PEOPLE IN THE ROOM. Eight, if counting the virtual presence emanating from the speakerphone sitting in the center of the conference table, barely audible, a deep background reverberation that might be mistaken for something electrical, or if animate then certainly not human, but I knew that it was actually the sound of Dortmund breathing and wondered how a man so clever could have failed to locate the mute-button.

The conference room had windows but they gave onto the embassy's central courtyard. The walls had tempest shielding and the speakerphone was connected to an encrypted line—the site was secure.

The ambassador occupied the seat at the head of the table. As it was his turf he was nominally in charge, but as soon as the four-star had marched into the room it had been clear who would be taking command. The ambassador's initial resentment was now mixed with relief at having had the burden of responsibility so decisively removed from him.

The general took a seat on the opposite side of the table from me. While waiting for the others to arrive he had given me a long hard stare, and I knew without asking that before leaving Qatar he had pulled my service record—evidently he had not liked what he read, especially the dishonorable discharge that was presumably the last entry in it.

I stared straight back.

The marines do not go in much for distinguishing ornamentation, but the army love their baubles and every soldier's biography is plastered across his chest. Since the general was a four-star, he was adorned like a South American dictator. I went through the many insignia.

Black-and-gold Ranger tab on the left shoulder, which meant that he had more than a basic infantry background, but there was not above it the Special Forces tab that was the army's equivalent of force recon. Unit citations above the right pocket, which can be ignored; it is the individual decorations above the left pocket that count. I first looked for the easiest to identify: Purple Hearts. He had none. I had two, which sounds impressive but is not, at least not in my case—you do not have to get banged up very badly to earn one. None of the biggies: Distinguished Service Cross (extreme gallantry) or Silver Star (just regular gallantry). Like me, he had a Bronze Star, but his did not have the V for valor: it had been awarded for meritorious service instead. That meant nothing: luck and opportunity are both beyond the power of men to summon, and for all I knew he could have been a Medal of Honor recipient, an award whose ribbon I did not know, having never seen one.

Above the ribbons was a combat infantry badge, which meant that at least he had been in a real shooting match. The only campaign ribbon I recognized was Gulf One, and I hoped that it was not the sole basis for the combat badge. On the pocket flap were para wings but no "mustard stains," the little gold stars indicating combat jumps. No freefall badge, so he was not high-altitude qualified like me.

The comparisons were absurd; those four stars on his shoulders trumped me hands down, even without the fact of the court-martial. The uniform itself was as crisp as if it had just come fresh from the quartermaster's stores, notwithstanding the hurried flight from Qatar. The general commanded US Central Command and was therefore a true military bigshot, just one step away from having it all: Joint Chiefs. CENTCOM is headquartered in Tampa, but since their area of responsibility covers the Middle East they have theater HQ in Doha, Qatar, and we had been lucky or unlucky enough that the four-star happened to be there when Miranda and I had shown up at the gates of the U.S. embassy in Abu Dhabi, soaked from the swim ashore after opening the sea cocks on the Alcazar, preferring the physical evidence of having shot and killed two men to disappear beneath the waves.

The general had with him two aides whose lapel badges revealed their specializations: a full colonel with an M-26 and crossed sabers—armor—and a major with the dagger and rose signifying military intelligence. The major made sense but I was not sure why the tank guy was here. No marines had been invited.

But the navy had shown up, two of them, having naturally but unconsciously taken seats on the opposite side of the table from the army. The commander wore a surface warfare badge, the lieutenant-commander wore one with a pair of diving dolphins: he was a submariner. Unlike the army officers they were open and voluble, and they reminded me more of their Iranian counterparts than their countrymen sitting across the table.

The last person sat apart from everyone else at the far end of the table. Mid-thirties, civilian clothing. He made no attempt to introduce himself.

Miranda walked in, returning from the infirmary. Strange to say, she had been shot: one of the rounds that had been fired at us from the wharf or the patrol boat had grazed an arm. The wound was so superficial that neither of us had noticed until it was revealed during the quick medical examination we had undergone on arrival at the embassy. Good enough for a Purple Heart, however: I had earned one of mine for much the same.

She looked fine for a girl who has just been shot: freshly showered, smelling of soap, and all the better for the few hours of sleep she had gotten. Someone had found clothes for her: khaki trousers and a white safari shirt rolled at the sleeves to reveal on her left bicep the bottom of the bandage. The shirt was several sizes too big and unbuttoned at the throat sufficiently to reveal that whoever had supplied the clothes had not found a full set of underwear. The army guys tried to look businesslike, but the naval officers made no effort to keep the pleasure from their faces.

The only person whose eyes were not pinned to Miranda was the civilian. His expressionless gaze continued to calmly sequence through the other players as it had the entire time, quietly evaluating them.

The ambassador stood.

"Miss Grey, I hope that you're feeling better."

"Fine, Mr. Ambassador. It was just a scratch; probably not even from a bullet."

She was lying: we had identified the entry and exit points in her clothing, and the wound was not a scratch from something sharp but the shallow groove characteristic of a gunshot graze—but her declaration had the intended effect of deflecting attention from her. All except the civilian, who looked at Miranda with sudden interest, and I could tell that he had somehow gained access to her medical report and was now wondering why she would deliberately play it down.

The ambassador looked out over the table. "Well, folks, perhaps we should begin with introductions. As I think you all know, my name is Bob Adamson, and I have the honor of being the U.S. ambassador to the United Arab Emirates."

He sat down with a look of deep self-satisfaction that might have been more understandable had the ambassadorship been the culmination of years of distinguished service in the State Department, but earlier today one of the staff had quietly told me that his was a political appointment made in reward for hefty campaign donations. Back home, Adamson owned a series of auto dealerships.

The general cleared his throat but remained seated.

"Kastoriano. US Central Command, general commanding." No first-name nonsense for him. He nodded to the man on his right. "This is Colonel Lloyd, whom I have assigned to take charge of the operation."

There was no operation to take charge of, at least not yet, but he was making the point to the ambassador and everyone else that whatever happened from now on was going to be his show. The Pentagon and Foggy Bottom are on opposite sides of the Potomac, but it might as well have been an ocean that separated them: Defense and State cannot stand each other.

Lloyd, having been introduced by his master, said nothing himself and settled for a nod. The major spoke up, although strict military precedence would have made the naval commander next.

"Major Dunbar, US Central Command, military intelligence." He tried to sound authoritative, but in the end he could not help glancing toward the civilian for his reaction, perhaps hoping not to see there a smile of condescension. The civilian remained perfectly expressionless. The naval commander spoke up next.

"I'm John Hartsridge, Flag ASW Officer, embarked on USS *Vinson*. The admiral commanding the battle group sent me to act as the point person for any naval element in...in whatever this is all about."

For as long as the *Vinson* battle group was in the Middle East the general sitting across the table from me technically owned it: his was a high-echelon combined command and so he had charge of all combatants in his AOR, not just the army. But there was a subtle message to the colonel in the commander's response: your boss can bully all he wants, but my boss is only under his authority temporarily; you and I should work together.

The lieutenant-commander introduced himself.

"Gary Riehl. I'm the submarine liaison officer on the *Vinson*. I'm a submariner by trade, which is why they sent me."

It looked like I was next.

"Lysander Dalton. No affiliation."

"Marine," Kastoriano said. It sounded like an accusation.

"Ex-," I corrected.

I could tell that he expected me to add a "sir," but all that stuff stopped when they stripped me of my rank and locked me up in Leavenworth. His eyes went to Miranda.

"Miranda Grey," she said. "I'm an out-of-work airline pilot."

The general looked at the last person in the room, the silent civilian.

"Tom Vannerberg," he said. "State." No one believed that he was from the State Department, but neither did anyone choose to question the assertion. "I have a colleague listening in on the secure line," Vannerberg added. No name; Dortmund did not wish to be identified.

The general turned to his colonel. "All yours, Bill."

Colonel Lloyd spoke for the first time.

"Captain Dalton, perhaps you can take us through everything from the beginning to make sure that we're all on the same page."

I would have liked to correct that *Captain*, which had been introduced to subtly assert his superior rank, but there were more important things at stake right now. I gave as succinct a briefing as I could, but even so it took twenty precious minutes. I ended with what I hoped was a hint that we should act first and save the discussions for later.

"It was obviously some sort of laser weapon," I told them. "It might be better to intercept the *Speed Graphic* before the thing gets delivered."

No one paid the slightest attention to my suggestion. Instead, Hartsridge asked me if I could draw a picture of it.

There was a whiteboard and some markers. I made a quick sketch.

"Perhaps ten feet high," I said. "Big heavy cables running back to a bank of power converters. That and the liquid nitrogen suggested heavy power use, presumably as an energy weapon."

"And this glass capsule?"

"Part of the vessel's structure, like I said."

"Optical quality?"

"I would say good. Kadri told me that he had the thing designed by a telescope builder."

"With the weapon in the capsule, what was the field of fire?"

"Limited in azimuth by the outer hulls, around sixty or seventy degrees I would guess. But high elevation, perhaps unlimited, all the way to ninety."

"What about down?"

"Down?"

"Could the laser point downward?"

"Yes, as a matter of fact it could."

"How far?"

"Perhaps straight down. Certainly close to it."

"So it actually had a one hundred-and-eighty-degree elevation arc?"

"I guess so, if shooting at the ground counts."

"It does at sea," the commander said. "During this demonstration, did you notice which way the laser was pointing?"

"I didn't get a clear look. I had the impression that it was moving from side to side, but whether it was pointing up or down I have no idea."

"I saw it," Miranda said. "I glanced up from my hiding place during the demonstration, and I can confirm that it was pointed down. Also, it was moving side-to-side as Captain Dalton says, like this."

She made a gesture, finger pointed down and swinging through a narrow arc. I could see both naval officers nod, as if they had already suspected this. The commander turned back to me.

"And this demonstration was made to the two submariners?"

"At the time I thought it was being made to the minister, and that the submariners were just in attendance because they had transported him. But I could be wrong."

"You saw the submarine dive before the demonstration?"

"Diving, yes. Not yet dived."

"And are you certain of the wavelengths?"

"Positive." I had made sure to remember the scales on those gauges, measured in nanometers: detailed intelligence like that can make all the difference in the success or failure of a reconnaissance mission.

Hartsridge turned inquiringly to the other naval officer, who nodded but said nothing: they had obviously discussed it earlier and already reached a tentative conclusion, something that our reporting had just confirmed. Hartsridge now addressed the army officers, with occasional glances down the table at Vannerberg the civilian.

"We don't think that it's a weapon. We think that it's a submarine detection system."

He was silent a moment.

"Like sonar?" the general eventually asked.

"Yes, sir."

"So, no real problem then?"

"No, sir, just the opposite. It is a big problem. It is more than a big problem, it is our worst nightmare."

"Care to explain that, commander?"

But it was the submariner who spoke up.

"General, I hope that you won't be insulted if we spend a moment going through submarine basics."

"Not at all. Go ahead."

"Sir, let me first state the golden rule: the only real threat to a submarine is another submarine. Yes, surface ships are equipped with sonar and weapons and so on, but the truth is that nine times out of ten a submarine could sink a surface ship before the latter even knew she was there. Commander Hartsridge is an antisubmarine specialist, and I think he will agree." Hartsridge nodded in confirmation, and Riehl continued. "It's basic physics really: in the war under the sea, sound is everything. Submarines can hear a surface ship from many miles away, but they themselves are practically silent. The surface ship must usually send out a sonar ping and detect a return echo to find a submarine, but all the sub needs to do is listen. In any case, submarine weapons far exceed the range of the surface ships' sonars. And as if that wasn't enough, submarines can of course see the surface ships while themselves remaining invisible. We therefore have a huge advantage before a shot has even been fired."

"Okay, but what about this thing Dalton found?"

"Imagine if the sea was as transparent as air. Imagine if submarines were as visible as surface ships. Sound would cease to be a factor, and submarines would no longer hold the advantage. In fact, it would be just the opposite: they would be easy targets—you could just drop homing torpedoes on them from the air at your leisure, and they would be all but unable to defend themselves. They would be sitting ducks."

"Go on."

"That's what this laser does, sir. It sees through the water."

The submariner sat back, allowing the other people in the room to absorb the news. Hartsridge took up the explanation.

"That's why there was a submarine at the demonstration: it was a test target to prove that the thing worked. Blue-light laser penetrates water, but not red light, which was why we wanted to make sure of the wavelengths observed by Captain Dalton. But there is a severe limitation: backscatter. The aim is to have the light pulse travel down, hit the target, reflect back up and be detected: 'seeing,' although in this case the seeing would initially be done electronically, and then the signal converted into a visible image on a monitor. The problem with this has always been water impurities. Sea water is full of small particulate matter from which the laser will also reflect, so how do you separate the return from the submarine and the returns from all the other stuff? It's like trying to see an aircraft in a cloud. Well, we think they've solved the backscatter problem. In fact, the vessel's name gives it away."

"*Speed Graphic*?"

"Yes. We presume she is called *Speed Graphic* because she is effectively a floating camera. But the name is even more specific than that. The *speed* in a Speed Graphic camera comes from the speed of its shutter, which operates like a little Venetian blind, opening and closing in just a tiny fraction of a second. We guess that this is what the laser device does: it sends down its phased energy, then continually opens and closes the shutter, very fast, first seeing the returns from, say, fifty feet only, then from sixty feet only, then from seventy feet only, and so on to the maximum depth. That way the backscatter from particles at fifty feet and sixty feet won't obscure the picture at seventy. All of a sudden you've solved the backscatter problem and have a clear view at every depth. You can see underwater."

"How come we don't have these?"

"There's a second issue: range. The maximum depth that a blue-light laser can penetrate seawater is about 150 feet. That is quite shallow. Most submarines can dive to 600 feet or so, U.S. boats twice that. Some of the old titanium-hulled Soviet hunter-killers could manage 3,000 feet. The depth that we actually operate at varies, depending on a number of factors, especially the temperature gradients in the water, but 300 feet is typical. Therefore, as a practical matter, a laser system with a maximum range of 150 feet is of limited use."

"So why is this thing your worst nightmare, commander?"

"Because the maximum depth of the Persian Gulf is 200 feet. Mostly it's much shallower. And even at 200 feet, a submarine itself has a 30-foot diameter pressure hull, not counting the sail. And of course submarines don't operate right on the bottom; we are very careful to avoid it, in fact. In practical terms, submarines in the Persian Gulf never operate below 150 feet. In the rest of the world's seas and oceans a laser would miss detecting most submarines. The exception is the Persian Gulf, because it's so shallow. This device effectively makes the Gulf transparent to whoever possesses it."

"Are you telling me that the Iranians would know exactly where our submarines were?"

"Yes, sir, they would. And I'm afraid it's worse than that, sir. The Iranians have submarines of their own: three Russian-built Kilo-class boats. They are the only Gulf state to operate submarines. If they know where ours are, then their own submarines can operate with impunity. Like I said at the beginning, the golden rule is that the only real threat to a submarine is another submarine. They can therefore now use their submarines to close down the Gulf at will. A quarter of the world's oil supply can be shut down overnight, and there would be nothing we could do to stop them."

The general sat back, and all the bravado was gone from him. There was a long silence, which eventually I broke.

"Excuse me, but shouldn't an order be put out to intercept the *Speed Graphic* now?"

In response, Commander Hartsridge shuffled through the folder in front of him, removing a photograph which he passed to me. It was an aerial shot of a harbor, but not Dar Al Jawan. The *Speed Graphic*, distinctive even from above, was alongside a wharf.

"Bandar Abbas," the commander explained, "the principal Iranian naval base. This image was taken several hours ago, Captain Dalton. I'm afraid that it's too late: the *Speed Graphic* has already been delivered."

XXXVIII

T HERE WAS A LONG CONTEMPLATIVE SILENCE in the conference room following the revelation that the *Speed Graphic* was already in the hands of the Iranians. Eventually I pushed my chair back and stood. Whatever was to come now, it was no longer my business.

"Where are you going?" the four-star demanded.

"I've told you all I know, general. I guess it's pretty obvious what comes next."

"What?"

"Destroy the *Speed Graphic*."

"Don't be stupid—we're not going to start another Gulf War over this."

"I wasn't thinking of an overt assault. A SEAL team could quietly take out the *Speed Graphic* and be gone before anyone was the wiser. Even if the Iranians suspected who was responsible they could never prove a thing."

Before he could respond the civilian spoke up, the first time since having introduced himself.

"Can I ask you something before you go, Captain Dalton?"

"What?"

"You said there were two lasers in this device?"

"Yes."

"What was the second laser for?"

"I assumed range-finding—we use red-light lasers for range-finding in force recon."

"But according to the naval experts here, red-light laser doesn't penetrate water."

"No."

"So range-finding doesn't make sense."

"No."

"Makes you think, doesn't it?"

Actually, I had not thought about it at all.

"I guess I just don't know what it's for."

"Would you mind having a look at these?"

Vannerberg removed a bundle of photographs from a folder, perhaps a score in total. He selected three and laid them out on the table in a row. I stood by him to examine them.

Like the one Hartsridge had shown me earlier, they were aerial shots, but these images appeared to have been taken with different cameras and so presumably from different satellites: they had been shot at a lower altitude and showed much better resolution. All three were black-and-white. The first one was without shadows: it had been taken at night, probably with an infrared camera. The date-time group was stamped in the lower left-hand corner. The time was in Zulu. I converted it to local; the image had been taken shortly after five A.M. The second shot had been taken at around ten A.M.

something confirmed by the westward leaning shadows. But the third shot was without shadows, like the first, although it had been taken in broad daylight at two P.M., not long before the meeting had begun. The grain was not as fine as in the first two, and I realized that I must be looking at an image shot not with visible light but with side aperture radar: a Lacrosse reconnaissance satellite.

All three images showed the harbor at Bandar Abbas. It was trident shaped, north-pointing, and with the long center arm occupied by commercial shipping. The eastern prong was obviously the naval base: there were a number of small warships, corvette-sized, alongside the wharves. It took me a moment to realize that the southernmost wharf, isolated from the rest of the base, was not empty as I had at first thought. There were two submarines secured alongside, their black hulls all but invisible against the dark water below.

The *Speed Graphic* was further up the harbor, nearby a dry dock. Her transom door was open to form a ramp leading down to the wharf. The landing deck was unoccupied: the yacht's helicopter had, like most else, been removed from her before delivery.

"That's her," I said, pointing to the spot.

"Would you compare the photographs, Captain, and tell me if you see any changes?"

I checked for the most obvious thing first: shipping movements.

"One of their missile corvettes put to sea."

"Yes, no doubt to patrol offshore, in case we were to attempt an immediate seaborne assault. Anything else?"

The *Speed Graphic* herself seemed unchanged in all three photos. I looked for activity on the wharf beside her.

"There's a truck in this last shot that wasn't there before."

"What sort of truck?"

"A cargo truck."

"Large or small?"

I checked the scale, but the comparison of the *Speed Graphic* beside her was all that I needed.

"Large," I said. I was starting to get it now.

"What do you deduce from these photographs, Captain Dalton?"

I sat back down.

"They're going to remove the laser device."

"That's what I think, too." He turned to face the rest of the room. "We've already identified the truck," he said. "It's an ex-Russian military vehicle of a type operated by the Iranian Revolutionary Guards. It's used to transport high-value weaponry, usually missiles, but in this case no doubt the laser. As I'm sure you all know, the Revolutionary Guards are the closest thing the Iranians have to elite troops. They guard the weapon labs, among other things."

The general spoke up.

"Are you saying they're taking the laser to a weapons lab?"

"That's what we assume."

"For what purpose?"

"To replicate it."

"You mean they are going to build more of these *Speed Graphics*?"

"No. That wouldn't account for the red-light laser."

"Then what?"

"There has to be some purpose for the red-light laser, general. Otherwise, why have it?"

"So what's it for?"

"To measure altitude."

A long silence, broken at last by Hartsridge.

"So this one is only a prototype," he said. "It was never meant to be seaborne: they are going to put them in aircraft."

Vannerberg nodded. "Thus the red-light laser, needed to measure altitude instantaneously. Take the reading from the blue-light laser, subtract the reading from the red-light laser, and that gives you the precise depth of the submarine. And thus also the lightweight servo components observed by Captain Dalton. Hence also the purchase by the Iranians of six aging Russian airliners that would no longer be of commercial use: they are going to convert them to airborne surveillance systems equipped with these sub-detecting lasers. Kind of complicates things, doesn't it?"

"Very much."

"Have they unloaded the laser yet?"

"Not at the time of this photograph, otherwise the truck would have left. Chances are they will wait until morning rather than attempting so delicate a task in the dark, which means that we have just tonight to do something about it."

The general checked his watch.

"Still four hours of light left, Mr. Vannerberg. Even if it could be mounted in time, which I doubt, running an operation in the hope that they'll wait until morning doesn't make much sense."

"We'll know for sure at 5:48 this afternoon, general."

Kastoriano was initially taken aback by the certainty of this declaration, but he soon figured it out. Photographic reconnaissance satellites run in roughly polar orbits, circling the earth about fourteen times a day. During those fourteen orbits they will pass over their primary targets just twice. The orbits are designed so that one of those two passes will always occur either in the early morning or the late afternoon, to get those shadows that are so helpful in image analysis. Bandar Abbas, being the principal Iranian military base on the Strait of Hormuz, was an obvious primary target, hence that infrared photograph at five this morning. The Advanced Keyhole satellite that had taken it would therefore make its second pass late this afternoon—presumably at 5:48—this time using visible light rather than infrared photography. If it found the truck still there then it was a good bet that the Iranians would wait until the next day before unloading the laser.

Vannerberg continued.

"If we begin planning now, we may be able to mount an operation to destroy the laser tonight. Should the last satellite image show that the truck is no longer there, then we can always call it off. But if the truck is still there, then we have one last chance to do something now before this thing disappears forever into some underground weapons lab, after which a few months from now the Iranians will gain absolute control of the Persian Gulf."

"It's not enough time to organize a special ops team," the general said flatly.

Vannerberg nodded in silent agreement. His eyes went to me, as I had suspected they would.

A long silence. I shrugged my shoulders; I had no real choice.

I turned to Hartsridge. "Do you have a submarine that can get me in close?"

"No, and no," he answered. "No submarine near enough, and even if we did it couldn't deliver you in close: the water is too shallow approaching Bandar Abbas; even their own submarines transit in and out on the surface."

"Small craft?"

"That corvette patrolling off the base would find it long before we could deliver you."

"Okay, I'll have to HAHO in." I turned to the four-star. "General, what type of aircraft did you fly over on?"

"C-130."

"Can I borrow it?"

"Borrow it for what, Dalton?"

"Insertion into Bandar Abbas."

"Forget it. I am not authorizing a flight into Iran."

"It will remain in international airspace the whole time, general. They'll file a flight plan, talk to ATC, squawk IFF, do it all by the book. In all respects it will be just a routine flight, except that by the time it lands I will no longer be aboard."

"It doesn't matter, Dalton. We do not conduct military operations against foreign nations without the approval of the national command authority. Like I said, I'm not going to start another Gulf war."

In the uncomfortable pause that followed this emphatic pronouncement there was just a single sound: a meaningful throat-clearing emanating from the speakerphone. It was to be Dortmund's first and last contribution to the proceeding, but it was an important one, prompting Vannerberg to withdraw a folded piece of paper from his coat pocket, which he then passed to the general without remark.

It had been torn from a roll, the way military signals are after they have been printed out on teletype machines.

The four-star read it, reread it more slowly, then silently passed it to the colonel. Lloyd read it through several times before passing it back. The general read it a third time.

"This is very loosely worded, Mr. Vannerberg."

"As they so often are, general."

I wondered where the signal had come from. There were not many levels above CENTCOM in the chain of command: the Joint Chiefs, the civilian leadership in the Pentagon, the National Security Council perhaps, and of course the White House at the very top. But whatever authority had issued it, the order had no doubt originated with Dortmund. As usual, he had thought through everything in advance.

Nobody said anything for a minute. Being the Washington insider that he was, Dortmund would have worded the order so that whoever had signed it could claim credit for success but accuse the general of exceeding his authority in the event of failure. If I screwed up, any chance Kastoriano had at Joint Chiefs would be gone forever. Every general must play the political game but sometimes they go over to the other side, and if this one had done so then his next action would be to demand clearer orders before proceeding, as was his right. I looked at Kastoriano now, wondering whether he was still a soldier, or if by this stage in his career he had become just another politician in uniform.

Eventually he folded the signal and put it in his pocket. He looked at me.

"Okay, let's hear it, Dalton. Big picture first."

Still a soldier. I tried to keep it brief and upbeat.

"Sir, I do a high-altitude drop from the C-130 and glide from international airspace into Iran. Too small for radar to detect: they won't know I'm there. Bandar Abbas is right on the coast, so getting in will be the easy part. From the drop zone I make my way down to the port, set timed charges aboard the *Speed Graphic*, then extract."

"Extract how?"

"As opportunity presents. I'll have a preplanned rendezvous tomorrow night with the navy in international waters. If I don't show up it's because I've decided to make my way overland instead. I'll arrive in Iraq or Pakistan sometime later, about a week from now."

"Why not fly out?"

It was Miranda who asked this strange question. All eyes went to her, and an awkward silence followed.

It was Major Dunbar who eventually spoke.

"Fly out how?"

"Steal an aircraft." Miranda had been glancing through some of the satellite images. She separated one from the others. It was not a shot of the harbor but of runways by the desert. "Where is this airfield, major?"

The major twisted his head and examined the photograph.

"That's Bandar Abbas International. It's a joint civilian/military facility. The civilian terminal is at the southern end of the field. What this shot shows is the military part, at the northern end."

"And these aircraft?"

She pointed to a series of what had at first looked to me like large dark oil stains on the tarmac, but then I noticed that they were all lined up neatly, and if you looked hard enough you could make out the shape of aircraft. Their camouflage paint scheme did a good job.

"They're F-4s. That is, Phantoms: old U.S.-built aircraft from before the Revolution. They belong to the 91st or 92nd Tactical Wing of the Iranian Air Force, which are headquartered at Bandar Abbas."

"Then why not drop in a pilot with Captain Dalton and simply fly away?"

The major smiled. "It's a very nice idea," he said in the condescending tone of a professional speaking to a well-meaning but hopelessly naive amateur. "But the thing is these are Vietnam-era aircraft, and the U.S. military stopped flying them years ago. Where are we going to find a pilot in time?"

"Me."

"I don't mean just any pilot, Miss Grey. I mean a qualified F-4 pilot."

"Me."

"Miss Grey, F-4s are military fighter-bombers. To have flown one you would have had to have been in the military, and given the age of the aircraft you would be in your late forties at least, which you obviously are not. In any case they are combat aircraft, and so under the rules of the U.S. military at that time it is not possible for a female to have flown them. I know you mean well, but we really must get on with mission planning, so perhaps you'll leave it to us for now."

Miranda ignored him and addressed the table at large.

"Before I got an airline job I had to get as many flying hours as possible. That's the main thing that the airlines look for when hiring: number of hours. The more experience you have, the more likely it is they'll give you a job. But getting hours is expensive, so I joined the Air National Guard. As the major points out, women are not allowed in combat roles, which means we usually end up flying transports. That suited me just fine because transport means multi-engine, and multi-engine hours are the best hours for landing a position with an airline. But instead they gave me the very worst flying job in the whole national guard. When the last F-4 squadrons were shut down they decided to convert some of the aircraft to pilotless target drones for live missile firings. They're better than regular drones because they are genuine high-performance fighters, so you can make them do more realistic combat maneuvers. But the conversion requires testing, and during the testing there has to be a qualified pilot in the front seat to take over and fly the aircraft manually if something goes wrong. No one wanted the job: it was dangerous, the aircraft were old and by then poorly maintained, the flying was unexciting because it was mostly done by remote, and there was absolutely no future in it, since the F-4s were already phased out. That's why I got the assignment: no one else wanted it. But hours are hours, and I was grateful for the job. As far as I know, I am the last person in America, male or female, to ever qualify on an F-4. And here I am."

XXXIX

MIRANDA AND I WERE ON PURE OXYGEN, and I wondered if since meeting me she was becoming weary of breathing from compressed gas tanks. Freefalls above 12,000 feet are usually done with hundred-percent oxygen, and tonight we would be jumping from twice that height. One of the two main problems in high-altitude work is hypoxia, and so to reduce the risk you go onto pure oxygen thirty minutes before the jump, thus flushing all nitrogen from the body.

I could see nothing of her face, covered as it was by the helmet and mask. She had both visors down, so I could not even see her eyes. The mirrored one is meant for daylight operations only, tinted and covered in reflective material to protect the eyes from raw sunlight unfiltered by the further five miles of the atmosphere through which it would normally travel before reaching the earth. But if she wanted it down she could keep it down: the less she saw the better.

The C-130 gave a big lumbering lurch. There was not much turbulence at 24,000 feet but we were close to the aircraft's operating ceiling and she was struggling through the thin air. It was an old C-130, a basic no-frills transport model, not one of the MC-130 Combat Talon variants with which I was more familiar: aircraft modified for special operations work. Like Miranda, she was Air National Guard. Military transports have tail markings that, as with a soldier's insignia, reveal much about them. There are two big letters indicating the home base, in this case *CI*: Channel Islands, an Air National Guard base in Ventura Country, California, and home of the 146th Airlift Wing. What an experienced eye looks for is not these two large letters but the smaller alphanumeric marking located lower down and forward on the tail. It is composed of the service designation and the year that the aircraft was ordered. This one read "ANG74": this particular aircraft was ordered way back in 1974 and was probably older than the pilots flying her. She showed her age: everything in her that was not already broken creaked and groaned as if about to snap. It was like being inside a sailing ship in heavy weather.

I looked at the woman sitting across from me. The noise of the engines would have made conversation impossible except by shouting, even without masks, and so we had hardly spoken since takeoff. She was still studying the sheets that had been hurriedly faxed to her during those precious few hours of planning we had managed prior to takeoff. It was a preflight checklist for an F-4E, the version most common in the Iranian inventory.

Gone now was the aloof patrician at Arlington, and gone too was the indulgent sensualist in the south of France, a creature lifted straight from *Luxe, Calme et Volupté*. Miranda had once again transformed herself, this time into a machine-like creature, someone

I felt surprisingly confident going into combat with. She was a changeling, someone you could never quite put your finger on. I could not help thinking of those quantum particles to whose intangible qualities physicists attribute the most whimsical of labels: up, down, strange, charm, beauty, truth. Miranda was an endlessly shifting amalgam of them all, a little quark burst into life.

I wondered if she was thinking of what was to come. In as much as it is possible to conclude someone's mood when their face is hidden, she seemed in good spirits, even content. This was probably a result of the pure O_2; I felt pretty good myself. The rest of her body was as well disguised as her face, for the other big threat in high-altitude work is frostbite. We had Nomex jumpsuits, but the colonel's supply people had been unable to locate the polypropylene thermal liners you normally wear beneath them—not unsurprising in the Middle East. The ambassador had shown himself to be more than just a political drone, asking his staff to go home and return with leggings and sweat suits and the like. Under our jumpsuits we now wore a mixed variety of civilian workout gear, layer after layer. I could not help smiling: heavily armed and heavily padded, Miranda looked like a militant Michelin Man.

I had used duct tape to seal the cuffs to our gloves and boots. HALOs are bad enough but HAHOs are worse, and it would be entirely possible to freeze to death while doing one. Military freefall is specific to special ops, and is not much like the parachute drops practiced by regular airborne. The aim of airborne is to get a lot of troops into the drop zone quickly, so the jumps are usually conducted from no more than a thousand feet and last less than a minute; there is no risk of hypoxia or frostbite. They leap out, one after another in rapid succession, each with a static line attached to the aircraft which when the jumper is clear automatically deploys the canopy, a dome of traditional parachute design.

High-altitude work is different. To begin with, we use rectangular canopies because the rigs are maneuverable. There are two basic jump profiles: HALO and HAHO. HALO is an acronym for *high-altitude low-opening*: in other words a long freefall followed by deployment of the canopy just before you go splat. The technique is used so that the aircraft can stay above opposition missiles during the insertion. HAHO means *high-altitude high-opening*: in other words almost no freefall at all: the canopy is deployed shortly after leaving the aircraft. From such a high altitude you can glide a very long way, as we would be doing tonight, gliding from international airspace into Iran. The advantage of a HAHO is that the aircraft can avoid opposition defenses entirely. The disadvantage is that you spend a long time at high altitude with the temperature well below zero.

The jumpmaster came back aft and held up two open hands in front of my face: ten minutes to run. I went forward with him to a position between the pilots and began the final prejump checks. Weather, unchanged: cloudless with a big bright three-quarter moon. According to CENTCOM's forecasters what little wind there was aloft this evening would be in our favor. On my left wrist I wore an altimeter and above that a compass, both of whose readings I verified with those on the cockpit controls. My instruments had battery-powered lights so I turned both on now—there is nothing as embarrassing as a night jump in which you leave the aircraft without having remembered to first switch on the instrument illumination.

I went back aft. We would be jumping in a buddy harness: that is, Miranda would be secured to me, her back to my chest, and we would be together under the one canopy—Miranda could not be expected to accomplish by herself as her first-ever parachute experience a nighttime HAHO insertion into opposition territory with full oxygen and combat gear.

The maximum weight for a military freefall is 360 pounds, and we would be near that limit tonight. I checked through the kit bag. Twenty M112 demolition charges, each block consisting of 1.25 pounds of C-4 plastic explosive wrapped in Mylar, and fitted with an adhesive strip to attach them to the target. Twenty-five pounds is a lot of boom, but I did not intend to leave that laser without making a mess of it. The detonators were stowed separately in a waterproof metal container and very carefully padded. Timer and wires. Some 50-grain detonator cord, a length of slow fuse, and two starters—I intended to configure an electrical detonation, but experience had taught me to always take along some det cord and slow fuse, just in case. Spare magazines, but only two apiece because of the weight problem. No carbines or grenades or assault vests, for the same reason. Water but no field rations. Entrenching tool and netting. Aluminum maglites. Field glasses. Bolt cutters. No radios, no signal flares, no comms gear of any kind: we were on our own.

I helped Miranda to her feet and we performed a final equipment check. Before landing we would release the kit bag on a tether. It would hit the ground a little before us, and so when we came down there would be less momentum to cause injury. But there are two items that you must keep on your person during a combat jump: a knife and a pistol. The knife is to cut away entanglements, the pistol is in case there is a meet-and-greet when you hit the ground, what the military euphemistically calls a *contact landing*.

The knives they had found for us were old fixed-blade KA-BARs, a weapon I knew well.

The pistols were Heckler & Koch P9S automatics, a handgun I had heard of but never seen before. Some special ops forces were equipped with them many years ago but they were long out of service, and this pair had come caked in Cosmolene, the hard synthetic grease with which weapons are coated for long-term storage. They were scratched up, having obviously seen much use in the past. Each had an extended threaded barrel and came with a large awkward suppressor. Despite the weapon's name, which reveals that they are normally 9mm, these particular examples were chambered for .45 ACP. This is a requirement for special forces use: not only do .45-caliber rounds have more punch than 9mm—they can weigh over 200 grains versus a nine's usual 124 or so—but regular 9mm rounds are transonic or even supersonic: that is, they have muzzle velocities well over 1,000 feet per second. There is little point in suppressing the sound of a weapon's discharge if the round goes on to produce a sonic boom. Almost all .45-caliber ammunition is subsonic, typically 900 FPS, and so back in the days before special subsonic 9mm rounds were available it made sense to use .45s.

They were blowback weapons with concealed hammers and single-action-only triggers. Just seven rounds in the magazine. There was a cocking/decocking lever on the left side of the frame, which in combination with the concealed hammer made it possible to safely keep an extra round in the breech, as we had done. I had briefed Miranda on its operation, but hoped that she would not have to use a weapon that she had never fired.

The jumpmaster gave me the five-to-run signal.

We took up a position at the rear of the cargo bay. We changed over to the oxygen bottles that we would be jumping with, and I hooked up the buddy harness. At three to run the jumpmaster latched onto his safety line and took his post. The C-130 has a large rear ramp but that is for cargo drops only: leapers like us exit via the side door. He opened it, and the combined roar of engines and buffeting air filled our ears.

At one to run Miranda gave me the thumbs up, as we had practiced. I gave the same signal to the jumpmaster, and we shuffled forward. Miranda put her boots together at the edge. I put mine on either side of hers, grabbed the sides of the doorway, and leaned back, arms outstretched.

The jumpmaster gave us ten seconds, then five, then go. I heaved forward, and we vaulted out into the void.

XL

WE WERE USING A RAM-AIR CHUTE and so needed to gain airspeed before deploying the canopy. It takes six seconds to reach terminal velocity, about 120 MPH. Six seconds does not sound very long but in a freefall it feels like an eternity. During that interval you must stabilize in the correct position, which is as if lying face down on a table—in fact, that is how they first teach it to you at freefall school in Fort Bragg. Your arms and legs are the control surfaces.

We were stable. After six seconds I activated the canopy release and we were immediately hit with the rapid deceleration that feels eerily like someone is pulling you back up again. Soon we were floating beneath the canopy.

I checked the compass but then realized that I had no need of it: visibility was unlimited, and far below I could see the moon-drenched waters of the Gulf sweeping up in a great silver arrowhead at whose tip shone the distant lights of Bandar Abbas. I set our course, adjusting a little for drift. It was an easy ride, and I wondered if like me Miranda was looking at the far horizon silhouetted by the moon. The earth's curvature was visible. In the dark and held near weightless by the canopy above, it felt as if we were astronauts suspended in space above a blackened and desolate planet.

The moonlight would help with landing, but it could be a problem, too. There was little chance of us being detected by radar, but on a pleasant evening such as this there was always the possibility of someone going outside to take the night air and, looking up in quiet contemplation of the stars, happening to suddenly notice a parachute floating down from the sky.

We were at 8,000 feet when we made the coast. I went into an orbit of the drop zone while continuing to lose altitude. Bandar Abbas is only a small city, but its position astride the Strait of Hormuz gives it importance beyond its size. It lies stretched along the coastline from the port at the western end to the airfield in the east. In the moonlight we could see the runways of the latter clearly, despite the absence of runway lighting; it was shut down for the night. The airfield was the last human feature before the desert, which stretches away east and north, all the way to the vast escarpment abutting the wide central plateau that occupies most of Iran. Our drop zone was the unpopulated flat stretch of dry brown earth directly east of the field.

I saw no movement at the airport, no lights suddenly coming on, no beams from vehicle headlamps piercing the desert, carrying out troops to greet the intruders. We were undetected.

On the last orbit I concentrated on the ground below, trying to pick a good landing spot clear of rocks and gullies. We came down. I flared at the last moment, and we landed on our feet without even falling over. I collapsed the canopy and hoped that the rest of the mission would go as smoothly as had the insertion phase.

Number fifty, I thought—I had been counting them on the flight over, and Iran was the fiftieth country I had visited, one way or another.

We unharnessed and took off our jumpsuits to get rid of the padding beneath. Miranda stripped down to underwear alone, and she was a beguiling sight in the moonlight, naked apart from underwear and combat boots. I was sorry when she put the jumpsuit back on. When we were dressed she gathered in the canopy while I went to the kit bag. Nothing was broken: there was nothing to break except the detonators, and if something had gone amiss with them we would not have needed an inspection to become aware of it. I took out the entrenching tool and began digging.

Soon we had the oxygen equipment and parachute gear buried. It was only a shallow ditch, but out here it might be decades before anyone ever found it, perhaps never. We did a quick equipment check and then began the march to the airport, about two miles distant across the desert expanse.

Normally there is a flood of intelligence before embarking on a recon job, so you generally have a good idea of what you will be encountering. That was not the case now, and so I was relieved when we reached the perimeter of the airport and found no electrification or guard towers or dog patrols, nothing but plain chain-link fencing. All we had were the bolt cutters, so anything more would have been a problem.

I did a quick survey of the airfield. There was a little illumination around the civilian area down to the south but the military hanger directly across from us was darkened—electrical shortages are chronic in Iran, and perhaps security was the victim. The field glasses were night-vision capable and so despite the darkness I could clearly see the F-4s arrayed along the apron. They are purposeful-looking aircraft, taught, powerful, belligerent. I could not wait to jump into one and get out of here.

I dug a shallow trench behind a small rise about a hundred yards clear of the wire. This was the position from which Miranda would keep watch over the military area on the other side of the runway while I was away blowing up the *Speed Graphic*. She had two duties to perform. The first was to establish the security routines: foot or vehicle, timing pattern, hangar area only or perimeter as well, and whether the control tower was used as an observation post. The second duty was to identify the likely location of the startup carts. It turns out that, like the engine of a car, a jet cannot start itself: it needs help. In this case the help is not a crank or a starter motor but an auxiliary power unit that provides compressed air to get the turbines spinning. Some aircraft have their own but not F-4s; Phantoms use an auxiliary power unit mounted on a trolley that the ground crew wheels out for engine startup. Without an APU, we would be going nowhere.

Miranda lay down on her stomach in the trench. I left her with the water and everything else from the pack that I would not need myself, then covered her with the camouflage netting. Even in daylight she would have been invisible to anyone not close enough to shoot.

"All set?"

"Yes."

"You want anything while I'm out?"

"Postcard," she said.

"Anything else?"

"Souvenir snow globe, if you can find one. My niece loves them; she's four."

"I'll see what I can do."

I began to walk away, but her voice stopped me.

"Hey, Lysander Dalton."

"Yes?"

"Keep your head down."

I HAD INTENDED TO GO BY FOOT DOWN TO THE PORT, but in front of the civilian terminal at the southern end of the airfield I noticed a lone bicycle in a rack. It was secured with a chain and lock, but I had the bolt cutters in the backpack. I was soon pedaling down the road toward the harbor area.

Like the airfield, the naval base was surrounded by chain-link fencing. I left the bicycle under a tree and surveyed the base through the binoculars. I was on the eastern side, where a road ran down by the fence. The wharf with the submarines was to my left, and all three of them were alongside now: the third had come in since the last satellite photograph I had seen this afternoon. There was lighting on the dock, but the boats themselves were darkened. Ahead of me were the wharves with the main surface combatants: corvettes and high-speed missile boats less than a thousand tons in size, too small for open-ocean work but suited to the Persian Gulf. I could see a watchkeeper by the gangway on the one nearest me, reading a newspaper to pass the time. Further docks lay beyond them, slightly to the right from where I lay and about four hundred yards distant. Alongside one was the *Speed Graphic*, large and impressive. The truck whose purpose we assumed was to transport the laser was still parked nearby. There were a dozen or so people on the wharf admiring the *Speed Graphic* and talking among themselves—she was something of a tourist attraction, and there would be no chance of me boarding her unobserved from the landward side.

There were fifty yards between the fence and the nearest water. It was open space, but it was unlit. I went across the road to the fence and cut my way through.

If you are not sure you are hidden, the best way to not attract attention is to act as if you belong. Once I had pushed through the gap in the fence I walked across the flat concrete expanse casually, as if I made the same journey every day. I came to the dockside. The only person visible was the watchkeeper on the rear deck of that surface combatant, but he was still immersed in the newspaper. There was a pontoon tied up a little further down, low in the water, with paint cans and roller brushes on long handles: it was used for painting the ships' sides. I clambered down onto it.

I was too low to be seen by the watchkeeper now. I slipped quietly into the water, and swam in a slow breaststroke down past the warships and around to the *Speed Graphic*.

There was no chance of me using a berthing hawser to board her as I had done last time: the people on the wharf would have seen me for sure. But her new Iranian crew was not the efficient team that Kadri had gathered: her bridge wings were deployed and she still had an anchor acockbill, either of which would provide an easy means for me to gain access. I chose the anchor, since it was easier to snag with the grapnel. I was soon aboard.

The bridge was unoccupied. I shook the water from the automatic, used the cocking lever to set the hammer, and began the journey down through the superstructure. I met no one. The interior was dark: it seemed that they had not yet figured out how to hook her up to shore power, or perhaps they had an incompatible supply, but in the vehicle deck someone had set up portable lighting. The transom ramp was down but the deck itself was empty—even the Cadillac was gone.

The electrical cable that powered the portable lights had an extension disappearing into the passageway leading to the glass capsule. That meant the laser was very likely under guard. If there was just one of them then the odds were on my side, even two would not be insurmountable. If there were more than two then I would be in trouble.

I made a last check of the weapon, took a deep breath, and swung into the passageway. There was just one of them, sitting on the deck, wearing a ragged uniform, and looking mightily bored. He glanced up sleepily but I shot him before he could react further, two rounds into the chest. The laser compartment was closed but not locked. I dragged the body inside with me, although if anyone came down that passageway they would have had to be blind not to see all the blood. Hopefully he had been assigned to keep watch for the entire night, and so no one else would be coming along.

The laser was stowed as I had first seen it, although this time it was not powered up. I threw down the pack and began exposing the adhesive strips on the blocks of plastic explosive, slapping them onto the machine as I did so. Wiring up the timer and detonators took much longer: you do not rush anything with detonators. I had only intended to use the det cord if for some reason an electrical detonation had not been possible, but then another idea occurred to me. The Iranians would be unfamiliar with the electrical wiring; they had not even been able to connect the *Speed Graphic* to shore power. If I ran the det cord along the wiring harness there was every chance that they would assume it was just another electrical cable, despite the bright red color. I ran out a length, leading from the explosives to the small cutout high up on the bulkhead where the wiring harness ran through the ship. I made a last check of the demolition charge and then exited the compartment. On the other side of the bulkhead was the ladder leading down to the starboard engine that Kadri had shown us when we first come aboard. I grabbed the det cord and took it down into the space. At the entrance were the engineering controls, including the fuel inspection port: the place from which samples of the fuel oil can be taken for analysis. It must necessarily lead down into the fuel tanks themselves. I opened the plug and stuffed the det cord down into it.

Ten minutes after having boarded her, I slipped back into the water. I left the way I had come, swimming across to the pontoon and finally making my way back through the fence. I was just picking up the bicycle and thinking that I had gotten clean away when the *Speed Graphic* blew up.

There were two explosions, the plastic and the fuel, a small but discernable fraction of a second separating them. I had not initiated the detonation: the timer was set for another forty minutes from now, by which time I would have been well clear and hopefully on the way out of town in the back seat of an F-4. Someone had found the explosive; perhaps the guards were on a rotation schedule.

In any delayed demolition you always set a tamper trigger in case someone finds the explosive before the time is up. This is often a mercury switch in the timer itself. A mercury switch consists of two electrical terminals inside a vial. One terminal is immersed in a small pool of mercury, the other is a ring terminal just above it. Any movement will cause the liquid to flow one way or another, and since mercury is a conductor it will complete the circuit. Result: boom. The natural reaction of a layman on finding an explosive with something wired into it which is ticking away is to very rapidly remove the thing that is ticking, which activates the mercury switch. That is why in the movies ordnance disposal people are always careful to cut the wires before moving anything else.

If you safely cut the wires and successfully disconnect the timer the next reaction, even for someone familiar with explosives, is to remove the plastic from whatever it is attached to. That was why in addition to the mercury switch I had embedded a second detonator and tamper switch assembly, inserted directly into the plastic itself and completely independent of the electrical circuit. Onboard the *Speed Graphic* someone had obviously moved something, and whether it was the timer or the explosives the result was the same.

Twenty-five pounds of plastic makes a big blast and despite being contained inside the *Speed Graphic* it was tremendously loud. But it was nothing compared to what came next, and most people recalling this night would remember no other, for the sound of the *Speed Graphic*'s fuel tanks exploding echoed deeply across the city, a huge bass concussion visceral in its impact. I was knocked to the ground, although I was a quarter-mile away. The heat from the fireball was sufficient to be painful. Debris fell like rain. When it was over the *Speed Graphic*, and much else surrounding it, was completely gone, entirely obliterated by the blast.

I got on the bike and began pedaling.

XLI

MIRANDA WAS WHERE I HAD LEFT HER, hidden beneath the camouflage netting in a shallow trench a hundred yards clear of the wire fence surrounding the airfield. I got in beside her and surveyed the scene. Much had changed. The control tower was lit up. The lights outside the military hangar were also on, illuminating the apron. Through the glasses the F-4s were now visible without the night vision tinge, revealing the yellows and browns of their desert camouflage paint. Two of them had their canopies raised, and around the second one ground crew were installing what looked like ammunition belts.

"I thought it wasn't supposed to go off yet," Miranda said.

"Someone must have found the explosives."

"I could see the fireball from here."

"I gather it woke up our friends."

"Yes," she confirmed, "But it's not all bad news. See those two aircraft with the canopies up?"

"Yes."

"They must be the alert aircraft—that is, the planes on standby. That tells us they are fully fueled, so that's one less thing we have to worry about. Better yet, the startup carts are already out there with them, so we won't have to find one."

"They're arming the one on the right."

"Yes, they finished the other one just before you arrived."

"What should happen next?"

"Depends on what their orders are. If they have been told to launch as a precaution the next step would be startup, then taxi and takeoff. But if that was going to happen I would have expected the pilot and weapons officer to already be strapped in and going through their preflight checks. So it's more likely that once the aircraft are armed that will be it. The aircrew will likely stay in the operations center or the briefing room, suited up and ready to go, until the stand-down comes."

"What about the ground crew?"

"If we're lucky they'll return to the hanger once they're done and wait for the stand down, too."

We were not lucky—when the ground crew finished arming the second aircraft and returned to the hanger they left one of their guys behind: perhaps the regulations did not permit an armed aircraft to be left unattended on the lines. He sat under the second aircraft, back against the nose wheel, and facing away from us toward the hangar, perhaps hoping to see someone coming out to tell him that whatever had happened down in the harbor was not the result of an air raid, and so they were standing down. Or perhaps he just wanted to watch the smoke still billowing into the night sky from the port facility to the west.

Someone would soon find the gap in the fence surrounding the naval base, and the alert for saboteurs would go out: we could wait no longer. We left our cover. I cut the wire and we were quickly through. The runway lights were still out, perhaps as a precaution against an air raid, and so we were easily able to make our way across the airfield unobserved. I left Miranda about fifty yards short of the concrete apron and crept forward by myself, keeping low, eyes always forward. The risk here was that the man I was approaching would hear me, or that I would be seen from the tower as I came under illumination from the hangar lights.

Eventually I was about thirty feet away—close, but handguns are inaccurate and I did not want to alert him with a near miss. I took careful aim and pulled the trigger. He slumped forward without a sound, as if he had just dozed off. I gave the all-clear signal to Miranda, and we approached the F-4. I dragged the body away from the nose wheel.

In addition to the fresh blood I noticed a small pool of hydraulic fluid on the tarmac. I looked up. It was dripping down from somewhere inside the aircraft.

"It's leaking," I whispered, pointing it out, but Miranda showed no concern.

"Good," she said. "Any F-4 that isn't leaking is probably empty."

There was a ladder attached to the side leading up to the forward cockpit. Miranda climbed it and got into the front seat. I went to the startup cart. It was already hooked up, and all I had to do was switch it on. I gave a thumbs-up to Miranda, and a moment later the quiet night air was pierced by the slowly increasing pitch of a jet engine beginning to spin.

I checked the control tower through the field glasses and saw someone looking straight back down at me, also with binoculars. No alarm yet, but it would not take long. The noise from the turbine became louder as the RPM increased, but then Miranda hit the engine start, and the volume changed from a piercing squeal to an almighty roar. The whole airframe began to shake.

This was my cue. I disconnected the cart and ladder, thrust them out of the way, then removed the chocks from under the wheels. At that moment the ground crew came pouring from the hanger, alerted by the noise and probably wondering what their colleague was up to. I removed the sound suppressor and took three quick shots. It had the intended effect: down they went. Some of them scrambled back behind the hanger. I wondered how far away their weapons were.

I jumped up onto the wing and climbed along the fuselage to the rear cockpit. Miranda started the second engine. Soon I was in the seat but rather than strap in I replaced the magazine and kept the reloaded .45 aimed at the side of the hangar, ready to shoot the ground crew if they came around the corner. But the opposition came from another direction: a truck emerged from near the control tower and came racing down the taxiway. It skidded to a stop about a hundred yards away, and I could hear the ground crew yelling to them, probably telling them to shoot us. The soldiers dismounted and took cover behind the truck or lay flat on the deck.

A bullet went zinging through the canopy still open above me.

"Let's get going," I urged Miranda.

We began moving, slowly at first, but quickly gathering speed.

"Close up," Miranda ordered, bringing her own canopy down. I emptied the remainder of the magazine in the direction of the soldiers and then closed my canopy, still functional despite the bullet hole.

Instead of turning away from the soldiers as I had expected her to, Miranda headed straight for them. She began firing the F-4's cannon, a six-barreled, 20mm Gatling gun that was the bigger brother of the minigun I had encountered at Caracol. Six thousand rounds a minute of thundering tracer poured out ahead of us, the loud staccato sound much heavier and deeper than the soldier's rifle fire. The recoil rattled the airframe as if to shake it apart. The rounds passed above the soldiers lying on the ground, but as the fire swung through the truck it was torn to shreds. Miranda kept firing as she swung the aircraft further around, now pointing back at the line of F-4s. I realized what she was doing: disabling the other aircraft, particularly the other alert aircraft, to ensure that no one came after us. As the rounds pounded into them their thin airframes folded as if made of aluminum foil. The other alert plane, full of fuel, exploded in an enormous fireball, making any further effort to disable the remainder unnecessary. Miranda thrust forward on the throttles, and we began racing across to the runway. She did not taxi on asphalt, instead taking the direct route right across the open ground. We were bouncing all over the place and I feared that the F-4 would fall apart before we could take off, but we soon made the runway. The cockpit was full of noise: the jet engines, the servo motors as Miranda lowered flaps for takeoff, the occasional loud impact of a rifle round hitting home, sharp and high pitched, but we had opened up a good distance and they were just lucky shots.

Miranda pointed us down the runway. There was not the usual pause: Miranda opened the throttles wide without allowing any momentum to come off. We quickly gathered speed, but then ahead of us a truck came racing onto the runway. It skidded to a stop, and the driver jumped from the cabin and ran for his life: they were using the truck to block our takeoff roll.

"Hold on," Miranda shouted.

Jet engines work by compressing air and mixing it with fuel to burn in a combustion chamber, the expanding gases from which create thrust. But military fighter aircraft have an extra feature in which they can inject raw fuel directly into the exhaust for an added push: afterburn, a way of getting some extra punch in a hurry, although at the expense of extremely inefficient use of fuel. Energy conservation was not our concern right now: Miranda engaged the afterburners, and I was thrust to the back of my seat as the power poured on.

It was simple from here: either we would gain sufficient airspeed to lift off, or we would plow into fiery oblivion when we hit that truck. It seemed that we were destined for the latter when at the last moment Miranda pulled back on the stick and rotated the F-4. The aircraft shot up like a rocket—nothing like a commercial takeoff: it was like being blown out of a cannon. We surged up and up. The landing gear slapped home beneath us, and we were away.

Miranda flew the Phantom in the same way she drove the Aston Martin: at full throttle. The airspeed indicator in front of me climbed rapidly. In the high six-hundred-knot range there was a brief nose-down buffeting—"Mach tuck"—indicating the transition to supersonic flight. Still she continued accelerating, past Mach 1, and then eventually past Mach 2. After takeoff we had initially shot up several thousand feet but Miranda had quickly brought us back down to below five hundred, not because we had no oxygen but because she wanted to keep low to avoid radar. I followed the compass headings as we turned southwest. Any mistake at this speed and altitude would quickly kill us both, but the stick between my legs moved smoothly and confidently: if Miranda was nervous, it did not translate through to her control of the aircraft.

Our destination was the US airbase at Al Udeid, but it was not to be: something went wrong. I heard the change in pitch from the engines behind me, and the aircraft jerked around before Miranda regathered it. Suddenly our airspeed was rapidly decreasing while our altitude was rapidly increasing. We were heading south now, straight toward the nearest coastline.

"Flameout," Miranda shouted. "They must have hit our fuel tank. Stand by to eject."

I strapped in about as fast as it is possible for a human being to strap in. There were two ejection handles, one between the legs and the other overhead, marked in alternating bands of yellow and black to indicate their importance.

"Ready," I yelled.

"On my third eject," she said.

"Got it."

I saw her hand go to the ejection handle above her head.

"Stand-by. Eject, eject, eject."

I pulled the cord and blew through the canopy. Tremendous acceleration: they say you briefly experience twenty g's when ejecting from a fighter aircraft. I was conscious, but it was a near thing, and my vision had tunneled right down, a brownout rather than a complete blackout as the force of the ejection drained blood from the brain. But it only lasted a moment and I was soon back with it. I looked around.

For the second time in the same evening, I found myself floating beneath a parachute canopy high over the moonlit waters of the Persian Gulf. There was desert directly below us: Miranda had crossed the coastline before ejecting. She was over to my right now, maybe fifty yards away, floating beneath her canopy. The F-4 was spiraling slowly down to the earth, the single yellow-orange dot from the remaining engine visible. But then that one flamed out too, and the aircraft was momentarily invisible until it crashed, a brief fireball in the desert far below, completely silent, as if on another planet. Further down the coast I could see a city all aglow, and among the many buildings there was a distinctively needle-shaped spire, much taller than all the others, that could only have been the Burj Khalifa—to my great relief, we were going to come down in Emirati territory.

XLII

THE SUMMER SEASON HAD SETTLED OVER D.C., the air thick, the heat oppressive, the trees of the Mall sagging under the burden of their foliage. To the southwest the sky was already filling with thunderheads, billowing towers which this afternoon would advance upon the city like evangelists bent on redemption, coming to wash away its sins.

Summer is tourist season in Washington and sightseers were all about, chirping like cicadas. I was wearing sunglasses and walking with my head down, lost in thought and not paying much attention to where I was going. Without meaning to I entered the Vietnam War Memorial, a shallow cutting dug into the surrounding land. It was walled with broad slabs of black granite inscribed with the names of the dead.

I had never been to the memorial. There was a fair-sized crowd. Many people were searching out names. Several were taking rubbings directly from the stones. Some placed flowers. One woman wept.

How long would people weep here, I wondered. Did it end with the last generation of personal memory? Does anyone weep at a World War I memorial anymore? Civil War? Surely not the Mexican wars, although for all I knew there might be someone at the Alamo right now, weeping for a lost ancestor. Perhaps Greeks still wept at Thermopylae.

I hurried back out into the open space of the Mall. The Lincoln Memorial loomed ahead, the man himself perpetually staring out upon the distant Capitol with stern disapproval, as if he knew the hearts of the people who served therein and was not pleased with what he saw. I reached the end of the reflecting pool that runs down the middle of the Mall and began the walk eastward, keeping to the northern side, counting the park benches as I went.

I reached the eighth bench. It was occupied, but not by whom I had expected. There was a family: mother and father in their late thirties or early forties, two children around ten years old. The father was giving a civics lesson of the type that a well-meaning parent might give in such a place. I stood a moment, wishing they would go away, but the lesson seemed nowhere near ending.

I checked my watch. Still early; I went over to a vendor on Constitution Avenue and bought a Coke. By the time I wandered back the bench was vacant. It was a pity in a way: the family had missed an opportunity to get a real civics lesson, straight from the source.

I sat and waited.

Suddenly he was beside me. Strange enough that he could have approached unheard, astonishing that his great bulk had come to rest upon the bench without its impact having alerted me. The usual black suit and tie despite the heat of the day and his abundant natural insulation.

He wordlessly passed me a newspaper. No greeting, no salutation; we were like an old married couple having passed beyond such minor pleasantries. I looked over the newspaper, a jumble of headlines that had little connection with me, and put it down.

"You've already read it?"

"I'm a winemaker, Mr. Dortmund. I don't read the *Wall Street Journal*."

"You should, Captain Dalton. Economics underlies all truth. Every political act is an exchange, and money is its ultimate measure."

I wondered what Lincoln would have thought of this theory. Dortmund picked up the newspaper and folded it to an article before passing it back to me. The headline read *French Oil Giant Secures Long-Term Iran Contract*. I scanned through the article, which filled in detail but added little to the headline. A big French oil company had done a deal in which they were to run several large Iranian oilfields, including a significant investment to rebuild infrastructure that had deteriorated under years of Iranian mismanagement and neglect. The price of the deal was undisclosed but the estimates were in the usual astronomical sums that have no real meaning to working individuals like me.

"Okay, so what?"

"So what? Has it never occurred to you to ask who made the laser, and why?"

"Kadri made it, and he did it for the money."

"Yes, yes, but that is like saying that the Vietnam War began because of the Gulf of Tonkin incident. Technically correct, but it misses the bigger picture."

The Vietnam reference made me wonder if he had come by the same route that I had. I gestured with the newspaper.

"Are you saying that the laser is related to this?"

"Naturally."

"The French built it?"

"Kadri formed a shell company, and it was the shell company that built it. But who supplied the shell company with the actual lasers?"

"I have no idea."

"Laurent, a large French electronics firm and defense contractor that is partly owned by the French government."

I looked again at the headline, more thoughtfully now. Dortmund continued.

"Avionière, an aviation parts maker for Airbus and Dassault, supplied the servos and guidance equipment. Avionière's majority shareholder is the French government. And lastly, the team of programmers and engineers who actually built it came from the Marianne space launch company. While doing so they were technically employed by Kadri—which gives the French plausible deniability—but by coincidence all fourteen of them returned to their jobs at Marianne after the laser project was completed. Marianne is 32.53 percent owned by the French national space agency, by the way."

"Are you telling me that the French government gave the laser to the Iranians in exchange for oil concessions?"

"A simplification, but essentially correct."

"But if the Iranians shut down the Gulf, wouldn't it have affected them, too?"

"You would never make an intelligence analyst, Captain Dalton—you miss small but important details. Where is the new terminal to be?"

I checked the article. There were to be pipelines constructed across Iran to transport the crude to a new shipping terminal that would be built at a port called Banda Beheshti.

"You forget, Captain Dalton, that unlike other Gulf producers Iran has coastline outside the Gulf. Bandar Beheshti is on the Indian Ocean. Any shut down of the Gulf would therefore leave it unaffected, although such a cutoff would stop all oil from Qatar, Bahrain, Kuwait, Iraq, the Emirates, and even Saudi Arabia. Imagine if that were to happen. What price would oil go to? A thousand dollars a barrel? Two thousand? Who knows? But one thing is certain: the Iranian government and the French national oil company would both reap huge rewards, profits beyond imagining. And the French state would remain supplied with oil, without the shortages that would likely cripple the rest of the industrialized world. The result would be a significant power realignment: France's GDP would rise relative to other industrialized nations, and with it her voice in world affairs. She would once again become a player, a country to be reckoned with. That, of course, has been the aim of French policy since the time of de Gaulle. It was a brilliant plan, most astute."

He spoke with genuine admiration, a sentiment that I did not share. I put the paper aside.

"What happens to Kadri now?"

"Happens how?"

"Legally."

"My dear Captain Dalton, he broke no laws. The U.S. arms embargo against Iran does not apply to France or French nationals."

"Moran's murder?"

"With you as a witness at a public trial, Captain Dalton?"

"I was thinking of something a little quieter."

"Extra-judicial, you mean? For what purpose would we do such a thing? Believe it or not, Kadri is a very useful man to us. His contacts are invaluable and he knows the rules of the game."

Which was why Kadri had killed Hanna but spared Miranda: in the rules of the game collateral deaths are acceptable, but you do not kill the other guy's people without a good reason; it is considered unsporting.

"You could get him for the white-slave trade."

"Don't be absurd. It is an activity without consequence in the affairs of nations and so is of no interest to us." In Dortmund's world human trafficking was a mere trifle, a sin so venial as to be unworthy of intervention, like jaywalking or neglecting to use the full nine-digit zip code. "What does have consequences, Captain Dalton, is your failure."

"My failure?"

"It was the simplest of missions: recover a notebook. A child could have done it."

"I got close."

"Close? Close only counts in horseshoes and hand grenades."

"No, it counts now, too."

"And just how do you figure that?"

In response I handed him a notebook of my own. It was wider than it was high, and the pages were unlined. He read the cover.

"Autographs? Captain Dalton, I do not give out autographs."

"I'm not asking for one."

He was about to say something more, but whatever it was never came out. His posture stiffened a little, and I could tell that he had already guessed what must have been inside the autograph book. Whatever else could be said of him, Dortmund was not a stupid man.

Nor a coward: he showed no fear, although he must have guessed the degree of ill will that I now bore for him.

He opened the book and briefly flicked through it, coming to a halt at the one page that was not blank. He looked at the signature for a long time, as if staring at the thing long enough would somehow erase the fact of it.

"When did you obtain it?" he asked.

"This morning."

"How did you guess?"

"The *Roosevelt* was diverted to the Caribbean before Hanna Moran disappeared."

Since returning from the Middle East I had mostly put the affair out of my mind, too busy with the vineyard to think about things, but driving to D.C. today I had come in across the Arlington Bridge. The last time I crossed that bridge had been in Miranda's Aston Martin, and recalling it this morning I suddenly realized what it was that had bothered me about our conversation that day, something that had lain dormant in the back of my mind ever since, a little seed of doubt waiting to germinate. Miranda's cousin told her that the *Theodore Roosevelt* was mysteriously diverted a week before, but Hanna Moran had picked up her dry cleaning the previous Wednesday. How could it be that the carrier was diverted *before* she disappeared? Once I had figured it out, a thousand little inconsistencies were resolved, from Dortmund's inability to obtain Moran's social security number to his persistent use of her name over an unsecured international telephone line.

After getting into D.C. I had left the car in a parking lot and bought the autograph book at a stationery store before hurrying up to Capitol Hill. When I called Stolper's office from outside the lobby I had only asked that an aide take the book up to him, but the senator himself had shown up, perhaps eager to cement a vote. He came bounding down the Capitol steps toward me, arm extended, practiced grin firmly in place.

We shook hands. He said a lot of upbeat sounding things very fast, none of which I absorbed; all I could think was: *How much did you know?* He signed the autograph book with a flourish and returned it to me. I tried to hand back the pen, which was his, but he insisted that I keep it as a souvenir. I looked at it more closely. Dark blue, and the seal of the United States Senate was stamped on the barrel.

He uttered some more stock phrases and turned to take his leave. But after a few steps he had stopped and turned back around, looking over his shoulder with a suddenly unsmiling expression.

"There were no other autographs in your book," he said.

"No."

Long pause.

"You don't actually collect autographs, do you?"

"No."

"And you're not really from Mississippi, are you?"

"No."

Stolper stood there for perhaps another thirty seconds, trying to figure out what it was all about. He must have thought better of asking, or perhaps he just did not want to know. He turned and continued back up the steps without saying anything more, but all the spring was gone from his step.

BESIDE ME, DORTMUND SIGHED.

"I should have arranged our meeting for the summer recess," he said. He closed the book and passed it back. "I'm amazed that you thought to get his autograph."

"Nothing beats hard intelligence."

"When did you see the notebook?"

"When Kadri killed Hanna Moran. It fell by the vehicle I was hiding under."

"Open, I assume?"

I nodded. We were quiet for a while.

"Who wrote it?" I asked.

"Composition, or physical script?"

"Physical script."

"One of my Harrys. In fact you've met her."

"The stripper?"

"No, the other one."

I had liked Harry-the-stripper and was stupidly disappointed that the elegant calligraphic penmanship I had seen in that notebook— so unlike Stolper's lazy backhand scrawl—had not belonged to her.

"She did an excellent job," Dortmund continued. "Switched pens, varied the style slightly from time to time, as if he'd been tired or writing in an awkward position—on the flight back to Mississippi perhaps. She even caused one pen to run out on the page, a nice realistic touch, I thought."

"Shouldn't you have tried to simulate his handwriting?"

"Very difficult to sustain, and anyway where would they get an example of the real thing to compare it with? No one physically writes anymore: everything is done on email or a word processor or some other electronic text system. The idea of an autograph hound never occurred to us."

"It might occur to them."

"No," he said with finality. "The operation has been a complete success: they have swallowed it hook, line and sinker."

"And the only reason you sent me was to convince them that you were trying to get the notebook back, and that therefore it must be the real thing?"

He shrugged his shoulders, as if the answer was too obvious to warrant a response.

"What if I'd gotten it?"

"What?"

"The notebook. What if I'd gotten it back?"

"It would have made no difference. In the unlikely event that you retrieved the original a photocopy, supposedly made by Hanna Moran, would have been made available to them. Whether or not you retrieved the notebook was irrelevant; the only thing that mattered was that you be observed trying to do so. Given your propensity for the overly dramatic, I had little doubt that you would oblige us. My own people are more subtle: they do not leave dead bodies lying about in airport departure lounges."

Dortmund delicately avoided the other obvious reason that he had chosen me: I was disposable.

"The men who followed me from Hanna Moran's apartment: they were yours?"

"We had to ensure that you did not fall too far behind, Captain Dalton. They were not pleased when you shot at them, by the way."

"And you had the apartment sanitized?"

"We have a crew trained for such work. If you were to play your part successfully it was essential that you find nothing to suggest that it was a safe house."

"What if I hadn't found the locker at the health club?"

"We gave you the key; how could you possibly have missed it?"

"I nearly didn't think of it."

"If it had become necessary I would have arranged a little prompting. One of my Harrys perhaps, posing as a friend of Hanna's, mentioning how much she enjoyed swimming there."

It was an elegant testament to his judgment of my abilities: not only had he taken it for granted that I would fail to recover the notebook, he had felt the need to give me help so that I would not fall hopelessly behind.

"And the purpose of the locker was for me to find the matchbook from Oblivion?"

"Of course."

"Which means that you sent Hanna Moran to Oblivion, too."

"Naturally. Zane and thence Kadri were the obvious way to go."

"You killed Hanna Moran."

"I employed Hanna Moran. Balthazar Kadri killed her."

"No, he just pulled the trigger."

"As you wish."

"Did you give her lunch at your club?"

This time he did not answer.

"I'll bet you did. My guess is that first of all you had your people hunt around for someone suitable. They probably compiled a list of likely candidates. You would have wanted an actress or a model, someone who could play the role. Blond, since they command a premium. And someone with no near relatives, or estranged from their family: someone who would not be much missed. Once the candidate was identified you would have moved in personally to consummate the deal. An invitation to lunch at the Mayflower Club, all very mysterious. She arrives full of curiosity. You're all courtly, apologizing for the inconvenience, thanking her for putting herself out. Then over the appetizer you tell her, not quite precisely, who you are. Drop the phrase *national security* here and there. *White*

House, too, probably. You let on that there might be a role for her, hint that her country needs her. You would have allowed her to believe that it's glamorous, that no one really gets hurt, and I'll bet that by the port and *petits fours* you had her clamoring to sign up. Is that how it went, Mr. Dortmund?"

"No, not really. Hanna Moran needed little convincing from me; she was someone coming to the end of a not spectacularly successful modeling career and was wondering what came next."

"And so you showed up as her savior?"

"Something like that, yes. As indeed I would have been, had she made it back. I offered her a very large sum of money, Captain Dalton, just as I offered you. Which reminds me."

He took a long manila envelope from his jacket and passed it to me.

I pulled out the contents. A single sheet of thick paper, not very high quality. The top two-thirds was white and mostly blank: just a line of typeface at the very top: file numbers, the sort of stuff governments everywhere print on their paperwork. Below that was my name and address positioned so that when the sheet was folded they would appear in the envelope's window.

At the bottom of the white section was a perforation and beneath it a check whose complex colorful background was probably meant to deter counterfeiters. It was drawn against the United States Department of Treasury. My name was listed as the payee. The amount was equal to the outstanding balance of my vineyard's mortgage. It was by far the largest sum of money that I had ever held in my hand, or was ever likely to.

I tore it in half, then again, then over again until I had it down to the smallest pieces I could manage. I scattered them over the grass at my feet. A pigeon came over and gave one of them an exploratory peck but soon moved on, apparently sharing my opinion of Dortmund's money.

We were quiet for a while. Dortmund eventually broke the silence.

"It is amazing to me, Captain Dalton, how many people mistake imprudence for decency."

"Forgive me if I don't hold your opinion of decency in very high regard, Mr. Dortmund."

"Miss Moran understood there was danger."

"You knew they would kill her."

"No: I expected her to survive. It is you whom I assumed they would kill."

There is not much you can say to something like that.

I stood. "Goodbye, Mr. Dortmund."

"Until next time."

"There will be no next time."

"Yes, there will."

"I would rather go bankrupt than do anything more for you."

"There will be no question of bankruptcy. Your little melodrama may have been momentarily satisfying, but it makes no difference: the sum that we agreed to will be paid directly to your bank in satisfaction of your mortgage. There is nothing you can do to stop us, and you can be sure that the bank will not send the money back, even if you ask them to."

"Then why would you imagine that I would ever work for you again?"

For once Dortmund did not immediately answer. Instead he stood and stretched a little. He looked around, taking his time. At first I thought it was automatic, routine surveillance resulting from habituated tradecraft, but it turned out that he was just taking in the scene.

"It is pleasant here, is it not?"

"I guess."

Long pause.

"The women are smiling, the children carefree."

"Yes."

Another long pause.

"Tell me, Captain Dalton, are these people happy?"

A strange question. I looked around for myself. The family who had previously occupied the bench was gone, but several facsimiles promenaded along the Mall, laughing, chatting, taking photographs. A young couple occupied the bench down from us, oblivious of all else except each other. A little boy ran about chasing pigeons, but he was barely walking and they were able to out-trot him, without the need to take wing.

"I suppose that for the most part they probably are."

"Yes," Dortmund said, "that's what I think, too. And thus they represent the successful product of the national imperative, do they not, for what is our country's purpose, if not the pursuit of happiness?" He turned to face me. "Now tell me this: *why* are these people happy?"

An impossible question. I shrugged my shoulders in reply. He turned back to survey the scene.

"Then I will tell you why. They are happy because unhappy men like you and I do what must be done." A long silence as he continued to inspect the people passing by, something he did with neither sympathy nor pity. "We are their invisible fairy godmothers," he said at last. "We grant them wishes they didn't even know they had, and of whose blissful benefits they remain forever unaware."

He picked up the newspaper and tucked it under his arm.

"Until next time, Captain Dalton."

He turned and trudged away, indifferent to any response from me. I watched him slowly recede in perspective down the Mall, a strange dark presence among the colorful crowd that eventually closed him from view.

I finished the Coke and looked around for a trash can, thinking about what he had said. Nothing Dortmund says can ever be taken at face value—he deals in lies for a living—but it seemed that there had been a civics lesson after all, although not the one I had anticipated.